I've travelled the world twice over,
Met the famous: saints and sinners,
Poets and artists, kings and queens,
Old stars and hopeful beginners,
I've been where no-one's been before,
Learned secrets from writers and cooks
All with one library ticket
To the wonderful world of books.

© JANICE JAMES.

LOTTIE TRAGO

Josh and Miriam Retallick return to Cornwall from Africa. There, they meet their niece, Lottie, abandoned by her mother, Jane. When Jane returns home, bringing gossip and rumour with her, she becomes involved with Marcus Hooper, a man who has no qualms about beating a woman or cheating a man. When Lottie must choose between two men, she has no idea that the sins of her mother could fall onto her.

E. V. THOMPSON

LOTTIE TRAGO

Complete and Unabridged

CHARNWOOD
Leicester

First published in Great Britain in 1989 by
Macmillan London Limited
London

First Charnwood Edition
published March 1991
by arrangement with
Macmillan London Limited
London

British Library CIP Data

Thompson, E. V.
    Lottie Trago. — Large print ed. —
Charnwood library series
I. Title

823.914

ISBN 0–7089–8578–5

Published by
F. A. Thorpe (Publishing) Ltd.
Anstey, Leicestershire
Set by Words & Graphics Ltd.
Anstey, Leicestershire
Printed and bound in Great Britain by
T. J. Press (Padstow) Ltd., Padstow, Cornwall

Book One

1864

Family Trees of the Retallick and Trago families

Retallick

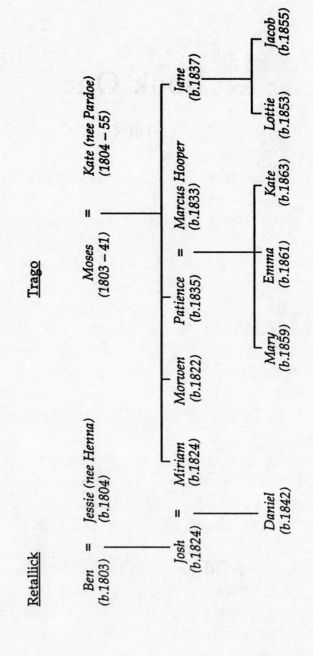

Ben (b.1803) = Jessie (nee Henna) (b.1804)

Josh (b.1824) = Miriam (b.1824)

Daniel (b.1842)

Trago

Moses (1803 – 41) = Kate (nee Pardoe) (1804 – 55)

Miriam (b.1824) | Morwen (b.1822) | Patience (b.1835) = Marcus Hooper (b.1833) | Jane (b.1837)

Lottie (b.1853) | Jacob (b.1855)

Mary (b.1859) | Emma (b.1861) | Kate (b.1863)

1

SLOWLY, the huge bulk of the SS *Great Britain* was eased towards Liverpool's Prince's Dock by two fussy, hard-working tugs, their paddles churning the dark waters of the river Mersey to a muddy froth.

Clustered about the giant three-masted vessel were small boats of every conceivable type and size, filled with awed sightseers and excited relatives of those on board. They had met the *Great Britain* at the mouth of the river, some anxious to catch a first glimpse of long-absent loved ones, others to marvel at the 322-foot length of the ship that had been launched as the largest vessel afloat.

As the strip of dirty water between ship and jetty was squeezed to nothingness and stout ropes began to stitch ship to shore, the wind toyed with a hundred delicate handkerchiefs held aloft in greeting.

Among the passengers crowding the rail were a man and woman who knew no one on the quayside, yet every excited glance from the shore rested upon them before moving on. Both had the deep tan common to those who have spent many years outdoors in the fierce African sun. He stood tall, with an impression of fitness, head and shoulders squared to blue skies and far horizons, unbowed by winter rains and chill winds.

Josh and Miriam Retallick viewed the scene on shore with a confused mixture of emotions.

3

Joy, certainly, but sadness too, together with anticipation and apprehension.

"You're hurting my shoulder!"

The surprised complaint came from the small girl standing in front of Josh and upon whose thin shoulders his hands had tightened unconsciously.

"I'm sorry, Anne," Josh apologised immediately.

"I didn't mind Miriam's hands squeezing *me*," Nell Gilmore gave her six-year-old sister a scornful look that contained all the superiority a sister senior by two years could muster.

"Having two young girls with us isn't how I imagined our homecoming would be." Josh spoke quietly so the girls would not hear, but Nell and Anne were too busy cheering along with three hundred fellow-passengers as the steel stern of the *Great Britain* bumped against the quayside.

"It's more than either of us could possibly have hoped for eighteen years ago . . . "

Looking past the waiting quayside crowd, Miriam saw the acres of dockland that were the pride of Liverpool . . . The thought made her smile. *Pride of Liverpool* had been the name of the ship taking them from England and home all those years before.

They had not been first-class passengers on that occasion. Josh had been a prisoner under sentence of transportation to Australia, convicted of a treasonable conspiracy. Miriam had taken passage on the same ship with Daniel, their three-year-old son, with little expectation of ever seeing England again.

When the *Pride of Liverpool* foundered on the Skeleton Coast of South West Africa, Josh and

4

Miriam were cast ashore in a land beyond the jurisdiction of Great Britain. Here, Josh had built a new life for his family and they prospered.

Eighteen years . . . She and Josh had been only twenty-two then. Almost the same age as Daniel was now. If only Daniel was returning with them now Miriam's happiness would be complete. But Daniel had established a profitable trade-route that extended across half the breadth of Africa. He would one day be a very wealthy man indeed.

"Look, there's a band!" Nell's excited cry broke into Miriam's thoughts. As the two young girls chattered excitedly at the scene in front of them she smiled, yet there was a sadness in her smile.

Nell and Anne Gilmore were orphans. Sole survivors of a missionary party which had trekked to the heart of Africa, totally unprepared for the perils they encountered along the way. One by one the members of the party had died. Nell's and Anne's parents had been among the first. When there was only one man and the two girls left alive they had been found by bushmen and handed over to Daniel Retallick. Soon afterwards the girls' companion also died, and Josh and Miriam took charge of the young sisters. When the opportunity occurred to return home to Cornwall, it seemed natural for the girls to come with Josh and Miriam. They had no one else.

Miriam reached across and took Josh's hand. His start of surprise indicated that his thoughts had also been far away. As he returned his wife's smile the final rope linking the SS *Great Britain* to the quay was secured. They had arrived in

England. Another forty-eight hours should see them home in Cornwall.

The ageing, leather-sprung coach slid and lurched from pothole to wheel-carved furrow as it negotiated the steep hillside road skirting the eastern rim of Cornwall's Bodmin Moor. On the high, exposed driving seat a coachman hauled on the reins and cursed the snorting, high-stepping horses as they shied at a steep, downward slope. He would have cracked the long, plaited leather thong of his whip about their ears had he not needed both hands to fight the long reins. Heavy showers in the last few days had made the indifferent road treacherous. A momentary lapse could result in coach, passengers and horses sliding off the road and plunging to the bottom of the mine-torn valley, seven hundred feet below.

Inside the coach the two young Gilmore girls squealed, half in fun, half through fear at the erratic movements of the vehicle. On the seat between them Miriam clung to both as well as she could. She had long given up uttering comforting platitudes, choosing to utilise her energies to prevent the girls from suffering injury.

On the opposite seat, Josh sat alone, impervious to the violent movement of the coach, so engrossed was he with the scene outside.

"We should be able to see Sharptor soon . . ." Josh slid along the polished leather seat and shifted his gaze to the window on the other side of the seat as the uncertain camber of the rough road tilted the coach away from the valley.

"Thank the Lord for that. It means the journey's

6

almost over. These last few miles have been worse than the storm we went through in the Bay of Biscay."

Josh looked at Miriam in surprise as the coach levelled out on a section of road recently filled and graded. "But we're almost *home*. This is Cornwall . . . the moor. Here, let me take Anne."

Reaching across the gap between the two seats, Josh took the six-year-old Gilmore girl from Miriam and sat her upon his knee. "Yes, we're almost home, young lady. This is where you'll be living — just around the corner of the next hill."

"I don't like it. There are too many chimneys and smoke . . . and things."

Josh met Miriam's raised-eyebrowed glance and he grimaced. "Those chimneys belong to the mines where men and women around here earn their living — but not enough chimneys are throwing out smoke. I'd say all isn't well with the copper-mining industry in Cornwall."

"I don't care about smoky old mine-chimneys. I liked it better in Africa."

Once again the two adults in the coach exchanged glances, but this time it was Miriam who spoke, "We've left Africa behind for good, Anne. Sharptor will be your new home. You'll enjoy it more when you see the house — and make friends to play with."

"Look! There's a pig . . . with lots of babies," Nell's excited observation caused the younger sister to wriggle free of Josh's grasp and join her at the open coach window.

"It's good to see them behaving as children should," said Miriam quietly.

Josh nodded, his eyes taking in another smokeless mine-chimney. Something was *very* wrong. It was mid-week and the mines — many more than he remembered — should have been in full production, smoke belching from tall granite chimneys, the clattering of ore stamps echoing from tor to tor. Yet less than half were working.

An unexpected shout of "*Whoa!*" from the coach driver brought horses and coach to a sliding halt.

Putting his head out of the open window, Josh saw a line of men standing across the road. They were dressed as miners, but the pick-axes and long-handled shovels they carried were not implements of work today. Each tool was held in the manner a soldier might hold a bayonet-fitted rifle, or a pike.

"Where you making for?" One of the miners, a burly, narrow-browed, bearded man put the question to the coach driver.

"Up to Sharptor," was the coachman's reply.

The miners closed in on the wagon. "What's your business on the tor? 'Tisn't a place for a coach and horses."

"He's taking me to my home," Josh swung open the door and stepped stiffly to the ground. He was puzzled by the attitude of the miners, but grateful for an opportunity to stretch his aching legs. "My wife and two young girls are inside. We've all been travelling for a long time, so I'd be obliged if you'd stand aside and let us pass."

"Who are you?" The miners' shovel-wielding

8

spokesman stood his ground. "I've not seen you before — and I've been working a core at the Sharptor mine for ten years."

"*I* know him, Marcus."

The words were spoken by a young, beardless miner, who could have been no more than seventeen years old. "It's Josh Retallick on his way home from Africa. he wrote telling my ma he was coming." The young man extended his hand towards Josh. "You won't know me, Mr Retallick. I'm Jethro Shovell — Cap'n Shovell's son."

Josh shook the young miner's hand warmly, "I'd have recognised you anywhere. You favour your mother. How is she — and your brother? He was no more than a babe-in-arms when I left Cornwall."

Jenny Shovell and Josh had been like brother and sister when both were young. It seemed a lifetime ago . . . It *was* a full life span for many of the young men employed in the highly dangerous copper and tin mines of Cornwall — as Jethro's next words proved.

His face displaying anguish, he said, "My brother was killed in a mine accident, two years ago. A ladder broke loose when he was on his way down. His death tore ma apart for a while."

"I'm sorry, Jethro. I really am." Josh seized at a means of changing the subject. "What's going on here? Why are you and the others mounting a guard on the road?"

Jethro Shovell looked suddenly ill at ease and the miner he had called Marcus answered Josh's question, "The machinery of the Sharptor mine's

9

been put up for sale. If we let it go the mine'll never work again — and neither will anyone in Henwood."

Josh was shocked, but not altogether surprised. "By the look of things it isn't the only mine to shut down hereabouts. Coming across the moor I counted more smokeless chimneys than working ones."

"The difference between us and them is there's still enough ore in Sharptor to give us all a living if the mine was properly managed. It's a *good* mine." Jethro Shovell spoke passionately. "But you'll know that yourself, you built the engine for the mine."

"That was more than twenty years ago, Jethro. Times change. So do mines — "

" — and mine *owners*," the interruption came from another of the miners, an older man than the others. "Theophilus Strike would have owned the Sharptor mine when you were here. He kept it until he died, only six months since. Nigh on ninety, he was, but a better man than his nephew, for all that."

There was a murmur of agreement from the other miners and Jethro Shovell explained, "First thing Leander Strike did was try and sell shares in the Sharptor mine. Said he needed to raise capital if the mine was to keep going. We all reckoned at the time he wanted to raise money to pay his gambling debts. Whatever the reason, it didn't work. There's been too much money lost in mining in recent years. With the price of copper dropping almost daily no one in his right senses would buy mining shares."

"So he's put the machinery up for sale?"

Josh looked at the grim faces of the miners as they nodded confirmation. There was something about a Cornish miner that was unmistakable. Josh would have recognised their origin and calling had he met with them anywhere in the world.

"He'll not find a buyer so long as we're here — and there are others guarding the roads from Darley and Barriow Bridge." Jethro Shovell spoke of the two other roads which approached Sharptor. Both merged in Henwood village, the houses of which were visible little more than a half-mile away.

Suddenly embarrassed by the intensity of his feelings, Jethro Shovell added sheepishly. "But you've had a long journey. You and Mrs Retallick will be wanting to get the girls home. We've held you up long enough listening to our troubles. You'll find a nice warm fire burning at your place up on the tor. My ma and yours must have cleaned and warmed the place through twice a day for weeks now. They're that excited about you coming back from Africa."

Miriam smiled at the young man. This was the homecoming she had dreamed about. If only Daniel were here . . . but she was determined to allow nothing to spoil this day for her.

As Josh climbed on board, the coach started off with an unannounced suddenness. Miriam had to hold the two girls tight to her to prevent them sliding off the seat. She smiled at each of them in turn. *They* were her family now. The girls had survived an ordeal that would have unbalanced the mind of a grown man, and they had no one else. She hugged them closer. Six-year-old Anne yielded to her embrace, but Nell, thin and wiry and two years senior to her sister, wriggled free and moved closer to the open window.

"Look . . . soldiers!" Nell suddenly pointed to where a small cluster of cottages and a tall, grey mine building had come into view beyond the yellow gorse and dark green fern, higher up the slope.

"It's militiamen . . . at the Sharptor mine," Josh peered from the window. "Jethro Shovell never mentioned anything about soldiers."

"He and the others probably know nothing about them. The militiamen will have marched across the moor from Bodmin. If the miners fall foul of them there'll be trouble. Serious trouble."

Not far from the road a young girl armed with a stick was noisily driving a small flock of goats away from the fern towards a grassier spot. Her faded and badly patched dress was much too small for her and had probably been handed down at least four or five times.

Calling from the window for the coachman to halt the vehicle, Josh shouted to the goat-girl, "You! Girl!" He needed to repeat his words three times before she turned her face towards him. "Come here . . . I want you."

The girl seemed reluctant to comply, but after shooing the goats farther from the dense-growing fern she came half the distance to the coach before stopping once more.

"What d'you want with me?"

"I need a message taken to some men waiting

12

along the road towards the Phoenix."

"I've got Mr Barnicoat's goats to look after. If I don't keep 'em out of the fern they'll eat it and blow themselves up fatter 'n pigs."

"Take the goats with you. They'll come to no harm. I'll give you threepence."

"I'll not put my job at risk for *threepence!*" The girl's voice was heavy with scorn, coloured by a rapid assessment of how much more she might ask from a man who wore a suit and rode in a carriage. "It'll cost you a shilling — at *least.*"

Miriam's chuckle was no salve to Josh's exasperation.

"If it wasn't so important I'd tell the little hussy to go to hell. As it is . . . !" Josh fingered a silver coin from his pocket, "All right — but hurry. You'll find Jethro Shovell up the road with some miners. Tell them there are militiamen up at Sharptor mine. They should keep clear of them."

The coin spun through the air and the girl pounced on it as it hit the ground. Backing away, she reached the goats before calling out, "The miners already know about the militia. Me and my brother saw them coming down off the moor and I sent Jacob off to tell Jethro. You must have passed him on the road."

"Why, you . . . !"

Miriam's laugh cut through her husband's not-too-serious anger. "Doesn't she remind you of someone?"

"Who?"

"*Me,* when I was ten or eleven and living in the cave, up on the moor."

13

Josh looked again at the cheeky, young goatherd. There *was* a certain likeness . . . but Miriam was calling through the window.

"What's your name girl?"

"Lottie. Lottie Trago. What business is it of yours?"

Miriam drew in her breath sharply. Her own maiden name had been Trago.

"What's you mother's name?"

"I ain't got no mother . . . nor a father, neither. I live with my Aunt Patience."

"I knew it!" Miriam was filled with a confusing mixture of emotions. "Patience is my sister! The girl must be Jane's daughter. That means Jane must be dead. She was the youngest of the family, too."

The ragged young goatherd had turned away and was driving her charges across the moor. She intended putting a good distance between herself and her duped benefactor in case he tried to retrieve his shilling.

"Lottie!"

The young girl turned her head, but kept walking.

"When you return home, tell your Aunt Patience to come up to Sharptor as soon as she has a minute to spare. Tell her . . . tell her Miriam's come home."

14

2

THE coach was brought to a halt for the second time that day as it skirted the Sharptor mine. This time the men standing in the road wore the scarlet coats of militiamen — and they were armed with long-barrelled rifles.

Before the part-time soldiers could ask the coachman his destination two men hurried from the mine. One was tall, thin and balding. His companion wore the unfamiliar uniform and insignia of a police inspector.

"I'm Leander Strike. This is Police Inspector Coote. Are you here to look over the mine machinery? You'll find it in splendid condition. The engine's a superb model." Leander Strike spoke eagerly . . . far *too* eagerly. "You'll find the price equally attractive, I'm sure."

"You have no need to tell me anything about the Sharptor mine engine — but I'm not here to buy mine equipment. I'm on my way home — though I'm being stopped and asked so many questions it's likely to take twice as long as it should."

Leander Strike's attitude underwent an immediate change. His eagerness was replaced first by disappointment, then by suspicion. "There's nothing on the moor beyond here but mine cottages — and you're no miner."

"I own the old farmhouse farther up the hill beyond the mine. I've been away for some years,

15

but now I'm home again."

The mine owner stared at Josh as though looking at a ghost, "My uncle sold the house and land up there many years ago . . . to Josh Retallick."

Police Inspector Kingsley Coote, a grey-haired man with a heavy, drooping moustache, frowned. "When I was a young constable in Bodmin I remember the arrest of a lad named Josh Retallick. Must be all of twenty years ago now. He took a leading part in a riot down at the port of Looe, if my memory serves me right. Convicted at Bodmin Assizes of conspiracy to treason and sedition — a capital offence. But instead of hanging he was sentenced to transportation. For *life,* as I remember."

"Your memory's excellent, Inspector." Josh met the challenge of the inspector's eyes. "I was convicted of a conspiracy. *Wrongly* convicted. I have a Queen's pardon in my luggage, together with a copy of the guilty party's confession. Now we've got that out of the way, I'd like to take my wife and these two young girls home. We've all had a long journey from the heart of Africa and are very weary."

"Africa, you say? Africa?"

Leander Strike was less impressed than his companion, "You might have a pardon, Retallick, but there's seldom smoke without fire . . . " He looked at Josh suspiciously. "I've got troubles with the men and their so-called 'unions'. Things have become so serious Inspector Coote's found it necessary to call out the militia. Now a man who's been convicted of stirring up sedition appears on the scene! I'd say that's more than coincidence."

"You can say whatever you like, Strike, but don't question my character too loudly or you'll find yourself in a courtroom. From all I've heard you can do without any further trouble. Ask the militiamen to stand aside if you please, Inspector. We're going home."

The police inspector waved the militiamen off the road, but before the coach pulled away, he said to Josh, "I don't doubt your pardon is on record, Mr Retallick," something in the policeman's voice left Josh in no doubt the inspector would check his story, "but you spoke as though you've been stopped elsewhere today. Is someone trying to prevent access to the Sharptor mine?"

"Not to my knowledge," Josh lied. "It would seem coaches are such rarities on the roads hereabouts that folks are insatiably curious."

The police inspector expressed neither belief nor disbelief. "Loaded ore carts are just as unusual as carriages these days, Mr Retallick, as you'll find out for yourself. It's rare too for a mining man to be *returning* to Cornwall. Most are leaving. I trust you'll let me know of anything you hear that might be of interest to me?"

Josh inclined his head absent-mindedly. He was thinking of the inspector's words and looking towards the tall, Sharptor mine engine-house. A great cast-iron beam protruded through an opening high up in the building. Inside was the engine — *his* engine. He had built it after serving a three-year apprenticeship at the Harveys foundry at Hayle. Had supervised its installation on this mine. The finest engine in the county, it

17

had been built to last a lifetime.

Incorporated in the great wooden beams which descended deep into the mine-shaft was a revolutionary 'man-engine', the first of its kind in the county. Nearby was the pumping-engine he had also built and installed . . .

Josh's gaze shifted to the police inspector and then on to Leander Strike, "Mining is a peculiar business, Inspector. You need to be a gambler to invest in a mine — and only the boldest gamblers succeed."

Josh and his father leaned side by side on the gate beside the stable at the rear of the house, saying little. There was no need for talk. Blue smoke rose lazily from the pipes clenched between the teeth of both men and each was content in the companionship of the other. The emotional reunions were over. Almost twenty years of separation had been bridged.

From where the men stood, high Bodmin Moor fell away to the Marke valley. Beyond the valley the land unfolded in a breathtakingly spectacular fashion to the wide plains extending on either side of the Tamar river. On the far horizon the western heights of Dartmoor rose, an irregular mass, from the plain. A brief, early-summer storm seemed to be following the course of the river that separated Cornwall from the rest of England. Behind the storm a soft-hued rainbow promised a crock of gold on either side of Kit Hill. The mine-embellished landmark reared a thousand feet from the valley floor to form a giant stepping-stone between the two moors.

Behind the two men Miriam called from somewhere in the house and she was answered by Anne's high-pitched, excited voice.

"It's been a long time since we last shared a pouch of tobacco," Ben Retallick broke the silence between father and son. "Your ma's had all her prayers answered by your return with Miriam and the two young maids for her to fuss over. If only young Daniel had come with you her happiness would be complete."

"Miriam would agree with ma, but Daniel's a young man with a life of his own — and a good trading business between Matabeleland and the coast. He's an important man in that part of the world. He'll be among the richest one day, I've no doubt."

"You've done well too, boy. Your ma and me are proud of you."

"None of us need ever go hungry," Josh conceded. "That's more than most can say, hereabouts. The mines seem to have fallen on hard times."

"Mining's always been an uncertain business — as much for the men who put up the money as for those who work below grass. Matters have grown worse these past few years. Every time the price of tin and copper drops more men are laid off. Many are leaving Cornwall and going to wherever there's work to be had. Mexico, Australia, America, South Africa . . . but you'll know something of this for yourself."

Josh nodded. He had successfully mined copper in South West Africa where many other minerals were being discovered and

19

worked by immigrant miners.

Ben Retallick knocked out his pipe against the heel of one of his heavy mining boots. He was now sixty-one years old, but until the Sharptor mine closed down he had been one of the mine's shift-captains, responsible for the smooth and efficient management of the mine during his tour of duty.

"Was the Sharptor mine being worked the way it should have been, before it went out of business?"

Ben Retallick shook his head vigorously, "It's been running down for years. Theophilus Strike was reluctant to hand it over to anyone else. I think he knew what that nephew of his would do. During his last years Theophilus was too old to visit us here and we couldn't get a sensible decision from him. We haven't had a decent engineer on the mine for years and the engines are costing twice as much to run as they should. Tom Shovell held things together while he was mine captain, but he retired a couple of years back and Theophilus wouldn't appoint anyone to take his place. Accidents were beginning to happen and the men were becoming edgy. You can't run a mine that way."

"I met Tom's son along the road today. He seems a nice enough lad."

Josh told his father of the miners who had brought his coach to a halt.

Ben Retallick nodded seriously as he refilled his pipe. "Jethro's a good lad but he's keeping bad company. Marcus Hooper's been struck off the books of every mine hereabouts. We've no

20

place for all this 'trade union' nonsense in the mines of Cornwall. It serves no useful purpose and gives the owners another excuse for laying off men. They have reasons enough, without being handed more."

Josh did not challenge his father's peremptory dismissal of the aims and usefulness of the trade unions. It was a subject on which they had never been able to agree. This, at least, had not changed.

"Is there still enough ore underground in the Sharptor mine to make running it worthwhile?"

"*Properly* run it could be the best little mine in the area. It'll never be as grand as the Phoenix once was — or make as much money as the Caradon — yet it could bring in a tidy profit. But it needs to have money spent on it — and Leander Strike's not a man to spend money on such a venture. What with his gambling debts and a son away at some expensive school near London, he's hard-pressed for money to live on."

"What's he hoping to make from the sale of the engine and machinery?"

Ben Retallick cast a speculative glance at his son before shrugging his shoulders. "There are more engines than pasties on sale in Cornwall right now. I've heard Strike is seeking at least five hundred pounds. I'd say he has more hope than expectation. He'll be lucky to get scrap value. Either way, it's the end for the Sharptor mine. It won't effect your ma or me too much. I've spent a lifetime burrowing in the ground like a mole. It's time I got to know the sun. It's the young miner I feel sorry for, especially one with a young family.

He's a choice of taking his wife and children away from everything they've ever known, or staying and watching them starve."

Ben Retallick sucked his pipe noisily into life and peered at his son through the blue smoke. "Are all these questions leading somewhere?"

Josh nodded before straightening up away from the gate. "It's possible, but let's go up to the house and see whether Ma and Miriam have managed to get the girls to bed yet." He shivered suddenly. "It may be early summer for everyone else, but twenty years in Africa's thinned my blood."

Miriam's sister, Patience, came to the house at Sharptor early the next morning. Seeing the two women standing together they were unmistakably sisters — but the similarities ended with the physical likeness. Patience was a washed-out drab woman of twenty-nine, already greyer-haired than Miriam although she was eleven years her junior. Part of the reason for this was revealed when she admitted to having lost two children before giving birth to the three she brought with her on her visit to Sharptor. The surviving children were all under five years of age. They played with the Gilmore girls in the garden, their clothes contrasting painfully. Nell and Anne were wearing new, good quality dresses, while the clothes of Miriam's nieces would not have been accepted for cleaning-rags by a fussy woman.

Patience was aware of the contrast in the children's clothing and she said apologetically, "It's difficult keeping them decently clad with things being the way they are. I can get bal-work on the mines sometimes — but Marcus couldn't get steady work, even when all the mines were working."

"Would that be Marcus Hooper?"

Josh put the question sharply and Patience looked at him quickly before shrugging her shoulders in a gesture of resignation. "I see you've heard of him already. He says he'd feel less of a man if he didn't speak up for what he believes in and I suppose he's right, but it don't make things any easier for me and the kids when there's no money coming in. I suppose I shouldn't complain, really. He gets angry with Lottie and Jacob sometimes, but he wouldn't see 'em without a roof over their heads, even though they're nothing to do with him."

"Our Jane's children? We met up with young Lottie yesterday," Miriam paused in the act of pouring boiling water on the tea leaves spooned into the cups on the table. "When did Jane die?"

"Jane's not dead! Oh no, not *that* one — though she might as well be as far as Lottie and Jacob are concerned. She ran off with one of the soldiers sent here when they were expecting trouble in the mines. I'm talking about way back, when Lottie and her brother were hardly more than babes. There never was no trouble, except what Jane brought on herself. She'd let the fathers of Lottie and Jacob get away with what they did . . . but she wasn't going to let this one out of her sight until he'd done the right thing by her. I suppose two bastard children by someone else would hardly strengthen her claim on him,

23

would it? Especially that Lottie. She's growing up as wild as the moor. Sometimes I think she deliberately sets out to anger Marcus."

Jenny Shovel was in the house and she came from the kitchen with flour halfway up her arms, in time to hear Patience's last words. Snorting loudly, she said, "It doesn't take a great deal to anger that man of yours. I sometimes wonder why you stay with him. Mind you, that young Lottie has enough cheek to try the patience of a saint."

"I've told her so myself, many times, but she doesn't heed me. The only one she'll listen to is your Jethro. If he so much as says 'Hello' to her you'd think she'd been given a shilling."

The mention of a shilling reminded Miriam of her introduction to her ragged niece, but a tight-lipped Jenny Shovell was talking again. "I've told our Jethro to keep away from her. She's trouble. Unless something's done about her she'll end up like her mother." Her face suddenly registered embarrassment. Turning to Miriam, she said, "Begging your pardon, Miriam. I know Jane's your sister, but there's no denying she scandalised Henwood with her ways."

Trying to hide a smile, Miriam said, "I seem to remember I did the same when I was Lottie's age."

As Jenny Shovell's embarrassment grew, Miriam allowed her smile to show. "I was very taken with what *I* saw of the girl. I'll try to persuade her to come here to Sharptor to live. She'll be company for Nell and Anne. Nell's a very prim little thing, they'll be good for one another. Tell her to come and see me, Patience."

"I will," said Patience, gratefully, " . . . when I see her."

Patience suddenly realised from the expressions of the others that she would have to explain further.

"It's Marcus. When he loses his temper with her she runs off, taking young Jacob with her. She did it again last night. I used to worry myself silly about her, thinking she wouldn't come back. But sooner or later there she is one mealtime, sitting at table as large as life, just as though nothing's happened. It'll be the same this time, I don't doubt."

"Where does she go?"

"Who knows? Could be anywhere. Lottie knows this moor as well as folks say you once knew it, Miriam. Although I doubt if she'll do as well as you. This house is *lovely* . . . and your clothes . . . Our ma would be proud had she lived to see you now."

"Yes, well . . . you drink your tea and I'll take you upstairs. I've a couple of dresses I don't need any more. They'll serve you a treat. There are one or two things the girls have grown out of too. They'll fit your eldest, at least."

3

LEAVING Miriam and Patience turning out clothes from the trunks which had travelled with them from Africa, Josh walked down the hill to the Sharptor mine. The sisters had much to talk about, he would not be missed.

The militiamen had left the mine the previous evening. They had been called to another mine a couple of miles away where out-of-work miners had caused damage to a mine-engine being dismantled for a foreign purchaser. It seemed a new militancy was in the air among the despairing miners.

Josh hoped to find Leander Strike at the mine, he had a proposition to put to the mine owner. However, the mine was deserted and Josh wandered among the buildings, saddened by the air of neglect he saw everywhere. Paintwork was cracked and peeling, broken panes of glass had not been replaced for years and some doors stood open, drooping on torn hinges.

Many timbers in the mine buildings were rotting away and the low roof of one sagged crazily. This building, beside the mine store, had once been the miners' changing-room. Here, Josh found signs that someone had been sleeping amid the accumulated rubbish. He thought immediately of Lottie Trago and her young brother, although it might just as easily be a sleeping-place for any one of the scores of vagrants who tramped the mining districts in a vain search for work.

Josh had been looking around the mine for almost half an hour when he heard the sound of a horse turning in to the mine from the road. It was Leander Strike — and he was not pleased to see Josh.

Still sitting his horse, the mine owner scowled down at Josh. "What are you doing here, Retallick? Your place is up the hill. This is private property. Neither you nor anyone else has a right to snoop around the Sharptor mine."

"I came looking for you."

Dismounting, Leander Strike said, "If you want to discuss work you're after wasting your time and mine. There isn't a copper mine in Cornwall can afford to take on an engineer. These are bad times, Retallick. You should have made some enquiries before coming back from wherever you were."

"I'm not here to beg for work. I've come with an offer to buy the Sharptor mine from you."

Three times Leander appeared about to say something and twice he was unable to find words. At the third attempt he repeated Josh's statement with some difficulty. "You . . . want to buy the Sharptor mine?"

As Leander Strike fought his disbelief he tried to remember what his uncle had told him of the man who stood before him.

Josh Retallick was a powerfully built, fit-looking man, his skin deep-tanned from many years spent in the fierce sunshine of Africa. He had earned a reputation as a fine engineer when still young — the name of Josh Retallick was invariably mentioned whenever Cornish engineers were being discussed. No doubt his skills were exaggerated with the passing of time, but Theophilus Strike had been convinced until his dying day that in Josh Retallick, the Sharptor mine had possessed Cornwall's finest engineer. Had Retallick not become actively involved in the twin evils of unionism and reform, Theophilus Strike believed he would have become the most skilful and inventive engineer Cornwall had ever known.

Trade unionism was anathema to Leander Strike. Irrationally, he blamed trade union activists for his own troubles, refusing to accept that he knew nothing at all about mining. Yet here was a convicted trade union agitator standing before him discussing the purchase of the Sharptor mine as though he were a gentleman!

"The Sharptor mine's not up for sale."

Now it was Josh's turn to show surprise, "But . . . you mistook me for a buyer when I arrived at Sharptor yesterday."

"I'm selling the engine and pumping equipment because it's past its prime. I'm not selling the mine. One day the price of copper might make it worthwhile opening up again."

"If that ever happens you'll have a hundred mines clamouring to buy any engine still available. Prices will be far beyond your reach. Even if you managed to obtain an engine there'd be no one left in Cornwall to work it. The Sharptor mine engine is still one of the finest in Cornwall and will serve for many more years. It just needs a little work carried out on it, that's all."

"It can be done elsewhere. The engine goes. If

you want to buy a few shares in the mine for old times' sake I'll be glad to oblige you. One and sixpence each was their last quotation. If Great Uncle Strike had sold when I suggested the mine would have fetched thousands and I would have inherited a fortune. Instead, I'm hanging around a useless mine, waiting for an engine-buyer who'll probably never arrive and talking to a convicted agitator. All right, so you've been granted a pardon, it doesn't alter the facts. Go back to Africa, or wherever you came from. Buy a mine there."

"I've been involved in mining in Africa — and my mines made good profits. So too could the Sharptor mine. If you have no interest in working the mine for yourself, at least think of the men and their families who look to the Sharptor mine for a living."

"Have *they* ever thought of *me?* No, they damned well haven't. *I* have a family to keep too, Retallick. If you precious miners had worked a damned sight harder over the years and not tried to squeeze every penny they could from my uncle, the Sharptor mine might still be producing copper. I don't doubt it's the same story in most other mines. It isn't enough for a man to earn an honest living these days. He needs to make believe he's as good as the man who gives him his livelihood. He wants to elect men to parliament. Some of the most dangerous agitators even talk of standing for election themselves! They dream of becoming gentlemen overnight — but without accepting any of a gentleman's responsibilities, of course. It takes hundreds of years to make a gentleman, Retallick. It's high time some of these 'unionists' realised that."

"By 'responsibilities' I presume you mean ensuring that men less fortunate than your 'gentlemen' are able to work?"

"I'm talking of *all* the responsibilities of a gentleman . . . but I can't expect *you* to understand. I've said all I have to say. The Sharptor mine's not for sale. That's an end to it."

"I doubt that. Mr Strike. I doubt that very much."

Josh walked away from the Sharptor mine trying hard to swallow his deep disappointment. He had been convinced Leander Strike would sell. The manner of the mine owner's refusal had not helped to make it any more palatable.

In the evening Josh and Miriam took the girls to Henwood chapel. Wrightwick Roberts, the minister, conducted a service of thanksgiving for the safe return of Josh and Miriam to the village of their birth.

Contrary to general Methodist practice Roberts had been the Wesleyan minister in the area for more than forty years and well remembered Josh's conviction and transportation.

An ex-miner himself, Wrightwick Roberts understood the miners' ways and had spent a lifetime fighting with all his God-given faculties for their souls and their temporal well-being. More than one man had ruefully declared that God had blessed Wrightwick Roberts with hard and mighty fists.

The ex-miner preacher was in his seventy-seventh year. He still possessed the broad shoulders of his

30

youth, but they were more rounded now and there was a gauntness to his great-boned frame. It was almost time he moved aside to make way for a younger man.

As Ben Retallick walked home in the darkness with Josh, Miriam and the children, he expressed his thoughts about the service and the Henwood minister. "He'll be hard to replace. Henwood needs a special kind of minister in these difficult times. Certainly not one trained in city ways."

Josh was carrying Anne on his shoulders and he shifted her to a more comfortable position before replying. "Wrightwick hasn't retired yet. When he does you mustn't judge his successor before he has a chance to prove himself. I've heard it said John Wesley wasn't too much to look at and without enough meat on him to fill a pasty, yet he didn't let it stop him from doing everything he set out to do."

"Perhaps. All the same . . . "

At that moment Miriam said, "Look! There's someone at the mine . . . but who'd be lighting a fire there at this time of night?"

"No one who's up to any good."

Josh had seen the shadowy figure of a man silhouetted against the flames. "That blaze is either in the store or the old changing-room alongside."

As he swung Anne from his shoulders to the ground he remembered the make-shift bed he had seen amid the accumulated rubbish in the derelict building.

"Miriam, run back to the village and get help, then take the children on home. Pa and I will see what we can do in the meantime."

Without waiting for an answer Josh ran towards the mine buildings, his father keeping pace behind him. As Josh neared the blaze he could see he had been right. The blaze was in the rubbish inside the old changing-room and it had already spread to the dry and rotting beams. Yet even as he made the observation he saw flames licking from another building many yards from the first.

Ben Retallick saw the new blaze too and was heading towards it when Josh called him back. "Leave it. We must try to get this one out first. I believe this is where Lottie and Jacob Trago have been sleeping."

Ben Retallick looked at his son with an expression of horror on his face, "You don't think they're inside now?"

"I don't know — but we'll need to find out."

The fire had gained a rapid hold on the accumulated rubbish inside the changing-room and it was impossible to go in through the door. The flames had not yet reached the far end of the building, but it would not be long. Smoke was already beginning to seep out from between the crooked tiles.

A pile of rubble from the workings was piled against the wall. Scrambling to the top, Josh climbed on the sagging roof of the building and began tearing off tiles.

"We need water. There's plenty down in the levels, but none up here . . . " Ben Retallick stood looking up at Josh helplessly.

"There's water been left standing in the engine's boiler. You know where the tap is. See if you can find a bucket somewhere."

Josh stopped talking abruptly. The dry wooden beams of the changing-room were burning with a sound that resembled the crackle of musket fire, fanned by a stiff breeze. But Josh had heard another sound. Ripping away another couple of slates from the roof and sending them spinning into the night, he crouched low over the hole he had made.

Straightening up suddenly, he turned an agonised face towards his father, "They're in here. The children. *I can hear them screaming!*"

Josh redoubled his efforts, tearing off the slates regardless of the broken nails and torn fingers he suffered in the process. He was working desperately when other figures climbed to the roof beside him. The villagers had seen the flames even before Miriam reached Henwood to sound the alarm.

Josh passed on his grim news without pausing in his efforts and as more roof beams were exposed the cries of Lottie and her brother could be heard more clearly. But it seemed all his efforts might have been in vain. The changing-room and the store beside it had been built at a time when there was no need for economy. The buildings were built to last. The roof beams were placed so close together Josh knew he could not slip between them and drop to where the terrified children were hidden by smoke. Meanwhile the flames were drawing closer with every wasted moment.

"We need an axe . . . now!"

As the miners looked blankly at each other,

Josh's heart sank. No one had thought of bringing one.

"Try the blacksmith's shop." Even as he spoke Josh remembered the steel door of the smithy, secured with a stout padlock and chain. By the time the men broke in it would be too late. Already the flames from the fire had advanced across much of the still-slated section of the roof.

Suddenly a slight figure appeared on the roof. It was Jethro Shovell. Turning a pale face towards Josh, he said, "I think I might just squeeze through the gap between the beams. Let me try."

"You might get inside — but I doubt if you'll be able to climb back out again." As Josh spoke a whole section of roof collapsed into the fire at the far end of the building, sending a column of sparks high in the air. They hung there for a moment before raining down upon the rescuers. Inside the building renewed screams arose from the two trapped children.

"I've got to try. That's Lottie in there." Jethro Shovell stripped off his coat and sat down on a beam, his legs dangling inside the burning building.

"Just a minute . . . " A miner scrambled to the roof. In his hand he carried a battered bucket filled with water. "I'll damp you down with this." Without waiting for a reply he tipped the contents of the bucket over the young miner.

The water was cold and Jethro Shovell gasped in sudden shock. Then, remembering the children, he grasped a beam and eased himself feet first into the burning changing-room. At first it seemed even he might be too large to squeeze through

34

the narrow space. Then he expelled the breath from his body and promptly dropped out of sight inside the smoke-filled building.

Once inside Jethro Shovell wasted no time. Barely twenty seconds after his disappearance the head and arms of Lottie Trago appeared between two beams. She was quickly pulled clear by Josh. She clung to him, quivering with fear until he lowered her to the arms of the men standing on the ground.

Josh could hear Jethro Shovell coughing inside the changing-room, and then the young miner's hoarse voice called, "Jacob is unconscious. I'll try to pass him up to you."

Smoke was billowing up through the almost tileless roof now and it had become unbearably hot on the wooden beams. There was a long silence broken only by the crackling of the fire. Then, after another bout of coughing, Jethro Shovell called with what remained of his voice, "Why didn't you take him . . . ?"

"None of us saw anything. Carry him closer to the wall." Realising it might prove dangerous for Jethro to attempt to find his way through the smoke and flames inside the burning building, Josh shouted, "Follow my voice . . . and bring the boy with you. Keep going until you come to the wall and then hand him up. Keep going . . . Don't stop. You must pass him up and come out yourself. *Quickly!*"

Josh was sliding down the narrow-angled roof as he was speaking. The reason for his sudden urgency was the collapse of yet another large section of roof. It sent flames chasing a fountain

35

of sparks high in the night air. The fire was advancing at such an alarming speed now that no part of the roof could be considered safe. Other miners, realising the danger, hurriedly leapt to the ground. Soon only Josh and one other man remained on the burning building.

"Are you there, Jethro? Hurry, man!"

"I'm at the wall . . . holding him up . . . "

Josh felt down through the choking smoke and his hands came in contact with a small body. He took a grip of the boy's clothing and heaved, hoping Jacob Trago's clothing was more substantial than that worn by his sister. They were not. Josh could feel them tearing in his grasp as he lifted. Fortunately, they held together long enough for him to pull the boy through the space between the beams and into the arms of the other miner on the roof. Moments later Jacob was passed down to the uplifted arms of the other miners.

The moment he released his grasp, Josh turned back to the burning building and called inside, "Jethro . . . can you hear me?"

There was no answer. By now the smoke was so thick Josh too was choking and the flames were perilously close.

"Jethro . . . *can you hear me?* Stand chose to the wall and lift up your arms!"

Josh groped through the roof, reaching as far as he could. He could feel nothing and the heat was scorching his cheek now.

"*Jethro!* For God's sake reach up. *You must . . . !*"

Josh thought he could hear coughing somewhere below him, but he could no longer be certain. The fire was making a great deal of noise and

36

the heat fast becoming unbearable. Another few moments and he would have to abandon his place on the roof.

The other miner was also feeling down through the roof beside Josh and he suddenly let out a triumphant shout, "He's here! I've got him. Give me a hand."

Josh hurriedly shifted his position and reached down. He found Jethro's hand clasped by the other miner. Reaching further he was able to grasp the young man's wrist.

Jethro Shovell was practically dead weight, but as Josh hauled on his arm, Jethro's other hand came up in a weak protest at the pain and Josh grasped this arm too.

"Heave!" As he called, Josh straightened up, bringing the body of the limp young miner with him.

Jethro Shovell took a blow on the head from one of the beams as he was hauled through the narrow gap, but he reached safety — and not a moment too soon. His clothes were smouldering and he had lost most of his eyebrows — but he was alive.

Josh and his fellow-rescuer swiftly followed the minister to the ground. Squatting beside him, they coughed up the smoke from their lungs. Less than a minute later the remainder of the roof crashed inwards with a roar that sent the men standing close to the blaze scurrying hastily to safety.

Jethro Shovell was retching and coughing and as he struggled to a sitting position men pummelled him on the back in a bid to rid his lungs of the smoke he had swallowed.

Through streaming eyes Josh could see Lottie apparently none the worse for her experience trying to reach Jethro.

When Jethro had partially recovered from the combined effect of smoke and pummelling, he called hoarsely to Josh, "Jacob . . . is he alive?"

Josh looked to where Jacob Trago was crying noisily, comforted by Patience Hooper.

"He's fine. He's a very lucky boy."

Josh climbed to his feet and rested a hand on the young miner's shoulder. "There's not much wrong with you either, Jethro. Lottie and Jacob owe you their lives — and I can see that Lottie, for one, will never forget her debt."

4

THE more Josh thought about the shadowy figure he had seen in the early glow of the mine fire, the more convinced he was that he knew the identity of the arsonist. However, he said nothing to Police Inspector Kingsley Coote.

The police inspector arrived at the Sharptor mine the day after the fire. He found some thirty ex-Sharptor miners cutting out charred and blackened wood and piling it well clear of the buildings. By doing this they hoped to ensure there would be no fresh fire should a strong moorland breeze spring up.

Inspector Coote wandered about the mine for some time, peering inside buildings and occasionally using the toe of his boot to stir the charred wood in an apparently aimless fashion. Eventually he came to where Josh and his father stood in the shadow of the engine-building, enjoying a rest and a smoke.

Inclining his head to both men, the inspector said nothing until he too had packed and lit a large pipe. Then, breathing smoke, he said, "To see the way the men are working today you'd hardly believe they've all been laid off."

"The Sharptor mine's been part of their lives for so long it comes natural to do whatever needs doing when something like this happens."

Inspector Coote nodded agreement with Ben Retallick's words. He drew deeply on his pipe before speaking again, "All the same, it was a Sharptor man who set fire to the place."

"You can't possibly be sure of that." This time it was Josh who answered.

"I can — and I am, although proving it will be something quite different. All the same, it was someone familiar enough with the mine to know exactly where to set four fires."

Josh had seen only two fires, but Ben Retallick nodded. "There were four fires started. Two never got going, but there were four, right enough."

"The biggest fire came very close to causing a tragedy, so I hear." Kingsley Coote might have been discussing the weather as he puffed contentedly at his pipe and gazed across the countryside. "If you hadn't known about those children I would have been looking for a murderer today, Mr Retallick."

"It was Jethro Shovell who went in after the children. He's become a hero overnight on account of it." Ben Retallick seemed unaware that Inspector Coote was pursuing his enquiries, albeit in an unobtrusive and seemingly diffident fashion.

Josh was not fooled. "I feared the children might be sleeping there. Their aunt came to the house and said they sometimes ran off and spent a night or two away from home. When I looked around the mine I saw someone had been sleeping in the old changing-room. I guessed it was Lottie and her brother — and in case you're wondering *why* I was poking into the mine buildings it was because I've offered to buy the Sharptor mine. I'd be a fool if I didn't know exactly what I'd be getting for my money. I know the engine well enough, and my father's told me all I need to know about the underground workings. I wanted to assess what there is above grass."

Ben Retallick stared at Josh open-mouthed. Josh had expressed great interest in the mine, but he had said nothing of his offer to Leander Strike.

"I'm aware of your offer, Mr Retallick. I went to see Mr Strike as soon as I was told of the fire. He would have come here with me today, but he has a bad attack of gout. He's convinced you started the fires yourself in a bid to persuade him to sell."

Ben Retallick put a hand on his son's arm, as though to prevent him from erupting in anger. But Josh was no longer the hot-headed young man who had been transported almost twenty years before.

"I'd say Leander Strike has more reason than anyone else to see his mine buildings burnt down. He'd receive more compensation from an insurance company than he'll make from selling off the machinery. However, I don't think this was his doing, any more than it was mine. You wouldn't need to look far to find a couple of hundred miners bearing grudges against Strike — but I doubt if you'll find any Sharptor man who'd start a fire here."

"That's pretty much the way I feel about it, Mr Retallick, but I'm obliged to you for your observations. Now I think I'll go and have a word with the guardian of those two runaways you were telling me about. I understand they have no parents of their own to turn to . . . "

41

When Police Inspector Coote went in search of Patience Hooper and her young charges, Ben Retallick put the surprise he felt into words.

"Were you serious when you said you've thought of buying the Sharptor mine?"

"I've done more than think about it. I made Leander Strike an offer."

Ben Retallick's looked at his son with something akin to awe in his eyes. Josh had risen above his station in life when he had qualified as a mine engineer. To consider becoming a mine *owner* was almost beyond belief.

"What did Strike say?"

"He made it perfectly clear he'd see the mine go bankrupt before he'd sell to me."

Ben Retallick's expression might have been either one of disappointment, or relief. "Oh well, all things happen for the best, or so they say."

The Sharptor mining community had hardly recovered from the excitement of Josh and Miriam's return, when another 'homecoming' occurred to threaten the tranquillity of everyday life in the small mining hamlet.

After her rescue from the burning mine building coupled with a stern warning from Police Inspector Coote about her future conduct, Lottie Trago was a much-chastened young girl for a while. So much so that the long-suffering Elias Barnicoat had grudgingly agreed to trust his goats to her once more.

Lottie's day began early in the morning when she took the goats to the high moor. She would remain here all day and return the goats to their owner in Henwood village late in the evening.

From her Sharptor house Miriam would watch her young niece driving the goats to the moor and they would exchange a wave if Lottie was not too lost in her own thoughts. Sometimes Jacob would be with Lottie, other days he might go off to find work for himself.

One day, Josh was unexpectedly called upon to help repair a damaged engine on a mine some five miles away. He left Miriam wondering what she should do with the pie she had prepared for his midday meal. Acting on a sudden impulse, she decided to take the pie to Lottie. She knew Patience was not in the habit of making up a meal for the young goatherd to take with her to the moor.

It was a fine, sunny, moorland day. As Miriam left the lush, dark-green fern behind her on the lower slopes, she felt the remembered ageless tranquillity of the moor reach out and envelop her. It was a peace that transcended physical senses, and remained untouched by the distant clatter of a stamp on an unseen tin mine.

A flood of memories returned to Miriam as she passed the strange chamber formed by huge, flat rocks, that had been her childhood home, high on the hillside. A few of the memories she had of this place were happy. Most were not.

Local superstition said this was a burial chamber, built for one of the ancient chiefs who had ruled the moorland tribes long ago, in the darkness of time. Whatever the truth of the superstition, this had been home for Miriam during the whole of her childhood. There had been a wooden door on the chamber then. Even from a distance Miriam could see it had long since been torn down, most probably for firewood. She felt no urge to go any closer and inspect the dark and brooding chamber.

Remembering the violent death of her drunken, bullying father, and the misery of her worn-out and defeated mother, Miriam felt no affection for the strange, moorland home. Indeed, merely looking at it caused her to shudder involuntarily. Miriam was relieved to turn her face to the sun-cleansed moor.

Miriam found Lottie resting on a tor-top rock that had been carved to the shape of an armchair by wind, rain and time. From here Lottie was able to keep watch on the forty-odd goats belonging to Elias Barnicoat.

The young girl was at first suspicious of her aunt's motives in coming high on the moor to find her. However, when Miriam explained and produced the man-sized pie as proof of her story, Lottie's mistrust gave way to greedy delight.

Lottie Trago ate like a young and hungry animal. In less than a quarter of the time it would have taken a grown man to eat the substantial pastry-covered meal of meat and vegetables, Lottie was cuffing the last crumbs of pastry from about her mouth and picking the odd fragment of food from her dress. None of the clothes Miriam had given to her sister had been passed on to Lottie. She still wore the same ragged dress Miriam had seen from the coach — and it was even dirtier now.

"Call in when you next pass the house," said

44

Miriam casually. "I've a dress of Nell's that should fit you. The one you're wearing is so far gone it's indecent."

Lottie was at least three years older than the eldest Gilmore girl, but she was small for her age. The dress would fit her well enough — certainly better than the one she was wearing.

"You don't have to give me nothing." There was an air of pathetic defiance in Lottie's voice. "This dress'll go on for a while yet. Anyway, Aunt Patience says it's quite good enough for herding goats up here on the moor."

Miriam suppressed an urge to hug Lottie to her. It would be a mistake. An unforgivable encroachment upon the young girl's fierce independence. The more Miriam spoke to Lottie the more she realised how much the young girl resembled *her* during her younger days. "I wouldn't want to disagree with your Aunt Patience, but I've been thinking of trying to get a school started in the village. You'll need something better than a goatherd's dress if you intend coming along."

Lottie's expression registered sheer delight for only a brief moment. It was quickly replaced by feigned nonchalance. "I won't be going to no school. *He* says learning and religion was thought up by rich folk, to teach us to keep things the way *they* want them to be."

"If by 'he' you're referring to your Uncle Marcus, that's exactly what I'd expect him to say. It isn't true, Lottie. Learning is a key that can open so many doors. Wouldn't you like to learn how to read and write? When I was your

45

age it was what I wanted more than anything else in the whole world."

Lottie discovered a random crumb she had overlooked. As she picked it up she shrugged. "It don't much matter what *I* want. If I don't tend Elias Barnicoat's goats there'll be little money coming in the house. I take home milk sometimes, too. *He* ain't going to let us lose all that just so I can go to some old school."

"There'll be no need for you to lose anything. Jacob can look after the goats for a couple of hours each morning while you go to school. Then he can go in the afternoon. I'll speak to your aunt Patience — and to Marcus — about it."

Once again Miriam glimpsed a brief flash of unguarded pleasure, but it disappeared as swiftly as before. "It won't make any difference. I won't be allowed to go to no school, neither will Jacob."

Lottie suddenly sat upright on the stone seat and looked out across the moor, "Here's Jacob now. If I'd known he was coming I'd have saved him a piece of pie . . . What's he doing up here? He's supposed to be working the bellows in the blacksmith's shop this morning. The Phoenix mine was sending a dozen horses in for shoeing."

Turning away from Lottie, Miriam could see a small figure running across the moor towards them. He was running hard and waving as he came. As he drew nearer, he shouted something, but he was still too far away for his words to be made out.

Jacob's pace never faltered. By the time he scrambled up the last rocky slope to where

Miriam and Lottie waited he was hot, excited and breathlessly speechless. Time after time he tried unsuccessfully to speak, his cheeks scarlet with frustration and excitement.

"Here, sit down and get your breath back," Miriam took the child's thin arm to lead him to the stone seat vacated by Lottie, but he shook her hand off impatiently, his eyes never leaving his sister's face.

Suddenly the words came tumbling out in disjointed excitement, "Lottie . . . It's Ma . . . *Our* ma . . . She's come back to us."

Miriam was watching Lottie's face as Jacob gasped out his incredible news. What she saw was a raw vulnerability that she would never forget, no matter what Lottie did in the future. Once again she felt an urge to put her arms about the young, ragged girl and protect her from the world in which she lived.

"D'you hear, Lottie? Ma's come home."

Lottie nodded. Close to tears, her voice came in a fierce whisper, "I knew she'd come back to us some day. I *knew* she would. Even when *he* was saying . . . all those things about her. I *knew* she'd come back."

As though caught up in a confused dream Lottie began to run down the slope in the directon of Henwood. Suddenly she turned about and looked at Miriam with an expression of dismay on her face, "I forgot about the goats. Elias Barnicoat . . . "

"Don't worry about them. I'll drive the goats to Henwood. You hurry on ahead."

Lottie began to run once more . . . and again

she turned. This time she ran back and, without a word, grasped her young brother's hand. As the two children ran across the moor towards Henwood village, Lottie could be seen urging her small brother to a greater speed than his tired legs could achieve.

With a choking lump in her throat, Miriam watched until the children disappeared from view behind a slight rise in the ground. She hoped the unexpected reunion with her mother would measure up to Lottie's high expectations. Miriam feared it would not, but she murmured a silent prayer that the vulnerable young girl would not be let down too badly.

It was with a heavy sense of foreboding that Miriam began rounding up the flock of grazing goats, impervious to their bleating protests at this disruption in their daily routine.

5

JANE TRAGO'S return to her home village disturbed the insular Wesleyan community more than any occurrence for very many years. The closure of the mines had been a gradual, eroding process. The impact of Jane Trago was an immediate and personal challenge to every woman in Henwood who had accepted the price that needed to be paid for 'respectability'.

Jane Trago did not return to the village on foot in the manner of a vagrant, as more malicious tongues declared she was. Neither did she arrive in style in a carriage, as had her sister. She rode into Henwood on the back of a farm cart, the driver having come three miles out of his way to deliver her to her destination. He was rewarded with a kiss that brought a rush of blood to his cheeks and scandalised the women who stood in doorways, or peeped through small-paned windows.

The only luggage Jane Trago brought with her was a large army knapsack, decorated with a number of regimental badges. All these details were carefully recorded by the women. Few of the men looked beyond Jane Trago herself. A tall, amply built girl with long dark hair, she wore a dress with a low-cut bodice which suggested her rich suntan extended far beyond face and arms.

As the farm wagon creaked away through the small mining village, Jane Trago lifted her knapsack and turned in at the doorway of her sister's home to find her way blocked by Marcus Hooper.

"Where do you think you're going?"

Marcus Hooper's gruff-voiced belligerence was not entirely due to the astonishing arrival of his errant sister-in-law. It was as much the result of a late night unionist meeting, called and funded by a visiting delegation from the coal mines of northern England.

The meeting had taken place in the private room of a tavern and drink and talk had vied with each other far into the night.

Jane Trago's dark eyes had daunted men with far more authority than Marcus Hooper. She used them to full effect now.

"What sort of welcome is that for your long-lost sister-in-law? I've come to see my family. Will you stand there and make me trip over you? Or are you going to lift this knapsack indoors for me?"

"We've not heard a word from you since you ran off with that soldier. No, nor had a penny to help support your kids. Yet you come back and expect to be given a welcome?"

"Had I learned to write I might have sent you a letter — though what use it would have been I don't know, *you'd* have needed to find someone to read it to you. As for money to keep Lottie and Jacob it's *me* you're talking to, Marcus Hooper. You'll have had them out working for you as soon as they were big enough to lift a tinner's hammer. By the look of things around here you should be grateful for young'uns old enough to do a full day's work without calling for a grown-up's food. But if it's money you need — "

Plunging a hand down inside her dress with a movement that revealed even more of herself, Jane Trago fished out a small purse made from grey elephant hide. Shaking out a guinea in the palm of her hand she thrust it at Marcus Hooper. "Here! Go and find a beerhouse and come back a happier man."

As Marcus Hooper took the coin he looked beyond Jane Trago and saw the doorways filled with inquisitive neighbours, each anxious to hear a snippet of what was being said, in order that they might repeat it as often as Jane Trago's return was the subject of conversation.

Pocketing the coin, Marcus Hooper said, "You'd best come inside the house — for now, at any rate."

"It's nice to see you too, Marcus." Jane could see Patience standing nervously inside the room, wanting to greet her sister, yet frightened to anger her husband. "Now, let me speak to that sister of mine."

Unceremoniously she pushed past Marcus and held her arms wide. "Patience! My God but you've aged — and you look so tired!"

Life had been hard for Patience. Married to a man who could not keep a job because of his unionist views, she had given birth only to watch her first two babies die. In addition, she had taken on the burden of the children abandoned by this woman . . . her sister. Many times she had fed her despair with thoughts of what she would say to Jane if ever they met again. Now the moment had arrived and, all her words of reproach forgotten, Patience held out her arms and burst into tears.

51

As the sisters clung to each other the years fell away. Both were more than ten years younger than Miriam and they had never been as close to her as they were to each other. There was an older brother too, Morwen, but Patience could hardly remember him. He had gone off to join the army when she was little more than a baby. She and Jane had grown up alternately supporting and relying upon each other until men entered the sisters' lives and their paths diverged.

Marcus Hooper watched the reunion with a growing anger rising inside him. He should never have allowed Jane Trago inside the house. All these years without so much as an enquiry after her children . . . Now she was being cried over by Patience. He fingered the guinea in his pocket. He would not take it to the inn where the northern unionists were staying. With money in his pocket they would expect him to buy drinks for them. There was a small, disreputable beerhouse in nearby Upton Cross. He would go there.

As he turned to leave the house Marcus Hooper tripped over Jacob Trago, who was coming in. Gripping the surprised boy by the shoulder, Marcus propelled him inside the cottage. Giving Jacob a shove that sent him staggering halfway across the room, Marcus said, "There, boy. Your mother's come calling. Say Hello to her quickly, before she goes off and leaves you again."

Disentangling herself from her still weeping sister, Jane Trago crouched down in front of the bewildered, wide-eyed boy. Resting her hands on his shoulders, she took in the ragged clothes and dirty, pinched face.

"Hello, Jacob. My word, you've grown into a fine young man." For a moment it seemed she might gather her son in her arms and hug him, but she felt him stiffen in anticipation and the moment passed.

Dropping her hands from his shoulders Jane stood up and smoothed the dress down over her stomach. Without taking her eyes from the son she had not seen for so long, she said, "I'd have hardly recognised you . . . but where's Lottie?"

Jane Trago asked the question hesitantly. Children began work as soon as they were able to swing a cobbing hammer — and the mines were notoriously dangerous places.

"She's up on the moor, tending Elias Barnicoat's goats. I'll go and tell her you're here . . . " Jacob spoke eagerly. His emotions were in such turmoil he needed to get away and allow his thoughts to fall into some semblance of order.

As Jacob ran from the house and up the track towards the moor, immense joy welled up inside him. His ma had come back! No longer could other village children taunt him with the cruel observation that even his own mother disliked him so much she had run off and left him.

Happiness was a rare sensation for Jacob Trago. Now it filled him to overflowing as he ran to share his news with the one person he knew would understand everything.

All the way from the moor to Henwood village Lottie berated her young brother because his short, aching legs could not move any faster. Yet, when they came within view of the cottages and she saw the women standing in their doorways, she slowed to a dawdling, uncertain pace.

Now it was Jacob who wanted to go faster, "Come on, Lottie. If you don't hurry up she'll be gone again."

Lottie pulled her brother to an abrupt, dismayed halt. "What do you mean? Hasn't she come back to stay with us? To be with us . . . for ever."

"Uncle Marcus doesn't think so. He said I should say hello to her quickly, before she upped and went again."

"You don't want to take notice of anything *he* says," Lottie spoke scornfully, yet she began walking more quickly, just in case . . .

"She's brought a bag with her. Like the ones soldiers carry on their backs when they're marching."

"There you are then!" Lottie spoke triumphantly. "She'll be carrying all her things in there." In Lottie's world few people owned more than they might carry in a soldier's knapsack. "It stands to reason she's going to stay if she's brought all her things with her."

In truth, Lottie was even more confused than her small brother. She still had indistinct, untrustworthy memories of the woman who had once held her hand when they walked together, but there were other memories too. Of smacks and shouted abuse — but the woman Lottie associated with these more unpleasant memories might have been someone else . . .

Far more perceptive than Jacob, Lottie was aware of the interest focused upon her as she walked through the village towards the cottage occupied by Marcus and Patience Hooper. The villagers formed small gossiping groups in the street and every head turned to watch the two young children as they walked past, hand in hand. Some of the women nodded and smiled knowingly. Others looked at them with an expression of tight-lipped disapproval on their faces.

Gripping her brother's hand so tightly he yelped in painful protest. Lottie walked with her head high, looking neither to left, nor to right. She too had been subjected to cruel remarks from her contemporaries — and she knew they had only been repeating what they heard from their parents. The difference was that Lottie ensured the other girls suffered for their abuse. It was by no means unusual for an irate mother to knock upon Patience Hooper's door with a tearful daughter in tow, complaining that the weeping child had been kicked, punched or deprived of the odd handful of hair. Lottie had learned to make her own way, seeking neither approval nor censure from the villagers, and disregarding both when they came her way.

Inside the house one of Patience Hooper's small daughters had fallen and struck her head on the hearthstone in the kitchen. She was crying noisily and for a minute or two neither woman noticed Lottie standing in the doorway beside Jacob.

Then, as though sensing her presence, Jane Trago turned slowly and mother and daughter stared at each other with eyes that were disturbingly alike.

"Hello, Lottie." Jane felt she should open her arms to her daughter, but she did not. Even a simple greeting proved difficult.

Lottie had longed for this day. The day when her mother would come back to her. Sometimes, seated on a rock on the moor, with only goats and the moorland birds for company she would warm herself against a chill wind by imagining what she would say when the moment arrived. Should she speak of the loneliness and heartache she had suffered? The torment she had gone through, not knowing where her mother was, or why she had left? Or should she speak of the love she had carried inside her all these years for the woman who had borne her?

Lottie's reunion speeches had been rehearsed and amended in her mind a thousand times. Now the wonderful moment had arrived.

"Why did you go off and leave me and Jacob?" It was all wrong. This was not what she wanted to say.

"You wouldn't understand, Lottie. Perhaps one day, when you're a big girl . . . "

"You didn't love us enough . . . *That's* why, isn't it, just as everyone says? Why have you come back now if you don't love us? We've got on all right without you. We don't need you — "

Lottie broke off her tirade and fled from the house. She ran through the single street of Henwood, not seeing the women who stared after her and raised their voices in smug variations of 'I told you so . . . '

Hardly noticing where she was going, Lottie did not stop until she gained a rocky shelter amid the gorse, high on the hill behind Sharptor. She crawled in on hands and knees, disregarding the

56

sharp green gorse needles reaching out to scratch face, arms and legs.

Once inside the shelter she sat down disconsolately. Drawing her legs up, she rested her forehead on bony, dirty knees. Suddenly a great sob escaped and she began to cry. It had all gone wrong. The one thing she wanted more than anything else had happened — and she had spoiled it. Now her ma would believe she didn't love her. She would probably go away again, never to return. Lottie did not know why it had gone so wrong. Perhaps it might have been different if only her ma had held out her arms to her . . .

Driving goats was a new experience for Miriam. In some perverse way she enjoyed it. The arrival of the animals in the single village street broke up the groups of gossiping villagers more quickly than anything else might have done — although they re-formed again immediately. Miriam had not been in the village for almost twenty years, but it had not changed. Dominated by the granite mass of Sharptor, the tiny cottages clung to each other beside the roadway. There was not one villager who did not know who she was and her arrival brought the excitement to a new peak.

There had not been such a day as this for as long as the villagers could remember — and it surprised no one that the Trago family was causing the stir. They had always been out of step with the rest of the community.

The noise of the goats brought Jacob Trago from the house and Miriam called him to her,

"Jacob, you know where these goats belong. Take them on home."

Jacob was unused to being in sole charge of the goats, but he was eager to be seen performing the task. He took over from Miriam and, flapping his arms and shouting in the unintelligible language he had heard cattle-drovers using, he shooed the goats through the village, hoping his mother could see him.

Miriam had not been to Patience's home before, but she had seen where Jacob had come from. She entered without knocking at the open door. It was gloomy inside the cottage and very small, but she could see the home contained very few material comforts.

"Well . . . and what do we have here?" Jane Trago advanced across the room and stood in front of Miriam, eyeing her from head to toe in a provocative manner.

"It's Miriam. I told you she was back." Patience, harassed by the crying child she held in her arms, made the introductions. "Miriam, it's *Jane*. She's come home."

For some moments Miriam and Jane looked at each other with guarded expressions that bordered on a totally irrational hostility — then it was gone and the sisters hugged each other and smiled their joy at meeting again after so many years.

Suddenly Jane drew back and wrinkled her nose in distaste, "You smell of goats!"

Miriam smiled, "I took over Lottie's goat herd so she could run home to greet you. If I hadn't been there I don't doubt she'd have abandoned them to find their own way home, she was so excited."

58

Miriam looked about the room, suddenly aware that Lottie was not there, "Where is she?"

Jane Trago shrugged. "The excitement must have worn off on her way home — or perhaps I didn't come up to her expectations. She gave me a mouthful of cheek about going off and leaving her, then she ran out. It doesn't matter. I wasn't expecting to come home and be showered with daughterly love. I *did* walk out on her. She's no reason to love me."

"But she *does,* Jane." Miriam was appalled that the reunion between Lottie and her mother had gone so disastrously wrong. Lottie would be heartbroken. "If anything she loves you too much."

"Then she has a damned funny way of showing it . . . But I'm as dry as an old man's kiss. Don't you have any grog in the house, Patience?"

Patience shook her head as she jogged her fretful child up and down in her arms, "Marcus enjoys a drink when he can afford one, but he never brings any to the house." She made the statement proudly, as if this was one of her husband's more admirable qualities. Beaming at each of her sisters in turn, Patience exclaimed, "I still can't believe we're all together. If only Morwen were here now we'd be a whole family again for the first time since Jane and I were babies."

Miriam had hardly given her brother Morwen a thought since her return. He and Josh had never liked each other and Morwen had been instrumental in Josh's arrest . . .

"You'll not be seeing any more of Morwen. At least not in this life." Jane spoke with such vehemence that the two other women fell silent and waited for her to explain the statement.

For a few moments it seemed Jane had said all she was going to on the subject. Then she lifted the army knapsack from the stone floor to the stained, wooden table and jabbed a finger at each of the badges attached to it, in turn. "You see these? Every one of them belongs to a regiment I've followed, most of 'em in India. I've been nurse, cook, washerwoman, seamstress — and mistress — in each."

Jane smiled when Patience drew in her breath sharply at her sister's disclosure. "Does it shock you? I don't see why it should. I daresay I've found more love and tenderness beneath a blanket than you've known with that man of yours."

Jane Trago looked at each of her sisters in turn, inviting argument. None came, although Patience looked deeply hurt.

Jane returned her attention to the knapsack, pointing to a circular badge on which was a raised crown and the figure '32'. She said, "This belonged to my man in the Cornwall Regiment. A sergeant, he was. A good man. He took me to India as his wife. He showed his colonel a marriage certificate for me too. It belonged to his real wife, but that didn't matter. He died at Lucknow. If he hadn't been killed he'd have won a medal for certain, he was that brave. Our Morwen was there too and I turned to him after my man had been killed." Jane Trago snorted bitterly, "Some comfort he was! He tried to sell me to the other soldiers in the regiment. Said we'd make enough to keep ourselves in drink for the rest of our lives. What he meant was, keep *him* in drink — and I'd have needed to take a great many men to do that, I can tell you. I told him I wouldn't lead such a life for him nor for any other man. He didn't care, he found a little Indian girl to make money for him, instead. Then her father came along and stuck a knife in Morwen for what he'd done.

"Our dear brother wasn't too badly hurt, but another soldier who came to his aid was stabbed to death. The girl's father died too — at the end of a regimental rope, but not before he'd given evidence against Morwen. Our devious brother might have got away with it even then, but one of the first men the girl had gone with must have been suffering from the pox. She put more soldiers out of action than the great Mogul.

"Thanks to Morwen I had to leave the thirty-second and find a billet with a regiment where he wasn't known. I ended up with the Bengal Light Infantry, up in the mountains of northern India. Men from Suffolk, they were. Good men too.

"Just before I left India I heard our dear brother had died in prison. As far as I'm concerned it was the best thing that could have happened to him."

Patience was dismayed. Morwen had been a source of pride to fall back upon. A means of escaping from the realities of her life of pitiful drudgery. He was a *soldier*, serving his queen and country. Now he was dead and her illusion had been shattered.

The revelation came as less of a surprise to Miriam. Morwen was closer to her own age and she had known him better than either of her two sisters. Morwen had hated Josh and she always feared what might happen if they were to meet again. Life would be better for the Trago and Retallick families without him.

"I must return to the house and see that the girls are all right. I left them with Josh's ma. She adores both of them, but she's getting too old to cope with them for very long."

Jane sniffed, "From all Patience has told me you're doing well for yourself these days. Practically the lady of the manor, by all accounts."

Miriam's smile was entirely free from malice, "I'm not complaining. Josh and I are very lucky — but where will you be staying? We've plenty of room up at the house on Sharptor."

"It would be too grand for the likes of me. I'll stay down here. Besides, it's closer to the inn. Can you put me up, Patience? I'll pay for my keep."

Patience hesitated, torn between a desperate need for money, however little, and fear of Marcus's reaction if she allowed her sister to stay in the cottage. "We've only the two rooms upstairs. You'd need to share with the children."

"Sharing a room with *children* will be a luxury — as you'd know if you'd ever shared a mud hut with fifty soldiers. More often then not there'd be animals and snakes and spiders too. It will do me fine."

Miriam gave her sister a faint smile. She had shared sleeping quarters with snakes and spiders — and worse — during her years in Africa.

"You'll at least come to visit me at Sharptor?

It sounds as though we have many experiences in common."

"I wouldn't be at all surprised," Jane's smile revealed the secret of why she was able to captivate the hearts of men so easily. "If I hadn't had two bastard children and run off with a soldier, Henwood would still be talking about *you*."

6

JESSIE RETALLICK had not tired of the two Gilmore children. Miriam found the three of them busy in the kitchen of Jessie's home, making bread. The two girls were elbow deep in flour and the smell of baking hung on the air.

Brushing back a lock of loose, greying hair with a flour-whitened hand, Jessie said, "I'd go away again if I were you. We'll be busy for another hour or two — and by the time we've done these two girls won't be a pretty sight. I'll clean them up and bring them to the house by bedtime."

Walking from the cottage to her own house, Miriam could not help comparing the lives Anne and Nell Gilmore had with the prospects the future promised Lottie. The ragged little waif must have been bottling her emotion up inside for all these years. That it should have all poured out when she was reunited with her mother was a tragedy. Miriam thought Lottie must be the unhappiest girl in Cornwall at this moment.

Looking up towards the high moor, Miriam's gaze fell upon a jumble of granite rocks surrounded and almost hidden by flowering gorse — and suddenly she knew where Lottie was. As a young girl Miriam had also found sanctuary in the rock shelter when she needed to hide her misery from the world.

In that instant Miriam knew she must go to her ragged niece. Lottie would need someone to cut away the tangle of hurt and bewilderment that had her firmly in its grasp.

Miriam went to her own house first, Josh was still away and she took a warm coat from behind the kitchen door. A chill wind was blowing and it was always stronger up on the moor.

It was the first time Miriam had walked on this particular part of the moor since her return from Africa. It brought memories of earlier days flooding back to her far more vividly than had meeting relatives and old friends. She had spent hours here with Josh when they were both children, and many more on her own. She had discovered every hiding-place; every long-forgotten 'digging'; the setts of badgers and the earths where foxes reared their playful families.

As Miriam had anticipated, the wind grew stronger as she climbed the rock-strewn slope to the tor. From here it was possible to see for miles around and count the tall chimneys that in the nineteenth century had replaced ancient granite crosses as landmarks.

At the entrance to the rock hideout Miriam stooped low and peered along the gorse tunnel she would need to traverse on hands and knees. It seemed much narrower and lower than she remembered. For a moment she hesitated, feeling faintly foolish. She was a grown woman now — a *middle-aged* woman — and middle-aged women did not crawl on hands and knees along gorse tunnels to reach the haunts of their childhood. Then she thought of Lottie. If the girl *was* in here . . .

Miriam's progress through the narrow tunnel proved every bit as painful as she had feared. Gorse branches brushed against her face and legs and sharp brittle gorse needles pierced the skin of her knees like wooden splinters. It was a great relief when she reached the end of the tunnel and could straighten up.

The rock shelter was low-roofed, triangular, formed by two huge flat rocks leaning against each other — and Lottie *was* here.

The young girl sat with her back to one of the stones, head resting on dirty, drawn-up knees. The fresh wind was carrying sound away from her and she was unaware she was no longer alone until she looked up suddenly and saw Miriam standing before her.

"Wh . . . what are you doing here?" Lottie's eyes seemed twice their normal size in her dirty, tear-stained face.

"I came to find you. I thought it might be a good idea for us to have a chat together." Miriam turned away for a few moments in order to retain her composure. There was so much hurt in the big brown eyes.

She looked out over the top of the gorse surrounding the hiding-place. Beyond the moor church spires dotted the landscape and farmers toiled in the patchwork of pocket-handkerchief fields, plodding patiently behind broad-flanked horses. All was as it had always been. It was a comforting and reassuring feeling.

"How did you know where to find me?"

Miriam turned back to Lottie and smiled, "It's where I used to come when I was a girl. If I had

66

a guinea for every hour I've spent here I'd be a rich woman today."

Lottie looked at Miriam in surprise. "Why? Why did you spend so much time here?"

"Same reason as you, I suspect. Because I was unhappy."

Lottie looked down at her knees again, misery returning as she remembered her troubles. Miriam knew what she was thinking. No one *could* be as unhappy as she was at this moment.

"You ma understands, you know. She expected you to be angry with her. After all, she *did* run off and leave you and Jacob. But she's back now. It will be many years before you begin to understand *why* she did it — if you ever do — but you must try your best to forgive her. She's returned, even though it would have been far easier for her to stay away. Make that a beginning, Lottie. Go back to her and make this the happiest day of your life, not one of the *unhappiest.*"

Lottie remained for a long time staring intently at her knees. When she looked up at Miriam once more it was as though she was waking from a dream. "Do you really think she — my ma — will understand?"

"Of course she will." Miriam held a hand out to Lottie, "Come on, before you go to see her again you'll come to my house. I've a dress there that's much too big for Nell. I don't know what I was doing making it so large. It'll serve you a treat."

It was an innocent enough lie. Miriam had made the dress only the day before with Lottie in mind. This was an unexpected opportunity to present it to her without fear of a refusal.

By the time Lottie and Miriam arrived at the Retallick house the young girl's anguish had been replaced by a rising excitement that was beginning to bubble over. Lottie bombarded Miriam with a whole barrage of questions, most of which she was unable to answer. At the time Miriam left England, both Patience and Jane had been too young for Miriam to know them well. She countered by questioning the young girl on her own sketchy knowledge of the Trago family, filling in what details she could.

The dress made by Miriam completed Lottie's renewed happiness. By the time she was washed and had her long, tangled hair brushed with a painful efficiency, Lottie Trago looked a different girl.

On her way from the house Lottie passed Jessie Retallick, who was bringing Nell and Anne home. Josh's mother was still shaking her head in disbelief when she entered the kitchen, where Miriam was burning Lottie's discarded rag dress.

Told of the reason for Lottie's transformation, Jessie's manner underwent a change, her mouth setting in a straight, disapproving line, "If Lottie's looking for approval from *that* one she's doomed to disappointment. I'm sorry, Miriam, I know Jane's your sister, but she's never cared for anyone but herself. There's nothing but hurt in store for anyone who cares for her."

Jessie gave Miriam a shrewd look. "It's not hard to see you're stricken with young Lottie — and I've no need to ask why. I've known you from the time you were a baby. You can see yourself in that girl, and so can other folk. Stay close to her, Miriam. Sooner or later she's going to need someone dependable to turn to."

When Jane Trago entered the tap room of the Cheesewring Inn, at the heart of Henwood village, it was as though landlord and customers were suddenly struck dumb. The inn was not busy. No more than five men sat drinking at a single table in the low-beamed room. Beyond them the leather-aproned landlord stood leaning on a stained and unpolished serving bar that guarded a gigantic barrel at the rear of the room. All six men stared open-mouthed at Jane Trago — and she was dressed to provoke just such a reaction. The outmoded dress she wore hugged the contours of her body more closely than most Cornish women would have thought decent, and threatened to evict her well-fleshed bosom.

"Er . . . are you looking for someone . . . ma'am?" The landlord was the first to find his voice, although he seemed uncertain how he should address his visitor.

"Do you always assume everyone who enters your inn has come looking for someone?" Jane Trago's glance took in the five men at the table before returning to the landlord. "It's small wonder you're short on customers."

"You're here to drink?" The landlord's astonishment returned once more.

"So help me! I swear I'd need to raise a bump on his head before he'd believe I was carrying a hammer." Jane Trago's remarks were addressed to the drinkers at the table and provoked a nervous laugh. "Of course I'm here to drink — and there's money to pay for it."

Slapping a silver florin noisily on the wooden bar, Jane Trago said, "I'll have a tankard of ale, landlord. I'd forgotten how much dust was raised in mining country. Do you have a name to serve up with your drinks?"

"Waldo Davey's *my* name. I can't say I've seen *you* in these parts before." As he spoke the landlord filled a tankard from a wooden tap set in the huge barrel.

"That's because you won't have been here many years." Jane Trago gazed about her at the almost empty taproom. "By the state of trade in here you're not likely to be here for very many more."

Waldo banged the full tankard down upon the counter, causing some of the contents to spill and form a foaming puddle on the stained wood. "So you know all about running a tavern, do you? Pity you're not an expert on mining too. Then you could get the mines running at a profit again and I wouldn't have time to stand about listening to advice from someone with no right to be drinking in a miners' bar."

"There's no law says I can't drink in a tavern when I've got a thirst — and I've worked in enough inns and beerhouses to know what men want when they come to one. I'm talking of places where *soldiers* drink, Mr Davey — and they spend well."

"Ah! Then you'll be the Trago woman. I heard you'd come back to the village. I should'a known.

It takes a brazen woman to walk into an inn by herself and order a beer. But from what I've heard you raised such a scandal when you left Henwood you'd need to be a brazen hussy to return at all."

"Only a desperate landlord would insult a paying customer, Mr Davey . . . but it's plain to see you're as desperate as any I've come across." Jane Trago appeared not to have taken offence at Waldo Davey's words. "I may know little about mining, but given a chance I'd put this tavern back on its feet again."

The customers seated at the table had ceased talking among themselves and were listening to Jane Trago's conversation with Waldo Davey with much interest. Davey glanced in their direction before returning his frowning attention to Jane Trago, waiting for her to say more.

She took a deep draught of her ale, emptying half the tankard, all the while looking at the landlord over the rim of the pewter mug.

Waldo Davey reached a sudden decision, "Come in the Cap'n's room and tell me about these ideas of yours. Otherwise they'll be all about the village before I've had time to so much as think about 'em."

Jane Trago followed Waldo Davey from the room pursued by catcalls and whistles from the five miners at the table behind them.

The landlord led the way to a room as large as the taproom. The furniture in here was less worn and the room was dominated by a huge table capable of seating more than twenty men around it. A great open fireplace occupied most

71

of one wall but there was no fire and the room was cold. Jane Trago shivered, but Waldo Davey seemed not to notice. He pulled out a chair for her but when she shook her head he pushed it back beneath the table.

"All right, tell me about your plans to bring men and money to my inn."

"You'll need to satisfy *me* about something first," Jane Trago assumed a briskness that was at odds with her soft, feminine appearance. "Are you an innkeeper because you want to make money? Or do you see your inn as a place for miners to spend all evening without buying more than a single pint of ale, just so they can tell each other how bad the world's treating them?"

Waldo Davey was not a quick-thinking man. He struggled to find the answer he thought she wanted to hear. "I do my best for the miners. They're having a bad time — "

"And so will you if you can't attract more than five customers in here at this time of the evening on a Friday. It must be settling night at more than one mine — and *some* are still working. How many of them pay out in here?"

The landlord looked shocked, "Few mines pay out in taverns any more. The Wesleyans didn't like it. They've helped to have the law changed — "

"The Wesleyans would put you out of business and shout 'Hallelujah!' Why should you think of them? Anyway, they're not calling the tune any more, the mine owners are. I've yet to meet a mine purser who wouldn't change his habits if there was the chance of making a few pounds from doing it. Speak to the pursers. I'll do it for you, if you'd feel better about it. Get them in here and make sure they pay out in notes — five pound notes, to the leading man in each core working on his mine, then they'll have to come to you for change. The banks charge sixpence for each note they change. You'll charge a shilling — unless the man changing the note buys drinks. Any man worth his salt is looking for a second drink when he's got *one* inside him, especially if I'm on hand to prattle to him. Those Wesleyans who've signed the pledge can either set it aside, or pay you a shilling for their principles. They'll do it, and willingly. The nearest bank is at Liskeard. A man would walk off sixpennyworth of shoe leather getting there."

Waldo Davey looked at Jane Trago slightly bemusedly. Her talk was too ambitious for a simple man, but she had more to say.

"How about credit? You *do* give 'tick' here?"

The Cheesewring Inn landlord shook his head. "That *would* be throwing my money away. Most of those who'd drink on 'tick' would be out of work. They'd never be able to pay."

"If anyone doesn't pay you take out a distress warrant against him. Most men have *something* of value that can be sold to pay their debts."

Waldo Davey shook his head again uneasily. "I couldn't see a man's family suffer because he'd been drinking on credit in my tavern."

Jane Trago looked at the landlord contemptuously. "There's more than one way of suffering, Landlord Davey. Which is worse, helping a man to forget his problems for a few weeks, then forcing him to face up to them, or letting him sink deeper into a pit of misery before he *needs* to do something about them? Sooner or later those miners who can't find work will have to sell up and go to where they can afford to support their families. If they leave it too long so many others will be ahead of them they'll need to move on yet again. You'll be doing them a favour. Making them face facts before it's too late."

The Cheesewring Inn landlord felt there must be a flaw in her argument, but he was unable to find it immediately. He turned the conversation to details he *could* understand. "What do you get from all this new business that'll be coming in?"

"Work here in the Cheesewring Inn — and you won't regret *that.* I can tell you. I'll run everything for you, house as well as tavern. All you'll have to do is sit back and think of ways to spend the money I'm making for you. In return I'll take a quarter of the profits."

"A *quarter?* In my own tavern . . . !"

"How much are you taking now? I'll wager it's not enough to keep yourself in 'baccy. I'm offering to bring in *money,* Mr Davey. Money you can jingle in your pocket, or go out and spend. Money you can count in pounds, not in pence."

"I . . . I'm not sure."

The prospect was sorely tempting to the landlord, but Jane Trago saw he needed one last push before he took the first uncertain step — and she was ready.

"Then let me convince you . . . "

In the taproom the five customers looked up in surprise as Jane Trago threw open the door

74

and advanced upon them. When she reached the table she stopped and looked at each man in turn before declaring, "Mr Davey's decided the Cheesewring Inn needs to become more lively, to have more going on. As a start, he's employed me. To celebrate I'm going to buy each of you men not a pint, but a *quart* of good ale — yes, and something a bit stronger to go with it, if you so wish."

The miners raised a resounding cheer, but she stifled it with a movement of her hand, "I knew that'd please you, but before you get your drinks you'll need to do something for me. I want you to go out and spread the word that Jane Trago's serving drinks in the Cheesewring. Those who come here to drink will hear me telling of some of the things I've seen in far-off India. Stories to make your hair curl. You won't dare go home and repeat them to the missus, I'll warrant. Not only that, so no one need feel left out, there'll be 'tick' behind the bar for those without money to pay for their pleasures. Off you go now, and remember, there'll be a man-sized drink waiting here for you on your return. A kiss as well if you bring enough friends with you."

As the five miners made a hurried exit from the taproom, Jane Trago gave the worried Waldo Davey a wink. "Cheer up, landlord. I've a feeling in my bones you'll see more business tonight than you've known since you came here — and tonight's only the beginning. Tomorrow I'll be paying a visit to the pursers on all the working mines around here."

Her bid to bring custom to the Cheesewring Inn succeeded beyond Jane's own ambitious expectations. Men who had not visited the inn for many months came to see and hear the woman who had been the subject of village gossip and speculation for years. Occasionally a great guffaw of laughter went up from within the inn and the general hubbub attracted many of the working miners on their way home from a shift. Most had some money with them. This was soon added to the colossal amount marked up against the names of men who had none, but who drank all the more because of it.

Outside a number of wives and mothers gathered for a while to voice their concern at the 'goings-on', or to reprimand a new arrival to whom they were related. But as the noise increased and the language reaching the ears of the women became worse, they accepted defeat and went home.

It was the early hours of the morning before Jane left the inn, leaving the merriment continuing behind her. She did not leave alone, nor did she immediately head towards the home of her sister. Instead, her whispering and giggling together with the low voice of the man who accompanied her faded in the darkness of a footpath that led to the thick fern growing on the slopes beneath Sharptor.

She did not see the small figure waiting in the shadows beyond the warm light escaping from the windows of the Cheesewring Inn. A small, forlorn figure who screwed up the material of her new dress, painfully tightly in her hands.

76

7

THE CHEESEWRING INN prospered exactly as Jane Trago had predicted. True to her promise to Waldo Davey, she paid visits to all the working mines in the district. The blatant use of her physical charm and her uninhibited manner did not endear Jane to every man to whom she spoke. Methodism had lost much of its eighteenth century power within the mining community, but it still had a firm hold on many mine managements.

More than one purser sent Jane on her way with dire warnings about the evils of drink and the prospects for her soul. Nevertheless, three pursers agreed to pay their men in the Cheesewring Inn, a decision that would boost Waldo Davey's trade by more than five hundred men a month.

The scheme did not please everyone. The wives of Henwood were particularly incensed by the increased business at the village tavern. Apart from the noise and the risk of molestation to women and girls who ventured from their houses after dark, they were concerned for their husbands. Not a dozen village men were in employment, and none of these were involved in the Cheesewring Inn pay-outs, yet the Henwood wives were fearful of the effect on the unemployed men.

Many out-of-work miners were drawn to the inn by the influx of so many miners on pay nights. There was always the possibility that work might be offered to them by an unusually mellow purser. In addition, news was circulated at the inn of future vacancies. There were old friends and acquaintances here too, men ready to buy a drink for a less fortunate miner.

With the unaccustomed fire of strong drink in his belly, more than one out-of-work miner threw caution and his many cares to the wind. As Jane had predicted, he turned to 'tick' — unlimited credit — to prolong his euphoric state for as long as his legs would support him.

There were many 'hangers-on'. Some, like the Henwood men, were genuinely seeking a promise of employment, no matter how tenuous. Others had little interest in work. These formed part of the army of vagrants who wandered the county in aimless dejection. Thrown out of work many times by mine closures, they now tramped the countryside from habit. So far behind were homes and families — and even hope itself — all reality had been lost to the tragic wanderers.

However, some vagabonds were pursued by the laws of the land and these were the men most feared by the women of Henwood. Sitting hunched beside the road near the Cheesewring Inn, ostensibly half-asleep, they missed nothing of what went on about them. Should a miner be foolish enough to leave the inn alone on paying-out night he would wake in the morning with a lump on his head, pockets turned inside-out, and not a single item of value left on his person. More often than not the victim would lose not only his money but boots, coat and trousers too.

Josh voiced the concern of the village women

to Jane when she paid a rare visit to the Sharptor house one Monday afternoon. She had come in search of Lottie, wanting her daughter to go on an errand to Liskeard for her.

"She and Jacob are on the moor with the goats," explained Miriam as she made a cup of tea for her sister. "Even if you were able to find her up there she wouldn't leave the animals. It's a pity you didn't mention you had need of her before she went out this morning."

"Lottie and I don't keep the same hours." Jane Trago's face was puffy, her eyes bloodshot. "I needed to sleep late this morning — as much as I was able, with the kids screaming their heads off, and Marcus letting Patience feel the back of his hand."

"He was hitting her?" Miriam was indignant.

"I doubt if he really hurt her. Besides, she needs a bit of livening up, that one. I can't imagine what Marcus ever saw in her."

"*He's* not exactly the world's greatest catch," retorted Miriam. "From what I hear, Patience and Lottie have brought more money into the home than Marcus Hooper, these last few years."

In a bid to head off a quarrel between the two ill-matched sisters, Josh said hurriedly, "At least the family won't starve now you're putting money into the house, Jane, but some of the villagers are upset about the manner in which you're earning it."

"Those who are complaining will starve long before I do — but it's no good our Patience depending on me to feed her family. Waldo Davey's said I can move into a room at the

79

Cheesewring Inn if I feel so inclined."

"You'll not go there?" Miriam was about to remark that Jane would set village tongues wagging by moving in with the widower innkeeper, but she bit back the words. Her young sister had a total disregard for other people's opinions. "What about Lottie and Jacob?"

"I can't take them to the inn with me. They'll have to stay with Patience. I'll pay their keep. She'll be grateful for the money."

"Lottie will be dreadfully upset when she hears."

"Upset? Oh no, not that one. There were times when I was away when I worried about her. All right, not *often,* but sometimes I did. I realise now I was wasting my sympathy. She doesn't give a damn whether I'm here or on the other side of the world. It's all the same to her."

Miriam remembered how upset Lottie had been on the day of her mother's return to Henwood, but Jane Trago dismissed the subject and addressed her next words to Josh, "I hear you've been keeping your hand in by repairing an engine on the Wheal Phoenix. One of the shift captains was drinking at the inn last night. He sounded well pleased with what you've done for them. Are you going back to mine engineering?"

"I doubt it. I had hoped to buy the Sharptor mine and set it to work again, but Strike won't sell to me. He'd rather see the engines scrapped and the mine lying idle. He's not the man his uncle was."

Jane's interest quickened suddenly, "Would you

be talking of *Leander* Strike? Has *he* inherited the Sharptor mine?"

"Yes. Do you know him?" Josh wondered how Jane Trago could possibly know the owner of the Sharptor mine.

"Oh yes, I know Leander Strike. He used to come to the Sharptor Mine to check on things for his uncle. I was a young bal-maiden then, trimming ore for two shillings a week. When he came riding up on his horse we'd be expected to drop him a curtsy and say, 'Good morning, Mr Strike, sir,' looking as though we were pleased to raise blisters on our hands the size of a hammer head just to put more money in the pockets of the Strike family. Oh yes, I know Leander Strike."

A strange expression appeared on Jane Trago's face and she looked at Josh for a long time without saying anything. Then, just as her stare was beginning to make him feel uncomfortable, she stood up abruptly and walked from the house without a word of farewell. Behind her, Miriam stood holding the cup of tea she had just made for her sister.

Miriam came to stand beside him at the window and together they watched Jane walking away down the hill. Miriam slipped an arm about Josh's waist. "I hope you realise how lucky you are, Josh Retallick. You've got the pick of the Trago girls."

Three days later Jane came to the house on Sharptor once more. It was lunchtime and Miriam had just set a meal on the table for Josh and the two girls. Jane did not knock at the door, and

81

spoke to Josh before greeting anyone.

"Leander Strike's down at the Sharptor mine. He wants to speak to you."

"To me? What for?" Jane's unexpected arrival and abrupt message took Josh by surprise.

"Don't sit there asking foolish questions. Get down to the mine and ask *Strike.* I wouldn't take too long about it if you still want to buy his mine. He's quick to change his mind about things."

It was an astonishing statement to make and one that posed numerous questions. Too confused to ask any of them, Josh rose from the table and hurried from the house, heading for the Sharptor mine.

A light carriage with peeling paintwork stood in the shade of the tall engine house. The coachman was dressed more in the manner of a gardener. He surlily jerked a thumb in the direction of the mine captain's office when Josh enquired for Leander Strike.

The mine owner sat inside the office, hunched miserably in the captain's chair. Both his hands were cupped about the silver cap of a walking-stick, and one leg was stretched out before him, resting on a cushioned stool.

After greeting the mine owner, Josh said, "I've been told you want to see me?"

Ignoring the greeting, Leander Strike said gruffly, "Are you still interested in purchasing the Sharptor mine?"

Josh's excitement quickened. It seemed Jane Trago had been right — and now was not the time to question why Leander Strike had changed his mind so unexpectedly.

"I am — if we can agree a sensible price."

"I'm willing to sell you half the mine shares, on the understanding you'll put up the money to start the mine working again. The other half of the shares will go to my son. He won't interfere with the running of the mine. He's only fifteen and still at school."

Josh's enthusiasm ebbed away. Such an arrangement would not work. Leander Strike could take his son's shares from him at any time, thereby creating an intolerable situation.

"I can't accept that, I'm sorry, it seems we're just wasting each other's time."

Josh turned to go, but Leander Strike banged his stick hard on the wooden floor and called him back.

"Dammit, Retallick, don't throw a perfectly sensible offer back in my face and stalk off. That's no way to do business. All right, take two-thirds. That'll give you a controlling interest — and the lion's share of all the profit you think you'll make."

Josh did some rapid mental arithmetic. "I'm prepared to meet all the mine expenses for a year if I hold at least four-fifths of the shares. I won't do it for less."

Leander Strike's anger flared suddenly. Forgetting his gout, he made as though to rise. Bellowing in sudden pain, he sank down again hurriedly.

"Damn this gout! Damn you too, Retallick — and the Trago girl. I won't be forced into giving the mine away. I'll see the inside of a gaol first."

83

"I know nothing of Jane Trago's part in this," Josh retorted. "I'm making you a perfectly good offer for the mine. A thousand pounds for four-fifths of the shares — and I'll meet all mining expenses for twelve months. That's a generous offer for a flooded mine. Far more than you're likely to get elsewhere."

It *was* a good offer. Better than Leander Strike had been expecting. The mine owner had anticipated a sale in the region of five hundred pounds.

"How long will it take you to raise the money?"

"It's available in a Liskeard bank right now. I'll give you a note for the full amount on the day the shares are transferred to my name."

Leander Strike looked at Josh with a new respect — but it was a respect tinged with resentment. Few *gentlemen* these days could call up a thousand pounds immediately. Yet here was this ex-convict speaking as though it were a trifling sum.

"All right, Retallick. The Sharptor mine is yours. I hope for my son's sake you can wring a profit from it. It's more than I've been able to do since it was left to me. I'll have my solicitor draw up the necessary papers and send them to you when they're ready. Now, help me up and think yourself lucky *you* don't suffer from a gentleman's disease."

Josh helped Leander outside to the coach, hardly able to contain his excitement. Buying the Sharptor mine was the culmination of an ambitious dream that had been with him since the day he and Miriam had decided to return to

Cornwall from Africa.

Josh's mind was filled with plans. He would set his engine to work and drain the mine of water. With the re-opening of the mine Henwood would come to life again. Men would leave home for work every day and women would have money to spend on their families.

Not until very much later that day did Josh pause to wonder just how Jane Trago had persuaded Leander Strike to sell the Sharptor mine to a man he so despised. Then he shrugged. The important thing was that the mine was his at last. Now he would bring work back to the men and women of Henwood.

8

BY late evening every miner within a five mile radius of Henwood village knew Josh Retallick was the new owner of the Sharptor mine. Most agreed it brought renewed hope to the community. Josh had been born in the small Sharptor cottage where his father, Ben, still lived. It was he who had built and installed the engine which had brought prosperity to the mine. He, more than anyone, stood some chance of bringing that prosperity back.

There *were* dissenters. These pointed out that Josh had been abroad for almost twenty years. He was out of touch with the problems of Cornish mining. Some suggested that by buying the Sharptor mine Josh had joined the ranks of the mine owners, and could be expected to behave as they did.

Nevertheless, dissenters and supporters agreed upon one thing. Josh Retallick would need miners to work his mine. The new mine owner woke the following morning to find a growing crowd of respectfully silent men gathered outside the gate of his house in the early morning mist. When Josh went out to them they broke their silence and began clamouring — *begging* — to be given work on the Sharptor mine.

Promising the men he would consider each one of them, he sent them off to wait outside the mine office for his arrival.

When Josh had eaten breakfast he walked to the mine — and discovered the number of waiting men had trebled. Women and children were there too, adding their shrill voices to those entreating Josh for work.

Pushing his way through the crowd, Josh gained the office, and found his father waiting for him, seated behind the mine captain's desk.

Rising to his feet, Ben Retallick extended a hand to his son. "Congratulations, Josh. You've got what you wanted — but I hope you haven't paid Leander Strike more than the mine's worth."

"I've given him twice the price he was asking for the machinery. In return I've got four-fifths of the mine shares. The remainder go to his son. With some work put in on the engine I could recover my money by selling it to an overseas buyer — if that was what I wanted. My boast that it's the best engine in Cornwall is not an idle one."

"I've never doubted it — but if the price of copper doesn't fall any more you'll have no need to sell. There's still plenty of ore below grass. A good mine captain will have no trouble keeping production going."

"That's something I need to talk to you about, Pa. You're sitting in the captain's chair. I'd like to see you there whenever I come in the office. No man knows more about the Sharptor mine, and the men who work best here."

Ben Retallick was taken aback by his son's words, "I don't know . . . You'd maybe do better having a younger man — or doing the job yourself. I haven't worked since the mine closed and your ma's got used to having me about the house. I don't know what she'll have to say . . . "

"I wouldn't expect you to spend every waking hour here — or involve yourself in underground work. I'll employ below-grass captains for that. There's no way I can take on the task of mine captain for myself. I need to work on the engine, perhaps take on the job of purser too. If we're to make a success of the mine I must keep a tight rein on finances for a year or two."

"I don't know . . . Mind you, it would be a worthwhile challenge to see the Sharptor mine on its feet again. Then there's that south-west sett. It was never worked seriously in Strike's time. I've always believed there to be good rich ore there. All the same, I'll have to think carefully about this, son."

Josh knew he had won. His father would not turn down an offer to run the mine that had dominated his life for so long — and Josh's mother would not deny him the opportunity to do so.

"Think seriously about it, Pa. I'm relying heavily upon you. In the meantime perhaps you'll help me take on men. You'll know most of them. I'd prefer to take on as many from Henwood as need work. There's a lot of labouring to be done on the buildings, the ladders to be checked, and there'll be plenty of underground work once the water level's been lowered. We'll also need a new shaft if this south-west sett's all you think it is. Once the men are started I'll ride to Looe and see about having timber and tools brought up here by rail . . . " There was a narrow gauge mineral railway, serving the moorland mines from the port of Looe, some thirteen miles away.

"There's be no need for *you* to do that. I saw Malachi Sprittle outside. You'll not find a better above-grass captain anywhere — and his brother is manager of the railway. Malachi will work out what you'll need, right down to the last nail — and get you preferential freight rates. Sam Clymo's outside too. He's the underground captain you need if you're going to sink shafts. He's a young man, and too quiet for some, but he'll have five fathoms dug while other captains are still scratching their heads, wondering where to site the shaft. *Your* most important task is to have the engine working well. You'll not begin making real money until the lower levels are pumped dry — and you're the engineer. All right, Josh, open the door and we'll start choosing our men . . . "

The Sharptor mine took on a hundred men that morning, but there at least eight men clamouring for each vacancy. Those who were unsuccessful went away with at least some hope for the future. Many of those taken on as 'tut-men' — labourers — were skilled miners. When the shafts were dug and tunnels drained, they would bid for the right to work a particular section of the mine, at an agreed rate for all ore brought to the surface. Working in teams, the rate they received would vary according to the difficulty of their particular pitch and the amount of ore found there. This was the gambling element of mining that was akin to 'gold fever'. Every miner dreamed of working a particularly difficult pitch — and of suddenly discovering a vast pocket of rich ore. It was a goal reached by few. Nevertheless success was achieved by a sufficient number to keep hope alive within the hearts of men who worked underground.

Lottie and Jacob drove Elias Barnicoat's goats past the Sharptor mine at the time when men were being taken on. They stood for a while watching and listening to the men quarrelling and arguing among themselves about their places in the long line of hopeful applicants.

"I suppose we'll be back working on the mine when it opens properly."

Lottie made the remark to her nine-year-old brother as they drove the goats on to the moorland grazing grounds.

"Why? Can't we stay looking after the goats instead?"

"*You* might be able to. You can't tell copper from rock and wouldn't get much more as a 'picky boy', anyway. But Marcus won't have me herding goats for a shilling a week when I can bring home two for crushing ore in the mine."

After a lengthy silence, Jacob said, "I don't want to look after the goats by myself. If you go to work on the mine I want to come with you."

Lottie's expression softened. "You can't stay with me for always, our Jacob. As soon as he can, Marcus will have you below grass, bringing home the sort of money *he* should be making."

Absent-mindedly slapping the rump of a coarse-haired goat which had stopped to graze the tender leaves of a young bramble bush, Jacob said wistfully, "Perhaps Ma will find a place for us so we can all live together . . . like a proper family. If she did I'd go below grass *now*. I'd work hard and make a lot of money. Then you'd be able to carry on looking after the goats and not go to work in a mine, if you'd rather. Ma could find another job too, and stop working at the Cheesewring . . ."

"I believe Ma *enjoys* working there. Enjoys it more than being with us, anyway."

The previous evening Lottie had been awake when their mother returned to the cottage. Marcus had been drinking at the inn and it sounded as thought he had drunk more than was good for him. Jane Trago brought him home and there was a great deal of giggling and whispering beneath Lottie's window before Jane Trago finally helped her drunken brother-in-law in through the door of the darkened cottage.

Lottie's remark had been made to her brother in anger, brought about by the hurt she felt at her mother's lack of concern for her two children. When Lottie saw her words had upset Jacob she reached out and grasped his hand. Squeezing it reassuringly, she said, "I expect it's just that she's not used to having us around. When she's been back a while she'll probably do like you say. Find a place for us all to be together."

"Do you really think she will?" Jacob asked the question eagerly. He trusted Lottie more than anyone else in the whole wide world. If she said things were going to work out all right, then he knew they surely would.

"Course she will. After all, she came back to us, didn't she?"

Jane Trago moved out of her sister's cottage three days after Lottie's reassurance to her brother. The move was precipitated by yet another late homecoming accompanied by Marcus Hooper. Once again Lottie listened to their vain attempts at drunken stealth as they approached the cottage. She heard them stumble in through the front door and waited for them to come upstairs to the two bedrooms — but tonight they seemed to be taking a very long time.

After many minutes of waiting Lottie saw a flicker of dim amber light beneath the warped and ill-fitting bedroom door, then the stairs creaked as Patience Hooper went downstairs.

A few moments later Lottie heard Patience's voice. She sounded angry — as angry as Patience ever could be. Aptly named, Patience rarely lost her temper. However, her voice was raised now. Then Lottie heard the distinct sound of a blow. It was quickly followed by another and Patience screamed. There was the sound of another voice, loud and shrill. Then the downstairs door to the stairs opened again and Lottie heard Marcus breathing heavily as he stumbled clumsily upstairs to the bedroom across the small landing. It was a sound Lottie had heard many times before. The sound of the head of the Hooper household going to bed drunk.

Marcus had left the downstairs doors open behind him and Lottie could hear the sound of talking — and crying. Shrugging herself down beneath the blanket, Lottie cut off most of the sounds and shut her eyes. Things in the Hooper household were back to normal.

The next morning Jane Trago awoke at the same time as her two children and as they watched, she rose from her mattress and began stuffing her few belongings back inside the army knapsack.

"Where you going, Ma? You're not going off and leaving us again?" Wide-eyed and pale-faced, Jacob threw the questions at his mother.

"I'm not going far. Just to the Cheesewring Inn, that's all." Glancing up, even Jane Trago recognised the fear on the face of her young son. "There's more room along there. I'll have a room of my own and won't be upsetting everyone when I come in late at night."

"You don't wake me, honest!"

There was desperation in Jacob's voice, but Jane was wrapped in her own thoughts.

"I may not wake *you*, but you're not the only one in this house. Your Aunt Patience finds my comings and goings disturbing. Life'll be easier for everyone if I move into one of Waldo Daveys rooms."

"Can me and Lottie come too? We wouldn't be a nuisance. I'd get work on the Sharptor mine . . . We could look for a place to live together. Just the three of us."

"You'd soon have enough of *me*, Jacob boy. I'm not used to having kids underfoot — especially my own. No, you're better off here. I'll pay your Aunt Patience for your keep — and I'll pay well — so just you let me know if you're not getting enough to eat."

As Jane Trago tightened the last strap on her knapsack, Jacob moved to stand beside Lottie, and his hand sought hers for reassurance.

"Can we come and see you sometimes?"

"There's nothing to stop you. But not in the evenings, mind. That's the busiest time in the Cheesewring. Better not make it the mornings, neither. Most days I'll be sleeping late. And don't come to the inn when there's customers to be served. Waldo Davey wouldn't take kindly to having you underfoot with customers around. Sunday afternoon's the best time, 'twixt three and five. Yes, that's the best time to come and see me if you've a mind to. Now, which of you's going to carry this knapsack to the inn for me?"

Jacob would have stepped forward eagerly to take the knapsack from her, but Lottie held on tightly to his hand.

Jane Trago looked from Jacob to Lottie and then shrugged her shoulders. "Well, please yourselves, I'm sure."

Fixing her gaze on Lottie, she said, "Haven't you got anything to say for yourself?"

"Would it make any difference if I had? If I said I wanted you to stay here would you change your mind about going?"

"No, I've made up my mind. I'm going to the Cheesewring Inn."

"Then I've got nothing to say to you."

Jane Trago glared at her defiant daughter for a few more moments, then shrugged once again. "You're too like your mother for your own good, girl." Tucking the knapsack beneath her arm she turned and left the room.

Not until their mother's footsteps reached the lowest creaking wooden stair did Lottie release her brother's painfully squeezed hand.

Rubbing some feeling back in to his fingers, Jacob asked, "Why wouldn't you let me carry the knapsack for our ma?"

"Why should you? Why should you *want* to? What's she ever done except *have* us in the first place? She didn't want us then, and she don't want us now. I don't care if I *never* see her again."

There was both hurt and anger in Lottie's outburst, but both emotions were quickly forgotten when she looked at her young brother's expression. His face was contorted with anguish and when he spoke his bottom lip trembled so much he could scarcely form the words.

"But . . . but . . . she's our ma!"

Lottie held out her arms and Jacob came to her. Clinging to her, he began to cry. Holding the little boy close to her, Lottie felt a deep, deep bitterness towards the woman who had given birth to them, only to cast them upon the world with such callous indifference. It would have been better — far better — had she stayed away and allowed Jacob to keep the romantic dream of the mother he *wanted* her to be.

"It's all right, Jacob. It's all right," Lottie tightened her skinny, bony arms about the sobbing boy. "You've got me to look after you. You'll always have me."

9

WITHIN two weeks of Josh acquiring the Sharptor mine work had progressed to such an extent that all but the lowest levels were free of water. Now work could begin on winning ore and raising it to the surface.

This was an exciting time for Josh and he put in more hours than any of the men working for him. While the smaller of the two mine engines was pumping out water he stripped the other and carefully put it together again, renewing every part that showed signs of wear. It was a long and arduous task, although the engine was in far better condition than he had dared hope.

It was a proud day when the furnace was lit from coal newly carried from Looe on the mineral railway. Tipped unceremoniously beside the track on the hill above the mine, it was packed on horses for the final few hundred yards. Eventually Josh hoped to build his own extension to link mine and railway — but that was in the future. For now it was enough to have pressure building up in the boiler of the main engine, bringing the moment closer when Josh would open the valve and bring power and life back to the Sharptor mine.

It was a rare, still, warm day. Smoke from the tall chimney rose in an expanding plume high into the air before breaking and drifting away across the high moor. The smoke could be seen for miles around, bringing women, boys and non-working miners from surrounding villages and hamlets. They stood in groups of constantly changing sizes, watching the increased activity about the mine. Some hoped to have a part in the future fortunes of the Sharptor mine. Others were merely indulging Cornish curiosity in a traditional way of life.

When Josh emerged from the engine house wiping the back of an oily hand across his forehead, he saw the waiting crowd for the first time. In the doorway behind him Ben Retallick smiled approval at the scene.

"This is a big day for every miner here, Josh. There's not a mine hereabouts has started working again after shutting down its engines. Costs are high enough on a mine in full production. Adventurers are reluctant to spend money draining flooded workings."

"When the new adit's completed we won't need to raise the water so far. The main engine will pump out the mine twice as fast — and at half the cost. The Sharptor mine will manage well enough just as long as the price of copper stays up and the men don't get too greedy."

"Amen to that!"

Josh ran a hand across his forehead once more, redistributing the grease. Suddenly he grinned. "There'll be time enough for serious thoughts the day after tomorrow, when we open the first biddings. The men have worked hard this last couple of weeks. Send some of them to the Cheesewring Inn. Ask Waldo for a couple of barrels of good ale — lemonade, too. If he complains that it'll make him short tell him I'll have some sent up on the train, tomorrow.

Miriam's up at the house with Ma, cooking. It may not be as fine a spread as they've seen the adventurers enjoy on settling days in the past, but it should give the men enough strength to produce a rousing cheer when I open the valve on the engine and pumping begins in earnest."

Josh received his cheer when the main Sharptor engine resumed work, but what began as a small treat became a celebration that continued until well into the night. The two barrels of ale became five as miners from miles around arrived to offer congratulations and help celebrate, many bringing ale and spirits with them.

One of the miners also brought a fiddle and soon the celebrants were singing, their voices echoing back from the rugged face of Sharptor.

"That's a sound I've longed to hear for many years," said Josh. He was standing in the doorway of the mine captain's office, a smoking pipe in one hand, a pint tankard in the other.

"It's been many years since miners hereabouts had anything to sing about," commented Ben Retallick. "But here's someone coming up the hill who has more problems than most . . ."

Patience Hooper was walking along the track towards the mine, her tired gait that of a woman far beyond her twenty-nine years.

Miriam had returned to the house to prepare more food so Josh put down his drink and set off to meet his sister-in-law. By-passing the crowd who were dancing to the music of the fiddler, Josh met her at the mine entrance.

"Patience! I was expecting you here earlier. Miriam's up at the house fetching more food, but we haven't run out of ale yet. Go up to the office, my pa's there. I'll fetch you a drink and leave word for Miriam to come there when she returns."

Patience stopped outside the mine entrance, seemingly reluctant to enter. "I haven't come to see Miriam. I'd like a word with you, Josh."

"I'm listening . . . but at least come and enjoy a drink. You look as though you could do with something."

"I've just finished work at the Wheal Whisper, at St Neot."

The village of St Neot was at least six miles away and Patience Hooper had walked home after completing a day's work there. It was hardly surprising she looked tired.

"I must get home as soon as I've said what I came for. I've left Jacob looking after the girls. They've been at Wheal Whisper with me and are tired out."

Josh was appalled. Patience had walked six miles to work that morning with her three young girls, spent the day breaking ore and walked six miles home again — no doubt carrying one or more of the children for much of the way. Josh had been away so long he had forgotten how hard women were expected to work in a mining community.

"I'm sorry, Patience, I've been so involved with the Sharptor mine I haven't had time to think of other people . . . *family.* There's work here if you want it. Something lighter than a bal-maiden's work."

"Thank you, Josh. I'll take you up on that . . . but I'm not here to ask for anything for

99

myself. It's Marcus — "

"Marcus? I haven't seen him today, but that doesn't mean he's not here. I'll have a look."

"You won't find him here, Josh. He'll be drinking at the Cheesewring Inn."

There was an unhappiness in Patience that went deeper than tiredness and concern for her husband's drinking habits . . . but she was talking again.

"It's rumoured you'll be setting the pitches in a day or two?"

'Setting the pitches' was the term used for auctioning each section — or 'pitch' — of the workings. The bidders were teams of miners who would work together to win and bring copper ore to the surface of the mine.

"That's right. All but the lowest levels can be worked now. Once the mine's completely drained there'll be more men working underground than on any other mine for miles around."

"Would you . . . take on Marcus?" The words came out in a rush after a hesitant beginning.

Josh frowned. "I'd prefer him to come and ask that question for himself."

"He's given up begging for work at mines. He says he won't give any mine captain the satisfaction of refusing him."

Josh made up his mind. "I won't turn him away. Tell him to come and see me."

Patience Hooper's face lit up with relief and for a few moments Josh caught a glimpse of the attractive girl she had once been. "You'll employ him?"

"I'll speak to him. If we're able to reach an

understanding on one or two matters I'll be happy to take him on."

Some of Patience's hopes seeped away. "You won't persuade him to give up his unionist ideas."

"I won't be asking him to abandon unionism. All I'll ask is that he takes up any grievances with me before stirring up the men. It will be to everyone's advantage. That shouldn't be too much to ask even the most ardent of union men."

"I'll ask him to come to speak to you . . . Thank you, Josh."

"Here's Miriam and some of the women returning. At least take some food home with you for the girls. There's more than enough."

Marcus Hooper came to see Josh at the mine early the next morning. He had neglected to shave, but the serge suit he wore was brushed and his frayed shirt was spotlessly clean. He entered the mine captain's office with his hat held respectfully in his hands, but his face wore an expression of aggressive suspicion.

"Patience said you wanted to see me."

Marcus addressed his words to Josh, although Ben Retallick was seated behind the mine captain's desk.

"Yes. I was talking to her yesterday and I suggested you might like to work on the Sharptor mine." Josh pretended not to see his father's surprise. He had said nothing about his conversation with Patience, and thought it might be better if Marcus Hooper thought the suggestion of employment had come from him.

101

"What'll I be doing?" There was no hint of gratitude in Marcus Hooper's manner. "I'm no tut-man. I'll not dig holes for others to make money.".

"That's all *I* can offer you, Marcus. If you want tribute work you must find men who'll have you working with them. If you do, I'll be happy to have you working at Sharptor — but you'll need to join a pare pretty quickly. We're setting the pitches at noon tomorrow and I want work to begin the day after."

A 'pare' was the miners' term for a team of men who would bid for, and work, a particular section, or 'sett'.

"I'll have no difficulty finding men to work with. I can mine as well as any man in these parts."

Marcus Hooper was almost at the door when he stopped and turned, "What about surface work? Can you find something for Lottie and Jacob?"

On his way to the mine that morning Josh had seen Lottie and Jacob Trago driving the Barnicoat goats to the high moor. Both children were singing a song that should have been confined within the walls of a less respectable beerhouse. Josh had smiled to himself and thought how much the comparatively free life of the open moor suited Lottie.

"I've nothing for them at the moment — although I'll find a place for Patience. With times so hard I'm trying to spread the work as far as possible. I'm hoping to put *some* money, at least, into every house in Henwood. If you've need of money right now I'll advance

102

you 'subsist', to see you through to settling day. Most men have taken some. I'll tell you the same as I've told them — I don't want to hear of it being spent inside the Cheesewring Inn."

"If I take subsist from you it'll be *my* business how I spend it." Marcus Hooper glared defiantly at Josh.

"Patience and the girls are family. That makes it my business too," Josh spoke quietly, trying hard to keep his temper with the man standing before him.

For a few minutes it seemed Josh's offer of an advance of pay would be refused on his terms. Then Marcus Hooper shrugged, "I'll take the subsist. You needn't worry about it being spent at the Cheesewring — not while Jane's there to see me right. You see, she's 'family' too."

When the door closed behind the departing miner, Ben Retallick leaned back in his chair and frowned up at his son. "I hope you'll not have cause to regret giving work to Marcus Hooper. The man's a notorious trouble-maker. There's not a mine captain in Cornwall will allow him near a working mine."

Josh remembered the man he had seen in the light of the flames on the night fires had been started on the Sharptor mine. He had always believed that man to be Marcus Hooper. But he had said nothing to anyone then, and would say nothing now. Instead, he replied "Marcus is married to Miriam's sister. I must give him a chance to work, at least. Keep a close watch on what he's doing. I'll expect to be warned if he starts stirring up any trouble. I'll give Marcus a fair chance, but I'll not let him do anything to put the Sharptor mine out of business."

10

AS they drove the goats back to the village the day after the party at the Sharptor mine, Lottie asked Jacob to return the animals to Elias Barnicoat. She intended having a bath in the stream that flowed through the gorse on the hillside near the mine.

Lottie was standing in the knee-deep water, naked, when she heard someone approaching along the narrow path through the gorse. Before she had time to leap from the stream and grab her clothes, Nell Gilmore appeared, and Lottie breathed a sigh of relief.

Continuing her ablutions, Lottie viewed Nell Gilmore with all the disdain her few years' seniority afforded. But their respective ages were not the only difference between the two girls. Lottie thought the older of the two Gilmore girls prim and priggish. No doubt she took after her parents. She had heard they had both been missionaries.

Lottie's opinion was confirmed when Nell told her she should be ashamed of bathing without clothes, within hearing of the Sharptor mine.

When Lottie replied with an oath that would not have shamed the coarsest miner, Nell was shocked into telling Lottie that God was listening, and would punish her for uttering such an obscenity.

Stepping clear of the spring, Lottie pulled her

dress on over her head. Easing the garment down over her wet body with difficulty, she said, "I don't know what God *you* worship, Nell Gilmore, but it can't be the same one everyone else here prays to. If it was you'd know He *likes* me having a bath. When I went to chapel once I was told John Wesley once said, 'Cleanliness is next to Godliness' — and he should know. He and God used to speak together lots."

Nell Gilmore was not very big, even when indignation swelled her almost to the point of bursting, "You're telling big fat lies, Lottie Trago. God doesn't talk to *no one* — except to the Jews, sometimes."

Lottie found Nell Gilmore boring. "So? Perhaps Wesley *was* a Jew. *I* don't care."

"I don't believe John Wesley said anything of the sort, Lottie Trago. You've made it up. You're a *liar,* that's what you are."

The younger girl was standing balanced on a mound of earth and coarse marsh grass, the sides of which had been eroded by decades of flood and drought. It needed only a comparatively gentle shove from Lottie's foot to push the mound over and send Nell sprawling in the black, hoof-churned mud of the marsh that surrounded the spring.

As Nell set up a wail of surprised indignation, Lottie grinned wickedly, "What you making all that fuss for, Nell? I'm sure God will love you just as much, even though you're smothered in mud and smelling worse than a farmyard pig . . . I'm not sure Aunt Miriam will, though."

The next day Lottie thought it wiser to find another route to and from the moor, avoiding the Sharptor mine. She was on her way back with the goats along an unfamiliar path when she saw a man sitting on the hillside, stripped to the waist. He sat in the sunshine, his back to a granite boulder, his head bowed as though he was dozing.

Lottie was on her own. Jacob had complained of feeling unwell earlier in the day and she had sent him home. She decided to give the dozing man a wide berth. Not all the jobless strangers wandering the county were honest, out-of-work miners. A girl from a nearby village had been attacked by two men in a lane near her home only a fortnight before. Another from a lonely cottage three miles across the moor had disappeared altogether — or so it was said.

The man did not raise his head as Lottie passed by, but suddenly she recognised him. It was Jethro Shovell. A few flicks of the switch she carried were sufficient to change the direction of the goats once more, sending them up the slope towards the young miner.

When she was still many yards away, Jethro spoke without looking up, "Hello, Lottie. What are you doing up here?"

"How did you know it was me?" Lottie had not taken her eyes from Jethro since she first recognised him. She would have sworn he had not seen her coming.

Jethro raised his head and smiled. "I knew it must be you. I could smell the goats."

"There's people who smell worse than goats,"

Lottie spoke defensively.

"Don't I know it! Tomorrow I'll be spending ten hours with a couple of miners winning ground at the end of a hot, cramped workings. By the end of the shift I'll be willing to give a week's pay to be back up here, smelling goats."

"You're starting work at the Sharptor mine then?" Lottie sat down on a long, flat rock and gave Jethro a sympathetic look. "Is that why you're up here today?"

"It's the last chance I'll have to enjoy the sunshine above ground for a while. We'll need to work all the hours God gives us if Josh Retallick is to make a success of the mine — "

"It's all right for Josh Retallick. *He* won't have to work below ground." Lottie sided aggressively with the young miner.

"Josh Retallick knows what working down a mine is all about. Now he's used his own money to give work to many men who feared they'd never work again — your uncle Marcus for one. It's lucky for him Josh Retallick is sympathetic towards unionism, even though he's suffered more than any of us because of it. I'll be working a pare with Marcus and a couple of others. Your aunt Patience will be pleased to have a man's wages coming in the house again, I've no doubt."

"The Cheesewring Inn will see more of Marcus's money than Aunt Patience will."

Lottie spoke scornfully. All the same, life would be more pleasant for her with Marcus out of the cottage for most of the day. When he was sober he was constantly pointing out her faults. Drunk, he became totally unpredictable.

Picking up his shirt from the ground beside him, Jethro pulled it over his head.

"Are you going already?" Lottie was disappointed. She rarely had an opportunity of speaking to Jethro when no one else was around. "There's still an hour or two of sunshine left.".

"I know, but I need to see Marcus and the others to sort out how we're going to work."

"You don't enjoy working below grass, do you? Why do you do it? Why don't you find something else?"

"What else is there? A man's got to earn a living somehow."

Jethro Shovell was only seventeen, but a young man matured early in a mining community — if the mines did not cut his life short. Jethro's mother had been widowed and left with a small daughter by the time she was Jethro's age. Tom Shovell, Jethro's father, was her second husband. Much older than Jenny, Tom Shovell had survived two roof falls and a misfired explosion that had claimed the lives of all the other men with whom he had been working at the time. He was one of the fortunate ones.

Walking beside Lottie towards Henwood village, Jethro tried not to think too much of what tomorrow would bring. Lottie was right, he *hated* working below ground. He enjoyed the feel of the sun on his face and body, and the sights and the smell of the moor. It was not merely that he disliked the hot, cramped darkness of underground work. He wanted something *more* from life. Something more than merely earning just enough to feed a family, uncertain of what the next day would bring. He wanted to be able to relish the thought of the future, not view it with fear. But he needed to work. His half-sister had married and moved to the other end of Cornwall and his father was a sick man. Since his brother had been killed, Jethro was the only wage-earner in the family.

"What would you most like to do, Jethro? I mean, if you could do anything you wanted? Anything at all?" Lottie's question brought Jethro back from his thoughts.

"I don't know. Perhaps be like the union man from the coal mines. The one who was here a few weeks ago. I'd like to do something to make life better for everyone who has to work down a mine."

"I didn't see all the miners rushing to shake his hand and join his union when he was here — although I hear he gathered quite a crowd at the Cheesewring Inn when he was buying."

"Our miners won't pledge themselves to any man who isn't a Cornishman. I *am* . . . " Jethro Shovell's enthusiasm enjoyed only a fleeting life. "But there's little sense talking of what I'd *like* to be doing. I know nothing except mining, and the Sharptor mine's the last hope for all us miners in this area. If it closes again there's nothing to keep me in Cornwall."

Lottie looked at her companion in dismay. The thought that Jethro might one day leave Henwood was too awful to contemplate — but she had to know more.

"Where will you go if the mine *does* close down again?"

110

"I don't know. Australia, perhaps. Or America, once the Civil War's over . . . South Africa, even. That's where Josh Retallick earned the money to buy the Sharptor mine."

Jethro might as well have been talking of going to the moon for all Lottie knew of any of these places. She had never been farther than Liskeard. One thing was certain, Jethro could not be allowed to leave Sharptor — and her life. The mine *had* to succeed.

"How about you, Lottie? What do you want from life?"

"I want to stay on the moor for ever. I don't want to go anywhere else."

"Well . . . why shouldn't you stay here? All you need do is wait until you're old enough and find yourself a good man. One who'll look after you . . . perhaps even buy you a goat herd of your own."

His words did not convey the reassurance Jethro intended. Lottie was thinking of the gap there would be in her life if Jethro went away. What future would there be for her then? Work on the mine, certainly. An early marriage perhaps . . . and children. An acceptance of her place in life. A mirror image of her aunt Patience — perhaps even to the extent of having a husband who would beat her frequently, to ensure she remembered she was only a woman . . .

Jethro reached out unexpectedly and ruffled Lottie's hair. "It seems strange to think that in only a few years time you could be married."

Unaccountably disturbed by his touch, Lottie shook his hand free. "You're only five years older

111

than me, Jethro Shovell."

Her statement seemed to surprise him, "So I am . . . but boys need to grow up more quickly than girls. Off you go now. You'd better get those goats home or Elias Barnicoat will come looking for them. I want to find Marcus and the others before they go to the inn to celebrate their return to work."

"Aren't you going to celebrate with them?"

"I'm not working ten hours a day underground just to give all my money to Waldo Davey. No, Lottie, I've signed the pledge. I've become a teetotaller."

Jethro's fears that all the other members of his pare would go off to celebrate at the Cheesewring Inn proved unfounded. Joseph Maddever, the senior member of the group was a staunch Methodist who frowned on the drinking habits of his fellow miners. One of the most experienced miners who would be working at the Sharptor mine, Maddever was well aware he had reached an age when most miners had already quit underground work. A childless widower who had lived cautiously and frugally all his life, there was no need for him to work now, but if the ageing miner shared any sin with his fellow men it was a love of money.

Joseph Maddever also had a strong dislike of Marcus Hooper. Only a last-minute plea by Josh Retallick had persuaded the pare leader to accept Marcus Hooper as a workmate.

The fourth member of the underground team was Kingsley Quick. Belying his name, Quick was a large, slow-thinking man in his mid thirties. He was married to a small, slim, energetic woman

112

whom he adored, and who dominated him as no man ever could. She had borne him four daughters and now carried his fifth child. Kinglsey Quick had no intention of upsetting his wife by spending an evening drinking in the company of Jane Trago.

Had he been so inclined, Marcus Hooper, too, might have found a reason for remaining at home on the night before the Sharptor mine began full-time working — but he did not. He made his way to the inn as usual, and discovered he had no more than a quarter of the regular customers for company.

Jane Trago slid a tankard of ale to him before he uttered a word. He nodded acknowledgement, making no move to pay for the drink.

Taking a deep draught of the ale, and smacking his lips in noisy appreciation, he said, "Where's everyone else tonight?"

"All the Henwood men are at home, making ready to begin work tomorrow."

"What is there to be made ready? A man goes to the mine, works his hours, then returns home. He isn't expected to give up all of life's pleasures because he has to work. That's playing into the hands of the employers and the churchmen. They tell us we're put on this earth to work — but that's only so *we* can keep *them* in idleness. It's an attitude the unions are fighting against."

"We all know about your unionism, Marcus Hooper — but I haven't noticed you going short of any of life's pleasures since I returned to Henwood village."

The wink she gave to Marcus was missed by

Waldo Davey. The landlord gazed about the taproom gloomily. "I thought we were going to make more money when the Sharptor mine re-opened. Look at it here tonight. If this is the sort of business I can expect in future I'll be the one giving up life's luxuries."

"You won't need to give up anything, Waldo. Tomorrow night when the miners come up to grass they'll have a thirst on 'em enough to drink us dry — and come settling day it'll be money coming across the bar, not just names."

"That's another thing. I've been looking at the tick you're giving. Some of the men owe more than they can earn in three months below ground."

"So? We'll take part-settlement. That means they pay us less that we're owed, but more than they think they can afford. When interest is added their tick will be doubled before the next month's half over. Soon we'll be collecting half the money paid out by the Sharptor mine in wages each month — and most of the other mines in the district too. That should be enough to pay for your little pleasures."

"It'll be all right as long as the Sharptor mine doesn't close down again. If it does I'll be a ruined man . . ."

Downing his second pint of ale, Marcus Hooper left the taproom to relieve himself. Refilling his tankard, Jane said, "Stop being such a Jeremiah, Waldo. If the mine stops working you need only to take your problem to the courts . . . but it'll never come to that. Josh Retallick won't fail, trust me."

"I hope you're right. You know Josh Retallick

114

better than I do. After all, he's *your* relative. Talking of relatives, you'd better not give Marcus Hooper too many ales tonight. He's trouble when he takes too much to drink."

"Don't you worry about Marcus Hooper. I'll see to it he's no trouble to anyone, tonight or any other night. Go upstairs and rest for an hour, Waldo. We'll not be rushed off our feet tonight. Off you go now."

Waldo Davey had gone upstairs by the time Marcus returned to the taproom. The miner stood talking to Jane across the rough board counter, interrupted only occasionally by other customers. Four or five of the regulars would remain drinking until the inn closed its doors at midnight. The remainder would leave as they finished their drinks.

In spite of Waldo Daveys warning, Jane allowed Marcus to drink more than any other man in the taproom. Marcus reminded her of soldiers to whom she had served drinks in India on the eve of a battle. He was drinking because he was afraid. Afraid of the mine, and of returning underground to work.

It was late when Jane told her brother-in-law he had drunk enough for one night. When Marcus growled irritably that *he* would be the judge of that, she silenced him with a look. In a low voice, she said, "You can please yourself about that, Marcus — but I'm having no drunken man in my room tonight, you understand? It's up to you, what's it going to be?"

By way of an answer Marcus downed the remainder of his drink and pushed the empty pewter mug across the stained wood counter. "What about Waldo?"

"Leave him to me. Go now and wait outside the back door. I won't be more than a few minutes."

Marcus Hooper left the inn, nodding an unspoken 'good night' to the other customers. A few lights were still burning in one or two cottages, but there was no moon and it was dark in the alleyway beside the inn. Once Marcus tripped over an untidily stacked pile of logs and he held back a curse as one fell heavily on his toe.

An upstairs window was open and he could hear Jane's authoritative voice calling for Waldo Davey to 'hurry up and get downstairs or I'll go to bed and leave no one serving in the taproom'. He shook his head, filled with admiration for his wife's sister. He had never known such a woman for ordering men around, but she *was* a woman, and a rare one at that.

At the back of the hotel Marcus made his way more carefully around a couple of empty barrels. He had been expecting to find them here. This was not the first time he had made his way to the back door of the inn during the hours of darkness.

He waited by the door for almost ten minutes before he heard the bolts inside being quietly and stealthily drawn back. Then the door swung open.

The sole of one of Marcus's steel-tipped boots scraped on the step as he entered and Jane hissed an admonishment.

The stairs inside the inn were uncarpeted

116

and they creaked alarmingly, but a couple of late-comers had entered the taproom and their raised voices obliterated the sounds of Marcus's clumsiness.

Jane's room was off a short corridor leading from the top of the stairs. Both room and corridor were in darkness. As Jane followed Marcus into the room he turned and took her roughly in his arms and his mouth found hers.

He smelled of ale and perspiration, but she accepted his embrace and the clumsy fumbling of his hands for a while before pushing him away.

"Just be patient for a few more minutes, Marcus Hooper. I need to talk to you before we do anything else."

"Where's a candle? I'll set a match to it . . . "

"We don't need a light for talking — and certainly not for what you want to do. Keep your hands to yourself for a while and listen to me. I don't need to be the cleverest woman in the world to see you're not enjoying the thought of working below ground in Josh Retallick's mine — "

"I'm not scared of working below-grass!"

"Shh! Keep your voice down. I'm not saying you're scared. Only that you don't *enjoy* working below ground. There's no reason why you should. I hated working on a mine — and I was at grass. But there's a way out, if you've a mind to take it."

"What way out? This is the first offer of work I've had for nigh on two years. If I don't accept this I'll never work again."

"And *why* haven't you worked, tell me that?"

"Because I've always been strong for a union

117

and mine owners don't want unionism to get a hold in Cornwall."

"Right! And hasn't there been a union man here from the coal mines of the north? Trying to gain support for an Association of all miners — coal, copper and tin."

"That's right. I offered to help him, but he wouldn't have me because I haven't worked on a mine for so long."

"He won't be able to say that after tomorrow. Do you know where to write to him?"

"No. But I know someone at the Wheal Whisper, over towards St Neot, who does."

"Good. Get the address and we'll have a letter sent off to him. If you do as I say you'll not need to spend the rest of your life underground at the Sharptor mine, waiting for an accident to kill you. But that's enough talk for one night . . . and don't drop your boots on the floor. The last time you were here Waldo Davey said it sounded as though I had a brewery horse in my room. If he knew it was you I'd lose my job — and *I* have plans for the future, too."

11

ON the day work resumed at the Sharptor mine, women, children and old men gathered about the engine house early to watch the miners descend the shaft on their way to the working levels. As steam hissed through the pipes in the engine room the great, forty-ton beam rocked soundlessly on its well-greased axle. Huge, wooden plungers, each as wide as a boy, screeched and creaked in protest as they dipped and rose in the shaft. The plungers worked pumps at the bottom of the mine and also served as a 'man-lift'. The lifts were simple affairs. A step was affixed to either end of the long rods. The miners rode up or down with the stroke of the engine, stepping off to a platform at the end of each stroke and awaiting the next step. All a man needed was a cool head and a sense of balance.

When the last man entered the shaft, the crowd thinned. A few people, mainly old men, remained throughout the day and saw the first ore brought to grass and fed through the jaws of the crushing machine. The noise of the steel rollers was a comforting sound and the women of Henwood went about their daily chores with a happy tune on their lips. All was well with the world once more.

Late in the evening, when the sun was dipping towards the moor behind the Sharptor mine the women and children returned to the mine to witness the return of their men to grass. It was not something they would do very often. On an ordinary working day few miners wanted their families to witness their exhaustion when they emerged from the shaft. But today was a special day. A day to be shared.

In the mine captain's office Josh closed the pages of the mine store credit book. Every man below ground had taken at least one item from the store, to be paid for on settling day.

"The first man should be coming to grass soon. Shall we go and show our faces?"

"Of course! I've waited a long time for this. I want to shake every man by the hand — "

Ben Retallick was still speaking when the engine took on a new and frightening note. The beam began to race, vibrating the tall, stone engine house to its very foundations. Then there was the sound of splintering wood accompanied by a crash that made the earth tremble.

Both men reached the door together and were in time to see a huge cloud of dust rise from the shaft and hang upon the air.

The engine had stopped racing almost as soon as it had begun, shut down by an alert engine-man. But Josh and his father knew what had happened, even before the screams of the women and children gathered about the shaft reached them. The Sharptor mine had suffered a catastrophic accident on the day of its grand re-opening. Some of the huge wooden pump plungers had broken away. It could not have happened at a worse time. The miners were beginning their ascent to grass — and the plungers doubled as a man-lift . . . !

Pushing their way through the women and children, Josh and Ben Retallick reached the shaft just as a young boy who could have been no more than eleven years old scrambled up the ladder from the shaft, a terrified expression on his dust-streaked face. He would have run past the two men had not Josh reached out and brought him to an abrupt halt.

"What's happening down there? Where's the break?"

Josh had to repeat his questions twice more before the boy took three or four deep gulps of air and stopped shaking long enough to reply. "The pump rods broke away . . . right below where I was standing . . . My pa was on it . . . I wanted to go back down, but Cap'n Clymo was there. He made me come up . . . "

"Where were you when it happened? At what level? Come on, boy. Pull yourself together. *We have to know*!"

The fierce questions were fired at the quivering boy by a small, bow-legged man who had pushed his way through the crowd at the top of the shaft. Malachi Sprittle was the 'above gradd' captain and his sharp words had their intended effect.

"Fifty fathoms . . . at the fifty fathoms level . . . " The boy recognised a woman struggling to push through the crowd to reach him. " . . . Ma! Ma . . . ! Pa fell away, with the man-lift . . . "

As the boy burst into tears and a wail of primitive anguish escaped from his mother, Josh Retallick gave his orders to Malachi Sprittle.

"Rig up a winch over the shaft — use the strongest cable you can find. We'll need to hoist some of the plungers clear. And have a skip sent down to the fifty fathom level in the whim shaft . . ."

The 'whim shaft' was the ladderless shaft used solely for raising ore to the surface in metal skips.

Josh lowered his voice so that only Malachi Sprittle heard his next words. "I'm going down there now. I'll have any injured men taken along the fifty fathom level to the whim shaft and you'll bring them up in the skips. Keep their families away for as long as you can."

Captain Malachi Sprittle understood the unspoken thought behind Josh's words. If there were bodies in the shaft it would be better to bring them up away from the eyes of the waiting families. The body of a man killed in a mine accident was a distressing sight for those who had once known him.

"I'll see to everything up top, Mr Retallick. You go on down. Both the skip and a winch wire will be at the fifty fathom level almost as soon as you."

Swinging himself on to the ladder descending to the depths of the shaft, Josh said to his father, "You'd best help Malachi get things organised up here."

"If that's your way of telling me I'm too old to climb down fifty fathoms of ladder you'd best think again. Unless you've a mind to dismiss me here and now I'm still captain of the Sharptor mine. My place is down this shaft. Off you go — and be quick about it or I'll be dancing on your fingers all the way down."

By the time the two men had descended three hundred feet into the depths of the mine, the choking dust had settled and they were able to see a myriad of lights twinkling beneath them. They had not passed a single miner on the ladders. There had been no panic among the men working below ground when the accident occurred. As soon as it was clear what had happened, every uninjured man in the mine made his way to the main shaft.

At the fifty fathom level the line of plungers came to an abrupt end. Everything below this level had been carried away by the weight of the falling plungers.

Taking a candle from a niche in the shaft wall, Josh leaned out away from the ladder, holding the candle close to the swinging rod. There was the dull gleam of metal in the candlelight and Josh swore softly. "Here's the cause of the accident. A new iron joint fitted only last week has snapped. It must have been a faulty casting."

"So no one's to blame for what's happened?"

There was relief in Ben Retallick's voice. All the way down to the fifty fathom level he had been torturing himself, wondering what had caused the accident. Wondering whether it was something he should have foreseen as the mine captain.

"No one on the Sharptor mine, but I'll have something to say to the captain of the foundry where that link was made. Let's go down further and see what's happened."

Three ladders down, they came upon the first of the injured. One had a broken collar-bone, the other two were suffering no more than cuts and bruises. All three realised how lucky they were to be alive.

From one of the victims Josh learned that the rods had broken without any warning, taking miners and pitwork with them until they had wedged in a mass of splintered pitwork where the shaft went off at a slight angle, about fifty feet below the spot where they were standing. The men thought miners were buried in the tangle of wreckage. What was less certain was the fate of the men who had been on the man-lift in the shaft beneath the break. The mine was being worked down to the hundred and fifty fathom level. This meant the fate of everyone in six hundred feet of workings was unknown. Beneath this were at least another hundred fathoms of flooded workings — and the accident had put the pumps out of action!

At that moment there was a clattering sound from the shaft above them and one of the injured men called a warning as a heavy steel cable snaked down the shaft.

Hurriedly passing on the warning, Josh and Ben Retallick scrambled down the remaining ladders to arrive at a scene of utter chaos. The ladders and pitwork had been torn away from the last few fathoms and the rescuers were using all their ingenuity in an effort to reach their colleagues. Ropes, timbers, and even spade-ended twist drills driven into the wall were being utilised to provide foot and handholds.

As Josh and Ben stepped gingerly on to the tangled wreckage, a miner was pulled clear. He seemed to be unconscious, until a sudden,

124

incautious movement by one of the men tugging on his arms brought a groan of pain from the injured man.

A second man, limp and still, was lifted on to a makeshift stretcher at the entrance to a working level only a few feet above the wreckage. As he was passed up to the grim-faced rescuers Josh saw the man's bloody face. It was Jethro Shovell.

Josh's ploy of bringing injured men to the surface via the whim shaft was successful only until the first rescued miner reached the surface. A cry went up from the waiting crowd as the man was lifted from the ore skip. The crowd immediately ran to surround the mouth of the whim shaft. Such was the crush there was a very real danger of someone being precipitated down the shaft and the rescuers protested they could not bring injured men through such a mêlée. Not until Captain Malachi Sprittle sent some of his surface workers to the shaft were the anxious families of men in the mine driven back and a path cleared for the injured men.

The first skip to reach grass carried three men. Two with leg injuries were unable to walk. The third was unconscious. The wives of the two conscious men rushed forward and hugged their husbands, tearfully grateful for their survival. The unconscious miner was much younger, no more than sixteen. His mother hurried to take his hand and accompany him as he was borne away on a litter. He would be examined in the captain's office by doctors from two nearby mines who had hurried to Sharptor as soon as news of the accident reached them. There were no tears from the mother, but her pale, tortured face bore tragic testimony to the anguish she was feeling. She had lost her husband and oldest son in a mine accident in West Cornwall some years before. Another son had been killed in a roof fall at a neighbouring mine that same year.

Only one man was brought up when the skip returned from its second descent to the fifty fathom level. He had suffered back injuries and was the most seriously injured of the men rescued so far.

As the skip rattled down the shaft yet again, Lottie edged her way through the crowd to where Jenny Shovell stood with a couple of other women. For Jenny too the accident brought back agonising memories.

"Is . . . is there any news of Jethro?" Aware that Jenny Shovell did not approve of her, or her family, Lottie asked the question hesitantly.

Jenny Shovell shook her head in a distracted manner. Suddenly there was a flurry of activity about the main shaft and Captain Sprittle ordered the newly rigged winch there to begin lifting cautiously. Josh had attached a double hawser to the broken section of plungers and a rope signalling system had been rigged. Three tugs would send down more cable, two was the signal to lift — and one brought the winch to a halt.

Slowly the cable tightened and the pitwork at the top of the shaft creaked and groaned as it took the strain. It was brought to a sudden halt by a tug on the rope.

The new scene of activity brought a buzz

126

of concern and speculation from the waiting relatives. The decision to begin raising the broken plungers from the tangled wreckage could have one of two meanings. Either all the men in the shaft at the time of the accident had been accounted for, or hope for any missing men had been abandoned.

As the winch at the main shaft resumed hoisting with painful slowness, the women and children moved uncertainly between the two shafts. As yet no one on the surface had any news of what was happening underground.

When the whim hoist clattered into motion, indicating the skip was on its way up with more casualties, the human tide flowed towards the smaller shaft once more.

There were three men in the skip this time. One was Jethro Shovell. There was still blood on his face from a gash on his scalp, but he had regained consciousness. However, he seemed to be in great pain. The second of the three was Marcus Hooper, nursing a patently broken arm. The third, a weary Ben Retallick.

There was a shriek from the crowd and Patience Hooper, carrying her baby and with two girls clinging to her dress, fought her way through the women. She reached Marcus, only to have him shoulder her away as she tried to hug him.

"Get away, you damned silly woman! Can't you see I've hurt my arm? Get off, I say."

Ignoring the children and nursing his grotesquely bent arm, Marcus walked to the mine captain's office, hunched over in pain. Patience followed after him, alternately laughing and crying. The

127

oldest Hooper girl was also in tears. The other two were so confused they could only stare about them, wide-eyed at seeing so many people gathered together at one time.

Jethro Shovell held a hand to his side both to support and shield injured ribs, and he too walked hunched over in pain. He reached out to clasp his mother's hand as she rushed to his side, overwhelmed with relief at seeing him emerge alive from the mine. When Jethro recognised Lottie's white face in the forefront of the crowd the brief, wan smile he gave her meant more to her than any words.

As the two injured men passed through the crowd on their way to the mine office and the waiting doctors. Ben Retallick help up his hand for silence. Despite his age, he had worked as hard as any other rescuer at the fifty fathom level, and now his voice reached every man, woman and child in the suddenly expectantly hushed crowd.

"You'll all have heard what happened in the main shaft, but so there'll be no rumours circulating about it, I'll tell you *exactly* what happened. A link joining two pump rods snapped at the fifty fathom level. One of the *new* links, fitted only last week. There must have been a fault in the forging."

Ben Retallick's statement effectively silenced those in the crowd who had been muttering among themselves about the dangers of opening an old mine, using ageing equipment.

"It was the sort of accident every miner and mine captain dreads. The accident it's impossible to guard against ... "

Ben Retallick found it necessary to hold up his hand for silence once more, "Fortunately my son put those plungers in with just such an accident in mind, some twenty years ago. He designed them so that in the event of an accident no plunger should fall farther than its length — twelve feet. Well, two of the safety stops broke away, but the third held. The rods fells only six fathoms — not a hundred and six, as they might have done. This could have been one of the worst accidents ever experienced in the area. Instead, thanks to good engineering, and the mercy of God, only eleven men have been injured. Those who've been worst hurt have already been brought to grass — you've seen them for yourselves. The others have no more than cuts and bruises — and a tale to pass on to their grandchildren. When I left the fifty fathom level just now every man underground at the time of the accident had been accounted for."

Ben Retallick's news was greeted with gasps of amazement that erupted in a wild burst of cheering. There had been no doubts despite an accident that might have been expected to carry tragedy into many homes in Henwood village — *and* spell disaster for the future of the Sharptor mine. The cheering was heard by those few villagers too infirm to make their way to Sharptor, and they too joined in the feeling of relief. It was the nearest thing to a miracle the villagers would ever know.

"What's more . . . " Ben Retallick addressed the crowd again, "what's more, Josh has asked me to tell you that no family will suffer hardship as a result of the accident. The mine will pay every injured man the same sum as that paid to the other members of his pare."

Ben Retallick walked to the mine captain's office with the cheers of the mining community ringing in his ears — only to come face to face with a reminder of the realities of life on a working Cornish mine.

Outside the office was a crowd of men, already some seventy strong, clamouring to be given the jobs of the men injured in the mining accident. The Cornish miner was a singularly *practical* man . . .

12

WILLIAM THORNDIKE travelled to Cornwall from the coal mines of Durham in the hot, late summer of 1864. A stocky, dour man in his early fifties, with close-cropped grey hair and bristling moustache. Thorndike had twice been lodged in North Country prisons as a result of his trade union activities.

More recently William Thorndike had travelled the country recruiting and organising miners into effective units, linked by a common cause. He would have found it difficult to hide his origins. Coal dust was ingrained in the lines of his forehead, and the rolled-up sleeves of his shirt revealed elbows stained black through years of close contact with the 'black gold' of the north.

Thorndike met with representatives from the Bodmin Moor mines in the taproom of the Boot Inn at Liskeard. Among those who came to hear him speak were Marcus Hooper and Jethro, both recovering from injuries received in the Sharptor mine accident.

The North Country miner described the problems facing the coal-miners and their families. He painted a picture that shocked the hard-working but easy-going Cornishmen. Thorndike spoke of blatant disregard by mine owners of recent legislation forbidding underground working by women, or boys under the age of ten. In many pits women still crawled along wet, dirty tunnels, stripped to the waist, towing baskets, or trucks of coal at the end of chains passed between their legs. Some continued such work even when they were in an advanced state of pregnancy. It was not unknown for their babies to be born underground and carried to the surface in a dirty pit apron, covered in coal dust. Many of the children were sent to the mines by parish poorhouses, to work for eleven hours a day without payment.

Conditions in the coal mines were far worse than in Cornish tin and copper mines, northern mine owners being less concerned for the welfare of their employees. Such attitudes had provoked a corresponding militancy among the coal-miners. Their disputes were accompanied by more violence than had been seen on Cornish mines.

There was both sorrow and anger in William Thorndike's voice when he reported that on more than one occasion northern mine owners had broken strikes by bringing in out-of-work tinners from Cornwall.

Coal miners were becoming increasingly bitter with the strike-breaking activities of their tin and copper mining colleagues. However, they appreciated the desperation of the Cornish miners and William Thorndike had travelled from the north in a bid to help them. The first step would be to organise an effective miners' union in Cornwall.

In this connection, Thorndike singled out Jethro Shovell and Marcus Hooper. Whilst sympathising with them on their injuries, he was quick to point out the advantages they afforded the two men.

"Those in authority are fond of alleging that men involved in trade unionism are pursuing their own ends and don't understand the problems of those they represent. No one can make such a comment about either of you. You are suffering as the result of injuries received in an underground accident — and have no doubt been cast aside by the mine owner to fend for yourself?"

"No. As a matter of fact the mine owner's paying us what we would have earned had we not been hurt." Jethro Shovell spoke out although he was aware it was not the answer William Thorndike wanted to hear, and he added, "But Josh Retallick's not the usual kind of mine owner. He's worked on mines himself — and been transported for his belief in trade unions."

"Ah! Would we had more like him," said the northern unionist, dishonestly. If all mine owners were as reasonable as Josh Retallick a union of miners would be doomed. However, there was little likelihood of such an idyllic situation being reached in the mining industry. "Tell me, are all the working mines in your area represented here tonight?"

"There are at least five mines with no one here — probably because the men are frightened they'd lose their jobs by coming. Until I started work on the Sharptor mine I hadn't done a days work for two years because of my trade union beliefs."

William Thorndike acknowledged Marcus's reply with a nod, but when he spoke it was to Jethro, "You seem a bright lad, would you have a Wesleyan background?"

"How could you know that?"

William Thorndike smiled and laid a hand on Jethro's shoulder, "A good Methodist can always tell another — and all the best union men are Methodists. But if there's likely to be trouble over unionism in Cornwall then we'll need to call it something else. A 'benevolent association' is usually looked upon favourably, the name doesn't matter, what does is that men pay a regular sum of money into something they can see will benefit them and their families. Sixpence a week is all you need ask from them. For that they'll get sick benefit, a burial grant — and a doctor's fee for sick children. Only one penny of their sixpence will go into the national union funds but it will suffice. One day we'll have enough saved to call the men out on strike and keep them from starving long enough for us to achieve our ends. You're young enough to see it happen, Jethro — and to reap the benefits from such a union. Stand for the union and you'll one day be the man all others turn to for guidance. You're still young for office, so I'm going to make Marcus the agent for this area, but I want you to assist him and learn as you go along."

The miners were crowding around Marcus, congratulating him on his appointment, when the door to the private room was flung open. A police sergeant entered the room, a number of tall-hatted constables filing in after him.

William Thorndike was momentarily taken aback at the sight of the police uniforms, and then he spread his arms wide in a gesture of despair. "Gentlemen, it seems your Cornish authorities are

134

no more tolerant towards unionism than they are elsewhere."

To the uniformed sergeant, he said, "Sergeant — you are a sergeant, I believe? — this is a private room and we are discussing the formation of a benevolent association in your district. We are all miners who care about the welfare of our fellow men. I doubt we're breaking any laws."

"I think you must leave me to decide that, Mister Thorndike. All I'm certain of at the moment is that you're a twice-convicted agitator, holding a meeting behind closed doors in my area. The Liskeard magistrate has asked me to ascertain the reason for your presence here. If he hadn't sent for me I'd be here anyway. Cornish miners have troubles enough of their own, they don't need you to add to them."

"I told you, Sergeant, we're discussing the formation of a benevolent association. To ease the distress of unemployment."

"I know what you *told* me, Thorndike. I prefer to find out things for myself. You're keeping minutes of this meeting?"

"It isn't a meeting. It's a discussion. A private discussion."

"Then you'll have nothing to hide and you'll not mind if I begin by taking the names of all those present at this 'discussion'. I'll know where to make a start if trouble *does* break out in my area."

The men in the room protested loudly. They were nervous about giving their names to a policeman. However, the sergeant was not a man to be dissuaded by a mild protest. Taking

135

the men aside one by one, he obtained each one's name, his address, and the mine where he was employed.

When he reached Jethro he asked the same questions and, as he was entering details in his notebook, he commented, "Shovell? Isn't that the name of the Sharptor mine's last captain?"

"That's right, he's my father."

The sergeant glanced up from his notebook. "What does he think of you being mixed up in unionism?"

"He spent a lifetime in underground mining. He approves of any attempt to improve conditions for miners."

The sergeant raised his eyebrows. "I doubt if he'd agree that stirring up violence will help Cornish miners — and that's William Thorndike's way of setting about resolving their problems."

"That's *slander*, Sergeant. I can claim the protection of the courts against such lies."

"As I said before, Thorndike, *I*'ll interpret the law. There's nothing slanderous about repeating the words of a judge of assize. Now, young Shovell, is there anyone else here from the Sharptor mine?"

"Only Marcus."

The police sergeant followed the direction of Jethro's glance. "Would that be Marcus Hooper, of Henwood?"

"That's right." Marcus Hooper tried unsuccessfully to produce a confident smile. "And I've never been convicted in any court, so I wouldn't say too much if I was you."

"I never say more than I need to . . . but I do

enjoy *listening* to some people. You're one of them, Mr Hooper. In fact, I so want to hear what you have to say that I'm taking you along to the police station so I can spend a few hours listening to you. There are a few questions I'd like you to answer."

"Me? Why me? I've done nothing wrong. You've no reason to arrest me."

"I've made no mention of *arrest,* Mr Hooper. All I've said is that I want to hear your answers to one or two questions." He nodded towards the constables who had entered the room with him and two of them stepped forward and took a grip on Marcus's arms.

As he left protesting his innocence, the room erupted in angry uproar. William Thorndike was loudest of them all, "You've no right to do this. We're having a private and peaceable meeting. You've no right coming in and arresting someone just for being here."

"You may carry on your meeting now, William Thorndike. I doubt if the absence of one man will make any difference to what you have to say — but remember, if we have any trouble in the Cornish mines after today I'll be looking for you, and the men here with you."

As he spoke, a series of discreet signals sent his constables filing from the room in the wake of those who held Marcus Hooper between them. When the last policeman reached the door, the sergeant touched a finger to his hat and went out, closing the door behind him. Immediately, the miners began talking excitedly among themselves about the events of the last few minutes.

Only Jethro Shovell remained silent. He had an uneasy feeling the sergeant had achieved the purpose for which he had entered the inn — and he believed it had little to do with the presence of William Thorndike.

At dawn the next morning the Retallick household on Sharptor was awakened by a prolonged hammering on the door. Fearing there had been another disaster at the mine, Josh put his head out of the bedroom window and learned that Patience Hooper was causing the commotion. A somewhat sheepish Jethro Shovell stood nearby.

When Patience saw Josh, she cried, "I need your help, Josh. It's Marcus . . . He's been arrested."

"Arrested? What for?" Newly awakened from a deep sleep, Josh's mind was not yet functioning as well as it should.

"For nothing, Josh. Nothing at all. You ask Jethro."

While Josh's mind was attempting to come to grips with this unhelpful piece of information, Jethro Shovell called, "That's about the truth of it, Mr Retallick. Me and Marcus was at a meeting in Liskeard with William Thorndike, the Durham unionist. A police sergeant arrived, asked our names — and arrested Marcus when he gave his."

Josh was beginning to understand, but now Miriam was beside him at the window and she called to her sister, "Come on into the kitchen. If you stir the fire up you'll be able to put the kettle on. Josh and I'll be down as soon as we're dressed."

Back inside the room the small, sleepy figure of Anne appeared at the door, "Something woke me up. Is it time to get up now?"

"No, it's still sleeping time," Josh swung the little girl into the bed he and Miriam had vacated. By the time he covered her up she was asleep once more.

As they hurriedly dressed, Miriam muttered darkly, "Family! If we'd had any sense we'd have settled somewhere else when we came back. Somewhere where we knew no one — and no one knew us."

Fastening his trousers, Josh nodded in the direction of the girl sleeping in their bed. "There's a little girl who'd give a great deal to have family of her own."

"I know," Miriam's expression softened. "I'm happy to have family too . . . but I'd rather they kept their problems for a reasonable hour — especially when Marcus Hooper is involved."

By the time Josh went downstairs to the kitchen he was thinking more clearly. While Miriam coped with her distraught sister he learned from Jethro the full story of Marcus Hooper's arrest.

"Are you certain this sergeant gave no reason for arresting Marcus?"

"He wouldn't even admit Marcus was being arrested. He said he was being taken to the police station to answer a few questions."

"Could anything said at this meeting with William Thorndike possibly be considered seditious?"

"We were discussing the setting up of a benevolent association. Marcus was appointed agent for the district."

"All right. I'll go to Liskeard and find out what's happening."

As he showed Jethro to the door, Josh asked, "Are your ribs healing well?"

Jethro's hand went to his chest automatically, but he nodded, "Most days are fine. Other times I can't move a muscle without pain and I never seem to have as much breath as I need." Jethro seemed embarrassed at having answered Josh's question so fully. "I expect to be ready to start work again before too long."

Josh knew Jethro's injuries had been more serious than perhaps the young miner realised. Two of his ribs had been broken in the accident and at least two more cracked. The doctor also feared a fragment of one rib had pierced a lung. Privately he expressed doubts to Josh about Jethro's ability to wield a pick again.

"Come and see me before you think of starting work. I've only a part-time purser working on the mine at the moment. I need a clerk to help him — and to help me. Someone who knows mining and could work in the office full-time. It isn't easy to find someone capable of doing such work, but your pa tells me you've had a good schooling — and I wouldn't expect you to start for a week or two."

Jethro nodded self-consciously. "Pa had me working with his mine purser for a year before I decided to work underground."

"Well, there you are!" Josh hoped his surprise sounded genuine. "You're ideal for what I have in mind. Give it a try and in a couple of years

I'll expect you to take over as mine purser."

It was a wonderful opportunity, as Jethro knew well. A purser's authority on a mine was second only to that of the mine captain. He was a man with considerable status, especially if he was fortunate enough to be purser of a *successful* mine. Yet Jethro hesitated.

" . . . I'll be happy for you to retain an interest in any aspect affecting the miners' well-being — just so long as it doesn't clash with your loyalty to the Sharptor mine."

"All right." It meant Jethro would be able to continue the work of the benevolent association for William Thorndike.

Josh nodded his satisfaction and Jethro left the house on Sharptor elated at his good fortune.

Josh rode into Liskeard two hours later. It was still early, but this was market day. Cattle, sheep and pigs were being driven to market, creating havoc with stallholders who were attempting to put up tables on which to display produce and wares. Thrifty housewives were here in plenty too, vying with servants from the great houses for the best bargains and freshest produce.

Given directions by a stallholder, Josh was soon heading towards an impressive building that had once housed a school. Now it was a police station, complete with a line of cells that on market days in more prosperous times would be filled with miners.

Inspector Kingsley Coote was in the police office. He greeted Josh courteously enough, but frowned deeply when he learned the reason for

141

the Sharptor mine owner's journey to Liskeard.

"You, of all people, should be aware that the unionism of these northern coal-miners is a spawning ground for trouble and those who thrive on dissension, Mr Retallick. Unless it's contained it spills over and taints all it touches. A few years ago William Thorndike would have been transported after his first conviction, and the country would have been better for it. Cornish miners are facing a difficult enough time today. They don't need William Thorndike adding to their troubles."

"When I was convicted and transported it came not as a result of evidence, but because of just such prejudice by those in authority. I'll not see another man suffer the same injustice."

"You're still a very new mine owner, Mr Retallick. Perhaps you'll think differently about things after a while. When you pay fair wages to a man you've a right to expect loyalty in return. There's no loyalty in a man who's pledged to two masters."

"I understand Marcus Hooper and the men with him were not discussing unionism, but a benevolent association. I see no harm in that."

"You can call a goat a kitten, Mr Retallick, but you won't change its smell. The men were discussing unionism — not that there's any law against that. Men can *discuss* whatever they wish."

"Then why have you arrested Marcus Hooper? I thought . . . ?"

"You thought he was arrested because of what was going on in the private room of the Boot

Inn yesterday evening? Oh no, had my sergeant wanted to *arrest* anyone, then William Thorndike would have been first on his list. I understand the sergeant went to great pains to assure everyone at the meeting that Mr Hooper was not being arrested. He was brought here in order that we might have a little chat about a few matters."

Josh was more puzzled than ever, until Inspector Kingsley Coote explained, "Marcus Hooper was brought here to answer a few questions about his movements on the night of the arson attack on your mine. An attack that might well have become murder, had you not appeared on the scene when you did."

While the inspector was giving his explanation, Josh remembered the figure he had seen leaving the mine, and his own suspicions.

"You don't seem surprised, Mr Retallick." Inspector Coote was a very shrewd man.

"What makes you think Marcus was involved?"

Hurriedly thinking back to the night of the fire, Josh believed he was the first on the scene. He was convinced no one else had seen the figure in the firelight.

"Not *what*, but *who*. It seems the two young Trago children were not the only ones intending to sleep on the mine that night. A vagrant was recently arrested for begging in the town. He told me he'd been warned off the mine by Hooper. Instead of going away, as he was told, he hid nearby in the fern and saw Hooper carry a burning rag to at least three buildings. The vagrant ran away when he saw you, afraid you might blame him for the fire."

"Why has he said nothing before?"

"Come now, Mr Retallick. The man is a vagrant. A homeless, jobless wanderer. A man at odds with the laws of the land and all who administer them. What reason would he have for running to us with his tale? I wouldn't have heard it at all had he not hoped to persuade me to speak for him in the courtroom."

"Did you?"

"Did I what?"

"Speak for him in the courtroom?"

"Nothing I had to say could have saved him from prison. The man has been convicted so many times he's deemed to be an 'incorrigible rogue'. But yes, I spoke for him. I told the court he was an old soldier who had served with distinction in the Crimean War, and that he had been helpful to the police. It made not the slightest difference. The judge was feeling dyspeptic after a less than agreeable lunch. He was sentenced to a year's hard labour, with a whipping before he's released."

Inspector Kingsley Coote had no discernible expression on his face when he spoke to Josh again. "The strange thing is . . . my informant saw you arrive at the mine before the arsonist had left. He felt quite certain you must have seen him too."

"I *thought* I saw someone but I wasn't certain and I couldn't possibly have identified him."

"You never mentioned this when we spoke before."

"I told you, I doubt if it *was* a man. It was probably no more than a shadow."

"The same 'shadow' seen by the vagrant,

no doubt?" There was sarcasm in the police inspector's voice.

"What do you intend doing with Marcus Hooper?"

"If Mr Strike is prepared to press charges I'll see that Hooper is brought to justice."

"Leander Strike is in Europe, 'for his health'. I understand he'll be away for at least a year. Anyway, he's nothing to do with the Sharptor mine now — and I'll not press charges."

Josh hoped Marcus Hooper had made no admission to the astute police inspector. Without it Coote would be forced to release the miner.

"You're making a grave mistake, Mr Retallick. A man prepared to commit arson for an imagined grievance should be in prison, where he belongs."

"You'll need to prove the case against him first, Inspector. As far as I'm concerned Marcus Hooper is one of my employees who has been injured in a mine accident — at my mine. He's also related to me by marriage. If I have to I'll go to a solicitor to arrange his release, but I hope that won't prove necessary. As you've said, Marcus Hooper hasn't been arrested. He came here of his own free will to answer a few questions."

Josh was calling the police inspector's bluff — and both men knew it.

Kingsley Coote looked thoughtfully at Josh for a while, then he shrugged. "It isn't worthwhile parting bad friends because of Marcus Hooper, Mr Retallick — but don't put too much trust in the man. He'll let you down because that's the sort of man he is. As for me . . . all I need is a little patience. He'll come again."

"Does that mean he can leave with me?"

"I'll have him brought from the cell now — it will save us the cost of his breakfast. Remember my advice, Mr Retallick. I assure you it's well intentioned. Don't get to thinking he's doing no more than you did all those years ago. I've read the records of your trial with great interest. You suffered an injustice, there's no doubt of that. Marcus Hooper is treading a very different path — and staying barely half a pace ahead of the law. One day he'll put a foot wrong and we'll overtake him. You — and he — can be quite certain of that."

13

THAT evening Marcus Hooper was in the Cheesewring Inn, declaring he had been arrested by the Liskeard police inspector because he was a trade union man. He had the full sympathy of his listeners. Cornish miners were a hardy, independent breed, resentful of any authority outside the mine. Marcus told them William Thorndike had left the Boot Inn at Liskeard immediately after his arrest, to return north. He declared he had been set free only because the authorities feared a strike of miners in which the Durham miners would join their Cornish colleagues. He made no mention of the part played by Josh Retallick in securing his release.

Jethro was the only man in the taproom who knew of Patience Hooper's dawn plea to Josh but he said nothing, keeping his thoughts to himself.

Jethro did not feel at home inside an inn. Although the other customers were miners, like himself, he was more used to their company below ground, working.

Jethro neither liked alcohol, nor the effect it had on other men. It was well known that many of the more serious underground accidents on the mine were caused by men whose thinking was befuddled by drink. It was also noticeable that more wives had bruised eyes and grazed cheeks the day after settling day, when their husbands had spent much of their wages in the inns and beerhouses.

However, despite Jethro's reservations about the truth of Marcus Hooper's story of his arrest and release, it was clear the local miners had none. As an expression of their indignation they clamoured to join the benevolent association of which he was the representative. They paid over their sixpences eagerly, pledging to continue to pay for as long as they were working.

As Marcus Hooper collected the money, Jethro carefully entered the names of the new association members in a book. He marvelled that men who would beat their wives senseless for wasting a few pence of their housekeeping should part with their money without bothering to ascertain what it would bring in return. He did his best to pass on what little information he had gleaned from William Thorndike, but most men did not bother to listen. Their money was more than a benefit payment. It was a gesture of defiance against the mine owners, the police — anyone with authority over them.

As more and more miners came to the inn to part with their money, Jethro ceased imparting his scant knowledge of the association. It seemed no one cared — and anyway, he was convinced the money would bring more good to the miners than if they spent it on ale.

As the evening wore on and the hot taproom filled with smoke and noise, Jethro closed his book and took a tankard of ginger beer outside. It was cooler out here and a man could listen to his thoughts.

He was seated on the wall outside the inn when Lottie came along the village street. She was on her way home, having just returned the goats to Elias Barnicoat. Her face lit up with pleasure when she saw Jethro, but not before he noticed how pale and tired she looked.

"Is everything all right, Lottie? You're walking along as though you have the cares of the world weighing on your shoulders."

"It's Jacob. He's not been well for a long time. He . . . he seems to be getting worse, instead of better." For a few moments Lottie seemed to be on the verge of tears, but she succeeded in fighting them back. "I'm worried about him. Marcus has put him to work in the Marke Valley mine, pushing skips of copper from the workings to the whim shaft. The work's too hard for him."

"There's certainly not much of Jacob for him to be doing such work," admitted Jethro.

The task of conveying ore from the working faces to the whim shaft, from where it was lifted to grass was traditionally work for boys — but it was not for the weak or unwell. "I'll have a word with Marcus about him."

Lottie's tired eyes expressed her gratitude, but she said, "You won't tell Marcus I've said anything to you?"

"No. I'll say I saw Jacob and thought he seemed unwell . . . " Embarrassed by the way Lottie was looking at him, Jethro said gruffly, "Here, have some ginger beer. There's far more than I can drink."

Lottie took the tankard and lifted it to her mouth but lowered it again without tasting it.

149

"Would you mind if I took some for Jacob? He's only ever had ginger beer once before. That was when Josh Retallick started up the Sharptor mine again. Jacob said it was the best thing he's ever tasted."

"Take it all — but bring the tankard back. I don't want Waldo Davey charging me for it."

"I'll see it's brought back," promised Lottie. "This might make Jacob feel better."

"Go on, off you go. I've work to do inside." Marcus had recruited more members for the miner's association and was shouting for Jethro to return to the taproom with the membership book. " . . . and mind you don't forget to return that tankard."

The gift of ginger beer seemed to lift Jacob's spirits. Lottie lay in the darkness of the bedroom as he slept and she imagined his breathing was a little less laboured than it had been recently.

Lottie was just dropping off into sleep when she heard Marcus returning to the house. She had no idea what time it was, but it must have been very late. She had heard the late-night revellers passing on their way from the Cheesewring Inn and Patience had been in bed for an hour or more.

From the noisy manner in which Marcus closed the front door Lottie realised he had been drinking heavily. His stumbling footsteps on the stairs confirmed her belief. She held her breath, willing him to fall inside the other bedroom and take his troubles to his long-suffering wife.

But luck was not on Lottie's side tonight. Marcus stopped outside the closed bedroom door and she could hear him mumbling and cursing to himself. Then there was the sound of matches being scraped into life, and a sudden strong smell of sulphur. The light of a candle showed through gaps in the ill-fitting bedroom door and moments later it crashed open.

Marcus stood swaying just inside the bedroom doorway for some moments, peering about stupidly, the arm he had broken in the mine accident held awkwardly. Lottie held her breath, hoping he would go away. Something in the way he looked at her when he had been drinking made her skin crawl. Now he was in her bedroom — and very drunk.

Marcus stooped to place the candle on the floor and succeeded at the third attempt. Advancing across the bedroom he stopped before he reached her. Standing swaying above Jacob, he suddenly reached down and shook the small boy roughly.

"You there . . . boy! Wake up, d'you hear me? Wake up."

Startled by his sudden, rude awakening, Jacob struggled to sit up on the straw mattress.

"That's better! What's supposed to be the matter with you, eh? What's wrong with you?"

Marcus tripped on the edge of the thin mattress and dropped heavily to one knee beside the still confused boy.

"Damn you, don't pretend you can't hear me. What's supposed to be wrong with you, eh?"

"He's sick! The work at the mine is too hard for him." Shrill-voiced, Lottie sprang to the aid of her brother.

"Too hard? When I was his age I was wielding

a heavy hammer and a borer, winning ore. He's not even doing a *boys* work properly. Are you?"

As he spoke, Marcus held Jacob in his grip, shaking him and suddenly the boy began coughing uncontrollably. Marcus never relaxed his grip and continued to shake Jacob, calling for an answer from him.

"Leave him alone! You'll choke him!" There was justification for Lottie's concern. Even in the flickering yellow light given out by the candle it was possible to see that Jacob's cheeks were a brilliant scarlet and he was having difficulty breathing.

"I'll let him go . . . when he's given me an answer." The words came out jerkily as Marcus continued to shake his small nephew.

A heavy, cracked chamberpot stood in a corner of the room. It had been used by Jacob and the two eldest Hooper children at bedtime. Taking it by the handle, Lottie swung it at the drunken miner. She had intended hitting him on the knee, but at the last moment his injured arm got in the way. The chamberpot struck him close to the recent break. Shrieking with sudden pain, Marcus released his hold on Jacob. At the same time he stepped back on the candle, extinguishing it immediately.

Marcus Hooper stumbled about the bedroom, trampling on his own children who added their frightened voices to their father's bellows. From the other room Patience's voice could be heard above the cries of the youngest Hooper child, demanding to know what was happening.

Lottie seized her brother's arm and propelled

him, still coughing, from the room and down the stairs. Opening the door they fled into the night, leaving the Hooper family to sort out the chaos in their home as best they could.

The two children spent the remainder of the night in a shed with Elias Barnicoat's goats. For much of the time Lottie nursed Jacob, cradling him in her arms. At times he coughed so hard she thought his lungs must burst. She feared Elias Barnicoat must hear him and come to investigate the noise in his goat shed. All the while Jacob's skin burned with a temperature so high she wondered it did not set fire to the straw they shared with the goats. She worried too. Never a large boy, Jacob felt distressingly delicate as she held him to her.

The next morning Jacob was still running a temperature, but his cough had eased and he insisted on going to work in the mine. Jacob was frightened of what Marcus would do to him if he failed to go to work. It would be bad enough facing up to him after what had happened during the night, even though none of it had been Jacob's doing. Nothing Lottie said could change her small brother's mind and it was with a sense of foreboding that she left for the moor with Elias Barnicoat's goats.

Lottie worried all day about Jacob. By the time she reached Josh and Miriam's Sharptor home on her way back to Henwood village, she was desperate to share her concern with someone. As luck had it, Miriam was at the gate of the house, waiting for Lottie. She had seen Patience that day. Marcus's down-trodden wife was sporting a discoloured eye and a badly split lip. Miriam knew Marcus must be the cause of the injuries, but Patience refused to tell her why. Miriam hoped Lottie might prove less reticent.

Hesitantly at first, because she was unused to discussing life in the Hooper household with anyone else, Lottie began to describe to Miriam what had occurred during the night. Suddenly, Lottie's reserve burst like a dam gate and her concern for Jacob and the story of his illness poured from her.

Miriam was appalled at Marcus Hooper's callous indifference towards the young boy. She was almost as angry with Patience. Her sister should have done far more for Jacob, even though her injuries proved how difficult life with Marcus was for her.

"Where is Jacob now?"

"He went to work this morning. He'll be at the Marke Valley mine for another hour yet."

"Return the goats to Elias Barnicoat as quickly as you can. Then get on down to the mine. Meet Jacob when he comes to grass and take him to the Marke Valley mine captain's office. I'll send someone for the Marke Valley doctor and get him to examine Jacob. If he says the boy isn't fit to work underground *I'll* speak to Marcus Hooper." Cutting short Lottie's thanks. Miriam said, "Hurry off now. I want to catch the doctor before he goes off somewhere."

Miriam was unsuccessful in her bid to summon the Marke Valley mine doctor. He had taken a wealthy patient to see a specialist in London. His work was being carried out by Dr Washington O'Rourke, doctor of the Phoenix mines.

Dr Washington O'Rourke did not enjoy his work as a mine doctor. He never had — and in recent months he had grown to hate his lot in life. The day was fast approaching when he would put Cornwall behind him and seek work elsewhere, even though this thought gave him little pleasure.

The truth was that O'Rourke was not a good doctor. He knew his shortcomings were likely to be even more apparent in general practice. It was for this reason he had decided to work for the Cornish mines, where most of his patients would be expected to die anyway. It was also the reason his drinking was beginning earlier every day.

Lottie met Jacob as he climbed clear of the shaft and his appearance pained her. He was on the point of exhaustion, and very close to tears. The Marke Valley mine had no mine-engine. Lacking the energy to climb fast, Jacob had waited until he thought all the men had gone off shift.

Unfortunately, one of the older miners had done the same, and for the same reason. Ascending the ladder behind Jacob, he had berated the sick young boy all the way up the shaft, blaming him for his own shortcomings.

The old miner was still grumbling at Jacob when he emerged from the shaft and Lottie rounded on him angrily. "There's no call for you to talk to him like that. If you were in such a hurry you should have got them to hoist you in the skip — or seen to it they put in a man-engine."

"Man-engine? There was no such thing when I was a boy. A ladder was good enough then, and so 'tis today — unless there's some young whelp to slow me down."

"When you were young they dug shafts no deeper than you could spit out of. You ought to be thanking Jacob, not swearing at him. If he hadn't been here you might have had to come to grass at the same speed as some healthy young miner and dropped down dead before you got halfway."

"Why, you cheeky young hussy . . . "

Without waiting to hear any more, Lottie hurried Jacob away as fast as his tired legs would allow. Fortunately, the aged miner was equally exhausted and the two children reached the mine captain's office while the miner was still complaining breathlessly about the 'impudence of modern-day children'.

The doctor had not yet arrived, but the mine captain allowed Lottie and Jacob to wait while he finished some paperwork. They were still waiting an hour later when the mine captain completed his work. Standing up from behind his desk, he was about to order the children from the office when he glanced through the window and saw Washington O'Rourke walking somewhat unsteadily towards the office.

There was drink in the office and the mine captain had no wish to become involved in a prolonged drinking session with O'Rourke. Snatching up his coat, he told Lottie, "The mine doctor's coming now. When he's finished tell the engine-man. He'll make sure the office is locked."

Having delivered this instruction, the mine captain went out through the doorway as though the devil was after him.

Dr Washington O'Rourke wore a peeved expression when he entered the office and looked accusingly at Lottie, "Wasn't that Cap'n Tobin I just saw leaving the mine?"

"He said we could use his office. The engine-man will lock up when we've gone."

"Damn! I especially wanted to see him." Crossing the floor, the doctor tugged at the door of a large cupboard in a corner of the room. It was locked, but O'Rourke tried it again before giving up. Turning back to the two children he displayed undisguised irritation. "I've had a message from Mrs Retallick to come here and examine someone. A child. What's wrong with you?"

He addressed the question to Lottie, but reaching out she took Jacob's arm and thrust him towards the doctor, "It's not me who's ill. It's him."

"Is it now?" Looking at Lottie, Washington O'Rourke thought she was probably older than he had first thought. Attractive, too, if she tidied herself up a bit . . .

Reaching out the doctor gripped Jacob's thin shoulder and pulled him closer without shifting his glance from Lottie.

"Well, what's wrong with you, eh? Don't like working underground, I suppose. Can't say I blame you. It's a place for moles and works and dead bodies. The Lord put the sun in the sky to give us life and warmth. Once you go below ground you're in the devil's own territory."

157

Jacob began to cough. It was a racking, choking sound that caused his whole body to contort uncomfortably.

Gripping Jacob's shoulder more tightly, Dr O'Rourke said, "There, d'you hear? That's what comes of working below ground. It's dust, that's what it is. You breathe it in while you're underground and coughing's the body's way of ejecting it. Cough away, my lad. It'll do you a power of good."

Releasing Jacob, the doctor said to Lottie, "How about you, young lady? How are you feeling? I find that dust about a mine affects young ladies far more than the men. You should have an examination. It won't be long before you'll be wanting to bring babies into this cruel world. You'll need to be strong and healthy for that . . . "

"You're not examining *me*!" Lottie had heard stories from the bal-maidens about Dr Washington O'Rourke's 'examinations'. One girl had referred to him as 'the greatest explorer since Captain Cook'. Moving away from him, she pointed to Jacob, "It's not me who's ill. It's him."

"Ill? The boy's as fit as anyone has the right to be in a mining area. He has a summer cold, aggravated by the dust, that's all. Be as bright as a new sovereign in a few days. Run along now, boy, while I have a little chat with your sister."

"You're not chatting with me. No, nor doing anything else, neither."

Lottie circled warily about the office, keeping as much space between herself and Dr O'Rourke as was possible.

158

"Come now, girl. You're being foolish. I'm a *doctor*. I'm merely thinking of you."

"Yes . . . and I know *what* you're thinking." As she talked, Lottie drew the over-friendly doctor farther away from the door. Suddenly seeing her opportunity, she ran for the door, taking Jacob with her.

Dr O'Rourke did his drunken best to stop her, but his outstretched hand grabbed air at least a foot behind Lottie. His bellow of angry frustration was cut off as Lottie slammed the door of the mine captain's office in his face.

The two children did not stop running until they were well clear of the mine and Jacob's coughing brought them to a halt.

"Well, that was a waste of time!" Lottie spoke indignantly. "You'd have done better to have seen him by yourself. He might at least have examined you then."

"You did your best, Lottie. It wasn't your fault. I expect he's right. It's just a summer cough. But it's nice having you care. I'll be all right tomorrow, you'll see."

14

TWO days after Dr O'Rourke's 'examination', Jacob collapsed when working at the two hundred fathom level in the Marke Valley mine.

The ventilation pump had broken down and temperatures in the lower levels soared to well above 100 degrees. Increasing humidity made the heat almost unbearable. Grown men worked stripped naked, perspiration giving them the appearance of having stepped straight from the Saturday night bath tub.

Work was being carried out in a dim, eerie light in the deeper levels, all but the most essential candles extinguished. It was believed a single candle burned as much air as a fully grown man could breathe.

Because of the reduced light only the prompt action of another boy saved Jacob from being run over by a heavily laden, rumbling skip, being taken along a narrow tunnel.

Jacob was pushing the middle skip of three, all on their way to the whim shaft. The boy behind him was panting like a spent dog and cursing Jacob for not pushing his skip faster whenever he could find a moment's breath to spare. It would be no cooler when the whim shaft was reached, but the air rising from the deepest levels caused a faint turbulence that produced the semblance of a breeze.

Suddenly, as he paused to wipe perspiration from his brow, the boy saw Jacob fall across the metal tram rail and lie still. There was no way to halt the slowly rolling skip in time but by squeezing through the narrow gap between tunnel wall and skip, the boy was able to reach Jacob in time to grab him and drag his limp body between the rails ahead of the skip until the heavy vehicle ground to a protesting halt behind them.

Jacob was taken up the whim shaft in an ore skip but by the time grass was reached he had regained consciousness. The mine captain was aware of the appalling conditions below ground, with no ventilation, and wanted to send the small boy home to recuperate.

Jacob was terrified of what Marcus Hooper might do to him if he handed over less than was expected on pay day and the mine captain eventually agreed to find work for Jacob above ground. He would be 'cobbing' ore — breaking off waste from the lumps of ore dug out of the mine. It was women's work and Jacob received cruel chaffing from some of the girls, but he felt too ill to care. Even though he was above ground now and away from the heat of the levels, he found breathing difficult. Twice during coughing bouts the world swung away from him and for a moment everything went black. It frightened him.

Finally, during the late afternoon Jacob felt so ill he could hardly lift his hammer. Then he realised he was going to be sick. He did not want to be ill in front of the others and hurried off as fast as his decidedly weak legs would allow. He had no need to say anything to the others, they would think he had gone to the privy.

Instead, Jacob made for a patch of rough ground beyond the mine workings. The undergrowth was so dense here there was little chance anyone would see him being sick and report him to the above-ground captain. Jacob feared being sent home, with the possibility of dismissal, far more than being ill. If he lost his job he would receive a leathering from Marcus, especially as the mine doctor had already said there was nothing seriously wrong with him.

Jacob had hardly reached the shelter of the bushes when he felt the world begin to swing about him once more. This time it was far worse than before. Inexplicably he found himself on his hands and knees and instinct drove him deeper into the undergrowth. Suddenly, and uncontrollably, he vomited. He had an impression of blood. Blood on the ground . . . and on his hands. His chest felt as though a giant hand held him . . . squeezing. Jacob fought desperately for breath . . . then he pitched forward on his face and remembered nothing more.

When Lottie returned to the Hooper cottage and discovered Jacob was not there she was concerned but not alarmed. He had probably stopped to talk to someone on the way home. Nevertheless, he had not been at all well and he might have found it necessary to rest somewhere between the Marke Valley mine and Henwood village. She decided she would go and look for him.

Ignoring Patience's plea for her to remain in the cottage and help feed and put the young

162

children to bed while she prepared a meal for Marcus, Lottie hurried from the house. Leaving the village behind, she headed along the track that led in the direction of the Marke Valley mine.

Lottie did not meet Jacob along the track, and when she reached the Marke Valley mine she was disturbed to find it almost deserted. They did not work around the clock here. However, the pumps were still operating, and after a search she found an engineer and two assistants toiling over the ventilation engine.

In answer to Lottie's question, the engineer shook his head, declaring he knew no one by the name of Jacob Trago working on the mine.

"Where was he working?" The question came from the youngest of the engineer's assistants. No more than four years Lottie's senior, it was apparent he found talking to her of more interest than helping to repair an engine.

"I don't know. Somewhere underground, pushing skips to the whim shaft."

The older man gave her a quick glance filled with sympathy. Pushing loaded ore skips was the worst job in any mine. He had begun his own mining career in the same way.

"He'll be a young'un then?"

Lottie nodded. "He'll be ten next month."

"You'd best hope he wasn't working in the lower levels," the younger man came back into the conversation. "They've had no ventilation all day. It's been hot enough to roast a pig down there. They brought one boy up in the whim skip earlier in the day. He'd collapsed at the two hundred fathom level."

Fear suddenly gripped Lottie, "This boy . . . the one they brought up . . . where did they take him?"

"Didn't take him anywhere, far as I know. By the time he got to grass he was feeling better. They set him to work with the bal-maidens for the rest of the day."

Lottie's brief panic subsided, but she was no closer to finding Jacob. "You don't know where the boy went after work finished?"

"When you've finished gossiping perhaps you'll consider helping me with this engine. That's what you're being paid for. If it's not working tomorrow there'll be no pay for any of us." The engineer broke into the conversation irritably.

The older man returned to work on the engine immediately. His companion grinned at Lottie apologetically, but before he too resumed work, he said, "Go and speak to Emma Hobbs. You'll find her at Upton Cross, in the cottage next to the pump. She's one of the bal-maidens on the mine here. She'll know who it was working with them. Tell her Wesley sent you . . . I'm her brother."

A further growl from the engineer forced the young man to resume work and Lottie set off for Upton Cross, a small hamlet on the brow of the hill, no more than a mile away.

Emma Hobbs was a cheeky, dark-haired girl of about fifteen. She quickly confirmed it *was* Jacob who had been working with them that day, but added, "Halfway through the afternoon he just walked off and never came back. Some of the women thought he didn't enjoy working with us and had gone home without telling anyone.

164

Anyway, we didn't tell the captain so he should still get his pay."

"Jacob wouldn't do that. He's too afraid of his uncle. Marcus would half kill him if he didn't bring home full wages on pay day."

"I was surprised when he didn't come back," admitted Emma Hobbs. "He didn't seem the sort of little boy who'd just go home without saying anything to anyone. He was working hard, even though he didn't look well."

"He's a very sick boy." Lottie's anxiety had increased as a result of what Emma Hobbs had told her. "He shouldn't have been at work at all, but Doctor O'Rourke said there was nothing wrong with him."

"O'Rourke?" Emma Hobbs snorted derisively. "Pa says he wouldn't let him treat our old sow — and there's not a man on the mine would let O'Rourke treat his wife, even if she were dying. The man's as randy as an old tom-cat."

Lottie hardly listened to the other girl's prattle, so concerned was she for Jacob. "Where can he be? What can have I happened to him?" Lottie did not know what to do next.

Observing the other girl's agitated concern, Emma Hobbs said, "I'll go and speak to my dad. He's in the garden, out back. There's cake on the table. Help yourself to a piece."

In normal circumstances Lottie would have taken full advantage of an offer of free food, but at this moment food would have choked her. She could not even stand still and paced the tiny room until Emma returned with her father.

"Emma tells me your brother went missing

from the mine this afternoon. She also says he hasn't been well. What's wrong with him?"

After asking a few more question, James Hobbs had an accurate, if sketchy idea of Lottie's and Jacob's situation. He watched her face intently as she gave her replies.

"All right, young lady, you come along with me. We'll get a few men together and have a look about the mine. If he's there we'll find him. Emma, go and speak to the other bal-maidens who live in the village. Ask if anyone saw which way he went when he wandered off."

The first call for James Hobbs was to the house of a Methodist lay preacher. A Bible lesson was underway but the men immediately gave up their evening to accompany James Hobbs and Lottie. More men and boys from nearby houses joined them when they learned what was happening.

As they were making their way towards the mine, Lottie saw Jethro Shovell coming along a track that merged with the one on which she and the Marke Valley miners were walking. On his way home from the Kit Hill mines, he had been recruiting miners to the miner's association. Leaving the men from Upton Cross, Lottie ran to Jethro and blurted out the story of Jacob's disappearance. When he agreed to join the search Lottie felt a great sense of relief. She was confident they would find Jacob now.

Before they reached the mine Emma Hobbs caught up with them. One of the bal-maidens had seen someone making for the rough ground beyond the mine, although she was not absolutely certain it was Jacob.

It took a mere five minutes of searching to locate the small boy. When the shout went up from one of the Upton Cross men, Jethro was nearby and he reached the scene before Lottie.

At first, Jethro thought Jacob was dead. The small boy lay face down on the ground, the granite rocks about him heavily spattered with blood. Jethro tried to prevent Lottie from seeing her brother, but she was too quick. Ducking beneath Jethro's outstretched arm, she reached Jacob as the man kneeling at his side straightened up.

"He's still alive. The Lord be praised! The child's still breathing."

"Emma!" James Hobbs called to his daughter. "Go and fetch the doctor. Tell him to hurry . . . "

"No!" The fierce cry came from Lottie. "I'll not let Dr O'Rourke see Jacob again. He said there was nothing wrong. Jacob could die for all he cares."

Lottie choked on her words and the Upton Cross men looked at each other in an embarrassed silence. Every man there was aware of Dr Washington O'Rourke's reputation, but no could think of an alternative.

"I'll take him to his home. To Henwood." Jethro's words solved their dilemma. Stooping down, he gently and easily lifted Jacob from the ground.

"A couple of us will come along and help carry the boy."

"Jacob doesn't weigh more than a good-sized pick-axe, Mr Hobbs, and my ribs are nigh mended now. I'll manage him well enough. I thank you and the others for coming out to look for him.

It was the act of Christian men."

"I still think he should be seen by the doctor. O'Rourke may not be the best doctor I've known, but he's better than nothing."

"If he needs a doctor we'll find one for him." Nodding his acknowledgement to the men, Jethro set off along the track, Jacob Trago in his arms and an anxious Lottie at his side.

Patience Hooper's reaction to the arrival of Jethro and Lottie with the unconscious Jacob was one of dismay — but her feelings were not entirely due to the seriousness of the small boys condition.

"I can't look after him. The baby's gone down with measles only today, and my other two will have it before the week's out. I've more than I can manage with them. I can't look after him too. Your ma's back in the village now. Go and see her."

Lottie was angry with her aunt, but Jethro's immediate concern was for Jacob. In spite of the assurance he had given to James Hobbs, the boy was beginning to weigh heavy in his arms. Even more alarming, the jolting had produced a trickle of blood from the corner of Jacob's mouth.

"We'll take him to my house. Ma will take care of him." Jethro turned and was back in the dusty village road before either Patience or Lottie could say anything more.

Whether or not Jenny Shovell would have taken care of Jacob was not to be put to the test. Halfway to the Shovell house they were overtaken by Josh, driving a two-wheeled

168

pony cart. He was on his way back to Sharptor after bidding for a small engine in a mine sale.

It took Josh no more than a few moments to learn the situation. "Get into the cart, all of you. We've room to look after Jacob at Sharptor. Hurry now. If Jacob's been lying unconscious for some hours he'll need attention — and quickly."

Josh's positive intervention relieved Lottie of much of her anxiety. She knew Jenny Shovell did not approve of her and been concerned that Jenny might refuse to have Jacob in her house. Now Lottie knew everything possible would be done for Jacob.

When they arrived at the Retallick home on Sharptor, Miriam was as concerned as Josh as the small boys condition. "He needs to see a doctor," she declared immediately, " . . . and I don't mean that charlatan, O'Rourke. Josh, send one of the stable lads on a horse to St Neot. There's a good doctor there. Make certain he knows it's urgent. Lottie, run down to the village and tell your ma what's happened."

"*She* won't want to know. She don't want to know nothing about us."

"It doesn't matter what she *wants* to know. She ought to be here."

"Your aunt Miriam's right. Your ma ought to know what's happened," Jethro observed the stubborn expression on Lottie's face and tried to avert an argument.

"Will you still be here when I come back?"

Before he could reply, Miriam said, "Jethro's earned himself a supper. He'll still be here. Hurry now and I'll have something ready for you too when you get back."

Lottie doubted whether she would be able to swallow so much as a crumb, but she ran all the way to Henwood village, just the same.

The Cheesewring Inn was packed with miners — but these were not the same type of men as those at the Upton Cross Bible meeting. Her progress through the crowded taproom excited more than one bawdy comment and she received a few pats on the head and one or two on more intimate parts of her body.

She found her mother working behind the stained wood bar, perspiring freely as she filled tankards with beer from the huge barrel and sent them sliding across the bar to a flustered serving-girl.

It was some minutes before Lottie was able to gain her mother's attention — and Jane Trago's response was hardly maternal.

"What are you doing? I said you weren't to come here during workings hours."

"It's our Jacob, Ma. He's been taken sick. He needs you with him."

"Nonsense! Jacob's as right as rain. Dr O'Rourke was in here only today. Nothing wrong with him, he said. No more than a summer cold, same as most folk have, this time of year. Besides, Waldo Daveys away visiting his sick mother and it's pay day at the Wheal Slade. I couldn't leave the inn tonight, not even if Jacob was *really* ill."

"He *is* really ill. We've taken him to the Retallick house, on Sharptor."

"Well then, if he's there there's nothing to worry

about. They'll take better care of him than ever I could — "

Turning to the harassed serving girl, Jane Trago said, "Yes, love? What was that order again . . . ?"

As Jane began serving once more and as Lottie waited uncertainly, a heavy hand fell upon her shoulder. "You heard what your mother said. There's nothing wrong with Jacob and this isn't the place for you. Get on home — and tell your Aunt Patience not to wait up for me. I'll be late tonight."

As Marcus Hooper propelled Lottie towards the door she wriggled free and angrily turned to face him. "Why should I bother to tell Aunt Patience something she knows already? She's got enough on her hands without having a drunken husband knocking her about. Stay out as late as you want. It's the best thing you could do for her — and you can stay away from *me* too while you're about it."

"Why, you . . . " Marcus Hooper lunged towards Lottie but she was far too agile for him. She was out of the inn while he was still trying to locate her in the crowd.

When Lottie reached the house on Sharptor she told Miriam she had passed on news of Jacob's illness. She lied that her mother would try to come to see Jacob as soon as it was possible.

"Good, he's been asking for her." Miriam looked at Lottie's pinched and worried face and said, "You look almost as ill as your brother. He's asleep now, for a while. Come in the kitchen with Josh and Jethro. I'll get you something to eat."

"No, thanks, Aunt Miriam. I'll go and sit with Jacob, in case he wakes up and wonders where he is."

The doctor from St Neot did not arrive at the house until well after midnight, explaining he had been called to a difficult confinement. He was as efficient as Dr O'Rourke was inefficient. He examined Jacob thoroughly, spending many minutes listening to his heart and lungs with the aid of a stethoscope.

When the examination was over, the doctor's expression was so serious that Lottie was frightened. "What is it, Doctor? What's wrong with Jacob?"

Aware of Lottie's extreme concern for her brother, the doctor said, "You're doing splendidly, girl. Splendidly. Just you stay here with him and be sure he keeps warm. If he asks for anything — anything at all — you can get it for him." Lottie's wide-eyed alarm was plain to see and the doctor added, "The boys desperately undernourished. He needs feeding up." Reaching out a hand he patted Lottie gently on the head.

Had the gesture been made by Dr O'Rourke, Lottie would have recoiled instinctively. Coming from this doctor, the gesture was as reassuring as it was intended to be. "You're doing a fine job, young lady. Keep it up. Keep it up."

Downstairs, in the kitchen, the doctor's manner underwent a change. When Miriam asked the same question as that posed by Lottie, the doctor replied, "The young lad's dying. His lungs are in such a state it's a miracle he's able to breathe at all. Unfortunately, the effort is putting too much strain on his heart. There's absolutely nothing I, or anyone else, can do for him. I'm desperately sorry for the lad — and even more concerned for the girl. There's a close bond between them."

Miriam nodded, not trusting herself to speak. After making a few more observations, the doctor declared there was no sense in remaining and he left the house.

"I'll go down and tell Jane Trago what's happening," said Jethro, wanting desperately to do something to help, but not knowing what to do for the best.

"No!" Miriam spoke suddenly and unexpectedly. "If anything happens to Jacob tonight I'd like you to be here with Lottie. She knows you better than she does us, Jethro. What's more, she *trusts* you. We'll all have a cup of tea first, then Josh can go and fetch Jane. She ought to be here — whatever *she* thinks."

It was half past one in the morning when Josh went to the village to fetch Jane Trago, but he came back without her, deeply puzzled.

"The inn was in darkness. I knocked loud enough to wake the neighbours, but there wasn't a sound from inside. I know Waldo's away so can only think Jane's lying abed in a drunken stupor."

Miriam was more in touch with village rumour and thought it more likely there was another, quite different reason why Jane had not come to the door. No doubt Patience was lying awake right now awaiting the return of her husband. Something would have to be done about the situation, but tonight there were more urgent matters for her attention.

"Here, I've made something for us to eat. Help yourself while I take some upstairs. Jethro is sitting in Jacob's room with Lottie. I fear she's going to need him before this night is out."

Jacob died at four-thirty in the morning, just as dawn was breaking. He died in Lottie's arms, holding Miriam's hand in the firm belief she was his mother. His passing was not laboured or protracted. He had awoken at 3 a.m., thoroughly confused. Convinced he was lying in Patience Hooper's house, he seemed to see only Lottie clearly.

He had lain half awake and half asleep for an hour and a half when he said suddenly, "I'm cold. Cuddle me, Lottie."

As Lottie held him close his hand slid across the bedclothes. Grasping Miriam's hand, he whispered hoarsely, "I'm glad Ma's with us, Lottie. We're a family now, aren't we?"

A moment later Jacob died, as easily and quietly as expelling a breath.

Miriam knew he had gone, but Lottie could not believe it. Miriam had to prise her away from her brother and carry her, struggling, from the room. Meeting Jethro in the doorway, Miriam explained, "He's gone, Jethro. Jacob's dead."

At Miriam's words Lottie let out a wail of anguish that was terrible to hear. Jethro immediately took Lottie from her aunt. As he held her to him she stopped struggling and began to cry as though her heart would break.

Jethro held Lottie in his arms for more than an hour, until there were no more tears left, only intermittent sobs. Suddenly she pulled away from his arms and stared at Jethro for a moment. It seemed she wanted to say something to him, but no words came. Turning away she ran from the room, and out of the house.

Jethro would have followed her, but Miriam's and stopped him. "Leave her, Jethro. You've given her comfort when she desperately needed someone. Now she has to come to terms in her own way with Jacob's death. No one can help her with that — not even you. Go home and sleep for a while now. You've helped Lottie as no one else could. She'll never forget it. Neither, I suspect, will you."

News of Jacob Trago's death reached into every house in Henwood, but it did not remain the sole topic of conversation for very long.

Patience Hooper's grief fought a losing battle with another, equally strong, emotion. Jealousy. Marcus had not come home to the cottage and Patience believed she knew where he had spent the night. Upset though she was at his absence, she also dreaded his return and the scene that would ensue. It would end in violence — and she would be the one to suffer.

She waited until mid-morning before accepting that the dreaded moment could be put off no longer. Taking up her courage and the three children of the marriage, she made her way through the village to the Cheesewring Inn. Women in doorways and at windows watched her progress, knowing where she was going — and why.

Patience went up to the front door of the Cheesewring Inn, displaying far more assurance than she felt. The door was closed, and apparently locked. She knocked loudly, but to no avail. No one came to the door. After five minutes of this, Patience shifted her attention to the back door, feeling somewhat bolder now.

Banging heavily upon the door, she called, "It's no use your hiding in there, Marcus Hooper. You've got to come out sometime. It's better sooner than later."

Her shouting, the crying of two of her children, and the banging on the door produced only the neighbours.

As the villagers gathered about the Cheesewring Inn there was be no doubting where their sympathies lay. Yet their growing anger was aimed not at Marcus Hooper but at Jane Trago.

"We should never have allowed her back in the village," declared one thin-lipped woman. "She was trouble before she went, and she's been nothing but trouble since she came back."

"'Tis shocking the way she treated that poor boy of her'n. Now he's lying dead and she'm carrying on like the worthless Jezebel she is."

"Shame!"

"Disgusting!"

"Women like her should rot in the stocks."

The women of Henwood village were working themselves into a state of wrathful indignation. One of them, emboldened by the silence from inside the inn, marched up to the door and hammered on it far more loudly than Patience had dared, despite her new-found bravado.

"Come on out of there, Jane Trago. If you don't, we'll come in and fetch you."

The woman's ultimatum provoked shouts of approval from the still-growing crowd outside but produced no response from within the Cheesewring Inn.

"Where's her window?" The militant woman who had assumed leadership of the crowd picked up a piece of granite the size of her fist from alongside the path. "I'll get an answer one way or another."

Suddenly the crowd fell silent. Mouthing threats was one thing. Carrying them out was another. Then an elderly woman with a deformed spine that bent her nearly double stepped forward.

"I'll tell you her room. It's the one nigh to the end. The one with curtains. Had me clean it out for her, she did, when I should'a been cleaning out the inn, not acting as servant to Lady Muck."

The cleaning woman's disclosure brought angry murmurs from the crowd. Without more ado the woman with the stone advanced along the side of the house until she was beneath the room occupied by Jane Trago. Drawing back her arm she threw the stone through the window.

The sound of breaking glass brought a great cheer from the villagers — but it failed to produce either Jane Trago or Marcus Hooper.

After a minute or two the cheering grew fainter and died out altogether. While the crowd wondered what they could do next, one woman, more charitable than the others, said hesitantly. "What if something's wrong? What if Jane Trago's lying hurt? I mean ... with Waldo away and

177

yesterday being a pay day . . . she must have taken a lot of money. What if someone broke in, knowing she was on her own?"

"She's not been on her own. My Marcus is in there with her. He must be. He hasn't come home."

Patience Hooper's plaintive words went unheeded. The seeds of doubt had been sown in the minds of those who a moment ago had been loudest in condemning Jane Trago.

"Ah, 'tis right, you know. There's men hanging about these parts who should have been fitted with a hangman's collar afore now . . . "

"She could be lying inside, killed for Waldo Davey's money."

"And Marcus Hooper might have suffered the same fate, for going to her aid!"

Patience Hooper's scream distracted the crowd for only a moment. A big man shouldered his way through the crowd, a sledgehammer in his hands, "No good standing out here talking of what *might* have happened inside. There's only one way to find out. Stand back, Mrs Hooper — and take those children out of the way with you."

The powerfully built man waited until Patience and her children were ushered back from the door then he swung the heavy hammer as though it were a stick, and broke the door from its hinges with his second blow.

The miner and a companion entered the inn together and the crowd waited about the door expectantly.

It was ten minutes before the men reappeared, and the man who had wielded the hammer said,

"You've all been wasting your time. Jane Trago's not here. Her bed's not been slept in so I'd say she's been gone for some time."

Looking to where Patience stood surrounded by her three wide-eyed children, he added, "Marcus ain't here, neither, missus. I reckon the two of 'em have taken off together — and I'll wager all of Waldo Davey's takings for the past few weeks have gone with 'em!"

"That won't be all," White-faced and haggard from lack of sleep, Jethro pushed his way through the crowd to where the two miners stood. "Marcus Hooper has all the money he and I have been collecting for the miners' association. More than a hundred and fifty pounds . . . !"

15

BY the time their absence from Henwood was discovered, Jane Trago and Marcus Hooper were many miles away. Their whole, dishonest scheme had been carefully planned by Jane. During the months she had been a serving-girl at the Cheesewring Inn, Waldo Davey had come to trust her with confidences he would have told to no one else. He took the inn takings to the Liskeard bank only once a month — sometimes only every two months. Between these trips the money was hidden beneath a floorboard in an upstairs cupboard. This was a secret he shared only with Jane Trago.

Her decision to rob the innkeeper had been made many weeks before. When Waldo was called away to visit his dying mother, it merely made her chance of being caught more remote. It also meant that for a while there would be not two but three months takings beneath the floorboards, including money taken by the inn on three mine settling days. It was more money than most miners would see in a lifetime of working.

Jane Trago's decision to include Marcus Hooper in her plans were made one night when he was boasting of the money he and Jethro had collected on behalf of the miners' association. Persuading him to go along with her was easy. Jane had learned many years before that the surest way of making a man do as she wished was to get him into bed with her. Marcus Hooper proved to be no exception.

Leaving Patience would cause Marcus no distress. Her spiritless subservience, constant whining and interminable child-bearing were a permanent source of irritation to him and he no longer gained any satisfaction from hitting her. Had she fought back it might have been different, but she never did. Instead, she accepted the beating as her due. If she spoke at all during a beating it was to plead that she 'loved him'.

As for the children, they were bearable only when they were not crying, or whining like their mother. He felt no uncritical affection for them. Nothing of the magic bond that was supposed to bind parent to child. Neither did he believe they loved him as children were said to love their father. They cried when he shouted at them, clinging to their mother for support. They were Patience's children, and always would be hers alone. No doubt it would have been the same had they been sired by any other man. Patience was a great 'earth-mother', her body no more than a framework for her reproduction organs.

Patience would never know the passion of love as demonstrated by her more wanton sister. Jane could drive a man to distraction with her abandonment in bed — or in the bracken of a moorland hillside. Marcus needed no other incentive to run away with her — and to bring the miners' association funds with him.

Between them they would have enough money to go far away from Cornwall and set up a tidy little business, somewhere where they were not known and where their money might buy respectability. Perhaps a beerhouse, or even a small tavern.

When the last customer had been ushered from the inn, Jane and Marcus left by the back door. Hidden inside the bundles they shouldered was the money collected by Jethro and Marcus, and every penny taken at the inn over a period of some ten weeks.

The runaway couple followed the mineral line almost to Liskeard. From here, soon after dawn, they caught a train that took them first to Plymouth and then on to the anonymity of London.

Once they had booked into a hotel on the edge of London's teeming East End, using the names Mr and Mrs Cornwall, Marcus relaxed. He and Jane had succeeded in their audacious theft. He, Marcus Hooper — or Marcus Cornwall, as he would henceforth be known — was a rich man on the threshold of a new and fuller life.

It was an occasion for celebration — and Jane's enthusiasm matched his own. First they enjoyed a meal in the tavern's dining-room such as Marcus had never before tasted. There were fish dishes, four kinds of meat, vegetables of almost infinite variety — many entirely new to Marcus — fruits he found equally confusing, and wine.

Wine was also a new experience for Marcus and although Jane prevented him from quaffing it as though it were ale, he drank enough to set his senses reeling long before they adjourned to the public bar. It was as noisy a place as the Cheesewring on pay night. Soon they were surrounded by a circle of new-found acquaintances, all happy to share in the celebrations of the free-spending newcomer.

Marcus woke the following morning convinced he had a smithy inside his head and a dry strip of leather in place of a tongue. He groaned, but the sound failed to filter past the leather. He tried to recall where he had been drinking the evening before. Suddenly he remembered where he was, and what had brought him here.

He reached out for Jane, but she was not in the bed beside him. He opened his eyes. The curtains were closed, but there was sufficient light filtering through the chinks to see that day must have broken many hours before.

It was equally apparent that Jane was nowhere in the room. She must have gone down to breakfast without him. Marcus's stomach heaved at the thought of food, but he sorely needed a drink. A pint of good ale should put his mouth to rights, at least.

Downstairs, the dining-room was empty and a clock in the hallway told him it was half-past eleven! Breakfast was long since over. However, the landlord was happy to supply Marcus with a tankard of ale. After an initial rebellion by his stomach, Marcus downed the drink and regained a modicum of control over his voice.

"Have you seen my wife this morning?" The voice was barely recognisable as his own and he thought it must be this that brought a frown to the face of the landlord.

"Aye, that I have, sir. I prides myself on always being about when a guest leaves, no matter how early they are, or how late I was working the previous night. It's a poor landlord who lies abed while his guests take their leave. Very solicitous of you she was, sir. Left strict instructions you wasn't to be disturbed. Took all the baggage off with her and said you were to follow on when you'd had your sleep out and settled the bill."

"Follow on? Follow on where?" Marcus stared stupidly at the landlord.

"Why, it's not my business to nose into the affairs of my guests, sir." The landlord's frown deepened. "But if *you* don't know, then I'd say we're both likely to have a problem. There's a few question that need the asking. You *are* married to the lady, Mr Cornwall?"

The name came as a shock to Marcus. For a moment he had forgotten, "Er . . . Yes, of course we're married. In a minute or two I'll remember where we're supposed to be meeting. It's just . . . It was quite a party we had last night."

"That it was, Mr Cornwall. You put away an alarming amount of brandy and was buying drinks for anyone who so much as poked his nose in through the door. I'm hoping it was *your* money you was spending, and not *mine*. All them drinks were charged to your account. Yours and Mrs Cornwall's."

"I've money enough to pay my account — and more." Even as he uttered the words Marcus had the feeling of a man teetering on the edge of a precipice. All the money collected for the miners' association had been wrapped in a flat bundle and hidden behind a heavy wardrobe in the room. If

Jane had taken that too he was in trouble. *Serious* trouble.

"I'm relieved to hear it, Mr Cornwall. Very relieved indeed. You see, I can't afford to lose the money you owe me for your stay here — and I doubt if you'd enjoy a lengthy spell in Newgate prison. I've heard it's highly insalubrious for them with no money and no friends."

"I've told you . . . I *have* money."

"So you have, sir. So you have — and don't think I'm doubting you. No, not the one minute. However, seeing as how your wife's gone on to some place you can't as yet recollect — and seeing as how she took all your baggage with her — I'd like to accompany you to your room and have you settle the bill there."

"There's no need for that. I'll bring it down."

"I'm sure you would, sir. But it's no trouble. If you don't mind we'll go upstairs and settle your account right this minute."

The landlord was a big man. His build and the way he carried himself marked him as an ex-pugilist. He was not a man to argue with once he had set his mind to something. Marcus Hooper, alias Cornwall, preceded the landlord up the stairs to the room he had occupied with Jane Trago.

Marcus knew his fate as soon as he entered the room. The heavy wardrobe had been moved. He should have noticed it when he awoke. He *would* have noticed it, had he not been suffering the effects of the previous night's revelry.

There was no more behind the wardrobe than inside the heavy piece of dark, wooden furniture. The whole room was empty. Not only had Jane

185

taken all the clothes purchased by Marcus upon their arrival in London, she had even picked up the small change he had emptied from his pockets and left lying on a sideboard.

The landlord watched in silence as Marcus Hooper's search became increasingly desperate.

"Am I to understand you haven't the means to settle your account, Mr Cornwall?"

The landlord had dropped his use of 'sir' and the significance of the omission was not lost upon Marcus.

"I . . . She . . . There must be an explanation. I probably wasn't listening when she told me where we were to meet up. She'll come back when I don't turn up there. I *know* she will."

The landlord nodded, "I hope so, for your sake, Mr Cornwall. When she does, I'll refer her to the local police inspector. He's a friend of mine and I'm quite certain he'll be delighted to secure your release in exchange for the money you owe me. I'm sending for the police inspector now, Mr Cornwall. While we wait for his arrival I'd be obliged if you would remain here, in your room. Please don't attempt to leave. I'll have one of the porters on guard outside your door. He's not very bright, but extremely strong. He'll likely put a dent in your skull if you as much as show your nose through the doorway."

Jane 'Cornwall' did *not* return to the East End inn and neither force nor inducement succeeded in persuading Marcus to reveal his or the missing woman's true identity.

When the heavy prison gates of Newgate

clanged shut behind Marcus 'Cornwall' he had been convicted of swindling the inn landlord and the judge deprecated his 'unhelpful attitude' by protecting, so the court believed, his missing accomplice.

Three months after being confined to prison Marcus was involved in a serious altercation between prisoners and warders. As a result he was convicted of maliciously wounding a gaoler. It would be seven long and tortured years before the heavy wooden gate opened and the sun shone once more on the prison-pale skin of the miner from Cornwall.

Book Two

1871

1

LOTTIE TRAGO sat on a bench beside Emma Hobbs in the shade of a crude shelter of wood and thatch on the Sharptor mine. Wielding long-headed hammers, both girls were 'cobbing'. It was hard, muscle-wearying work. Nearby, beside a huge mound of ore, eight more girls sat in pairs, similarly occupied.

It was a hot day and Lottie paused to wipe her hands on the rough hessian apron she wore, before tucking a tress of lank, black hair back beneath her bonnet.

"If the weather's like this at Liskeard tomorrow it'll be as hot as the Devil's oven among the crowds at Midsummer Fair."

"No doubt the men'll use it as an excuse to drink more than they should. They'll say 'tis the only way of keeping cool."

"Since when has a miner needed an excuse to drink too much?" retorted Lottie.

"Since Nell Gilmore began preaching against the evils of drink, I reckon."

Lottie's derisive snort caused Emma Hobbs to smile. She and Lottie had become firm friends in the seven years since the tragedy involving Jacob brought about their first meeting. Five years before, the Marke Valley mine had drastically reduced its work force. When Emma was put out of work Lottie took the opportunity to repay the debt she felt she owed her.

Lottie had lived with the Retallicks since Jacob's death and when she spoke to Josh he readily agreed to employ Emma as a bal-maiden. He never regretted his decision. Emma was a good worker and had an infectious good humour.

"Is Jethro taking you to the fair?"

"No doubt he'll be going to Liskeard, same as everyone else."

"That isn't what I asked," Emma persisted. "Has he asked you to go to the fair with him?"

"I expect we'll get together and have a look at what's there — when he's finished preaching at some old teetotal meeting."

"Ah!" Emma looked at Lottie sympathetically. "What you really mean is, Jethro's going to Liskeard with young 'Holy Nell'?"

"I don't mean anything of the sort," Lottie hit a piece of rock so hard with her hammer that much of the ore was reduced to dust while pieces of rock were sent flying. "Jethro's been strong against drink for as long as I can remember. I admire him for it. Nell *will* be at the meeting, I've no doubt. She'll go wherever there's folk with nothing better to do than stand about and listen to her — and you know miners. They'll stand around gawping at a young girl for as long as she's prepared to make a fool of herself."

"I've heard she preaches a powerful sermon. It's said she takes after her parents who died preaching in Africa. I expect that's why she's so keen on religion, because of them?"

"That's what she *wants* folks to believe. As long as she throws in a couple of Hallelujahs! she can flaunt herself in front of stupid men for as long

192

as she likes without upsetting the women — " A second piece of ore suffered a similar fate to the first. "There's a name for girls who get men all excited without giving 'em anything — and it's not 'Evangelist'."

Emma Hobbs sympathised with her friend. Nell Gilmore was now an attractive sixteen-year-old. Fair-haired and dark-eyed, her skin seemed to have retained the tan imparted by the African sun. She had no need of artifice to have men take notice of her.

"I'm fed up with this. I'm going for a walk." Throwing her hammer to the ground, Lottie rose from the bench and walked away from the pile or ore without a backward glance, heading for the high moor beyond the mine.

"Huh! It's all right for some among us!" The acidic comment came from the oldest of the bal-maidens, a widow in her mid-fifties. "If I'd thrown my hammer down and walked off the mine when I was her age I wouldn't have had a job to come back to."

"That's because your uncle didn't own the mine," retorted Emma Hobbs. "If Lottie wasn't so independent she needn't work here at all. I know for a fact Josh Retallick would give her the same money each month, whether she works or not. But Lottie won't be beholden to anyone. She'll make up for any time she's lost when she comes back."

What Emma Hobbs said was the truth. Refusing to have anything to do with Patience Hooper, Lottie had lived at the Retallick home since Jacob's death, doing her share of work about the house. When Elias Barnicoat died and his goat-herd was sold off, she asked Josh if he would find a place for her at the mine.

Josh had suggested she attend the school started in Henwood by Miriam instead. Lottie replied that if she could not work on the Sharptor mine she would need to find both work and a home elsewhere. Eventually she and Josh had arrived at an agreement. She would work on the mine in the mornings and attend school during the afternoons. This Lottie did until she had learned all she felt was necessary for her. Then she became a full-time bal-maiden, turning over half her pay to Miriam each month as her contribution to the household expenses.

Lottie was part of the Retallick household and every effort was made to make her feel at home. She had her own room and was consulted, with the Gilmore girls, whenever important family decisions needed to be taken. Yet, for all this, Lottie never felt she belonged. But then, Lottie never felt she really belonged anywhere.

Leaving the noise of the mine behind, Lottie headed up the ferned slope towards the high moor. This was the only place in the whole world where, if not entirely belonging, at least she felt at her ease. The moor was prepared to accept her as she was. It tolerated her, as it tolerated all those who knew and loved its timeless beauty, but man would never *belong* here. Men and women were merely brash interlopers in this ancient place. It would always be so, although the moor was prepared to share peace and solitude with those who genuinely sought these two elusive states.

Lottie had long ago accepted that her sense of loneliness emanated from within herself. No one could have been kinder to her than Josh and Miriam. They were both very fond of her and showed her as much affection as they did their two adopted daughters.

Squatting in the rock hideout among the gorse with knees drawn up beneath her chin, Lottie wondered whether either of the Gilmore girls ever entertained doubts about their own place in the Retallick household. She thought it probable that Anne did. The younger of the two Gilmore sisters was a thoughtful, sensitive girl. But Nell . . . ?

Lottie squirmed with angry indignation when she thought of Nell Gilmore. Narrow-minded, bigoted, self-opinionated, self-righteous . . . Nell Gilmore was *all* these things. She was also clever, skilful with words, and supremely self-confident, and she was a powerful orator. When preaching to a crowd Nell displayed a passion that seemed alien to her very nature. Jethro Shovell held her in awe for all these qualities.

Jethro's admiration for Nell was, in itself, sufficient reason for Lottie to dislike the Retallicks' adopted daughter even had there been no other flaws in her character. Lottie adored Jethro as much now as when she was a barefoot young waif looking after Elias Barnicoat's goats. She knew Jethro was fond of her too and their futures had been converging quite satisfactorily — until Nell Gilmore began her youthful evangelising.

Lottie realised Jethro and Nell were drawn together only by their mutual love of Methodism

195

but the knowledge did not make her feel any better.

Since John Wesley's death, a number of dissenting Methodist groups had formed breakaway Churches to espouse their own particular views on worship and evangelism. One, the Bible Christians, encouraged women preachers and Nell, naturally, had been keenly interest in such a Church. As Jethro was a Wesleyan Methodist, Lottie hoped Nell might join the rival Church.

However, Wrightwick Roberts, the strong and respected preacher of the Henwood chapel for almost fifty years, had always put the saving of souls foremost in his thinking. To achieve this end he did not restrict his preaching to Sundays, nor did he mind whether or not he had the roof of a chapel over his head when he prayed. He went out among the mining communities, sometimes holding day-long services on the moor, attended by thousands.

Jethro was one of Wrightwick's helpers. When he pointed out to his fellow churchman the advantage of having a fiery and dedicated young woman evangelist at their meetings Nell had been invited to preach at an outdoor meeting.

She was an immediate success and had remained so ever since, large crowds gathering wherever and whenever she preached.

Lottie could only stand helplessly by as she saw Jethro and Nell drawn closer together by their shared interest in Methodism. However hard she might try there was nothing she could do to prevent it happening.

Methodism vied with trade unionism as the

main interest in Jethro's life and Lottie had tried attending chapel with him. But she found herself unable to accept the constraints Methodism place upon its followers, and she was too honest to pretend.

Methodism was becoming an increasingly teetotal religion, and Lottie saw no harm in this. She had seen for herself how a heavy-drinking miner could destroy the very fabric of his family's life. But the Methodist preoccupation with abstinence was not confined to alcohol. Music was deemed 'sinful', and dancing and singing 'occupations of the devil'. All social gatherings other than those organised for an interpretation of the Bible were frowned upon. It was thought they brought girls and men together in 'lustful temptation'.

Such restraints were not for Lottie. She would not accept that God's guidelines to His people might only be interpreted by crusty old killjoys in the stark, whitewashed interior of some chapel. God was the supreme being who had given the birds their song, the wind and moorland streams their music, and the flowers their exotic fragrance and form. She felt the messages passed from God to his people via the chapel-going policy makers were being seriously garbled somewhere along the way.

At one time Lottie had been able to tell such thoughts to Jethro. To discuss her doubts with him. That had been before Nell Gilmore's rise to fame as an evangelist. Lottie had hoped the visit to Liskeard Midsummer Fair with Jethro would help restore the closeness between them. However, it seemed he was more interested in temperance — and Nell Gilmore.

Lottie's chin came up from her knees. Damn Nell Gilmore! Damn Jethro Shovell too. *She* was going to Liskeard Midsummer Fair to enjoy herself. She would enjoy herself. With, or without Jethro . . .

In the Sharptor mine captain's office, Josh, Ben Retallick and Captain Malachi Sprittle sat around the desk on which sat a squat, half full, ball-stoppered brandy decanter. In front of each man was a partially filled tumbler.

A large, leather-bound ledger lay open on the desk and Josh turned the pages slowly, running a finger down each column of figures. Occasionally his finger came to a halt as he noted a particularly significant entry and he would read the figure aloud for the benefit of the others. Each new figure provoked a shaking of heads and a murmur of disapprobation.

Eventually Josh reached the last page of neatly written entries. He read out three sets of figures from here before he closed the heavy leather volume without another word. He poured generous quantities of brandy into the three tumblers, then sat back in his chair and looked at each of the other men.

All three wore grim expressions. Indeed, there had not been the hint of a smile inside the office for more than half an hour, as Josh gave a summary of the Sharptor mine operations for the previous twelve months.

"There you have it, gentlemen." Reaching out, Josh raised a tumbler to his mouth, grimacing as the brandy fumes assailed his nostrils. "We've raised more copper ore to grass in the last year than in the previous two — yet we've made a loss. If we hadn't decided to mine tin as well as copper the loss would have been catastrophic."

"Now the price of tin is beginning to fall again." Malachi Sprittle followed Josh's example and reached for his glass. "It only needs to drop a couple of shillings a ton and it'll be worth no more than copper — and that's what will happen by Michaelmas, you mark my words."

"How long can you afford to run at a loss, Josh?"

The question was asked by Ben Retallick. Now sixty-eight years old he was still a powerfully built man, but he was beginning to look tired. He had handed over the captaincy of the mine to Malachi Sprittle four years before, but he was in the habit of paying a visit to the mine at least once a week.

"I've almost reached the end of the road." Josh looked almost as tired as his father, and there was far more strain showing on his face. "I can keep the Sharptor mine running for no more than another three months. If the price of copper rises before then we'll survive for a few more weeks — but I can't see beyond mere survival. There's still plenty of copper down below, but it's so deep the cost of pumping is making it uneconomical to go after it."

"So the Sharptor mine's likely to close again?"

Josh nodded unhappily. "Unless a miracle happens in the next few weeks."

"Will you tell the men, or would you rather I broke the news to them?" Malachi Sprittle asked the question sympathetically. He knew how much the mine meant to both Retallicks.

"I'll tell them . . . but not until after the Midsummer Fair, tomorrow. Let them enjoy that, at least."

2

THE morning of the Liskeard Midsummer Fair dawned bright and clear. It promised an occasion that would justify months of excited anticipation. Before the coming of the mineral railway to the moor the Midsummer Fair could be enjoyed only by those fit enough to walk to Liskeard. Now it was possible to ride on the train to within a mile of the mid-Cornwall market town. Everyone able to place one foot before the other was expected to go. Henwood would be a near-deserted village for this one day.

There was no comfort on the train. The 'carriages' were open ore trucks, especially cleaned by an army of women for the occasion. Bracken was strewn on the rough wooden floors and most of the women carried cushions with them. The journey itself was a huge adventure for the children of the mining community. Young boys and girls spent a sleepless night, awaiting the first sign of grey dawn through their curtainless bedroom windows.

The small train was not due to leave the Sharptor siding until 8 a.m., but families started climbing the hill from Henwood village soon after seven. No one would be left behind, but latecomers would be crammed in the centre of a crowded truck. They risked their companion being someone to whom they had not spoken for years. Those who arrived earliest were able

201

to secure a few inches of space at the side of a truck of their choosing.

Lottie was one of the earliest but she did not choose her carriage immediately. Instead, she joined the small group of girls gathered about the locomotive. All pretended to admire the gleaming brasswork and spotless paint of the open-platform locomotive. Most flirted outrageously with the young engine-driver and his younger fireman. Unused to such attention the fireman retreated to gaze red-faced into the firebox so often that the engine-driver complained the draught would result in them burning fuel enough for two journeys.

Eventually, Jethro came up the hill from Henwood village, Bible and prayer-book in hand. When he reached the train he looked along the line of trucks, as though seeking someone.

"Hello, Jethro. We've both arrived at the same time," Lottie lied. "Are you looking forward to the fair?"

"Eh? Oh . . . yes." Jethro's glance continued to move over the crowd.

"We'd better get on board or all the best places will be taken."

Lottie needed to repeat her words before Jethro reacted to them.

"Yes. I suppose you're right, but perhaps we should wait just a few minutes."

"If you want a space for someone in particular you'd better get on the train now, or you'll not be able to choose where you go. Besides, I've to save a place for Emma."

There was sense in Lottie's words. Preoccupied

though he was, Jethro recognised the fact. "All right. Here, I'll help you up."

The wooden sides of the trucks were down and on any other occasion Lottie would have hitched up her skirt and clambered inside without effort. Today she seemed inexplicably awkward. Jethro took a grip on her waist and lifted her to a sitting position on the side of the wagon, to the accompaniment of whistles from other youths and men on the train.

Emma arrived soon afterwards and with her friend on one side and Jethro on the other, Lottie chattered away happily.

Ten minutes before the train was due to leave, a couple of railway employees came along to put up the sides of the trucks and secure them into place. By now, Jethro was biting his lip but Lottie pretended not to notice as she asked him to help her to her feet.

Soon, thick smoke began belching from the tall funnel of the locomotive and hissing steam escaped from every joint. Departure was imminent.

Just then someone could be seen running up the hill, her dress flapping in the morning breeze, one hand firmly holding a hat to her head, the other hand clutching a Bible. It was Nell Gilmore.

By the time Nell reached the train, cheered on by the young men and boys, her face was the colour of the red leather binding of the Bible she carried.

Jethro was quick to help her over the high side of the truck and he made a place for her. When Nell saw Lottie was in the same truck her eyes became as hot and angry as the skin on her face.

When the train jolted into motion to the cheers of its passengers, Jethro said to Nell, "That was a close call. I was beginning to fear you'd changed your mind about coming."

Nell cast a look of angry accusation at Lottie. "I'd have been as early as everyone else had some of my clothes not been hidden."

"Oh dear!" Lottie assumed an expression of exaggerated and infuriating innocence. "What was it you couldn't find?"

"You know very well, Lottie Trago. You don't need me to tell you."

"Yes, I do. At least tell me what it is I'm supposed to have hidden."

Aware that the other passengers in the truck were following the conversation with considerable interest, Nell looked out over the side of the truck as the train gathered speed. "It doesn't matter."

"But it *does.* You can't go accusing folk of hiding things without telling them what it is they're supposed to have hidden."

"I've said it doesn't matter. I'm here now so your efforts were wasted." Nell was in command of herself once more. "Jethro, give us a hymn, to help us on our way."

Jethro began singing and a number of older passengers joined in. Then, from the adjacent carriage some of the younger passengers began singing a bawdier but jollier song than that written by Charles Wesley. It proved more popular than the hymn with the young miners and soon drowned the efforts of their elders.

"What was it Nell couldn't find?" Emma Hobbs shouted the words in Lottie's ear as other voices rose in assorted song about them.

"I don't think she could find her drawers."

Emma Hobbs looked at Lottie in admiration, impressed by her ingenuity, "I wonder where they went?"

Lottie shrugged and gave her friend a grin. "I've no idea — but they'll look just as well on the cows in the field next to the house as they will on *her*. Anyway, there were far too many frills on 'em for a girl who has as much religion as she claims to have."

Emma Hobbs's grin was as broad as Lottie's as she mused, "I wonder if she had to come out without any on?"

Lottie shrugged, "It doesn't matter very much. There's no one at the Midsummer Fair — or anywhere else — likely to find out."

A couple of miles farther along the track the train was reversed into a siding and more trucks added. These were already filled with miners and their families from the Caradon group of mines. Site of the first mine in the area to produce copper in any quantity, Caradon was still the richest mining area, despite the drop in copper prices.

The additional trucks increased the noise level on board the trucks three-fold. There was good-natured rivalry between miners of any workings, and enough young women in the trucks for the young men to want to make an impression on them. Nell Gilmore was still making a valiant attempt to rouse religious fervour among the passengers but, for the moment at least, ribaldry had a more enthusiastic following.

An enclosed wagon was also added to the train

at the Caradon sidings to provide accommodation for mine captains and their wives. It was here Josh and Miriam joined the train.

Most of the men and women knew each other and by the time the train rejoined the main line they had divided into two groups. While women caught up with news of families, the men sat about a table on which cups and plates bounced with the movement of the mineral train and discussed the state of mining.

At the table was a man Josh had not seen before. Tall, thin and serious, the empty right sleeve of his jacket was folded and pinned low on the shoulder. The stranger sat quietly for a large part of the journey before one of the mine captains introduced him to Josh as Captain Samuel Coolidge, adding, "this is the man you ought to have gone to see right away, Captain Coolidge. Josh Retallick owns the Sharptor mine. He's able to take his own decisions, without considering whether or not any adventurers will approve."

Shaking the stranger's left hand, Josh asked, "Are you in mining, Captain Coolidge?"

Captain Coolidge appeared startled for a moment, then he smiled his understanding, "No, Mr Retallick. It was the Confederate army gave me the rank of captain . . . " he shrugged the empty sleeve forward, "and I lost this in a damned silly civil war."

The man's accent took Josh by surprise. It was American, and the product of one of the Southern states, Josh judged.

"I'm over here on behalf of the Mexican government, looking for good second-hand engines.

I've seen only two so far. I expected there'd be many more with the state of mining in your country. Would you know of any good beam engines it might be worth shipping back?"

Josh named four mines where he knew there were engines for sale, adding, "The one at Darley's probably your best bet if you're looking for a good sixty-inch engine. I helped make it during my apprenticeship at Harvey's of Hayle. With the exception of the Sharptor engine there's not a better one in these parts."

Skilfully using his one hand, to make notes in a small, leather-bound pocket-book, Samuel Coolidge expressed his thanks. When he returned the book to his pocket, he said, "It's not often one meets with the *sole* owner of a mine. Most seem to prefer to spread the risk among a great many other shareholders."

"With the present state of the market they're probably very wise," commented Josh, ruefully. "But I wanted to see the Sharptor mine working again. The only way I could do that was to buy four-fifths of the holding."

"It must have been a good investment, or you wouldn't still be in business when so many other mines have closed down."

"We're surviving — but I wouldn't like to predict or how long." Aware that other mine captains were listening to his words with great interest, Josh changed the subject.

"Are you staying on the moor for a while, Captain Coolidge?"

Samuel Coolidge shook his head, his eyes revealing that he knew the reason why Josh had changed the subject so abruptly. "I'm meeting someone in Liskeard and must return to London for a few days. But I intend coming back to the moor soon. When I do I'll take a look at the Darley engine you've mentioned. It's not often I have an engine recommended by someone with your experience."

Others joined in the conversation now, but more than once when Josh looked towards Samuel Coolidge, he caught the American looking at him with a thoughtful expression on his face.

The train must have been no more than a mile from Liskeard when the men in the enclosed carriage heard shrieks and shouts from those travelling in the open wagons.

Josh was first to a window and he looked out briefly before pulling his head back hurriedly. "Keep in! Keep your heads inside."

As the occupants of the carriage hurriedly obeyed his shouted warning, Josh gave an amused explanation, "It's some of the town lads. They come out here to the bridge on Midsummer Feast day and waylay the trains. They make up balls from coal dust, mud — and more unmentionable substances — and pelt the trains coming down off the moor. Some of our lads are ready for them, I think. I saw them collecting rocks from the mine this morning. It's safer to keep your head inside the carriage until we're well past the bridge. It's all good fun, but a direct hit could spoil a fine new dress or suit."

One person who did *not* consider it at all funny was Nell Gilmore. A missile containing a high percentage of coal dust landed on her flower-trimmed straw poke bonnet. The hat was not exactly the height of fashion, but Nell had been well pleased with its effect. It suited both her face and her personality. Unfortunately, the missile carried away some of the flower decoration and heavily stained the straw before disintegrating and spattering all those about her.

Holding the hat in her hands and surveying the damage, Nell tried to ignore the draught whistling through the gaps between the floorboards of the railway truck. She had not believed the absence of drawers would make such a difference to her comfort. She tried to console herself with the thought that the ancient saints of Cornwall had suffered far more discomfort and humiliation in the Lord's service. It helped only a little. She had a feeling this was not going to be one of her better days.

3

BY the time the train from Sharptor came to a halt in the sidings at Lady Park, younger passengers had already scrambled over the side of the wagons. After racing the engine along the track they set off in a bid to be first to reach Liskeard, no more than a mile away. They had a great deal of company on the road. Miners and farmworkers from miles around shared the highway with sheep, cattle, horses and goats, being driven to market by farmers.

The Sharptor revellers were in time to witness the arrival of the funfair and its accompanying parade. After performing at Truro fair a week before, the travelling entertainers were now working their way slowly eastwards across the country. It hardly mattered that they left a plethora of unsolved crime in their wake. They were vagabonds in the mould of Robin Hood and his band of Nottingham Forest outlaws. Robbing the rich, they brought great pleasure to the poor.

The cavalcade extended for almost a mile along the road, representing the whole spectrum of entertainment. Gaudily bedecked riders, lumbering bears, muzzled and hobbled; clowns; top-hatted showmen; and carts bedecked in the manner of Chinese pagodas. The latter were driven by men sporting Chinese-style moustaches and carefully made-up slant eyes. However, when cursing the children who stole rides on the back of the highly decorated carts the 'Chinamen' were able to call on a surprisingly rich English vocabulary.

Nobody cared if the wagon drivers were not what they appeared to be, or that paint on the carts was peeling or the gaudy clothing exceedingly dirty. They excused the sequinned ladies who peered about them bleary-eyed and with an accumulation of stale alcohol on their breath. This was The Fair. The annual midsummer event for which even the poorest families tried to set aside a few shillings of hard-earned and painfully spared money.

Last place in the procession went to the travelling players. Everything needed for their performances was piled on a number of rickety carts, pulled by bony horses that looked as though they belonged inside a glue pot.

The actors, too, were less than impressive. The best were seedy, the worst downright villainous. However, this was their early-morning travelling look. In the afternoon, inside their canvas theatre they would be transformed into kings and queens, lovers and heroes, knights and fair damsels. For the duration of a performance their talents would transport a simple country audience to another time, another place. Performing deeds and mouthing words handed down and modified by generations of strolling players, they were beloved by their audiences.

Yet not all who travelled the same road as the entertainers and performers approved of their lifestyle. Many turned off when they reached the houses of Liskeard, heading for the field where the teetotal rally was to be held. It would be a

211

well-attended meeting.

Jethro and Nell Gilmore had stayed with the Sharptor mine contingent until now and Jethro seemed reluctant to bid farewell to Lottie. He made a last minute attempt to persuade her to come with him.

"Won't you come to the rally, Lottie? It will be a grand meeting. Men and women are coming from all over Cornwall. I'd like you to be there."

For a moment Lottie was almost swayed by his evident sincerity, but then she looked at Nell. Standing nearby in her stained straw bonnet, Nell's expression showed undisguised disapproval of all who followed in the wake of the Midsummer Fair procession.

"If I attend your meeting this morning, will you come to the Fair with me this afternoon?"

"I'd like to, Lottie, I really would — but I've promised to help with the preaching throughout the day."

Lottie shrugged nonchalantly, "I've come to Liskeard to enjoy myself — and that's what I intend doing. If you'd rather spend the day with Nell Gilmore, that's up to you, I'm sure."

"It isn't that I want to spend the day with Nell, Lottie. It's God's work I'm doing. It would please me greatly if you'd join me — "

"Jethro, are you coming? We promised Minister Kernow we'd be at the meeting early. I'm starting off the preaching, remember?"

Lottie held her breath, waiting for Jethro's reaction to Nell's imperious words.

"I'm coming. Just a minute . . . "

Lottie turned and walked away, before Jethro

212

had finished what he was saying. He had made his decision. She had no intention of allowing him to see how much it hurt.

Emma Hobbs understood. A couple of years older than her friend, she had suffered more than one disappointment from the opposite sex. Linking arms with Lottie, she led her towards the market where hoarse-voiced stall-holders offered a bewildering variety of goods to cure all ills; clothe a miner's wife like a queen, or furnish her house in the manner of a palace.

During the course of the morning Lottie bought herself a gilt and glass ring. The stallholder assured her it was an exact replica of a ruby ring presented to Queen Victoria by a fabulously rich Sultan of India. She also purchased a shawl, a lace-edged handkerchief — and a clay pipe for Josh.

Whenever Lottie and Emma Hobbs met up with other girls from Henwood village they stopped and compared their various purchases. All were looking forward to the afternoon when the sale of farm animals would cease and the entertainments of the funfair begin in earnest.

Yet even as she professed to be enjoying herself more than at any previous Midsummer Fair, Lottie found herself listening for the hymns from the teetotal rally. Sometimes they could be heard above the noise of the busy market place and she would wonder whether Jethro was really enjoying himself there.

The anti-drink faction seemed to be having a successful day. Try as she might, Lottie could not help wondering what part Jethro and Nell Gilmore were playing in the gathering — and whether it would bring them closer to each other.

Leaving Miriam to walk around the fair with the wives of some of the mine captains, Josh went to Webb's hotel, where the captains traditionally gathered to drink, eat and talk. There were fewer this year, and each man present was aware that his might be one of the missing faces at the next Midsummer Fair.

The conversation was of dwindling sales, falling profits and closing mines. The mining community faced an uncertain future. After a couple of hours Josh had heard enough depressing news. He decided to take a walk before returning to the hotel for lunch.

As he stepped form the hotel into the street with it's noisy crowds, someone hurried towards him. "Mr Retallick. Could you spare me some of your time? I doubt if it will be wasted."

Turning, Josh saw Samuel Coolidge. "Certainly. Shall we return inside?"

"I'd prefer to walk a while. Is there a place where we're not likely to be bothered by the speculation or curiosity of others?"

"I suggest we walk towards Lady Park. There's a teetotal meeting being held on that side of town, but the roads will be clear enough."

Samuel Coolidge nodded his agreement and the two men walked along in silence until the crowds of the fair were behind them.

"I've learned a great deal more about you since we travelled on the train together, Mr Retallick. You've led an adventurous life."

Josh said nothing, waiting for the other man to come to the point.

"I'm told you know engines better than any other man in Cornwall; you're used to getting your own way and you're not afraid of taking a risk — but then, if you were you'd hardly be the owner of a mine."

"You're talking in riddles, Captain Coolidge. Is there something you want to ask me concerning engines?"

"Not exactly. It's the life you've led that prompts me to put a proposition to you. You see, finding engines is not my *main* reason for coming to Cornwall. I am by profession a chemist. I was a very *good* chemist until I complicated life by losing an arm fighting alongside Jubal Early in the Shenandoah valley. It would have been a worthwhile sacrifice had we won — but there are no winners in a civil war, Mr Retallick. Only losers . . ."

Samuel Coolidge shrugged away his memories. "Now my knowledge as a chemist is used to help farmers — especially those who grow cotton. I've discovered that arsenic is one of the best possible chemicals for controlling the boll weevil, one of the cotton growers' most pernicious pests. That's my main reason for being here. To procure a regular supply of arsenic on behalf of the Mexican government."

At last Josh thought he understood the reason for Samuel Coolidge's secrecy. The mortality rate among those who worked in arsenic production was appallingly high. The trade unions, steadily gaining ground among the workers, were focusing special attention upon this particular aspect of mining — yet Josh was still puzzled why the American had singled *him* out for his attentions.

When he expressed his thoughts, Samuel Coolidge nodded his head, "A fair question, Mr Retallick, and I'll give you an honest answer. It seems your mine owners — 'adventurers' I think you call them — are scared of causing unrest by working arsenic on any large scale. I respect their feelings. Times are hard enough without setting out to meet trouble halfway. But their motives are probably very different to yours. They invest in mining to make a profit. Again, I'll go along with that. Only a fool throws his money around. But in you I think I've found the man I've been looking for. Someone who is mining not only to make money, but also to keep his countrymen in work. Moreover, someone who understands the problems of designing new machinery."

Josh looked at Samuel Coolidge quizzically, "Are you suggesting it's more important for a man to have employment than to have good health, Captain Coolidge?"

"No, Mr Retallick. I'm suggesting that a man can have *both.* The production of arsenic is dangerous — but so is mining. Men die from both. What I'm saying is that with care, one need be no more dangerous than the other — and this is where your engineering skill will prove invaluable. I've gone into this very carefully and I'm convinced that if my instructions are followed to the letter then producing arsenic can be a profitable exploit for both you and your work force. I don't doubt there will be opposition from the men's trade unions, but that's why I think you're the right man for a project such as this. You're not afraid to stand up for what you believe is right. I'd like you to give me the opportunity to prove that mining and calcining arsenic can save your mine, Mr Retallick — and many other mines on Bodmin Moor."

Josh was still sceptical, "I'm still not clear why you think *I'm* the one to help you with this scheme . . . "

"Why does a man choose one particular woman to be his wife when it seems there are tens of thousands with identical attributes to recommend them? I believe you're a man I can work with, Mr Retallick. Indeed, you're the man I *want* to have working with me. But allow me to send you the diagrams for my calciner. Look at them and see for yourself whether or not my ideas are sound. An exceptionally tall chimney will disperse the poisonous fumes long before they can do any damage at ground level. Other dangerous fumes escape through the furnace doors — in fact, more men die from these than from any other cause during arsenic production. I have a design for doors that should prevent this happening — but only if they are properly made. Just look at them, Mr Retallick. Even if you decide not to join me in this venture I will value your opinion."

"If I agree to consider your ideas — and it's a rather big 'if' at the moment — where will the money come from to buy all the new equipment and buildings we'll need?"

"You just leave that to me, Mr Retallick. There are a great many influential — and rich

— gentlemen in Mexico who'll willingly provide money to ensure a regular supply of arsenic for their crops. Their situation is quite as desperate as the mining industry in Cornwall. Ruination is staring them in the face."

Josh frowned, "I'll consider what you've said to me, Captain Coolidge, but even if I consider it to be feasible I'll need to consult my mine captains before I reach any decision."

Samuel Coolidge beamed and extended his hand, "That's all I ask of you, Mr Retallick. I'm confident that once you realise the potential of my offer you'll be eager to give your mine a new lease of life. I shake hands confident that this day will open a new page in the life of the Sharptor mine."

The two men were still shaking hands when a new sound reached them from the town. While they were talking the sound of hymn singing from the teetotal rally had been clearly discernible. Now the singing had been replaced by the roar of a great excited crowd. Mixed in with it were the screams of women.

The two men, their new accord temporarily put aside, looked at each other in consternation. Then they began running towards the field where the teetotal meeting was taking place.

4

FOR Nell Gilmore the day of the 1871 Liskeard Midsummer Fair was a page in the book of her life she would happily have torn out and forgotten for ever. Not that it was *all* bad. After such a frustrating and infuriating beginning, the day had seemed to go well once she reached Liskeard.

Nell was quite aware how hurt Lottie would be if Jethro spent the whole day with her at the teetotal rally. She knew it had been Jethro's intention to spend at least part of the day with Lottie at the Fair. But Jethro was so thrilled at the thought of preaching to such a huge gathering he would do nothing to upset Nell and put such an opportunity at risk. Nell made quite certain Jethro did not forget it was *her* influence that had given him this opportunity. Anyway, it served Lottie right. There was no doubt in Nell's mind who had hidden her undergarments — or why.

Nell Gilmore was a good speaker who enjoyed rousing a crowed to near fever pitch with words. It excited her when a vast crowd responded to her entreaties to 'Follow the Lord and forsake the demon drink for ever'. She believed her parents must have known similar joy when they preached in remote African villages and succeeded in converting the heathen natives to Christianity.

Nell often thought of her parents — her real

parents. She believed they would have been proud of her evangelising. She too was bringing sinners to the Lord. The thought gave added fervour to her remarkable preaching.

This morning after preaching the opening sermon she had been followed by a succession of preachers of whom Jethro was but one. He had given a nervous but honest sermon that satisfied those who were already members of the Methodist Church. However, Nell thought he was unlikely to attract new members, or persuade sinners to begin a new life inside the Church.

When it was her turn to come to the front of the platform and speak once more she launched straight into a fiery, evangelising tirade. Praising those who accepted her way of finding the Lord, she poured scorn on those who wasted their lives and money on alcohol.

Unfortunately for Nell, those very men she was castigating were in her audience in considerable numbers. Word had gone around the inns and beerhouses that Nell Gilmore was preaching on the edge of town against the evil of drink. The hard-drinking miners thought it would add to the fun of Midsummer Fair day if they went along and put their point of view.

Nell was quickly made aware of their presence. After she had called for a Charles Wesley hymn a large section of the rally began singing a different tune — with words that had certainly not been composed by the founding Methodist minister!

The assembled teetotallers struggled on to the end of the hymn against a growing chorus of loud, if not particularly tuneful, miners, singing in opposition.

When both song and hymn came to an end, Nell attempted to carry on with her preaching as though the dissenting miners were not there. But they refused to be ignored.

Nell was a powerful speaker. On occasions she had been known to rouse her listeners to a state of religious fervour that made them eager to pledge themselves to life-long abstinence, or follow the Lord in His march against evil. But Nell was used to preaching to an assembly gathered to *listen* to her. She had never before met with open hostility.

This lack of experience led her to attempt a dialogue with the leader of the noisy miners. When she urged her listeners to give up drinking and sign the temperance pledge, there were shouts of "Why? Tell us why, missie?"

"Because it's *evil*. It's the devil's brew, made in hell."

"No 't'ain't. 'Tis brewed by Walter Hicks along to St Austell. I see'd it writ on the barrel wi' me own eyes."

The exchange brought howls of glee from the miners.

"It doesn't matter where it's brewed, it's the devil's recipe, made to weaken men in the face of temptation."

"How d'you know, missie? Have you tried 'en for yourself?"

"No, and I never intend to — "

Nell Gilmore's heated statement brought howls of derision from the miners and one of them,

221

a giant of a man, pushed his way through the crowd to the edge of the platform. In his hand he carried a stoneware flagon from which he had been drinking during the exchanges between Nell and his colleague.

"How can you stand up there telling us we mustn't touch alcohol when you've never tried it for yourself?"

"I've no need to try alcohol. I've seen what it does to people — and I don't like it."

"I've seen what religion does to folk. *I* don't like that, either. You're telling us it's better than drink. I say you should try a drink for yourself before you tell us whether it's good or bad."

The big man's statement brought a howl of approval from the miners.

"That's right, Silas."

"You tell her right, Silas."

"Give her a drink. Make her down a pint of good ale before speaking out against it."

The last suggestion was taken up with gusto and soon the miners were chanting in unison, "Give her a drink! Give her a drink!" Their voices blotting out the protests of Nell's teetotal supporters.

At the edge of the platform, a number of miners joined their large colleague. Gathering about him they attempted to lift him up to the platform.

A number of men already on the platform immediately rushed forward to push the miner back. They succeeded, but it was a temporary victory. Not only did the miners have their large colleague back on the platform, but all around them other miners began scrambling on the wooden structure in order to prevent his ejection once more.

In a matter of a few minutes a pitched battle was raging on and about the platform. Jethro became one of the first victims of the anti-teetotal faction. He was not a heavily built young man. Attempting to push back the flagon-bearing miner, he was plucked from the platform with ease and sent over the miner's head to land with flailing arms and legs in the mêlée at the front of the crowd.

The big miner gained the platform, knocking over any man who looked as though he might oppose him. When he reached Nell he seemed uncertain of what to do next — until she drew back her hand and struck him across the face.

It was the worst thing she could have done. Passing the flagon of ale he was carrying to another miner, the big man pinned Nell's arms to her side with his great hands.

"Give her a taste of good ale!" He shouted the order to his companion.

The second miner held the flagon close to her face, but Nell moved her head desperately from side to side, making it impossible for the man to pour any ale in her mouth.

The giant miner immediately released one of his hands. Wrapping an arm about her body he took a grip on her hair and pulled her head back cruelly.

Nell opened her mouth to scream — and choked desperately as ale from the flagon poured down her throat.

A great deal of ale went inside her mouth, more cascaded down her face, over the front of her dress and even in her hair. When the big man released her she fell to the ground, coughing, choking, retching helplessly.

"That's enough. She's had a taste of 'en. She'll never again be able to boast that never a drop's passed her lips."

"She don't seem to think much of ale, Silas, do she?" The two men spoke to each other, seemingly oblivious of the fighting, brawling, cursing men about them, both on and off the platform. "She's coughing and spluttering fit to choke."

"You're right, Billy. Perhaps we should help her bring it up again."

Reaching down, the giant miner grasped Nell's ankles and lifted her in the air as easily as though she were a small baby. He held her over the edge of the platform — and all fighting stopped immediately. It was replaced by a sudden shocked silence. Earlier in the day Lottie had expressed the opinion to Emma Hobbs that no one at the Liskeard Midsummer Fair would even know whether or not Nell Gilmore was wearing her drawers. She was wrong. In that hushed moment some five thousand men, women and children bore witness to Nell's enforced lapse of modesty.

Suddenly the whole rally erupted in a roar that was a mixture of delight and dismay, the one quite equal to the other. How long Silas might have held Nell's nakedness up to view would never be known. So many men had clambered on to the stage that their combined weight was too much for the wooden structure. With a horrendous rending of wood it collapsed, sending most of those standing upon it crashing to the ground, and releasing Nell Gilmore from her unhappy embarrassment.

The collapse was the signal for another outbreak of fighting, but now help was at hand. Backed by some thirty or forty constables, police Superintendent Kingsley Coote, lately promoted, charged into the midst of the brawling mêlée, hauling miners out from the wreckage of the platform and passing them back to be handcuffed and marched off to the town's new gaol.

One of the men who had earlier been cheering those who opposed abstention now helped Nell to her feet. Too well dressed to be a working man, he downed two jeering miners as he led Nell to the edge of the crowd where Josh was trying to reach her. At sight of Josh, Nell burst into tears and clung to him. As Josh comforted her the well-dressed stranger walked away before anyone thought of asking his name or even really looking at him.

On the other side of the crowd Lottie and Emma clung to each other, scarcely able to stand, so overcome were they with mirth.

"Lottie, I wouldn't have missed that for worlds. To see Nell . . . and without her drawers!"

Howling with delight, the two girls leaned on each other for support as crowds of dejected teetotallers made their way past them. Nell Gilmore's unexpected exposure following so closely upon the heels of the violent fight had put an effective end to the teetotal rally for today.

It would be many, many months before Nell was able to take the platform at a teetotal or evangelical meeting without some irreverent unbeliever demanding proof she was wearing drawers.

Lottie's day was brought to a happy conclusion when she and Emma met Jethro wandering around the fair in a state of utter bewilderment, a bloody handkerchief held up to his nose. After satisfying herself he was not seriously hurt, Lottie mopped him up, washed his face in the leat at the bottom of the hill and spent the rest of the day enjoying with him the pleasures of the funfair.

Jethro was far too embarrassed to mention Nell, and Lottie was content to accept his silence and enjoy his company.

5

THE man who had rescued Nell from the miners at the Liskeard Midsummer Fair rode into the Sharptor mine late in the afternoon, a week later. Emma Hobbs saw him first and she nudged Lottie excitedly, "Look who's just come calling! Do you think he was so taken with what he saw of Nell he's come to see her face?"

"I doubt if he'll be able to tell the difference," retorted, Lottie maliciously. "In fact, if she pulled her drawers over her head perhaps she wouldn't go around preaching so much nonsense."

Lottie and Nell had fallen out yet again that morning and once more Jethro Shovell had been the cause of their quarrel. The previous evening he had come to ask Josh's advice on a union matter. When he was ready to leave, Lottie said she would walk to the village with him. Nell had immediately brought up a minor chapel matter. She pursued it in such detail that by the time it was resolved it had been too late for Lottie to walk to the village with Jethro.

One of the older bal-maidens sniffed disdainfully, "I don't know what young girls want with such fancy folderals. I've never worn any such things in my life. It ain't natural. You wouldn't catch my old man letting me wear them things."

Once inside the mine entrance the horseman guided his mount to where the girls sat working.

"He's coming across here," exclaimed Emma

unnecessarily. "What do you think he wants?"

"Whatever it is, his business won't be with us."

"Pity!" Emma spoke without taking her eyes from the approaching horseman. "Have you ever seen a more handsome man, Lottie?"

Lottie looked at Emma with amused surprise, "Don't tell me you're smitten by a gentleman, Emma Hobbs? I thought you had more sense. Gentlemen are interested in bal-maidens for only one thing."

"I've yet to meet a man who's any different — 'less it's that Jethro of yours, but he's too good to be real . . . "

Conversation between the two girls died away as the young horseman reined in his mount on the edge of the circle of bal-maidens and looked boldly from girl to girl. Emma tried hard to meet his eyes, but when he spoke it was to Lottie.

"I'm looking for Joshua Retallick, the mine owner. Do you know where I might find him?"

"What do you want with him?"

Lottie's unexpected question took the young man by surprise. His eyebrows drew together angrily at Lottie's seemingly impertinent reply.

"That's between Mr Retallick and myself. All I want from you is his whereabouts — if you know them."

Lottie shrugged nonchalantly, "The reason I asked is that if you're calling on business you'd best see Cap'n Sprittle, up at the office. If it's personal you'll need to go to his house, for that's where he is right now."

The horseman looked hard at Lottie, clearly not certain whether or not he had misjudged her motives. Still uncertain, he said, "He sent a message for me to meet him — on business. But if he's at his house I'll go there to find him. Where is it?"

"They'll tell you at the mine office — same as they would had you gone straight there when you arrived."

This time the stranger was not in doubt and anger suffused his face, but suddenly he laughed. "You're damned impertinent, girl, but it shows spirit, and that's a quality I most admire in a woman. What's your name?"

"Lottie Trago. And what's yours . . . *sir*?"

For the second time the man's laugh was not immediate, "Hawken Strike. I own a share of the Sharptor mine. That makes me your employer, I believe. I trust you'll bear that in mind when next we meet."

Turning his horse, Hawken Strike rode to the mine office, leaving a buzz of excited conversation behind him. No member of the Strike family had set foot on the Sharptor mine since Leander Strike sold out to Josh Retallick, seven years before.

Josh hurried to the mine to meet Hawken Strike, accompanied by his father and Samuel Coolidge. Earlier in the week, backed by mine captain Malachi Sprittle and more reluctantly by Ben Retallick, Josh had reached a decision on the production of arsenic.

As it would be a new venture and not without a degree of risk, Josh felt it necessary to acquaint Hawken Strike with what was happening. After all, the son of the previous mine owner still held

229

a fifty share of the mine.

Josh found Hawken Strike settled in the mine captain's office. After introducing his father and Samuel Coolidge, Josh sat down and informed the younger man of Coolidge's offer.

Hawken Strike listened in silence until Josh ended his narrative, then he frowned. "Isn't this arsenic a very dangerous substance to produce?"

"It's dangerous — but so is mining."

"We've learnt from past accidents." Samuel Coolidge felt Malachi Sprittle's terse statement needed amplification. "We've introduced far more safeguards than there were a few years ago."

"Can you convince the miners of this? Or will this scheme fail like so many tried in other mines, because the miners and their confounded union won't accept it?"

Josh inclined his head to where Jethro Shovell sat at a desk, apart from the others. "Jethro is the best man to answer that question. As well as keeping our mine accounts he's also secretary of the miners' union for this area."

Hawken Strike's glance in Jethro's direction was one of stiff hostility, but Jethro seemed not to notice.

"I've already discussed the prospect of producing arsenic with the men. They're prepared to do whatever's necessary to keep the Sharptor mine alive."

Hawken Strike's derisory snort suggested he had little faith in miners' promises. He directed his next question at Josh. "All this talk of redeeming the flagging fortunes of the Sharptor mine sounds splendid — but surely it's only theory? If producing arsenic is the answer why isn't every failing mine turning to arsenic production? Is it because it requires new capital? If so then my answer is an emphatic 'No!' The Sharptor mine has made a useful profit over the years, Retallick and I'm grateful for that. It helped me complete my schooling and gain a commission in the army. But the dividends have been dwindling in recent years. I believe you need to face facts. The mine's life is over. Putting money into a worked-out mine is a certain path to ruination. I'll not allow the Sharptor mine to ruin *me*!"

"Perhaps you'll allow me to allay Mr Strike's fears, Josh?"

Samuel Coolidge's calm, soft-voiced American accent cut short Josh's reply. Smiling in a placatory manner, the American said, "I quite understand your fears, sir, but other mines have not attempted to produce arsenic in any quantity because there has been no certain market for it — until now."

The one-armed American shifted position on his chair and leaned forward, his gaze fixed firmly on Hawken Strike. "Before the civil war in my country my family were cotton growers. In the years since the war ended, I, and many other growers, have been trying to rebuild an economy shattered by four years of bitter war. Then the Mexican government offered me land in their country if I'd go there and help them with their cotton growing. I accepted and had some success until a small insect known as a boll weevil put in an appearance. It's no exaggeration to say that unless this insect is brought under control the whole of a promising cotton industry in Mexico will be destroyed. In America too, if the insect can't be kept out. Through experiment I've discovered that arsenic is extremely effective against this pest. Unfortunately, we are unable to produce the vast amount of arsenic needed in America and Mexico — but *you* can. That's why I'm here. The Mexican government considers my mission so important they've authorised me to meet the cost of building a calciner to produce arsenic when I find a sound, reliable source. I believe I've found it right here on the Sharptor mine. I'll pay for the calciner and take all the arsenic you can produce. I have no doubt you'll be able to buy raw materials from other mines to supplement your own. I estimate that when you're in full production you'll be able to provide us with as much as a hundred tons a month. We're currently paying ten pounds a ton."

Ben Retallick gasped in surprise. The figures were impressive in an age when a miner was lucky to take home three pounds a month in wages.

"That takes no account of any profit we'll make from the tin we recover during the same process," added Josh. "And I already have the machinery we'll need for that."

Hawken Strike looked at Josh with a vexed expression on his face, "If things have progressed this far, why have you asked me here? You've never before asked my opinion on anything connected with the operation of the Sharptor mine."

"We've never before had to make a decision that will change the character of the mine. If we decide to accept Samuel Coolidge's offer Sharptor will no longer be a copper mine. We'll become first and foremost an arsenic producer. Copper and tin will become by-products. You might not be happy with such a drastic change."

"What will you do if I'm not?"

"Offer to purchase your share in the mine."

"And if I refuse to sell?"

Josh smiled apologetically, "I'll go ahead with the plan to produce arsenic — and pay you a monthly dividend. Nevertheless, I felt you should know what we're doing and at least have an opportunity to express your views."

Hawken Strike returned Josh's smile with a grudging respect, "I'm sure it won't have escaped your notice that by informing me of your intentions you've fulfilled any legal obligations you might have to me. I can't stop you. You're a shrewd man, Retallick — but I'll do nothing to thwart your scheme. For a fifty share of a thousand a month I'd support the devil himself. It's a pity the opportunity didn't come a year or two earlier. It would have guaranteed me promotion and I might have stayed in the army. As it is . . . with what my father left, together with Great Uncle Strike's inheritance, I'll be quite comfortably off."

Leander Strike had died in Europe the year before. Josh had sent his condolences then, but his letter had never been acknowledged. He murmured a few words of sympathy now, but Hawken Strike shrugged them off.

"He was a mean, cantankerous old man who squandered all the money he could lay his hands on."

"He left you a share in the mine," Josh reminded the other man.

"Only because he couldn't bear to see you taking everything. He thought it was worthless. Anyway, it had been Great Uncle Strike's intention to leave it *all* to me. Did you know that?"

Josh shook his head.

"Oh yes, I took a great interest in the mine when I was a boy. Great Uncle Strike brought me here often. He enjoyed pointing out the engine you'd built and the man-engine you'd designed. It was Joshua this, and Joshua that . . . the only reason *I* never took up mine-engineering was because I could never have matched your achievements."

"Theophilus Strike was a good man. He gave me the opportunity to become an engineer, the least I could do in return was become a good one."

Talk of Theophilus Strike had unexpectedly warmed Josh to this arrogant young man. "Now we've agreed the future of the Sharptor mine perhaps you'll come to the house and have a drink before you set out on your journey home? You'll come too, Samuel, of course."

Hawken Strike seemed surprised at the invitation, but after only the slightest hesitation he inclined his head, "I'll be delighted."

As he followed Josh from the mine office, Hawken Strike thought a visit to the house of an ex-convict who had returned from transportation to become a successful mine owner should provide him with a tale he would repeat on many occasions in the future.

Nell recognised Hawken Strike as soon as he

234

walked into the room — and Strike recognised her. Interrupting Josh's introduction, he said, "We've met before. I was at Liskeard when she was up-ended for her beliefs."

Nell's face was the colour of the ribbon in her fair hair, but she managed to say, "I would have suffered far worse indignities had you not rescued me. I never thanked you then. I do so now, I'm deeply grateful to you, Mr Strike."

"I *knew* I'd seen you somewhere," Josh exclaimed, "I'm grateful too. I believe you managed to down some of the hooligans who shamed Nell. *That* I would have been delighted to witness."

"It sounds as though Mr Strike had a very satisfying day. I saw him during the evening, after he'd enjoyed a visit to the theatre." Still dressed in her bal-maiden's clothes Lottie had entered the room unnoticed.

Hawken Strike was both confused and uncharacteristically embarrassed. Confused by the presence of a bal-maiden in this house, which was much grander than he had been expecting. Embarrassed because he was not certain exactly when Lottie had seen him. He had watched a play at the Midsummer Fair, but later, in the privacy of a cloth-hung cubicle behind the stage he had enjoyed the equally well-rehearsed performance of one of the actresses.

Unaware of Strike's embarrassment, Josh said, "This is Lottie, my wife's niece. She lives here with us."

"Mr Strike and I have also met before," said Lottie with a disarming smile. "He stopped to ask the bal-maidens the way when he arrived at the mine."

"And you kindly advised me how I might find you uncle," Hawken Strike had recovered his composure now. "I apologise for thinking you no more than an ordinary bal-maiden."

"No apology is necessary," said Lottie sweetly. "I *am* an ordinary bal-maiden."

"Lottie's far too independent for her own good," explained Josh, puzzled by the apparent undercurrent in the conversation between Lottie and Hawken Strike. "There's no need for her to work at all, but she insists on paying her way."

"An admirable trait." Hawken Strike's eyes had not shifted from Lottie since she had arrived in the room.

"She's happier working with her friends, I'm sure." Nell broke in on the conversation. Lottie had occupied Hawken Strike's attention for long enough. He had not rescued *her* from a hostile crowd. "How do you occupy your time, Mr Strike?"

Hawken dragged his gaze away from Lottie reluctantly. "Since I left the army I've kept myself busy looking after the family interest in London and in Cornwall. But, please, the name is Hawken." As he spoke Hawken Strike was looking in Lottie's direction once more.

Hawken Strike remained in the Retallick house for more than two hours. He was a lively and witty guest. His stories of life as an officer in a cavalry regiment were as amusing to young Anne Gilmore as they were to Ben Retallick. Some of his tales were rather risqué but he was careful

236

not to overstep the bounds of propriety.

Miriam thought Hawken Strike was trying very hard to create a good impression. She wondered why.

Eventually, Hawken Strike pulled a beautifully engraved watch from his pocket. Flicking open the case he seemed astonished when he saw the time.

"I never realised how late it was. If I don't go now I won't be home before dark and my horse has an unfortunate habit of shying at shadows."

Standing up, Hawken Strike looked about him as though seeking something, "I believe I must have left my riding-coat in your office, Mr Retallick, and I fear it will rain before I reach home."

"The office will be locked, but I have a key. Lottie will fetch it for you."

"I'll go with her and ride on from the mine . . . "

Miriam wondered whether it was her imagination, or whether Hawken Strike had sounded just a little too eager to accompany Lottie to the mine office.

She watched as Hawken Strike, leading his horse, walked beside Lottie down the hill from the house. Occasionally he brought his head close to Lottie's in a bid to hear what she was saying above the noise of the strong wind.

Miriam knew the intimacy suggested by the innocent gesture was probably a figment of her own imagination. Nevertheless, it disturbed her. Hawken Strike was a highly personable young man, but his background was very different from Lottie's.

Miriam also suspected there was a wild streak in the young man's nature that he had gone to great pains to conceal during his visit to the Retallick house. It had a kindred spirit in Lottie although she kept it under control for Jethro's sake.

Hawken Strike and Lottie both possessed characters that were disturbingly alike. Miriam hoped they would see no more of the young man on Sharptor after today. She feared he could bring great trouble into all their lives.

6

"WHY do you live with the Retallicks? Are your own parents dead?" Hawken Strike put the question as he and Lottie walked towards the mine.

"I never knew my pa, and ma went off some years ago." Lottie made it clear she had no intention of amplifying her reply.

"The Retallicks seem nice people. They've certainly led very interesting lives."

"They're all right."

"Mind you, I have the distinct impression you and Nell don't see eye to eye. Doesn't that make life difficult at times?"

"I didn't think life was supposed to be easy. Anyway, why should Nell make any difference? She's no more a Retallick than I am. They found her and Anne somewhere in Africa. Her parents died through preaching to people. If Nell's not careful she'll end up the same way."

Hawken Strike grinned wickedly, "She ended up the *wrong* way at the Midsummer Fair. I wonder she didn't die of embarrassment."

"She almost did." Despite the reservations she had about Hawken Strike Lottie found his grin infectious. Recovering quickly, she added, "She's really very grateful to you, you know — and so she should be. A crowd of drunken miners out for sport at Midsummer Fair don't go to a temperance meeting to sign the pledge. Neither, I suspect, did you."

"I had business at the fair and found I had a little time to spare."

Lottie's sniff might have been the result of a minor nasal irritation, but Hawken Strike was quick to turn the conversation away from the events of Midsummer Fair day.

"Does Nell work as a bal-maiden?"

"Our Nell do such work? No, she's employed by the Lord on far more important things. When she's not preaching a sermon she's writing one. If she's doing neither than she's *thinking* about doing one or the other — or so she says. Mind you . . . " Lottie added grudgingly, "she's a sight better than most men preachers I've had to listen to."

They had arrived at the mine captain's office now and Lottie opened the door. It was gloomy inside and she thought Hawken Strike stood much closer to her than was necessary. Locating his coat quickly, she handed it to him and immediately slipped out through the doorway. She was waiting for him when he followed, shrugging on his coat.

Locking the door, Lottie was twenty paces away before Hawken Strike realised she intended returning to the Retallick house without so much as a wave of her hand.

"Wait!"

Swinging up to the saddle, Hawken Strike overtook Lottie and brought his horse to a halt across the pathway.

"You were leaving without saying a farewell?"

"What does it matter? A word more or less from

me won't make any difference to you. I might as well save my breath for the walk home."

Lottie moved to pass in front of Hawken Strike's horse, but he urged his mount forward to block the path once more.

Staring down at her, he said, "You're a strange girl, Lottie. I don't think I've met anyone like you before."

"As you're such an expert on the ways of girls, I suppose I'm supposed to take that as a compliment. Mind you, the actress who let you out of her dressing-room at the fair had left girlhood a long way behind."

"True. Mrs Partridge is, as you so rightly say, no young girl. She was only a few years younger when I called on her to give her details of her husband's death in action during the Abyssinian wars. He was a trooper in my company. Since then she's earned a somewhat precarious living with a travelling theatrical company."

"Oh! I . . . I'm sorry. I didn't know. I thought . . .

Lottie never completed her explanation of what she had thought. Neither did Hawken Strike reveal that Dolly Partridge had been a minor actress with the same ribald theatrical company on the first occasion he met her. Or that a full bottle of brandy had been consumed during his night-long 'comforting' of the trooper's widow.

Nevertheless, Lottie was no fool. Looking up at Strike, she said, "But I did see her kissing you. She must be a very *friendly* widow."

Hawken Strike had the grace to smile, "Yes, we have become good friends."

Lottie inclined her head, "I would like to pass now, if you please."

Hawken Strike backed his horse from the path, but Lottie had gone only a few paces when he called, "Wait, I want to see you again."

"You know where I work, and when."

"I'd prefer to meet you in more congenial surroundings. I've invited the Retallicks to visit my mother and me at our home in a couple of weeks' time. Come with them."

"What will your mother think about entertaining one of your bal-maidens at her home?"

"I'm inviting you as a ward of my senior partner in a business venture. Anyway, the house belongs to me. Will you come?"

"I'll think about it."

"Good! I look forward to seeing you there."

As Hawken Strike rode away Lottie found it difficult to make up her mind about her feelings for Josh's young partner. She could not decide whether she really *liked* him or not – but one thing was not in doubt. She found him extremely disturbing.

When she reached the back doorway of the Retallick house, Lottie was confronted by Nell, who was fairly bristling with indignation.

"You've been gone a very long time for someone who just had to find a coat hanging in the mine captain's office."

"What's that to you?" Pushing past the angry younger girl, Lottie unfastened her cloak and hung it behind the kitchen door.

"I don't want Hawken Strike thinking everyone in this house is like you, that's all. He's a

242

gentleman, not one of your miners."

"Oh! So we've all got to pretend we're ladies now, have we? Just because a rider on a fine horse comes visiting?"

Nell glared at Lottie. "I wouldn't expect *you* to understand. If you hadn't come to live in this house you'd still be wandering barefoot and ragged over the moor. Godless and with no more morals than a mine cat."

"And where would *you* be if Uncle Josh hadn't taken you in? A heap of bones in Africa, or the wife of some tribesman, no doubt. I do believe you're jealous. Over Hawken Strike too! Holy Nell's fallen for a womanising ne'er-do-well. Why? Because he put an arm around your shoulders, walked you through a crowd and punched a few noses along the way? Don't make a fool of yourself over Hawken Strike, Nell. He'd have you before breakfast and have forgotten you by the time he was halfway through his first boiled egg."

"You've a filthy mind, Lottie Trago – but I wouldn't expect anything else of you. At least *I* know what happened to my mother – and who my father was . . . "

As Lottie rounded on the other girl the inner kitchen door opened and Miriam entered the room. "What's going on here? Your voices can be heard all over the house. What's all the shouting about?"

Lottie bit back a sharp retort, "There's nothing wrong, Aunt Miriam. I was just telling Nell that Mr Strike's invited me to go with you when you visit his house. I was saying how

243

interesting it should be. I think Nell wishes she was going too."

When the day came for the visit to the Strike home Miriam needed to remind Lottie of her own words and persuade her to take her place in the light carriage Josh had borrowed for the occasion.

The reason for Lottie's reluctance was the invitation which had been received from Isabelle Strike, Hawken's mother. It was extended to the whole of the Retallick family. Both Nell and Anne would be going. Lottie had no intention of spending the day vying with the elder Gilmore girl for Hawken Strike's attentions.

Samuel Coolidge was also included in the party. The American and Josh had good news for Hawken Strike. Work had begun on the Sharptor mine calciner and the refining furnace needed to cope with the large quantities of arsenic Coolidge wanted to purchase. News of the project had travelled fast around the Bodmin Moor mining communities. Already Josh had been visited by the captains of a number of ailing mines, each desperate to keep his own mine in production. They promised to provide Josh with a plentiful supply of mispickel, from which the arsenic would be extracted.

The tin mines would also supply Josh with arsenic 'soot', recovered during the tin-smelting process and requiring only a final refining. Samuel Coolidge was assured of a plentiful supply of arsenic to help his cotton growers escape the depredations of the hungry boll weevil. Of even more importance to Josh, it meant that the Sharptor mine could look forward to a new lease of life.

As the carriage rumbled through Launceston, the ancient capital of Cornwall, Josh pointed out the crumbling, round castle that had dominated the area centuries before Europeans had settled in America.

Samuel Coolidge and the others in the party were impressed by the size of the mansion house occupied by Hawken Strike and his mother. Josh had seen the house many years before. As a young apprentice engineer he had paid a call on Theophilus Strike, the then owner of the Sharptor mine.

Much to the Retallicks' surprise there were a great many people in the extensive gardens surrounding the great house, and tables were set out holding food and drinks.

Hawken Strike hurried to meet the carriage and explained that the district was celebrating the local saint's day. It was traditional for the occupiers of the manor to provide a feast for all who resided in the nearby village, and on the adjacent farms.

"I thought you might find it a little less daunting if you visited us when others were here," added their host. "My mother can be a little overbearing when she has nothing else to occupy her mind."

All the time he was talking, Hawken Strike's glance kept returning to Lottie, but when he proffered his arm for the walk to meet his mother, it was to Anne Gilmore. Blushing with all the self-consciousness of a shy fourteen-year-old, Anne took his arm and led the small procession to where Isabelle Strike stood in dutiful conversation with the vicar — and Superintendent Kingsley Coote.

Josh had recognised the policeman when he and his constables had broken up the riot at the Liskeard teetotal meeting, a few weeks before, but the two men had not had an opportunity to speak. Indeed, they had not spoken for many years.

As the two men shook hands warmly, Isabelle Strike informed Josh in a loud voice that Kingsley Coote was being considered as a candidate to take charge of the county's police, "and it's not before time," she added darkly. "The police force needs a strong man. These miners have to be taught a lesson. It's the mine owners who give them a living, not the leaders of these so-called unions. All *they*'ll succeed in doing is *destroying* the industry. As a mine owner yourself you'll know what I'm talking about, Mr Retallick."

Josh did *not* know, but Isabelle Strike had turned away to speak to Miriam.

Kingsley Coote took Josh's arm and led him away. "Isabelle Strike shares her late husband's hatred of unionism, but I want you to meet my wife. She doesn't often accompany me to such functions and she's wanted to meet you for a very long time. I told her years ago about you and your fascinating travels . . ."

As the Retallick family was absorbed in the gathering, Lottie found Hawken Strike at her side. Handing her a glass of punch he took her elbow and led her to a spot at the side of the

246

house where a stone balustrade edged a lawn. It overlooked a lake that had a rather unkempt appearance. There were a few people standing near, but they too were trying to escape the crowds on the main lawn and made no attempt to speak to their host.

"I'm glad you decided to come," said Hawken Strike, smiling at Lottie. "I somehow thought you would."

"Did you now?" Lottie's eyebrows rose a fraction. "You're very sure of yourself, Mr Strike."

"My name is Hawken — and one of the few things the army taught me was never to indulge in self-doubt. 'It *is*, because I say so.' That's the way British generals win their battles."

"What if the general on the other side thinks the same way?"

"Such thoughts are restricted to *British* generals, but should it happen then you would lay the blame for your defeat on the enemy's superior numbers, or the cowardice of your own inexperienced troops. There're dozens of books filled with excuses for losing battles — and not a hint of self-doubt in any one of them."

Lottie laughed. It was an open, uncomplicated sound that brought a smile to the lips of those who heard it.

"You should laugh more often, Lottie. In a room filled with beautiful women a man wouldn't look at anyone else once he'd witnessed your laugh."

"Flattery comes far too easily to you, Mr Strike. Did the reason you left the army have something to do with a woman? Tell me 'No' and I won't believe you."

Lottie's question caught Hawken Strike off guard. It came too close to the truth. He *had* been implicated in a scandal involving the wife of an officer senior to himself. Strike's resignation had made an official inquiry unnecessary.

"I left because promotion would bring additional expense. My father wasn't a careful man and what assets my great uncle left me were in land and mine holdings . . . "

As he was speaking, Hawken Strike saw his mother bearing down upon them, shepherding the two Gilmore girls and Samuel Coolidge ahead of her.

"So this is where you're hiding, Hawken." Isabelle Strike's glance lingered on Lottie for a few moments. "I thought you'd deserted your guests."

"I was showing Lottie the lake and was about to tell her of the plans we have to drain it and stock it with fish."

"Of course, dear, I should have guessed. Do you know, it's something Hawken has wanted to do since he was a young boy. His great uncle was already an old man when Hawken first came visiting and the place was showing signs of neglect. Hawken would walk around the house and grounds telling everyone what he intended doing when the house and lands became *his.* It amused Theophilus. But Hawken must have impressed him for when Great Uncle Strike died he left everything in trust for him."

Isabelle Strike's gaze returned to Lottie. It was noticeably lacking in warmth, "You'll have heard enough about the Strike family for one day, dear.

Tell me something of yourself."

Lottie shrugged, "There's really nothing to tell . . . "

"Lottie's being far too modest," declared Nell, innocently. "Uncle Josh swears she's the most independent girl he's ever come across. She *insists* on working as a bal-maiden, on the Sharptor mine."

"And what exactly is a 'bal-maiden', dear?"

"I sort and trim the ore when it's brought to grass," declared Lottie, in a voice that carried to those standing about them.

"Really! How terribly interesting." Isabelle Strike's expression reflected her thoughts with more honesty than her words. Rounding on her son, she said, "Hawken, take . . . 'Lottie' to meet Sally and Deborah." Smiling sweetly at Samuel Coolidge, Isabelle Strike explained, "They're Sir John Weston's daughters. Such *nice* girls. If only their dear mother could have lived to see them now. She would be *so* proud of them . . . "

Dutifully leading Lottie away, Hawken said in a low voice, "Mother is being her devious best. Sally and Deborah are probably the two most socially aware young ladies in the county. We'll give them a miss, I think. Instead I'll take you to see the vinery that Great Uncle had built. We might even find a ripe grape, or two . . . "

"You'll do no such thing. Your mother wanted me to meet your friends. All right, let's meet them — unless you'd rather not introduce me to them?"

Lottie looked at Hawken Strike challengingly. She accepted that he was attracted to her, but she believed it was no more than physical attraction. She was something he would like to enjoy, at the same time keeping her away from his family friends.

To her surprise Hawken Strike did not argue. "As you wish — but don't say I haven't warned you about them. They are both dreadful bores."

The Weston sisters were standing together in the centre of a small group of young men and women. Lottie realised she had noticed them before. Indeed, it would have been impossible not to have seen them. Dressed for a London *salon* rather than a Cornish garden, the two daughters of Sir John Weston wore the very latest Grosvenor fashions. Not for them the hooped skirt which had convinced the natives of Queen Victoria's far-flung empire that British women were deformed from the waist down. Instead, Sally and Deborah Weston wore dresses that Josh suggested to Miriam had probably been designed to fit a bushman woman. All the fullness of a hooped skirt had been gathered in to form a bundle upon the wearer's posterior. It was the first such dress Miriam had seen. However, since returning to England she had followed fashion sufficiently closely to know such an innovation was known as a bustle.

Lottie had no such awareness of recent fashion. She viewed the dresses of the Weston sisters with an incredulity that was quickly replaced by barely controlled amusement.

At first the introductions went exactly as Isabelle Strike had planned. It took no more than a couple of simple questions for the sisters to ascertain that Lottie was no more than 'a common village girl', as they would later refer to her.

Once this was established, putting Lottie firmly in her place became not only acceptable, but a necessity. Hawken Strike was one of the county's most eligible bachelors. True, the family home was one of the *minor* manor houses, but enough land went with it to make it respectable — and Hawken Strike was known to be a very ambitious, if slightly irresponsible, young man. Girls with Lottie's upbringing needed to know such men were not for them.

"My dear, what a pretty little dress you're wearing. You made it yourself, of course? How *clever* you are."

"Yes, I made it myself," Lottie replied disarmingly. The dress was a simple affair of cotton gingham edged with narrow lace. "I bought the material at Liskeard Fair — off a *real* Indian."

Somewhere in the small crowd about them a girl tittered. If Lottie heard she chose to take no notice, "Your dress is *really* lovely, but . . . why do you wear such a peculiar bundle at the back?"

"My dear, it's the very *latest* in fashion. I'll wager there's not another dress like these in Cornwall. No, not in the whole of the West Country."

"I don't doubt it. But . . . the lump? What's it there for?"

"It's not supposed to *do* anything. It's . . . well, it's fashion. London fashion. I don't expect you to understand."

"No, I've never been taught about such things.

It just seems a great pity to have something like that on such a beautiful dress, that's all."

"It's . . . it's *fashion*. It's what they're wearing in the smartest circles of *London*. Soon everyone will be wearing a bustle like this. At least, everyone who *matters*."

"You mean . . . if someone broke an egg on their head in London — in the fashionable circles — then everyone else would do the same? Not people like me, of course, but people who matter?"

At this there was a great guffaw of laughter from the men in the crowd. The women too had great difficulty controlling their delight at the exchange. Lottie had spoken with a disarming innocence and Sally and Deborah Weston were not the most popular girls in Cornwall.

Scarlet-cheeked, Sally Weston snapped, "Some people apparently find your ignorance amusing, *I* find it offensive. Come, Deborah. It's time father took us home. I don't think this is *our* kind of gathering."

As the two sisters stalked away, their bustles bobbed from side to side and the giggling increased.

Looking up at Hawken Strike, Lottie said, "I seem to have offended your friends."

"It might distress Mother. *I* find it something of a relief. You have shown up Deborah and Sally for what they are. Frivolous and unthinking young women."

Taking Lottie's arm, Hawken Strike led her towards the drive that circled the house. "I'm going to take you to see the vinery — and if

252

there's a whole bunch of grapes they shall be yours."

Before Lottie and Hawken disappeared from view, Isabelle Strike correctly guessed their destination and sent Nell and Anne Gilmore off in pursuit, suggesting they ask Hawken to show them the vinery too.

Nell Gilmore was still young, and she belonged to a religious sect which Isabelle Strike secretly despised. Nevertheless, the young evangelist was clearly smitten with Hawken — and she patently hated Lottie. She might prove a useful obstacle to place between Hawken and the attractive young bal-maiden until Isabelle Strike could find something better.

7

JOSH went to the Sharptor mine early the next day. He wanted to speak privately to Jethro, but had to wait for more than an hour before Captain Malachi Sprittle left the office to carry out an inspection of the underground levels. Now that the mine was going into serious arsenic production a great deal of arsenic-bearing ore previously regarded as waste would need to be brought to grass.

Jethro was perturbed when Josh sat on the edge of his desk and said he wished to have a serious talk with the Sharptor Mine's young purser.

"What about, Mr Retallick? Have you found a mistake in the accounts? I go over everything at least twice to make certain . . . "

"I'm more than satisfied with your work here, Jethro, but I was at Hawken Strike's home yesterday. So was Superintendent Coote. He's now the police superintendent responsible for law and order in this part of the county. He asked about you and passed on a warning for you not to become too involved with mines away from your own area."

"Why should Superintendent Coote feel favourably disposed towards me? Most policemen would rather convict a trade unionist than a felon. I'm surprised too that Strike should entertain a policeman who feels that way. Strike blames the union for the failure of the Sharptor mine when

254

it was owned by his father. I've heard rumours that he's cooking up something for miners in the Gunnislake region — and hopes to throw the union in the pot with them."

"That shouldn't concern you — and it certainly won't interest Strike. The Gunnislake mines are miles from here."

The mines were situated on the banks of the River Tamar, Cornwall's border with Devon and at least eleven miles away.

Jethro looked at Josh in surprise, "I thought you knew. Hawken Strike has a majority share in the largest mine in the Gunnislake area — and minority shares in many others there."

It was Josh's turn to be surprised. He would have expected Hawken Strike to mention his other mining interests when they were discussing the future of the Sharptor mine. There was no reason why he should, of course, and it would make no difference to Josh's plans for the mine. All the same . . .

Josh shook off the feeling of vague disquiet the news had engendered. "The troubles of the Gunnislake mines should be none of your concern. It's outside your area as union secretary."

"It *should* be. The trouble is they've had no union secretary since Tom Coumbe left for Australia. I was preaching over that way a couple of weeks ago and some of the miners asked my advice. They have a problem at Strike's mine. His mine captain's just put them on a five week month. There's also talk about doing away with some of their holidays. A couple of men went to the captain to complain when the orders were

255

issued. Both were sacked on the spot."

"The five week month's caused trouble wherever it's been tried. Strike's mine captain must be aware of that."

"Probably. But it's one way of cutting costs. Things are bad in mining at the moment. The captain probably believes the men will be afraid of complaining for fear they'll be sacked too."

Josh knew Jethro was right. Mines were closing every month. Out of work miners were to be seen standing in groups outside every mine in the county, hoping for the opportunity to replace an injured or dismissed employee.

"It's a problem that has no answer. Certainly not as far as you're concerned."

"That isn't so. There *is* away for the miners to stop captains taking advantage of them — but only if they're all of the same mind and don't allow threats of dismissal to beat them."

"You're talking of men withdrawing their labour from the mines?"

"Yes. A captain can replace a few men, but if they *all* refuse to work a mine can be brought to a standstill."

"Be careful, Jethro. The law isn't weighted as heavily against trade unions as it used to be, but it's still not on your side. Whatever you do, don't leave yourself open to a charge of incitement. Stand in court on such a charge and the police won't need any evidence against you. Judges take the mere wording on the indictment as justification for a stiff gaol sentence."

"I have no intention of inciting anyone, but I'll be attending a meeting at Gunnislake after service this Sunday and advising the miners there to stop work."

Josh stood up and looked down in Jethro in silence for a few moments. "I wouldn't expect you to do anything else, Jethro, but remember what I've told you. Superintendent Coote passed on a clear warning. Be very, very careful."

In the doorway Josh passed Lottie. She had a message for Jethro from Captain Sprittle. She arrived in time to hear Josh's parting words.

"What was that about? Why must you be careful?"

"Nothing . . . It doesn't really matter. What's going to happen will happen, no matter what anyone says or does."

That evening when work at the mine ended Jethro found Lottie waiting for him when he left to return home. This time she would not be put off. She wanted to know why Josh had warned Jethro to be 'very careful' — and she refused to be fobbed off by his repeated statement that it 'didn't matter'.

When eventually Jethro repeated what Josh had said, Lottie was quiet for a long time. Suddenly she said, "Josh is right. You *do* need to be careful."

"I appreciate your concern, Lottie, but you know nothing about such matters."

Jethro's manner was so condescending that Lottie bridled immediately, "I've seen enough of Kingsley Coote to know he's not a man to be taken lightly. When I was a girl he warned me that if I didn't behave I'd likely end up behind bars. It was after the fire at the mine, when you pulled me out

257

of the burning changing-room. His words are still branded on my brain. I never doubted then that things would happen exactly as he said — and I don't doubt it now. If the police want to break up your union they'll do it — and you're the obvious man to have arrested. Josh might be able to help you if you were arrested around here, but not at Gunnislake. I don't think Hawken Strike would involve himself in any scheme to have you arrested, but I doubt if he'd put himself out to *stop* it."

"Oh? One visit to his home and you're familiar with the way Strike — I'm sorry, the way *Hawken Strike* — thinks, are you?"

"I know more about him than you and I don't believe he has time to bother with what goes on in some old mine. He has far too much to do taking care of the farmlands owned by his family."

"One day spent hobnobbing in a rich man's home doesn't make you an expert on the way he thinks, however much he might have turned your head."

"Jethro Shovell! I do believe you're jealous! Is it because of me — or would it be because Nell was at his house too?"

"It would take more than one visit to the Strike house to turn Nell's head. She has more sense."

"Meaning *I* haven't?"

"You're certainly not behaving as though you have."

Jethro regretted his words as soon as he had spoken them. It was the first time he and Lottie had ever quarrelled and he could see she was hurt.

"What business is it of yours? You don't have the faintest idea of how I behave — or how I think, either. Most days you wouldn't even know whether I'm alive or dead. When you're not working you're busy with your preaching, your old trade union . . . or Nell."

"I think of you as much as I always have, Lottie. But, yes, religion and trade unionism are important to me. The miners have need of both. As for Nell . . . she's a great preacher. She's brought more men to the Church than ever I could. I admire her very much, but it doesn't mean I've stopped caring for you, or stopped being concerned about what you're doing."

"You're like Nell, Jethro. You both have plenty of *words* to give away. They cost nothing — and mean very little more. You probably haven't noticed, but I'm not a ragged little girl of ten or eleven who's willing to hang around you in the hope of being noticed once in awhile. I'm almost twenty years old and I expect more from a man than an occasional pat on the head, or a sermon on the company I'm keeping. You remember *that* when next you find time to think of me."

Turning, Lottie hurried back along the path, her eyes burning with the heat of the tears she was determined to hold back. She was in a turmoil inside because of their quarrel.

Had she looked back she would have seen Jethro staring after her, a strange expression on his face. He remained, lost in his own disturbing thoughts, until long after she had disappeared from view.

8

TWO months after work began on building the arsenic calciner it was in full production. Even so it came too late for many of the nearby mines. Prices on the world's metal markets had taken another sharp dip. Copper ore was fetching less than five pounds a ton and tin prices had tumbled by 20 per cent.

Wise men in lofty London offices sat back in their leather chairs and dismissed the crisis as casually as though it were tobacco smoke. The metal markets had been distorted by the unexpected appearance of thousands of tons of ore from South American mines (most worked by migrant Cornish miners). The situation would soon right itself. Demand for metals was rising. There was no cause for alarm.

But for too many mine owners, alarm had become despair. They had been clinging to uneconomic mines in the forlorn hope of a price rise. They could live on hope no longer. Mine shut-downs spread throughout Cornwall in an economic plague of alarming proportions. Only those mines able to pare their expenses to the bone stood any chance at all of survival.

All this had happened before, of course. Mining was an uncertain way of life. But the miner in the second half of the nineteenth century was a very different man from his predecessor. Chartism and trade unionism, coupled with mass emigration and sporadic return, had all contributed to the miner's recognition of his worth and a just claim to dignity as a man. He was also beginning to realise that his family had the right to a reasonable standard of living.

There were some who believed that any attempt to improve the miner's standard of living was a waste of time. They pointed to the bands of ragged vagabonds who roamed the countryside. This, they declared, was the *natural* lot of the mining man. It was true the ranks of the vagabonds were constantly being swelled by desperate, out-of-work men, but an increasing number of miners were leaving Cornwall to seek a new and better life in other lands. They emigrated in their thousands — and then in *tens* of thousands. They travelled to every place in the world where mines were being worked — America, Australia, New Zealand, Mexico, the list grew with every passing month. Some miners travelled alone. Others, unwilling to subject their families to the rigour of the workhouse carried them off to an uncertain, yet exciting future.

Josh and other forward-thinking mine owners deplored the departure of so many miners. They predicted that when the price of metals rose — as they earnestly believed it one day would — there would be too few miners left in Cornwall for mining to resume on the scale they had known.

Josh kept the Sharptor mine open while others around him were closing, but he was bringing only arsenic-bearing ore to grass now. The mining of copper and tin was temporarily suspended. He also found it necessary to redistribute work at the mine, to ensure some money, at least, went into as many households as possible. This was the reason Lottie found herself temporarily out of work.

Hawken Strike was delighted with the new arrangement. He had made a point of visiting the Sharptor mine at least once a week since the meeting with Josh. Ostensibly checking on the progress of the arsenic calciner, Strike always managed to spend some time with the bal-maidens. Sometimes he would wait until work ended for the day and walk with Lottie to the Retallicks' home. When he suggested Lottie should ride to the Strike house one Sunday and spend the day there he was astonished to learn she could not ride.

Two days after Lottie stopped working she looked from the kitchen of the Retallick house and saw Hawken Strike approaching along the path.

She was at the door awaiting his knock, yet when it came she delayed opening it to him for some moments. When she did, Hawken startled her by taking her hand and leading her towards the gate, ignoring her protests.

Outside were tethered two saddled horses. One Lottie recognised as belonging to Hawken. The other was an attractive grey on which was strapped a tooled-leather side-saddle.

"You told me you couldn't ride and had no time to learn. Well, you have time now and I'm supplying you with the means. Now you run along and fetch a coat while I ask Mrs Retallick to allow you to come with me for your first riding lesson."

262

Miriam had her doubts about the wisdom of allowing Lottie and Hawken to go riding without a chaperone. "You should really ask Josh first . . . "

"I've already spoken to Mr Retallick. I also asked him if he would object to keeping the grey in your fields. He said he had no objection — if you approved."

"You mean the horse is to be kept here . . . for me?" Lottie was as excited as a young girl.

"It's yours for as long as you care to use it. Learn to ride well enough to give me a decent race by the end of the month and I'll make you a present of the beast. Her name's Pearl, by the way."

Lottie was so delighted Miriam knew she could not possibly refuse permission for her to ride with Hawken. Nevertheless, she determined they would not go out unaccompanied after today.

Miriam's assent was rewarded by one of Lottie's rare hugs, before she ran inside the house for her coat. She returned so quickly she might have been afraid Hawken and the grey horse would disappear if allowed out of her sight for too long.

It took Hawken a few minutes to adjust the straps and settle Lottie safely upon Pearl. Then he mounted his own horse and led the grey away. Clinging to the pommel, Lottie protested that she would never be able to maintain her balance for longer than a few minutes.

Watching the two riders heading up the slope to the moor, Miriam had very mixed feelings. For years Miriam and Josh had tried to persuade Lottie to learn to ride and enjoy the many other pursuits Josh's money and position made possible. Lottie had always refused, not wanting to increase her obligation to her aunt and uncle. Now Hawken Strike was succeeding where she and Josh had failed. Miriam should have been pleased. She *would* have been pleased had the change of heart been brought about by anyone else. No matter how hard she tried, Miriam could not bring herself to trust Josh's young partner.

Miriam would have thought her worst fears were being realised had she been able to see the two riders no more than twenty minutes later.

After a brief trot, Lottie shrieked that she was falling. Leading her horse from the saddle of his own mount, Hawken Strike did not bring the animals to a halt until he saw Lottie was actually losing her seat. Then he sprang from his saddle and caught her as she slipped to the ground.

Lottie's laughter was brought to an abrupt halt as Hawken Strike's mouth came down to hers. For a moment she made no resistance, then she pushed him away as his hands began moving over her body.

"Is this the reason you've brought me a horse and promised to give me riding lessons? So you can get me alone on the moor and behave as though I'm an actress with a travelling theatre?"

"I've already explained that and no, it isn't the reason I want to teach you to ride — although I wouldn't want to miss any opportunity of being able to kiss you."

Lottie smiled unexpectedly. "At least you're being honest with me at this moment."

She stepped back quickly as Hawken interpreted

her smile as an invitation.

"Let's get a few things settled here and now. I enjoy your company and I'm delighted you want to teach me to ride, but it doesn't mean I want you mauling me. If you won't accept that I'll say goodbye now and leave you to explain to Uncle Josh why I decided to walk home."

Hawken looked at Lottie speculatively for a few moments, wondering whether she meant what she said or was merely playing hard to get. He decided she was serious.

"You're a tantalising woman, Lottie Trago. All right, I promise not to maul you, if that's the way you view my clumsy expressions of affection, but it doesn't mean there won't be an occasional lapse when I'll give you a kiss — but only in moments of extreme excitement, of course," he added wryly.

Smiling, Lottie said, "I'll accept that, and you never know, I too might occasionally have one of those 'lapses' you mention."

Before he could make anything of her statement she turned away and, hot-cheeked, took up the reins of her horse.

"You brought me here to teach me to *ride*, so help me back on the horse. I think I'm going to enjoy this!"

Lottie *did* enjoy horse-riding. Trotting across the moor with her long hair streaming out behind her, she felt a new freedom. It reminded her of the days when she had spent many solitary hours on the moor taking care of Elias Barnicoat's goats. There was also the challenge of learning to master the magnificent grey horse brought to Sharptor for her by Hawken Strike.

265

Lottie found Hawken exciting too. She knew he was a womaniser and would take advantage of her if she gave him the slightest encouragement. Yet he was attractive and she enjoyed his company.

The two riders spent the whole day on the moor and were on their way back to Sharptor that evening when they encountered Jethro on the track leading to Henwood. He looked tired and defeated. As she approached him Lottie felt ridiculously guilty that he should see her with Hawken Strike when she was feeling so happy.

Flushed and excited, Lottie reined in beside Jethro and expressed surprise at meeting him so far from the Sharptor mine at a time when he would normally just be finishing work for the day.

"Josh gave me the day off," explained Jethro, preferring not to look at Hawken Strike. "I had business at Gunnislake."

"You've not been to Gunnislake and back today? Why, that must be close on twenty-five miles!"

Jethro produced a tired smile. "We don't all have horses to ride."

Hawken Strike recognised Jethro as the purser of the Sharptor mine — and secretary of the miners' trade union.

"What was your business at Gunnislake? I trust you haven't been stirring up any trouble. There are problems enough with the market the way it is. We can do without industrial unrest."

"Your interests haven't suffered, Mr Strike. I was asked by the men to speak to your mine captain. He's introduced a five week month and done away with some holidays. Now he wants to cut their pay."

"I know exactly what he's doing. These are difficult times in the mining industry, as you know full well. A mine needs to cut its costs to the bone if it's to survive. If a miner wants to keep working and save his family from the poorhouse sacrifices must be made."

"A tut-worker at your mine takes home two pounds and five shillings a month — and this for a five week month now. A tributer might make three pounds if he's working a good level. On that he has to provide for his wife and family. Last year the mine paid out seven and a half thousand pounds in dividends. Yes, Mr Strike, sacrifices must be made — but I'd like to remind you that 'a sacrifice' meant one thing to Pontius Pilate and something quite different to the man he crucified."

Hawken Strike flushed angrily, "You're being impertinent, Shovell. I shall speak to Mr Retallick about you. In the meantime stay away from my Gunnislake mine."

"I have no reason to go there again. The men are too scared of being put out of work even to consider the justice of the situation. Your captain has won, Mr Strike . . . for now. But mining's a peculiar business. Right now mines are closing. Next year it might be impossible to meet the demand for tin and copper. If that happens you'll find so many miners have left Cornwall there won't be enough of them left to go around. Then *they'll* be dictating the terms on which they'll work."

Turning away from the mine owner, Jethro

spoke sorrowfully to Lottie, "I think I prefer the company you kept when you were a barefoot girl looking after Elias Barnicoat's goats. Enjoy your ride, Lottie."

"Why, the impertinent . . . " Hawken Strike urged his horse after Jethro, but Lottie moved her own mount in front of him.

"Leave him."

"He was damnably rude. He needs to be taught a lesson . . . "

Lottie reached out and put a hand on Hawken Strike's arm. "Jethro and I have been friends far too long for anything he says to upset me. He's an honest man, Hawken. He speaks the way he does because he really *cares* for the miners. To Jethro it's part of being a Christian. Promise you'll make no mention of this to Uncle Josh?"

Secretly Lottie was proud of Jethro. To speak as he had to Hawken Strike required great courage.

"I think you have too generous a nature, Lottie. His rudeness deserves a reprimand, at least."

"Please, Hawken . . . " It was the first time she had called him by his Christian name. "It's been such a lovely day. I don't want it to be spoilt in any way."

"When you put it that way how can I deny you anything? I'll say nothing to your uncle."

Hawken Strike would keep his word. Josh would learn nothing of his meeting with Jethro, but he intended discussing Jethro's activities with Superintendent Kingsley Coote. Jethro Shovell would regret speaking to him as he had.

Jethro's thoughts were far more confused than

268

those of the mine owner. He knew he had gone too far when speaking to Strike. It would have been easier to accept his failing had he honestly believed he did it because of the injustice suffered by the Gunnislake miners. Jethro was an honest man and he knew his rashness had sprung from a more personal grievance. He had denied it once before when Lottie had taunted him, but Jethro realised he was jealous of her friendship with Hawken Strike.

Hawken Strike returned to Sharptor to take Lottie riding the next day, but he was not to have her to himself again. Miriam had watched them returning together the previous evening. She knew enough of life to realise the dangers of allowing a young couple to spend time together on the moor.

Both the Gilmore girls could ride and after Miriam had a serious conversation with Josh he acquired a horse for Nell and a moorland pony for Anne that same night. Both were saddled and ready for their riders to accompany Lottie when Hawken Strike called to take her for the next riding lesson. Hawken's disappointment was ill concealed, but he made the best of the situation.

Painfully shy in every other respect, Anne was by far the wildest rider of the quartet. She ranged far and wide, for much of the time at a furious gallop. Nell moved from Hawken's side only when he complimented Lottie on the excellent progress of her riding. She felt obliged to demonstrate her own superiority in the saddle of a horse.

After this experience, Hawken Strike came to Sharptor less frequently to take Lottie riding. However, he was sometimes fortunate enough to arrive on a day when Nell was away preaching, or perhaps teaching on one of the chapel schools. On such occasions Anne was the sole chaperone and Hawken and Lottie were able to talk privately for much of the time.

On the days when Hawken did not come to Sharptor, Lottie took to going off riding on her own. Miriam did not mind. Lottie would come to no harm on the moor. She knew it better than anyone else and was familiar with every quaking area of bog, so deadly treacherous at certain times of the year. Lottie also knew where clumps of grass and heather hid mineshafts dug by miners of an earlier century. They had claimed many lives over the years.

For Lottie each ride was a renewing and exhilarating experience. Revisiting each remembered spot where she had once walked and talked with Jacob, she shed tears remembering the two unwanted children they had been then, loved by only each other.

Sometimes Lottie wondered what had happened to their mother, but she would dismiss such intrusive thoughts immediately. They had no place here, amid so many happy memories.

One evening Lottie was making her way homewards after a particularly exhilarating ride alone on the high moor. Autumn was in the air and there was a chill, cutting edge to the ever-present moorland wind that rattled the dying bracken.

As she neared Sharptor the faint path passed

through a narrow, high-sided gully that might have been an ancient tin-working, long since collapsed. It might equally have been a road carved out when history was an unwritten page. The moor had once supported a great many flourishing communities.

Lottie was well inside the gully when she saw a movement at the far end and two ragged, disreputable-looking men came into view. There were many such men wandering the countryside. Most were harmless beggars. A few were not. It would be foolish to take any chances here, beyond the hearing of mine or village.

Lottie turned the horse to return the way she had come — only to find more men had emerged from the undergrowth behind her. It was the perfect place to set a trap. So steep and high were the sides of the gully there would be no escape that way.

Letting out a shout, Lottie sent her startled horse bounding forward . . . but she was already too late. Before the horse could get into its stride, a black-bearded rogue leapt at its head. Grasping the bridle, he brought the horse to a nervous halt.

Lottie carried a riding crop in her hand and she struck out at the man with far more force than she would have used on the horse.

The first blow struck the bearded man across the cheek. He shrieked in pain, but did not release his grip. When the next blow fell he was prepared for it. Grasping the crop he tugged hard and Lottie fell from the saddle.

She was up in an instant and tried to scramble to safety up the side of the gully. She succeeded only in bringing a section of the steep bank sliding down beneath her before she was yanked roughly backwards. As she hit the ground she was pinioned by her captor.

Five or six men came to stand over Lottie as she fought desperately. But all resistance was in vain.

Suddenly her captor growled, "If you don't stop struggling I'll turn you over to the others and leave them to pay you back for this cut on my face."

Lottie stopped struggling, frozen in horror. It was not his threat that had such an effect upon her, but his voice. It was one Lottie had listened to many times, years before. A voice she had hoped never to hear again.

Lottie had been seized by Marcus Hooper.

9

MARCUS had been sentenced to twelve months' imprisonment. The magistrate believed he and Jane Trago had set out with the deliberate intention of defrauding the landlord of the inn where they were staying. Marcus's silence on Jane's present whereabouts was taken to be an intent to prevent her apprehension.

Being confined in a communal prison cell came very hard to Marcus 'Cornwall'. Within the grimy grey walls of the gaol he lived an unreal mockery of a life, where not even his name had any real meaning. His broad Cornish accent was unintelligible to the cockney criminals who shared the cell, and who spoke a language understood only among themselves.

Marcus received no visitors, nor did he have friends to send him an occasional meal to relieve the meagre and often putrid prison fare. He had not made friends easily in his home county. Here, among criminals who cared nothing for him and his plight, he withdrew farther and farther into himself. Rarely speaking he was as ready to fight for his food as any wild animal. Gradually he became a butt for the cruel humour of his fellow prisoners. They would goad him in order to entertain their visitors and themselves, pretending to want to steal his food at mealtimes.

The gaolers too gained amusement from teasing him, making him perform tricks, in the manner of some circus animal before they would hand over his daily bowl of 'swill'. One gaoler in particular enjoyed this cruel sport, and it was he who finally became the target for the pent-up anger and frustration of Marcus 'Cornwall'.

One day the gaoler's demands were even cruder and more impossible than ever and Marcus refused to perform.

"Please yourself." The gaoler dropped the ladle back in the cauldron of foul-smelling potato and cabbage stew and smirked at the Marcus's fellow-prisoners. "If Tommy Tucker won't sing for his supper he'll need to go hungry until tomorrow. Your belly'll be singing loud enough to keep everyone awake by then."

As the tormenting gaoler turned to leave the communal cell, Marcus leapt at him with a scream that contained all the fury and frustration of his months of tormented confinement.

Marcus's immediate target was his departing meal. Had the gaoler relinquished possession of the pot and made good his escape only his dignity might have suffered. Instead, bellowing his anger, the gaoler tried to snatch back the heavy ladle as Marcus carried it to his lips.

In the ensuing fight Marcus regained possession of the ladle and as his cell-mates cheered him on he used it to beat the gaoler to the straw-strewn floor of the cell.

The cowering man tried in vain to ward off the blows being rained upon him as the other prisoners urged Marcus to "Kill him!" Then gaolers began entering the cell from nearby sections of the prison, driving back the prisoners surrounding their colleague.

Marcus was overpowered by the sheer weight of numbers of the rescuers. Later, heavily manacled and with blows raining upon him, he was dragged away to the dark, dank solitary cells reserved for prisoner who broke the rules or were known to be violent.

Meanwhile, the other occupants of the cell were brutally subdued with the aid of long batons and the gaolers carried their unconscious colleague to safety.

For four weeks Marcus lay chained in his dark cell, suffering regular beatings at the hands of his gaolers and given only sufficient food to keep him alive.

When it became clear the injured gaoler would recover from his injuries, he appeared in court for the second time in a year. White as a maggot from his weeks in solitary confinement he stood manacled in the dock, making no reply when he was charged with the attempted murder of the gaoler.

Not one witness was called on his behalf. No prisoner was prepared to give evidence against a gaoler. Marcus left the dock to begin a seven year sentence of imprisonment, the judge showing unusual clemency by allowing it to run concurrently with the twelve months Marcus was already serving.

Ironically, the sentence went some way towards restoring Marcus's manhood. He returned to Newgate prison with a reputation as a man who had almost killed a gaoler. His companions in the prison now treated him with a degree of respect.

Marcus soon learned to make use of his new status. New arrivals who had friends outside were bullied into supplying him with an occasional meal. As time went on he became a leader of the harsh, closed society, able to call on support to force respect from new inmates. On the rare occasions it was not forthcoming, Marcus would use the black dark of a Newgate night brutally to emphasise the power that was his within the small, warped community of the gaol.

Marcus learned new skills too: how to pick a pocket, or bludgeon a man into insensibility without actually killing him. This latter refinement did not spring from a sense of humanity, but because there was less likely to be a hue and cry if the victim survived. Most important of all, Marcus learned that whatever he did, and however he did it, he should never own up to anything. If at all possible the blame should always be placed on someone else.

Yet, although he learned new ways and new criminal skills, Marcus never forgot the past. Every morning when he opened his eyes and looked up to the dirty stone ceiling of the prison, he breathed the stench of unwashed prison bodies and cursed the woman responsible for putting him there. Every night when he lay down upon the straw in the darkness and listened to the sounds about him, the snivels and coughing, whispering and groaning, he hoped Jane Trago might suffer a similar fate.

Each morning at about eleven the men crowding about the barred window overlooking the exercise yard would make way for Marcus to come among them. He would stand gripping the bars watching the women as they shuffled from their cells for a daily exercise walk in the yard. Unlike the other men, Marcus did not shout obscene appreciation when one of the women lifted her skirt above her waist. Nor did he catcall when a shoulder strap on a loose dress was deliberately dropped down from a shoulder.

Marcus was interested in seeing only one woman's flesh. One day he hoped he might peer between the bars and see Jane Trago dressed in drab, rough-spun prison garb, shuffling in line with the other women prisoners.

If this day ever came Marcus would move heaven and earth to gain revenge on the woman who had brought about his downfall. The women occupied a separate section of the prison, but there were ways to cross the divide between the two with the help of a suitably bribed gaoler.

Should Jane ever be incarcerated in Newgate gaol she would wake one night to feel Marcus's hands about her neck. He would ensure she knew whose hands they were before he squeezed the life from her with no more compunction than she had shown in destroying his.

Such a moment never arrived.

Marcus had made no attempt to mark off the days of his imprisonment. Counting the passing of more than two and a half thousand days would have been a depressing exercise at best. Fortunately, perhaps, it was beyond Marcus's capabilities. It therefore came as a complete surprise when one day he was escorted to the prison governor's office and told he was to be released the following morning.

The next twenty-four hours had an air of unreality about them. One moment excitement would well up geyser-like inside Marcus. Then he would be filled with apprehension at the thought of being cast upon a world that had moved seven years into the future while he was locked away in Newgate gaol. It caused him to have a sleepless night.

When morning came Marcus was taken from his cell to a ribald chorus of good wishes from those he was leaving behind. In the guardhouse, beside the great studded door through which he had entered Newgate seven years before, Marcus went through the formalities of his release.

He had a shock when his clothes were returned to him. They were of sufficient vintage, certainly. A film of green mildew confirmed this, but they were not the clothes he had handed in. Marcus 'Cornwall' had been wearing clothing of sufficient quality to gull a landlord into allowing Marcus and Jane Trago enough credit to warrant a twelve-month gaol sentence. These clothes were little better than ill-fitting rags. It seemed one of Newgate's incorrigibles, wise in the routine of prison release, had audaciously left Newgate wearing Marcus's clothes.

It was no use complaining. After seven years as a prisoner Marcus knew he had no rights within Newgate. The unknown releasee had put his cunning and prison-taught skills to good use. Marcus would need to do the same.

As the heavy door closed behind him and the iron bolts were noisily slammed home, Marcus stood on the uneven pavement and shivered. There was a light drizzle, but it was not cold that chilled him. It was apprehension.

A well-dressed man hurried towards him and Marcus stood back to allow him to pass. The man went on his way without so much as a sideways glance. In that moment Marcus found himself. He was a free man! He could go where he wanted. Do whatever he wished! But first he needed money and respectable clothes.

It had been Marcus's intention to leave the surname of Cornwall behind him and become Marcus Hooper once more. But the time was not yet right. Marcus Cornwall must exist for a while longer.

Putting Newgate gaol behind him, Marcus wandered the back streets getting used to his unaccustomed freedom. Emerging from an alleyway he found himself in Ludgate Hill. A hansom-cab pulled up alongside him and an elderly man stepped down, at the same time withdrawing a purse from his pocket. Extracting a couple of coins, the elderly man passed them up to the cab driver. The fare was evidently not as generous as the cab driver had been expecting. Spitting on the coins he slipped them in a waistcoat pocket and whipped up the horse without so much as a thank-you.

Returning the purse to a pocket and grumbling about the manners of London cab drivers, the elderly man stepped back from the kerb hurriedly to avoid being splashed from a fast-passing carriage — and collided with two passers-by. There were a few moments of confusion in the crowded street as the elderly gentleman and the pedestrians sorted themselves out — and it was long enough for Marcus.

Three quick paces took him to the heart of the mêlée. Brushing past the elderly man he was back inside the alleyway again within ten seconds — and clutched in his hand was the man's purse. Long before the theft was discovered Marcus had disappeared into the alleyways, twisting and turning among the narrow thoroughfares until he knew he was not being pursued.

There were two golden guineas and some silver inside the purse. It was not a fortune, but it was a good beginning. Much of the silver was spent in a busy beerhouse close to the River Thames. Most of the other customers were labourers employed on London's rapidly expanding underground railway. Their clothes were as ragged as those Marcus wore, and even dirtier. He was not out of place here and could sit without calling attention to himself for as long as he had money with which to buy drink.

As he sat sipping ale, Marcus thought seriously about his future. He could remain in central London, living on the proceeds of petty crime, but sooner or late he could expect to be caught again and returned to Newgate gaol. Marcus had not had time to decide what he wanted to do, but whatever he decided, it would not include a return to prison. Once was more than enough in any man's lifetime.

Marcus remained in the beerhouse until about an hour before dusk. By now he knew what he would do. Downing the last of the beer in the

280

tankard in front of him he walked outside to the busy London street.

Following the north bank of the river for a while, Marcus eventually turned off into more alleyways. He was heading for the Strand, one of the busiest thoroughfares anywhere in the land. Marcus had seen little of London before being cast into gaol but he knew something of its geography and the characteristics of its streets. Almost all his fellow prisoners had been Londoners and they would spend the days, weeks and months telling Marcus about their city. The places to avoid; where to hide; where to drink; where to find a woman.

There were many eating houses in the vicinity of the Strand, but Marcus was not here to dine. He searched until he found an eating house that suited the purpose he had in mind. It was in a narrow street off the main thoroughfare. The clientele here were neither too well dressed, nor seedy but the noise from within indicated that money was being spent and drink liberally consumed.

Marcus located a deeply recessed doorway from which a narrow stairway rose steeply to rooms above a tailor's shop. From here he would have a good view of the eating house door.

Seated on the bottom stair, Marcus settled down to wait. In prison he had learned to ignore the passing of time. For two hours he sat patiently waiting for the opportunity he was certain would come his way. Then, unexpectedly, a girl came to stand outside the doorway, partially obstructing his view. Thin to the point of scrawniness, she wore a cheap cotton frock and lightweight, badly stitched shoes that were parting at the seams.

Marcus had not noticed that the girl had walked past on more than one occasion, but she had seen him. Without turning to look at him she spoke from the corner of her mouth, "You . . . the geezer in the doorway. You looking for a tart?"

"No. Go away."

"That's not a nice way to treat a girl who's only trying to 'elp you. 'Specially with you only just out of quad an' all."

"How do you know I'm just out of gaol?" Marcus was startled.

"Gawd 'elp us . . . ! First-timer, was you? Must 'a been for something good. You don't get a Newgate tan like yours till you've been inside a year or two. I 'spect that's why the rozzer down the road's got 'is eye on you. I thought it was me he was after till I saw you."

"A constable watching me?" Marcus stood up, filled with alarm. "Where?"

"Sit *down*!" The girl hissed the words urgently. "If 'e thinks I've warned you 'e'll 'ave me inside instead. Look, mister, you got any money on you?"

"No." The lie came naturally to Marcus.

"That's what I thought. Pity. If you 'ad you could 'a come back to my place for 'alf an hour or so. The rozzer might think that's why you'd been 'anging around. It wouldn't need to be for longer than that. 'E'll be going off duty then, unless 'e nabs someone."

"I'll have money later tonight. I could pay you then."

"You've got a bleedin' cheek! If it's tick you

282

want you'll need to go to Uncle's, the shop round the corner with three balls hanging over the door — but even 'e can't give you what I've got to offer."

She looked around at Marcus. It was a long, unfathomable look that revealed nothing of what she was thinking.

"When did you get out of clink?"

"Today." Marcus's reply was terse. The constable might be on his way to arrest him at this very moment.

"Strewth! No wonder you're so nervous about going back in. How long did you do inside?"

"Seven years."

The girl looked at him again and there was awe in her expression now. "*Seven years!* I've never met anyone who's spent *that* long in clink. 'Ere, you mean to say you've gone for seven years without 'aving a woman?"

"I could last longer."

The girl's expression became quixotic as she continued to look at Marcus. She thought he probably wasn't bad-looking beneath his heavy black beard . . .

"All right."

Marcus's thoughts were still on the unseen constable, "All right what?"

"You can come to my place and pay me later — but I'll take scissors and a razor to that beard of yours first."

It took Marcus only a few moments to realise the suggestion would suit him well. One of the first things he had intended doing when he had a little more money was to have a shave and a haircut. What was more, going off with this girl was one way of escaping the constable's clutches.

"Come on. Let me take your arm and we'll walk right past the rozzer."

As Marcus emerged into the gas-lit street the girl wrinkled her nose in disgust at his appearance. "Your clobber don't do nothing for you. Dressed like that there's not a rozzer in London worth his salt who'd let you out of his sight." Taking his arm, she added, "It's a good thing I found you. Left on your own you'd have been back inside before dawn, that's for sure."

The attitude of the police constable standing on the corner of the street bore out her remarks. He stared suspiciously at the ill-matched couple as they walked towards him. Marcus held his breath, the hair on the back of his neck rising as they passed him by. He expected to feel a hand on his shoulder at any moment.

The fear did not dissipate until he and the girl turned into a narrow lane. He realised he was perspiring freely and his legs felt suddenly weak.

"Where d'you want to go? My place, or the room where I usually take me blokes?"

"What's the difference?"

"A couple of miles and a few more hours. I rent the room by the hour — and one's all I'll give you on tick. My place is in Hoxton, two miles away."

"I need to stay here." Marcus spoke hesitantly. He was not as certain of his plans as he had been an hour or two before. The narrowly averted encounter with the constable had unnerved him.

"Look, luv. I don't know what you're up to, and you don't 'ave to tell me, but you were talking of paying me later tonight, right? The only way *you're* likely to raise the ready is by bludgering someone. Now, if it was someone from that eating house you was watching, you're on a loser right from the beginning. Most of 'em there are gaffers from Scotland Yard, just round the corner. They'd have been down on you like coal down a chute. I think you'd better come with Maisie, duckie. You're not safe to be left on your own. Not yet you're not."

10

MARCUS awoke the next morning to the unfamiliar sounds of a horse and cart on a cobbled street and the hoarse cries of a coalman alternately advertising his wares and cursing his horse. Light streaming through a chink in grubby curtains was also a near-forgotten luxury.

"About time too! I thought you was going to sleep all day," Maisie stood in the doorway between bedroom and living-room. Dressed in a non-too-clean shift, she held a mug of steaming tea in her hand.

Entering the room she took a sip from the mug before offering it to Marcus. "Here, it'll have been a long time since you last had a nice cup o' tea in bed."

Marcus raised himself on one elbow and discovered he ached from head to toe. During the last twenty-four hours he had used muscles neglected for seven years. Even walking was an unaccustomed exercise. Taking the tea from her he took a sip and smacked his lips noisily.

"Is that good, lovey?" Smiling at him, Maisie sat down on the edge of the bed and slipped a hand beneath the coarse, brown blanket. "You was good last night. Best I've ever known."

Marcus was naked and her hand stroked his chest, his stomach . . .

"Here, take this." When Marcus held out the

286

tea she looked concerned.

"Don't you like it? D'you want more sugar in it?"

"It's *you* I want. I'll have the tea later."

"Again? Cor, you're a randy cove and no mistake." Even as she made her mild complaint Maisie stood up and let the shapeless garment she wore slip to the floor about her ankles. She was proud of her body and she ensured Marcus was aware of it as she took the mug of tea from him and walked across the room to place it on a chair. Turning, she walked back and stood brazenly by the bedside until Marcus reached up and grabbed her, pulling her down to him . . .

Maisie awoke suddenly. Sitting up she saw Marcus was dressing.

"What you doing?"

"What's it look like? I'm dressing. I'm not likely to get rich lying abed with you."

"You're not going up west to try to bludger someone again? Don't do it, Marcus. You stick out like a boil on a bishop's nose up there. Stay here until your Newgate tan's wore off and you've got some decent clothes, at least."

"How am I supposed to get clothes — leave a note for the *knockers*?"

"I don't know nothing about no knockers, but we can both live on what I make. There won't be a lot to spare, but we'll manage."

"You wanting to set me up as a *pimp*?" Marcus bellowed the words angrily. Of all the men sent to Newgate, the pimps — those who lived on the earnings of a prostitute — were the most despised. They could expect to suffer at the hands of their

287

fellow-prisoners. "I'd rather go for the drop."

Maisie shuddered. "Don't say such things. My pa used to take me to watch the hangings outside Newgate. I'd have nightmares for weeks afterwards."

Swinging her legs to the floor, Maisie sat in a round-shouldered posture, watching in silence as Marcus finished dressing. Her thoughts were troubled and the eyes that never left Marcus were older than her nineteen years.

When Marcus finished tying the laces of his heavy boots and stood upright, Maisie said, "Nothing I can say will make you change your mind, will it?"

When Marcus shook his head she shrugged her thin shoulders in resignation. "All right, if you won't change your mind then I s'pose I'll have to 'elp you."

"What do you mean, you'll help me? What can you do?"

"A sight more than you'll do on your own. If I can't stop you then I'll need to help you make it worthwhile — *and* keep you out of trouble. How well do you know London?"

"I learned something about it when I was in Newgate."

"That's what I thought. You *don't* know it at all." Looking up at Marcus, she said, "For Gawd's sake sit down! I'm cricking me neck looking up at you and I can't think properly while you look as though you're going to run out the door any minute."

Marcus glowered, but sat down as ordered.

"Now look 'ere, lovey. Before I tell you what

288

I've been thinking about let's both face the truth, eh? And the truth is, because of what I am *I'm* not likely to have suitors tripping over each other in their eagerness to marry me, am I . . . ? All right . . . " Maisie assumed a hurt expression, "you needn't make such a business of agreeing with me, but it's the God's truth, ain' it? But then, you're not likely to be the most sought after bloke in London . . . 'less it's by the rozzers. Look, if we 'adn't met each other what would we both be doing now? I'll tell you. I'd be getting ready to go up west hawking me pearly to some geezer I'd probably never seen before and who, likely's not, I'd hope never to meet again. After paying through the nose for a room I'd come 'ome with just enough money to buy food, pay me rent 'ere, and catch an 'ansom back up west to do it all again."

Maisie sniffed and promptly cuffed her nose, "As for you . . . you'd get 'ungrier and 'ungrier, till you was so desperate you'd do something stupid and be caught in no time. I ask you, Marcus, what sort of life is that for anyone, eh? Is that all you and I 'ave to look forward to in our lives?"

"Get to the point. What is it you're trying to say?" There was enough truth in what Maisie said to make Marcus irritable.

"What I'm trying to say is . . . I think we suit one another, you and me. We could get along. What's more, if we worked *together*, I reckon as 'ow we'd make a very nice living."

Marcus was beginning to understand what Maisie was suggesting, but he waited for her to continue.

"Look at me, Marcus. I'm not a bad looker, am I? I've got a good body. You imagine me all dressed up like them fancy tarts what ride in Hyde park. I could go places and pick up men who 'ad real money. Men who'd pay with gold and not 'old out their 'and for change or take out a purse and ask twice how much it is while they count out their silver and coppers. I'd pick 'em up and take 'em to a place where you'd be waiting to bludger 'em and lift their money and valuables. You'd 'ave to be dressed well too. Well enough for any passing rozzer to touch a finger to 'is 'elmet and wish you good evening, instead of 'iding in some doorway to see what you was up to. Wouldn't you like that, Marcus? I know *I* would."

"You and me working together? Dressed up like nobs?" Marcus frowned in concentration as he pondered the implication of her suggestion. "Where'd we get money for clothes like that?"

"Who said anything about needing money? I've got *friends.* Well, what d'you say? We going to give it a go?"

Marcus looked from the still-naked girl to his own ragged and rotting clothing. He had very little to lose.

"Why not?"

He had to fend Maisie off as her enthusiasm threatened to overwhelm him.

"You won't be sorry, Marcus, I promise. You and me'll never be short of money again."

Maisie would have been happy to spend the evening celebrating the new partnership with the aid of the bottle of gin she took from the coal cupboard, but Marcus insisted the bottle be returned to its hiding place. He was impatient to enter on his new 'career'. He had no intention of fouling it up because he'd drunk too much. There would be time — hopefully money too — when they had claimed their first victim.

Reluctantly Maisie agree to go along with his determined self-denial. When she was dressed she took him out of the house and, leaving Hoxton behind, led him south-eastwards. They passed through a maze of streets where the houses had tiny yards instead of gardens, and the occupants stepped out directly on to the unmade litter-strewn streets outside.

They eventually reached a wider street which Maisie said was Hackney Road. Here were many shops and workshops and Maisie headed for one which sported three golden balls suspended in a triangular formation above the door.

Before they reached the pawnbrokers, Maisie brought Marcus to a halt. "You wait 'ere for a few minutes, lovey. I'll go in first and have a few words with old Uncle Gropey before I let him see you. Try to be nice to him. With any luck he'll take any jewellery off us that we pick up. If he likes you he'll pay a lot more than if he don't."

While he waited for Maisie to return, Marcus looked in the windows of nearby shops. There were cobblers, tailors, haberdashery shops — and a number of gin-houses. There was also a pie-shop where a sign advertised 'pie, mash and gravy for threepence-halfpenny'.

The aroma from this last establishment made

291

Marcus's mouth water. However, the proprietor did not view Marcus with reciprocal relish. Maisie had trimmed Marcus's beard and cut his hair to a reasonable length, but nothing could alter the appearance of the rags he wore. Scowling, the proprietor flapped a large and spotless linen dishcloth at Marcus from the back of the shop, mouthing for him to "Clear off!" and threatening to call a constable.

It was a full twenty-five minutes before Maisie emerged from the pawnbrokers. Her transformation was amazing! The dress, shawl and bonnet she wore might not have been the very latest fashion, but they would not have looked out of place in any coffee-house or eating-place in London's West End. It was equally certain they had never before been worn in this area of London. Most probably they had been stolen elsewhere and pawned in Hackney Road for a fraction of their value.

Maisie was delighted with Marcus's reaction. Pirouetting for him on the pavement, she said, "There! Told you I wouldn't let you down, didn't I? I reckon I could turn a parson's 'ead in this get-up. It's your turn now, go on in. Old Gropey's got some togs in there good enough to get you a seat in the 'Ouse o' Lords."

Oskar Gropius was a wizened little man who might once have been a tailor. Shirt-sleeved, he wore an apron that reached down to his ankles. A *yarmulke* almost hid the bald patch on the crown of his head and around his neck was draped a tape measure.

"Come in. Come in." Gropius stepped back to allow Marcus to enter his shop. Peering out through the doorway as though afraid of who might have seen Marcus enter, the pawnbroker turned back and studied him for a few moments with a critical eye. Finally, he threw up his hand in despair as he muttered, "That Maisie! She comes to me for miracles now. A satin purse from a dog's ear? Come in the back room. Come. Are you a God-fearing man?"

Pulling aside a dark-green, slightly threadbare plush curtain, Oskar Gropius ushered Marcus inside a small room. "God-fearing men believe in miracles. If you're to make Maisie's fortune — and she believes you are — we'll need to make a gentleman of you. That's the first miracle we're hoping for."

"Maisie's the one who needs to be able to turn men's heads. All I need do is — "

Oskar Gropius threw up his arms and Marcus stopped talking.

"I don't need to know what you're up to. I don't want to know. You pray, I'll work. That way the miracle might just happen."

A large amount of clothing was heaped on and about a chair. Oskar Gropius sorted through the pile, casting some aside, placing other items carefully on a table. All the while he kept up a muttered, unintelligible conversation with himself.

Eventually the diminutive pawnbroker checked all the items on the table once more and then returning his attention to Marcus, "You'll need shoes too." Looking at Marcus's feet he asked, "Are those boots the right size?"

"They're a bit too large."

"That's what I thought. I've got just the thing for you in the shop." Pointing to the clothing on the table he ordered, "Be putting that on."

By the time Oskar Gropius returned, Marcus had on a shirt, tight striped trousers and a high-necked waistcoat. There was a cravat too, but Marcus was having trouble with this. The pawnbroker tied it for him, all the while clicking his tongue against the roof of his mouth to express his displeasure.

When he stood back he said, "There! That's the way *gentlemen* do it. Get Maisie to help you next time. She's good at such things. Now try these boots on."

The boots were much lighter and slimmer than those Marcus had worn into the pawnbroker's shop. Made of shiny black leather they had elasticated sides and were comparatively easy to pull on.

Finally Gropius handed Marcus a single-breasted frock coat and a bowler hat with a bell-shaped crown and narrow, curled brim. When Marcus donned these final items of clothing, Oskar Gropius beamed for the first time since Marcus had entered his shop.

"So! I make a miracle after all. Come, we show you to Maisie."

Maisie was waiting inside the shop and when she saw Marcus she clapped her hands in delight. "Marcus, you look *wonderful*!"

Kissing Oskar Gropius on his forehead, she said affectionately, "Uncle Gropey, you're a wonder! I don't know 'ow I'll ever be able to thank you."

The wink that accompanied the statement was

294

for the pawnbroker's eyes only.

"My name is *Gropius,* as well you know. Words of gratitude I can take, or I can forget. Your *business* is what will make me a happy man. Bring me lots of nice things and my smile will make the sun shine on Hackney Road. But don't bring me trouble. Trouble I don't need. If the police come here I don't know you . . . and you don't know me. You understand?"

"Course we do, Uncle Gropey. Don't you worry about nothing. Marcus and me'll make you even richer than you are now."

As Marcus and Maisie left the shop Oskar Gropius was correcting Maisie about his name yet again.

When they reached the pie shop Marcus stopped to savour the aroma once more, but this time the proprietor hurried outside to speak to them.

"Come in, sir, madam. You'll never have tasted such pies — and the potatoes . . . fresh from the country yesterday, all swimming in the most delicious liquor you've ever tasted . . . "

The pie shop proprietor stared open-mouthed after them as Marcus walked Maisie away. As they went, Marcus explained exactly why he had told the pie shop proprietor what to do with his meat pies.

11

MARCUS and Maisie's first foray to the West End proved highly successful. They took a hansom-cab to the Haymarket, at the heart of London's vibrant theatre-land. Here, in one of the theatres, Maisie found a seat in the saloon, a place where high-class prostitutes plied their trade. When she picked-up a likely customer she would take him to a small court in one of the alleyways at the upper end of the Haymarket. Here Marcus would be waiting.

Instead of a pleasant little interlude with Maisie, the victim would wake in the gutter with a sore head and empty pockets.

Before taking up her place in the theatre saloon, Maisie had showed Marcus the court where she would lead her victim and Marcus selected the spot where he would make his move. It had already been decided that Marcus would be in the saloon when Maisie picked up her man. He would be less conspicuous there than waiting for her in the courtyard. Dressed in the fashion of most men about the Haymarket he would arouse no suspicion as he walked along behind Maisie and their intended victim.

All went exactly as planned. Maisie's unsuspecting customer was a middle-class businessman from Oxford. In London to find additional markets for his goods, he had drunk enough to behave with a foolish lack of caution. Within twenty minutes of sitting down at her table, the businessman was accompanying Maisie into the small court, unaware of Marcus close behind.

When Maisie paused, ostensibly to remove a small stone from her shoe, Marcus muttered a polite, "Excuse me", and made as though to push past. As the out-of-town stranger put out a hand to steady Maisie, Marcus hit him with a short, home-made cosh filled with lead.

The man fell to the ground without uttering a sound and Maisie and Marcus rifled his pockets swiftly and efficiently. They took a few sovereigns from his pocket and Marcus lifted the man's splendid gold hunter watch together with its heavy gold chain.

It was Maisie who thought of checking for a money belt. As her fingers felt below the waistband of his trousers she gasped excitedly, "He's wearing one — and it feels heavy." It took her a few moments to release the belt and, taking it from her, Marcus stuffed it inside one of his pockets.

"Let's go."

Emerging from the court arm in arm they were swiftly swallowed up in the crowds emerging from the theatres.

In Trafalgar Square they hailed a hansom-cab. Seated together inside, they opened the money belt. In the light from the street lamps they counted their ill-gotten gains and could hardly believe their good luck. The night's work had netted them thirty-one guineas and seven shillings — plus a high quality gold watch.

In the darkness of the cab Maisie hugged

Marcus, unable to contain her delight. "We've done it, Marcus. We've made a *fortune* tonight."

"It's been a good night's work," agreed Marcus, more cautiously. "But it's not enough for us to retire on just yet."

"Who's talking of retiring? We're only just beginning. But let's enjoy what we've made so far. I know a place in Haggerston that stays lively until the early hours. We'll go there. You won't 'ave 'ad much to sing and dance about these past few years. It'll do you the world of good."

"All right," Marcus agreed. There was not much sense in making money if you couldn't enjoy spending it.

Maisie stood up and called back to the hansom-cab driver, giving him new directions with the adjunct that he was to 'whip the 'orse up a bit'.

Dressed as he was, Marcus would not have chosen to spend his money in the Scawfell had it not been Maisie's suggestion. He did not miss the nudges and lowered voices that heralded his entrance. However, the atmosphere changed once it was realised he was Maisie's 'bloke' and not one of her customers. When a small, sly man sidled up and shook Marcus's hand, reminding him they had shared the same communal cell in Newgate for a year, Marcus's acceptance was assured.

It soon became apparent that Maisie was both well known and popular here. The women crowded around to admire her 'up west' clothes and as men passed by they would occasionally nudge Marcus and declare with a cheery wink that he had 'a good 'un' in Maisie.

With a few drinks inside him, Marcus warmed

to the occasion and the company. After joining in a sing-song he called for the landlord to provide everyone in the crowded tavern with a drink at his expense.

Maisie was at his side before the cheering had time to die away. She intercepted the money he was passing to a potman, "Just a minute! What d'you think you're doing — and with *our* money?"

"I'm buying drinks for your friends . . . for *our* friends."

"Let them buy their own drinks. You're boozed out of your mind already. I should 'ave 'ad more sense than to bring you 'ere. After seven years in Newgate you'll 'ave no stomach for strong drink."

"I'm enjoying myself. That's what you brought me here for, remember?"

"I remember. I also know I need to go up west to buy more clothes tomorrow. If I wear these I've got on too often I'll soon get myself recognised."

"Why do you have to go up there? Old Gropey saw you all right before. He'll do it again. He fancies you . . ."

"Shut up! Don't mention his name in here," Maisie hissed at him angrily. "You've 'ad enough. It's time I took you 'ome."

"The night's just beginning. I'm enjoying myself."

"You open your mouth too wide when you've 'ad a few. It's 'igh time we went. Come on."

"Don't you tell me what to do — " Without any warning Marcus rose unsteadily to his feet and struck Maisie across the face with the back of his hand. The blow was hard enough to send her staggering backwards and crashing into a nearby table.

Most of the tavern's customers lived in the East End districts of Hackney, Shoreditch and Hoxton where violence was part of the pattern of everyday life. It had always been so. It probably always would be. But although it was part of their life, violence was governed by certain unwritten rules. First and foremost of these was that they protected their own. Another was that there would be no fighting in the taverns where they gathered to enjoy themselves.

Maisie was Hoxton-born and had lived all her life there. Marcus was a stranger. A brash, overdressed stranger at that. Before he had time to consider whether to hit Maisie again or sit down he was knocked to the floor. Still dazed he was picked up and thrown out in the street to the cheers of the other customers.

In Newgate gaol Marcus had grown used to being treated with deference by the other prisoners. He was not accustomed to such treatment. Scrambling to his feet he charged the jeering group in the doorway, his arms flailing wildly.

Before a single one of his wild blows landed, a straight right jab from one of the tavern's customers put Marcus on his back once again. The customer stepped forward to finish what he had begun but as he stood over Marcus, waiting for him to rise, Maisie forced her way through the crowd in the doorway. Flinging herself across Marcus, she shielded him from the man who had knocked him down.

"No more, Jimmie. Don't 'it 'im no more. 'E didn't mean to 'urt me."

The customer lowered his fists reluctantly, as though disappointed he was not to be allowed to bring the fight to an end in a more satisfactory manner. "He's *your* man — but you'd better warn him not to hit you again, especially when you're among friends in the Scawfell. Take him away and try to keep him sober — for his own good."

"Why, you . . . " Marcus heard the other man's words and struggled to rise to his feet. "I'll show you just how drunk I am . . . "

Holding Marcus down with great difficulty, Maisie hissed, "Don't be a fool, Marcus. Jimmie Goss is the greatest prize-fighter in London. Probably in the whole country. I've seen 'im down three navvies with as many punches. 'E's a bad man to cross and I suspect 'e's been drinking heavy too, tonight."

Marcus was not so drunk that Maisie's warning failed to get through to him. He stopped his struggling. A few minutes later the customers of the Scawfell returned inside the tavern, disappointed they were not to see a fight between their champion and Maisie's bloke.

Not until Maisie was satisfied the pugilist had re-entered the tavern did she release her grip on Marcus. Shaking himself free he rose to his feet and brushed himself down, his pride severely dented.

"I only did it for you, Marcus. Jimmie's a killer with the drink inside 'im. I didn't want to see you get 'urt bad."

"I've met men in prison who thought they were

tough. They soon learnt not to mess with Marcus Cornwall."

"I'm sure they did, but you're not in Newgate now, Marcus. This is Haggerston. The East End. You'd end up fighting everyone, not just Jimmie. Forget it now and let's go 'ome. I don't feel like any more celebrating."

"All right, we'll go home, but in future I'll choose where we go to celebrate — and how I spend the money in my pockets, you understand?"

"Course I do. Let's go now. We'll celebrate in our own way, just me and you. We don't need no one else to 'elp us."

The 'fortune' Maisie and Marcus stole from their first victim did not last as long as Marcus had anticipated. Pawnbroker Oskar Gropius took the watch in payment for the clothes he had supplied and much of what was left after their evening at the Scawfell went on new clothes for Maisie.

When they next went to the heart of London, Maisie was dressed almost as fashionably as before, although it was apparent she lacked the dress-sense of the woman whose clothes had found their way to the Hackney Road pawnbroker's shop.

Their second victim was neither as drunk nor as gullible as the first. When Marcus attacked him in the same court as before he was not taken entirely by surprise and fought back fiercely. Marcus's cosh made him drop to his knees but it took a rain of blows to render him semi-conscious, by which time his cries had aroused the residents of the court.

It was possible to make only a cursory search

302

of the groaning man and it yielded only four pounds. It was little enough for which to risk a life sentence.

That night Marcus and Maisie walked home. This was contrary to all Marcus's plans for the way of life he and Maisie were to lead. He firmly believed it was essential to get well clear of the area as rapidly as possible after committing a robbery. Before too long the police would be looking for a well-dressed couple hurrying away after a robbery had been committed. It would be impossible to stop and search every hansom-cab travelling through the heart of the city late at night — but a couple of foot would be vulnerable.

They reached Maisie's Hoxton home tired and bad-tempered and the blisters on Marcus's feet did nothing to improve his mood. Maisie took another beating that night, but she accepted it as part of her lot in life. The tears did not come until Marcus awoke from a nightmare shouting for someone named Jane.

Maisie received another beating a week later, after a celebration at an inn on the fringe of the East End, when Marcus had seemed attracted to a young 'dollymop', out for an evening of profitable excitement.

With Maisie's help Marcus had robbed their third victim of twenty pounds and some fine jewellery, for which Oskar Gropius gave them another ten pounds, ignoring Marcus's protest that it was worth at least seven times this amount.

The money had to last longer than usual on this occasion. One of Maisie's eyes was severely bruised by Marcus's fist, and it was impossible for her to work.

This enforced period of inactivity led to more violent arguments, but Marcus had learned a lesson. He was careful not to strike Maisie in places where a bruise would show. He also took to going out alone in the evening, returning so drunk he wanted neither to take Maisie, nor to beat her.

Frequently in a drunken sleep Marcus would repeat the name Jane and eventually Maisie asked who the mysterious girl was. At first Marcus would not answer. When she persisted, he informed Maisie that Jane was the woman he would 'swing for' if ever he met up with her again. His expression when he made the frightening statement was such that Maisie pursued the matter no further.

In fact, Maisie found it such a relief to learn Jane was not a rival that she was particularly loving towards Marcus that evening. He too was in an unusually mellow mood and said he would go out and buy some brandy for them to enjoy a quiet evening at home.

On his way to the ale house where he knew he could buy his drink, Marcus heard loud singing. Then he saw three men coming towards him, their arms about each others' shoulders. As they drew nearer he recognised the one in the centre as Jimmie Goss, the prizefighter who had struck him at the Scawfell tavern. The incident had rankled with Marcus ever since.

Standing well back in the shadows of a half-completed hospital they were building in Hoxton,

304

Marcus waited for the trio to pass by.

It was clear that Jimmie Goss and his companions had been drinking heavily. Marcus had heard rumours Goss was in training for another championship fight, but prizefighting had fallen into disrepute recently and it seemed Jimmie Goss was not taking his training very seriously.

When the three men were almost level with Marcus, Jimmie Goss detached himself from his companions. Mumbling something to them, he weaved his way towards the spot where Marcus stood. With a waving of hands, the other two men continued on their way, shouting for Goss to meet them in the Scawfell later.

Jimmie Goss passed no more than two paces from where Marcus pressed back into the shadows. A few moments later he heard the prizefighter relieving himself against a half-built wall.

Suddenly something moved behind Marcus and there came the sound of metal falling against metal. Reaching back, Marcus discovered he was leaning against a pile of iron rods, intended for railings around the outside of the hospital.

Jimmie Goss heard the sound and called out, "Who's that? Who's there?"

When Marcus made no answer the prizefighter repeated his question and made his way in Marcus's direction.

Marcus made no attempt to run away. When Jimmie Goss drew closer, uncertain of the source of the sound he had heard, Marcus was waiting, an iron rail in his hand.

Still hidden by the shadows he stepped forward and swung the iron bar in a low, vicious arc. The

305

iron rail hit Jimmie Goss, as was intended, on the knee-cap and Marcus heard the bone shatter a moment before the prizefighter began screaming in agony.

By the time help reached the crippled man Marcus was at the alehouse. Having purchased his drinks, he returned to Maisie's house well pleased with himself. Goss would never enter the prize-ring again. The years would see him decline into a drunken old has-been who would spend the remainder of his life sponging off anyone willing to listen to stories of his past glories. Marcus had exacted revenge for the humiliation he had suffered at the hands of Jimmie Goss.

The last excursion to the Haymarket in search of a victim was as disastrous for Maisie as the first had been successful.

It was the evening after she and Marcus had spent a happy night together at home, while the whole of East End London was agog with the story of how their prizefighting champion had been crippled. The general belief was that the savage attack had been carried out by supporters of his opponent. Someone, perhaps, who would have lost too much money if Jimmie Goss won his championship fight.

Maisie and Marcus discussed the incident on their way to the Haymarket in a hansom-cab. Marcus was magnanimous in his sympathy for the seriously injured prizefighter, agreeing the perpetrator should be discovered not by the police but by Goss's vengeful friends in Haggerston.

Tonight Marcus had decided Maisie should

tout for business in a fashionable eating-house close to the Haymarket Theatre. He had never been inside before, but had been impressed on an earlier trip to the area by the number of men of obvious wealth who entered the premises alone and left with well-dressed women.

Maisie and Marcus entered the eating-house separately. Marcus took a table close to the door, while Maisie sat in a more conspicuous spot near the centre of the room. Ten minutes later Maisie was joined at the table by a large, elderly and decidedly flabby man whose fingers were adorned with a number of expensive-looking rings and who had a habit of consulting a heavy gold watch. He just as frequently mopped his perspiring brow with a large linen handkerchief edged with a thin band of lace.

Marcus was just congratulating himself on being in luck when a sudden, unexpected silence fell upon the room. Glancing around, Marcus saw two helmeted constables standing in the doorway. With them was the man who had been his and Maisie's second victim. He was pointing across the room to where Maisie sat talking to her prospective customer, unaware of the new arrivals.

Only by calling upon all his will power was Marcus able to remain seated as the man and the constables walked towards him. Had his nerve failed there was no doubting he would have been recognised and arrested immediately. As it was, their earlier victim walked within an arm's length of Marcus, his gaze fixed firmly upon Maisie.

She did not see the constables until they stopped beside her chair. In the moments before he made his own hurried exit Marcus saw the expression of fear that sprang to her face.

As he hurried through the doorway Marcus thought he heard someone shout after him. He did not wait to find out. Taking to his heels he sprinted along the corridor and down the wide staircase, heedless of all in his path.

He did not stop when he reached the street, but sprinted northwards along the pavement, not pausing until he was well inside the skein of ill-lit alleyways where few constables would choose to follow.

Emerging in Shaftesbury Avenue, Marcus hailed a hansom-cab. Speed was essential. He wanted to reach Maisie's home before the police. He needed to clear out his few possessions and find the money he believed Maisie had hidden there. He did not think Maisie would deliberately implicate him. Not immediately, anyway, but it would not take the police long to find out where she lived. They would want to search her rooms for any incriminating evidence.

It took Marcus longer than expected to locate Maisie's hidden hoard. It was not enough to bring any comfort to even the first year of a long prison sentence had Maisie been able to find a way to have it taken to her in prison.

There was little else of value in the house but, almost as an afterthought, Marcus rolled Maisie's clothes into a bundle and took them with him when he left the house.

Oskar Gropius's shop had the boards up at the window, but there was a thin ribbon of yellow light showing beneath the door.

Gropius took a long time to come to the door in answer to Marcus's repeated heavy knocking. Eventually a shadow cut off most of the narrow band of light and a querulous voice demanded to know who was visiting him at such a late hour.

"It's me, Marcus Cornwall."

"Who?"

"Marcus Cornwall . . . Maisie's friend."

"Oh, *you*. I'm closed, come back tomorrow morning."

"I can't. Maisie's been arrested . . . " Marcus fell silent until two curious passers-by walked beyond hearing. Then, lowering his voice, he said, "I've got some stuff here. I need to get rid of it quickly."

"What stuff? What is you got, eh?"

"Open the door and you'll find out — but be quick or we'll *all* be in trouble."

There were a few moments of silence before Marcus' heard the sound of heavy bolts being drawn back.

"What you got?" Oskar Gropius wasted no time on niceties. Neither did he mention Maisie. Many of his customers spent long periods of their life in gaol. While they were out he would offer a friendly smile and a 'no questions' payment for their goods. When they were in prison he forgot even their names. It was better so.

Picking through the bundle Marcus had brought for him, Gropius looked up in disbelief, "Clothes? All you have to offer me is *clothes*?"

"They're good clothes. They cost me a small fortune."

The pawnbroker snorted in derision. Pulling

open a drawer he took out a small metal box and removed a five pound note. "Here, they're not worth so much, but I'm being generous because of who once wore them."

When Oskar Gropius turned to place the box back inside the drawer Marcus hit him with the lead-filled bludgeon that had been intended for another victim that evening.

The blow landed awkwardly and the pawnbroker was only knocked to his knees. When he looked up at Marcus there was no fear in his expression. Only pain — and a deep loathing — "I hope they catch you. I hope you hang by the neck and die slowly — "

Marcus hit the old man again and again. Even when Oskar Gropius stopped moaning and twitching and lay, a still, crumpled form upon the floor, Marcus's frenzy did not end until the muscles in his arm had no more strength left in them.

The key was still in the metal cash box. Turning it, Marcus opened the box and cursed his luck. He had hoped to find all the pawnbroker's takings inside. Instead there were only a few notes, eight pounds in all.

Marcus ransacked the pawnbroker's shop swiftly and thoroughly. He located a large steel safe in a back room but, unlike Maisie, Oskar Gropius had found a secure place for his money, and Marcus could not find the key.

There was little else of any great value on the premises and when Marcus let himself out of the shop he had only thirty pounds and a fairly new suit of clothes with which to face the world.

12

MARCUS did not relax until he was seated in the carriage of a train travelling towards Bristol and the close-packed jumble of London streets was replaced by a patchwork of green fields.

At Paddington railway station uniformed constables had been very much in evidence and Marcus needed to steel himself each time he walked past one of them. It was highly unlikely the body of Oskar Gropius had yet been found. Even when it was, there would be nothing immediately to link Marcus with his death. Nevertheless, Marcus felt the eyes of each constable was probing his mind in search of the guilty secret he had there.

Marcus had no plan in mind. He was heading westward, closer to the place where he could become Marcus Hooper once more, his alias remembered only in the name of the county of his birth.

But it was not time to return to Cornwall just yet. The train was carrying Marcus *Cornwall* towards Bristol. It was a city he had never visited but it would do for now.

In Bristol Marcus found lodgings at the Greyhound Inn, some little way from the heart of the city's busy dockland area. The inn was comfortable enough and Marcus soon discovered that one of the chambermaids who cleaned his room was willing — eager even — to provide him with favours far beyond the requirements of her hotel duties. Marcus found her amusing and Bristol was a fascinating city, yet it was not long before he began to tire of his aimless existence.

One night, walking back to his inn from a rather less reputable tavern on the fringe of the docks, Marcus came upon a party of celebrants leaving a well-lit and noisy tavern. By the time he had forced his way through the happy party, apologising politely, Marcus had collected two wallets and a watch.

Back at the Greyhound Inn, he examined his haul. The watch was a plain silver affair with no means of identification and he tucked it in his waistcoat pocket, standing in front of the room mirror to admire the silver chain looped across his stomach. He thought it added to his air of respectability.

When Marcus examined the contents of the wallet he was delighted to find a total of forty-three pounds in banknotes. It was a useful sum.

Had Marcus been able to read, his pleasure would have been quickly replaced by dismay. Documents in one of the wallets identified its owner as one Inspector Henry Fox of the Bristol Constabulary.

Inspector Fox was enjoying a pleasant evening out with friends, touring the city's inn when one of the party made the discovery his wallet was missing. Other members of the party immediately checked their own pockets and the loss of a pocket watch and Henry Fox's wallet came to light.

Fox had an excellent memory. He recalled the man who had passed among them when they spilled from the last inn. A man wearing London-type clothes, yet who apologised in a voice that carried the accent of Cornwall.

Smarting under the embarrassment of his own loss, the policeman determined this was one pickpocket who would not escape justice.

The following morning Marcus rose at nine still feeling pleased with life. He had a good breakfast before going for a walk. There had been a high tide that morning and he passed time watching the arrival of a number of foreign merchantmen in the city centre docks.

Returning to the inn, Marcus was climbing the stairs to his room when he was confronted by the chambermaid who shared his bed whenever circumstances allowed. Extremely agitated she clutched his arm, at the same time glancing over her shoulder fearfully. He opened his mouth to ask what was the matter but before he was able to utter a word she clasped a hand firmly over his mouth.

"Shh! Two constables are waiting in your room . . . " her hoarse whispering was interrupted as she cast another agonised glance over her shoulder. "They came looking for a man who looked and dressed like you. The landlord took them to your room. I think they found something there . . . "

Marcus cursed himself for a careless fool. After removing the money he had left the two stolen wallets hidden beneath clothes in a drawer. He should have taken them out with him this morning and cast them into the murky waters of the dock . . . Not that it would have made any difference. They had his description. Someone must have seen him dip into the pockets of his victims the previous evening.

At that moment there was the sound of a door opening in the corridor beyond the top of the stairs and Marcus could hear a man's voice.

"It's them! The constables!"

Marcus waited to hear no more. He went down the stairs in headlong flight. Charging through the inn lounge to the door he scattered startled guests and customers from his path.

He never stopped running until the noise of the busy thoroughfares at the heart of the city faded far behind him. Breathing heavily he leaned against a wall and looked about him. He was in an old and dingy part of the city. Mopping a handkerchief over his face he tried to think of his next move. The first thing was to change his clothes. The police had a description of those he was wearing.

Marcus found a second-hand clothes shop, run by an old woman. She had the appearance of a half-wit, but her business acumen would have done credit to a London street trader.

The woman sold Marcus an outfit of clothes that might once have belonged to a sailor, except that a sailor would never have spent the money on them that she charged. Well-worn, the garments still had plenty of life in them and he offered his own, far superior clothes in exchange. She refused, suggesting he should look elsewhere. Reluctantly he was forced to accept her deal, leaving his London clothes for her to 'pass on to a rag-and-bone dealer'.

Leaving the shop owner carefully brushing off the suit prior to displaying it on a hanger in the shop window, Marcus set off in the direction of the railway station.

There were constables here but they took no notice of Marcus, taken in by his new identity. Bristol was a seaport, merchant seamen commonplace.

Marcus excited no more attention at the ticket office when he bought a third-class ticket to Plymouth, another great seaport. Had anyone paused to think about him they would have assumed he was a sailor leaving his ship at Bristol and travelling to Plymouth to board another.

An hour later Marcus was on a train steaming out of the station, heading along the broad gauge line towards the port that lay just short of Cornwall's borders.

Marcus found a lodging-house not far from Plymouth Hoe. It was not as comfortable as the Greyhound Inn, but he felt less conspicuous there. He could drink in the sea-front beerhouses without needing to put on an act and pretending to be someone he was not.

There were easier pickings here too: merchant seamen from all the ports of the world, many of them strangers in England, and sailors from the men-of-war moored in the nearby Royal Navy dockyard. Some had just been paid off after two or more years abroad. Marcus learnt to recognise such men. He discovered that with patience it was possible to follow the sailor to a quiet spot and relieve him of his hard-earned money.

Marcus remained in Plymouth for six weeks. During this time he acquired more money than he spent. Careful not to become too familiar with his fellow-lodgers, he allowed no one to see his money, which for safety's sake he carried with him at all times.

One night Marcus had kept watch on a homecoming sailor for more than three hours before the man left the beerhouse where they were both customers. Marcus followed as the sailor weaved an erratic course towards the nearby Barbican where there were more women to be found in the beerhouses.

The sailor disappeared into an alleyway lit only by a single, defective gas-lamp which hung at a dangerous angle from the wall, and Marcus closed in. He was about to draw the bludgeon from his pocket when he heard a sound behind him. He spun around — but was too slow. A pair of muscular arms went about him, pinning his own arms to his side.

Marcus was dragged back to the dim, inefficient gas-lamp where four men dressed as sailors were waiting.

"Is this him?"

One of the sailors asked the question, at the same time tangling his fingers in Marcus's hair, pulling his head back so the feeble yellow light shone on his face.

Another man, fear showing on his face peered at Marcus closely, "That's the one . . . At least, I *think* it is."

"What's going on? I've never seen any of you before. I'm just a poor Cornishman, stranded here for the night. I've got little money left and I'll be on my way home again in the morning."

"Shut up! Hold him tight while I search him. We'll soon see whether we've the right cove, or not."

It took the speaker only a few moments to find the lead-filled bludgeon, hidden in Marcus's inside pocket.

"Well, well, well! And what's a 'poor, stranded Cornishman' doing with this in his pocket, eh?"

"It's for killing fish. Sometimes we get a shark in the nets. They fetch good money in the right places. They need to be stunned before they're brought on board . . ."

"You hear that, lads? He uses it to stun sharks!"

Suddenly the speaker shook the bludgeon in Marcus's face, "You're a liar, mister! I'll tell you what you use this for. You use it to batter poor, half-drunk seamen unconscious, so you can rob 'em of their pay. *That's* what it's for, matey."

This last assertion was accompanied by a tap with the bludgeon that was hard enough to be painful.

"No, you're wrong! I've told you. I only came to Plymouth today . . ."

"Well now, I've seen you in beerhouses at least twice this week, and Charlie watched you walk out after a shipmate of ours who was picked up unconscious only half an hour later with all his money missing. Tonight we saw you doing the same thing. If we hadn't been behind you I

317

don't doubt it would have ended in the same way. You're a thief, matey. A lying, coshing, coward of a thief, at that . . . "

Marcus thought he felt an almost imperceptible slackening of the arms about him. Throwing his arms wide with all his strength, he broke the man's grip and scattered the surprised sailors. He might have escaped had he not tripped over someone's foot.

Marcus scrambled to his feet but the sailors were upon him. Fighting desperately, he was beaten to the ground with his own bludgeon.

When he regained consciousness, Marcus was alone, lying on his back in a gutter in the centre of the dimly lit alleyway. There was the taste of blood in his mouth and his body felt as though it had been subjected to a severe kicking. His first thought was for the money he had in a bag fastened to a string about his waist, beneath his shirt.

It was gone! The shirt front was torn, the string cut from about his waist. Marcus's pockets had been rifled too, the linings turned inside out. He groaned. Every penny he had in the world was gone.

Standing up with difficulty, Marcus groaned again, but this time the cause was physical pain. His head hurt from the battering he had taken and every muscle in his body cried out in protest. What was worse, someone had trodden on the fingers of his right hand. It felt as though two of them had been broken. It could be the result of an accident, or it might have been deliberate. Either way the result was the same. Marcus would

318

pick no pockets for a long time to come.

Marcus spent that night in an empty fish cellar on the waterfront in the company of two vagrants, both of whom stank far worse than the cellar. The next morning he prevailed upon a ferryman to convey him across the River Tamar to Cornwall, pleading he had been robbed while on a visit to Plymouth and pointing to his bloody face and swollen fingers as corroboration of his story.

The ferryman was sceptical. He had heard many such stories before and Marcus looked little different from the hundreds of vagrants he encountered when carrying out his duties. Nevertheless, there could be no doubting that Marcus was as Cornish as the ferryman. As there was only one other passenger in the boat the ferryman agreed to take Marcus across the river to Cornwall.

For two months more Marcus lived the life of a vagrant. In common with his fellows he begged or stole in order to survive. His fingers mended, but they would always be stiff. Never again would he be able to practise his skill as a pickpocket.

Gradually Marcus gravitated closer to the moor from whence he had originated. By the time he finally arrived there he had gathered about him a gang of men who threw terror into all law-abiding citizens who met up with them.

On the moor they stole an occasional sheep, or begged food from remote farmers and cottagers too frightened to deny them anything for which they asked.

One day Marcus saw two riders far out on the

moor and hid himself in the midst of a gorse thicket. As the riders drew near he recognised Lottie. It was at this moment he formulated his plan to return to the home and family from which he had been an absent husband and father for so many years.

It was time to leave the past behind and become Marcus Hooper once more.

13

"I SEE you recognise me, girl. Well, haven't you anything to say for yourself? How about, 'Welcome home, Uncle Marcus'?"

Pinned to the ground, Lottie tried to keep her fear from showing as she looked up into Marcus's face, "Why have you come back? What do you want?"

"I'll be the one to ask questions — and you'd better have answers for 'em, or I'll turn you over to my friends here. They've been wanting to get to know you ever since we first saw you riding with that fine, fancy friend of yours. If you're anything like your mother you might like to enjoy their company *before* we have our little chat. What's it to be, eh?"

His words brought howls of approval from the ragged men who stood looking down upon Lottie. One, slow-speaking in the manner of a simpleton, said, "Let's have her first, Marcus. You said we might if we helped you catch her. I ain't never had one like her before . . . not one who's all clean and pretty."

"Shut up!"

The growled order silenced Marcus's companions and he returned his attention to Lottie. "Where's Patience? What's she been doing while I've been . . . away?"

"Same as she did when you were here. Earning money to keep herself and your kids."

321

Marcus laid a forearm across Lottie's throat and applied enough pressure to cause her to choke. "Don't you try to be clever at my expense, girl. You're too far from home for that. Where's your ma — and don't you try lying to me."

"How should *I* know where she is? No one's seen her since she left Henwood with you."

"Left with me? Is that what folk think? No, girl, you've got it all wrong. She ran off with all the union money and I went after her to get it back! I'd given her the money to look after for me, you see. I thought with all the money she was keeping at the Cheesewring Inn she'd have a safer place for it than I had. Then I found she'd run off with my money — the Cheesewring's too, I didn't doubt. I went after her, to get it back. Followed her all the way to London, but I couldn't find her. I tried, mind. Been searching all these years, following rumours from one place to another. I suppose I should have come back, or let folk know what I was doing, but I was ashamed, you see. Ashamed of what Henwood folk would think of me."

Lottie knew Marcus was lying. He had never cared a damn what Henwood folk, or any other folk, thought about him. Wisely, she said nothing.

"Did the police search for your ma for long?"

"They *never* looked for her — nor for you neither. You could have come back years ago for all anybody cared."

"What d'you mean, they never looked for us? What about the money your ma stole from the Cheesewring Inn? They must have gone after her for that, same as I did."

"No reason why they should. Any money that

322

was missing belonged to Waldo Davey, and he was away looking after his sick mother. When he came back he found he owed so much money to the brewery he upped and went in the night — just like you and ma. He was the one the police were looking for, but they never found him. Some miners came back from Australia a year or two back and said they'd seen him out there, working on a sheep farm."

Marcus was devastated. Jane Trago would never face retribution for stealing Waldo Davey's money, yet because of her *he* had spent seven years in prison. Seven wasted, humiliating years . . .

"What about the union money? What happened about that?"

"It seems the union wasn't legal, so it couldn't own any funds. If it *had* no funds they couldn't be stolen, could they?"

Marcus stared down at her, unable to take in the information she had just given him.

"Anyway, Uncle Josh paid the union what they'd lost — and Jethro paid him back half over the next few years. So you see, unless you do something stupid now you're not wanted by anyone. Not by the union, the police — nor by Aunt Patience if she has any sense."

"Watch your tongue, girl." Marcus leaned on her throat again. "Will you keep it still about me and my friends if I let you go?"

Lottie nodded stiffly, unable to speak and Marcus raised his arm from her throat, "In that case you can do something for me. Tell Patience I'm back. Tell her I've learned my lesson and

323

want to come back to her. Ask her if she'll stand by me."

Lottie could not keep the scorn she felt for Marcus Hooper from her voice, "You've been away for more than seven years without bothering to send a word to her — yet now you've the gall to ask Patience if she'll have you back? You've got a nerve!"

"Do as I tell you, d'you hear? If you want to be able to ride around with your fine friend you'll do your damnedest to persuade Patience to take me back. Horse-riding!" Marcus spat his disgust at the ground, "Does that brother of yours ride a horse too?"

Marcus's question caught Lottie off guard. As she remembered the brutal way this man had treated Jacob her eyes filled with tears, "He's dead. He died the night you and ma run off together."

"I've told you, we never went off together. You'd do well to remember that. So Jacob's dead, eh? Best thing that could have happened to him. He always was a weakling."

At that moment Lottie hated Marcus Hooper more than she had ever hated him before. More than she had ever hated anyone, but she dared not allow it show now.

Suddenly Marcus released her and stood up. He looked down at her as she brushed grass and dust from her clothes. "You go and speak to Patience — today. Now. Tell her I want to come home. Then come back here and tell me what she says."

"How do I find you when I've got Patience's answer?"

"Just come up to the moor, same as you've been doing these past few days. I'll find *you* — but be sure you do come back. If I have to come looking for you I'll have you before giving you over to the others — and I'd enjoy that."

The vagrant Lottie had decided was a simpleton began to protest loudly, "Don't let her go away, Marcus. We helped you catch her. You said we could have her when you'd finished with her — "

Marcus cuffed the other man so hard he staggered backward drunkenly, "I've told you twice to keep quiet. I won't tell you again."

To Lottie, Marcus said, "You'd better go before young Seth gets out of hand. His last love was a ferret he stole from someone's back yard. He crushed it to death because it wouldn't answer when he spoke to it."

As Lottie rode away the vagrants were still laughing at the memory of Seth's foolishness.

Lottie was badly shaken by her encounter with Marcus. She had been lucky to escape from the ordeal with no more than a bruised throat. She was also confused and uncertain what to do about Patience. Lottie had refused to speak to her aunt since the night of Jacob's death, seven years before. She had no wish to speak to her now, but Lottie had no illusions about what might happen to her if she failed to carry out Marcus Hooper's instructions.

Josh was standing in the garden of the house when Lottie returned to Sharptor and unsaddled her horse in the adjacent field. He was waiting to take the saddle from her at the gate and looked at her in concern. "Are you all right, Lottie? You're as pale as if you've just seen a ghost."

"Perhaps I have, Uncle Josh."

Grateful for the opportunity to share her experience with someone, Lottie told Josh of her encounter with Marcus and his friends, leaving out details of the method he had employed to ensure she paid attention to what he had to say.

"Are you quite certain it was Marcus? I mean, after seven years you could be excused for making a mistake . . . "

"It was no mistake. I've just met Marcus. What's more he wants to return to Patience. He's asked me to speak to her. To ask her to have him back."

"I can't believe it . . . To come back after so long. What's he been doing?"

Lottie repeated what Marcus had told her, adding, "I don't believe him. I still think he and ma ran off together. Either she gave him the slip or they ran out of money. Anyway, he's back now. What do you think I should do?"

"You're going to have to speak to Patience. I'll come with you. Miriam and Nell are down at her house visiting right now. If Patience has any sense she'll say she wants nothing more to do with Marcus. If she does, I'll get some miners together and run him off the moor. But if Patience had that much sense she'd have found herself a good man to take Marcus's place before now. My guess is she'll have him back."

When Lottie and Josh reached Patience's small home Miriam and Nell were about to return to Sharptor. The room into which Lottie and Josh

326

were shown was in a chaotic state. It did not appear to have been tidied for many days.

The three women in the room were taken by surprise at Lottie's arrival. Everyone in the village knew Lottie blamed her aunt for contributing to Jacob's death and had not set foot inside the house for more than seven years. Patience stared at her niece, uncertain whether she should throw her arm about Lottie in welcome, or order her from the house.

In the end she did nothing and it was left to Josh to break the awkward silence, "Patience, Lottie has something to say to you. It's about Marcus."

Fear replaced uncertainty and Patience's eyes widened, "You've heard from Jane . . . from your ma. He's dead, isn't he? Marcus is dead?"

As tears welled up into her aunt's eyes, Lottie looked at her disdainfully. "It would be better for everyone if he was. No, Marcus is back. I met him on the moor not an hour since. He wants to return to this house. To you."

Three times Patience attempted to speak, but speech was beyond her. Suddenly she began to cry like a child and Miriam moved in to comfort her.

After some twenty minutes Patience's blubbering had eased to the point where it was possible to carry out a conversation in the same room. Josh made Lottie repeat what Marcus had said about coming home, and his reasons for staying away for so long.

"Of *course* I'll have him back. He's my husband. The father of my children. But what about . . . the things everyone said he did?" Now the wide, watery eyes were turned upon Josh.

"What things? The Union's been paid back and Waldo Davey's long gone. Folk will talk, but I don't doubt Marcus has survived worse while he's been away. All the same, be sure it's what you really want, Patience."

"Of course I do! Go and find him, Lottie? Tell him to come back to us?"

"Hallelujah!"

Startled, everyone in the room turned towards Nell who had cried out with joy.

"Hallelujah, I say! This is a glad occasion. A time to praise the Lord. The prodigal has returned. Hallelujah!"

"I seem to remember the prodigal son returned home filled with meekness and humility. That description certainly doesn't fit Marcus Hooper. He's the *devil*'s man. Henwood will rue this day, you mark my words."

With this declaration of her opinion, Lottie walked out of the house, leaving the others staring after her.

14

THE return of Marcus Hooper to the bosom of his family was no more than a five minute wonder in Henwood. The novelty was soon over, too, for Marcus's children. The youngest of the three girls, Kate had been only a year old when her father had left home and Mary had been five. In between was Emma, then aged three. Only Mary had a vague memory of the man who now moved in to dominate the household.

At first they were as excited as Lottie and Jacob had been about the return of Jane Trago. Gradually they became more sullen, resenting the attention their mother paid Marcus at their expense. They began to appear with large bruises, too, and neighbours nodded their heads knowingly. Marcus Hooper had always been heavy-handed with those about him.

If he heard the remarks, Marcus gave no sign that he cared. Josh had given him work at the Sharptor mine and Marcus went about his business taking little notice of his workmates. They displayed an equal indifference to him. He was not popular and few men took pains to hide their feelings.

Marcus's task on the mine was to keep the furnaces burning in the calciner. It was hot and thirsty work and gave him an excuse for spending much of his money on drink. Not that he was alone in this respect. Many other miners did the same.

329

When he first returned, some men brought up the circumstances of his hasty departure, using it as an excuse to pick a fight with him. They quickly learned that fighting with Marcus was a foolish and painful experience. Years in prison had left him a vicious and determined fighter. No man in the area was any match for him.

One day police Superintendent Kingsley Coote paid a visit to the Sharptor mine. He had heard of Marcus Hooper's return to the area and wanted to have a few words with him. He spoke to Marcus for an hour and a half without learning anything new. No, Marcus had not known the extent of Jane Trago's dishonesty. Yes, he had gone after her with the sole intention of getting back the union's money. Indeed, he had followed rumours of her whereabouts that led him from London to the coalfields of Yorkshire and the north of England. No, he could not remember any specific addresses where he had lodged.

Afterwards the police superintendent visited Josh in the mine office. It was the end of the day and Jethro was just finishing off his day's accounts.

"Did you get any of the answers you wanted from Marcus?" Josh asked the policeman.

"Not one. That man's so adept at evading questions I'm amazed he ever got through a wedding ceremony."

"Do you think he was actually lying to you?"

"Through his teeth. When a man's been away for seven years he usually wants to tell everyone of the things he's seen. Marcus Hooper won't say a word of where he's been, or what he did. It's

330

my guess he has something to hide and I won't rest until I've found out what it is."

"Does it matter?"

"To me it does. Marcus Hooper is a hard man — and it wasn't mining made him that way."

Jethro slid a large, leather-bound ledger into a drawer of the desk at which he had been working, turned a key in the lock and stood up.

"If you don't need me any more I'll be going."

Jethro's expression gave no hint of his thoughts on the police superintendent's comments about Marcus.

"Of course. See you in the morning, Jethro."

Murmuring a polite good evening to the superintendent, Jethro walked from the office. When he had gone, Kingsley Coote said, "You employ a number of men others wouldn't care to have about them, Mr Retallick."

"I'm fortunate to be able to employ anyone, Superintendent. Not many mines can these days. But you were talking of Marcus Hooper, or do you have someone else in mind?"

"I'm talking of the other man involved in collecting funds for the miners' union at the time Marcus Hooper and the money went missing. The reason there'll never be a prosecution is merely a technical one. Stealing money is a felony in my book, no matter who it's stolen from."

"Jethro Shovell had nothing to do with the disappearance of the money. Even so, he spent the next few years repaying half the loss. He's a fine young man. An honest, God-fearing young man who cares for others."

"It's often the well-meaning people who give me most trouble, Mr Retallick. It's no doubt the reason why your Jethro Shovell is spending time listening to the grievances of the Gunnislake miners. He'd do well to keep away from the Gunnislake area. If you have a regard for the young man, you'll tell him so. Find some extra work to keep him here. The police are often accused of persecuting the trade unions. We don't, but I am against what they're doing. Giving a man ideas above his station is no good for anyone. If your young purser is a man of religion he'll know the way to salvation is through hard work. It's as true today as when my father used to tell it to me. Mind you, there's little enough work to go around in Cornwall these days. Some of my colleagues are inclined to say, 'Good riddance to the miners,' declaring we'll have a quieter life without them. But, like yourself, I'm from a mining family. I believe the mines and those who work in them are the very heart of Cornwall. If ever they're lost altogether then Cornwall, as we know it, will die."

Superintendent Kingsley Coote rose stiffly to his feet, "I'm getting too old to be spending so much time in the saddle. I'll bid you good day. I'll no doubt be seeing you again before very long."

"Good evening, Superintendent. I'm sorry your ride was wasted today."

"Did I say that? Oh no, it certainly hasn't been wasted. Marcus Hooper may have told me precious little about himself, but he let enough slip about his late companions to arouse my interest. I'm bringing in the militia to make

332

a sweep of the moors hereabouts. You'll sleep safer in your bed at night when Marcus Hooper's friends are behind bars — and perhaps some of those we flush out will be able to tell us a little more about Mr Hooper himself."

Watching Kingsley Coote riding away, Josh was glad the police superintendent was not after *him*. He was a dogged and determined man. If Marcus Hooper had something to hide he would need to have covered his tracks well.

Winter came early to the moorland communities in 1871. Snow fell during the first week of December and remained on the tors and in the shadowed gullies for much of the season.

One of the weather's first victims was Henwood's Methodist minister, Wrightwick Roberts. Now in his eighty-fourth year, the indomitable old man slipped and fractured his ankle while on his way to conduct a mid-week evening service. Carried back to his house by two burly miners, the old preacher's main concern was that the Lord's work should not be disrupted as a result of his misfortune. Not until Jethro came to the house and assured Wrightwick he would conduct the service with Nell's help did the old preacher take to his bed and await the arrival of a doctor.

It would be a long wait. So many mines in the vicinity had closed, those remaining could not afford to employ their own doctor. The nearest now was at St Cleer, some miles distant. It would not be safe to send anyone floundering through the snow until daylight.

Jethro and Nell were quite capable of

administering to the spiritual needs of Henwood's Methodist community, but not everyone approved of having a woman preacher. It was an issue that had helped bring about fragmentation of the Methodist Church elsewhere. Primitive Methodism, eager to use any means to take God to the people, used women preachers. So too did Bible Christians. The Wesleyan Methodist movement remained more conservative. Women preachers were still a rarity. Nell Gilmore was only allowed to preach because Wrightwick Roberts said she could — and he was not a man with whom to argue. He had been their minister for fifty years and the Henwood villagers respected the old preacher's wisdom and goodness too much to question his decisions.

For many years the Reverend Solomon Bligh, superintendent minister of the Methodist circuit which included Henwood, had wanted to replace Wrightwick Roberts. Such was the popularity of the aged minister, however, that Bligh had dared do nothing. He knew he would have to wait until Wrightwick Roberts died or, far less likely, took a decision to retire. If Bligh acted precipitately he knew there was a danger of losing the whole community. For many years Bligh had been forced to contain his growing disapproval of Wrightwick Roberts's preaching methods, powerless to take any action. Now, at last, he believed the opportunity had arrived.

The Sunday after Wrightwick Roberts's accident Solomon Bligh rode through the snow to Henwood village. He arrived at the injured minister's house two hours before the evening service. After an hour Bligh came to the cottage door and asked a child playing in the street to go and fetch Jethro Shovell.

As Jethro disappeared inside Wrightwick Roberts's house the villagers watched unashamedly from their doorways and windows. They saw lamps lit in the bedroom where Wrightwick Roberts lay and the shadows of the visitors on the curtains.

Five minutes before the service was due to start, the superintendent minister emerged from the house, a well-worn Bible tucked beneath his arm, Jethro Shovell at his side. As the two men made their way through the snow to the small church, the villagers extinguished the lamps in their own homes and followed them. All knew this would be a momentous occasion.

The chapel was filled to overflowing. Every seat was occupied and villagers stood in the aisles, and in the doorway. No one who could walk was absent.

Jethro conducted the service and then handed over the pulpit to Solomon Bligh for the sermon. Preaching on the theme, 'Only The Lord is immortal', Bligh talked at such great length that even the most dedicated chapelgoer began to fidget.

Not until he had thoroughly exhausted his theme did the superintending minister bring his sermon to an end with an echoed and fervent 'Amen' from his congregation.

Gazing about the chapel, Solomon Bligh nodded his approval, "It warms my heart in this cold weather to see so many of you here for this service — yet I am sad it should be on such an occasion as this. When my duty requires me to announce the end of a ministry of service to the Lord that is unequalled in my own long experience.

"You all know of Minister Roberts's accident, of course, and the seriousness of such an injury to a man of his years. I had a long talk with Minister Roberts before coming here tonight and it is with the deepest regret that I must tell you I have accepted his resignation as your minister."

The sigh that rose from the congregation reminded Jethro of the noise made when the moorland wind played in the scaffolding about the new calciner chimney at the Sharptor mine. Both signified change. A new and unfamiliar order of things.

Wrightwick Roberts *had* indeed tendered his resignation, but only after a great deal of pressure had been brought to bear on him by the superintending minister. Not until Wrightwick Roberts was warned that the people of Henwood would effectively be without a minister during his slow recovery did the aged man finally surrender.

The Reverend Solomon Bligh went on to inform the Henwood congregation that Jethro had been asked to take care of the chapel and its people until a new minister was appointed.

Jethro had agreed to take on the temporary responsibility, but he was secretly concerned about the appointment of a new minister. He was aware that Solomon Bligh thought Wrightwick Roberts allowed his part-time preachers too much responsibility.

Wrightwick Roberts, on the other hand, scornfully dismissed Bligh as a Methodist 'bishop'. He pointed out that in the towns where Bligh had spent all his years the chapels were attended by an increasingly affluent congregation. In the villages, especially the mining villages of Cornwall, affluence had passed them by. 'Threadbare but clean' was the description for Sunday-best clothes here.

Jethro hoped the new minister would be 'country' and not 'town'.

"A penny for them, Jethro."

Lottie's words startled Jethro, so wrapped up was he in his thoughts. He was walking home from the chapel and Lottie fell in beside him.

"Why are you looking so worried? Is it the responsibility of taking over the chapel? I thought you'd be delighted Wrightwick chose you."

"I am. I was worrying about the new minister. I hope that whoever he is, he'll understand our ways."

"You mean, you hope he'll let our Nell carry on preaching? Everyone knows Minister Bligh isn't in favour of women preachers. If he appoints someone who thinks the same way then Holy Nell will be out."

"You shouldn't poke fun at her, Lottie. No . . . Nell has worked hard for the Church in Henwood. If it weren't for her we'd be losing members, same as most Methodist chapels around here — and that includes Minister Bligh's own chapel."

"You have to thank Uncle Josh for that, too.

If he wasn't keeping the Sharptor mine working the Henwood miners would go abroad to earn a living, same as so many others from Cornwall."

"True." Jethro thought it time he led the conversation away from Nell. Lottie and Nell Gilmore did not get along and neither could see any good in the other. "I was pleased to see you in chapel today. You haven't attended very often just lately."

"No, I ride with Hawken most Sundays. It's the only day he has free."

Jethro was quiet for some minutes, then he said, "Putting Hawken Strike before the Church must mean he's important to you, Lottie."

"He's fun, I like him."

Lottie's reply left Jethro feeling empty inside, and decidedly unhappy. "Don't get *too* fond of him. You and me live in one world, Hawken Strike belongs to another. I'd hate to see you get hurt."

"We can none of us go through life without being hurt by *someone*, Jethro Shovell. Hawken Strike won't be the first man to hurt me."

With this ambiguous remark, Lottie stalked off through the snow towards Sharptor, leaving Jethro staring after her, wondering why his warning had upset her so much. It had been given with the best of intentions.

Shrugging his shoulders in bafflement, Jethro took the track that led to a small line of cottages built on the hillside. He had been born here and had never been away from Henwood. He was twenty-four years old now and was beginning to think he would never be able to go anywhere else. Long ago, when thinking of his future, he had expected to be married before this — but he had always expected too much from life.

Seven years ago he had hoped to make a career in the trade union movement, then struggling for a foothold in the industries. Jethro had dreamed of one day leading a miners' union to respectability and increased status in Cornwall. Improving life for men who, like his father, could look forward only to ill-health in their retirement.

Marcus Hooper had put an end to *that* dream for a long time. Josh Retallick had reimbursed the miners' union for the money taken by Marcus — or by Jane Trago, if Marcus's story was to be believed — but not before the union had sent an official to Cornwall to enquire into the loss. Jethro had been cleared of any dishonesty, but his naivety was strongly criticised and he was only now making up the ground he had lost as a result of that unfortunate incident.

Preaching also meant a great deal to Jethro. Had his circumstances been different he would have liked to be considered for the ministry. Unfortunately it would have meant living away from home, earning a mere pittance. He could not afford to do this. Jethro's money was the Shovell household's only income. It was needed for his mother and elderly, sick father.

Jethro had not married for the same reason. A year or so ago he had wanted to ask Lottie to marry him. He still would, if things were different. But Lottie and his mother did not get along with each other and he could not afford to run *two* homes.

More recently he and Lottie seemed to have drifted apart. It caused him great unhappiness and he became very depressed at times because Lottie meant more to him than anyone else — but still he could not tell her. It would not be fair.

He tried to accept that Lottie would one day marry someone else, but he found the thought unbearable. Yet there seemed to be nothing he could do about the situation.

Letting himself into the house Jethro heard his father's desperate coughing coming from the bedroom. His mother was there too. Jethro could hear her soothing voice as she sat her husband upright and massaged his back.

Hanging his hat and coat behind the kitchen door, Jethro walked heavily upstairs, calling as he went, asking if he could be of any help . . .

15

THE Reverend Wilberforce Beckett might have been especially created to the order of Superintendent Minister Solomon Bligh. Small and bespectacled, he was fresh from a long period spent on mainly clerical duties at the Churches' City Road Mission in London and he bitterly resented being sent to a Cornish backwater.

One of his duties had been to take notes at the many meetings held by the ministers of the London circuit, men who influenced the policy-making of the Methodist Church. Wilberforce Beckett had listened for many hours to the arguments propounded by the most brilliant theorists in the Methodist movement. Following every argument and counter-argument studiously, Beckett was convinced that he, more than any other Wesleyan Methodist minister realised where the true future lay for the movement.

It was for this reason Beckett had thrown in his lot with those who placed consolidation and respectability ahead of evangelism. He believed mainstream Methodism would win through and successfully cast off the image of a working-class movement. His reasoning had the weight of history to back it up. Popular movements tended to burn with a fierce but brief flame. Wesleyan Methodism would have a much longer life.

Wilberforce was a cold, but very efficient little

man. Although he was quick to pay his respects to the ailing Wrightwick Roberts, he declined to lodge in his house, preferring to take an empty cottage on the far side of the village. He did not want to be in the ageing minister's debt, neither did he want others to think he had anything in common with the man he had succeeded.

A few days after his arrival, the Reverend Wilberforce Beckett paid a visit to the Retallicks' Sharptor home. Josh had been expecting him, the minister had already visited a number of mine captains and owners in the area.

Miriam and Josh entertained the minister to tea and they spoke about the inclement weather and the poor price of tin and copper before the minister asked whether Nell was in the house.

"No," Miriam answered as she poured more tea for the minister. "She's ridden to Liskeard with Lottie, my niece, and Hawken Strike, who owns a share in Josh's mine."

"Ah yes, I've heard of Hawken Strike from some of my London friends. I intend paying him a visit as soon as the weather improves sufficiently to take a pony and trap on the roads."

Taking the tea from her, Wilberforce Beckett nodded his thanks. "It's rather a pity Nell isn't here. She has a most interesting, albeit sad, background, I believe."

"Yes, her parents died on mission work in Africa. She and her young sister were the sole survivors from a large party."

"That would explain her keen interest in preaching. Wishing to follow the example set by her parents is highly commendable. However,

342

I am not in favour of women preachers. They drive salacious men towards the devil, rather than to Our Lord. However, if this girl has had a reasonable education — and I have no doubt at all you will both have attended to *that* — I'll find a place for her. She can teach the girls in Sunday school — at least, until she marries and takes her rightful place in her own home."

The explosion Josh anticipated from Miriam did not occur. Instead, she asked, "You are married, of course, Minister?"

"Alas, no. My dedication to the Methodist movement has left me little time to find someone who might provide me with those comforts I envy when I visit homes like yours."

"I'm sure you'll find someone one day, Minister. The world must be full of girls who ask no more from life than to provide home comforts for a man who understands women as you do. No doubt she'll have the opportunity to teach Sunday school too — if she has sufficient education, of course."

The Reverend Wilberforce Becket paused with the cup held halfway to his mouth and looked suspiciously at Miriam. Then his expression cleared, "Yes, no doubt . . ." Returning his attention to Josh, he said, "You have experienced no trade union troubles here."

"None at all."

"I'm pleased to hear it, Mr Retallick. One hears all too often of labour problems in areas where Methodism is strongest. I blame the Primitives, of course. Their disregard for discipline encourages men to rebel against authority. We were quite

343

right to expel them from the Methodist Church. Unfortunately, we are all too frequently blamed for their shortcomings. We must all work hard for respectability, Mr Retallick. It gives me great pleasure to know I have men like you in my flock. Men who understand the needs of our Church. Thank you for your hospitality, Missus Retallick. I look forward to welcoming you to my chapel on Sunday, when I shall be putting my views on the future to the Henwood Methodists."

Returning to the house after walking Wilberforce Beckett to the gate, Josh found Miriam in the kitchen, noisily bringing pans from a cupboard and banging them down with considerable force upon the kitchen table.

"What are you doing?" Josh asked, in all innocence.

"What do you *think* I'm doing? I'm busying myself in the kitchen as a 'good little woman' should. Out of my way, or you might end up with a skillet dropped on your toe — or somewhere even more painful!"

"Steady on!" Josh protested as Miriam brushed forcefully past him, causing him to take two backward paces across the kitchen. "My name's not Wilberforce Beckett."

Miriam glared at him for a moment or two then her body relaxed and a sheepish smile came to her face. "I'm sorry, Josh. That man made me *so* angry. What is the Church thinking of, sending a man like Beckett to a Cornish mining area? Why, he wouldn't be accepted if he were *Cornish*."

Josh hugged Miriam. "You and I have known

344

worse ministers, Miriam. We've also met very much better ones."

He kissed Miriam before releasing her, "I'm going to have a word with Wrightwick." Suddenly smiling, he said, "I shall expect you to have a meal waiting for me when I return. If you can throw in a hymn or two I'll recommend you to our new preacher for his Sunday school . . . !"

Wrightwick Roberts was seated in a chair by the window of his small cottage. He had once been a large and powerful man but now Josh thought the aged preacher looked like a man whose skin had been hung carelessly over his frame. However, his mind was still as clear as ever.

When Josh casually introduced the subject of the Reverend Wilberforce Beckett into the conversation, Wrightwick said, "I know what you're going to say, Josh. You think Beckett is the wrong man for us here."

"Don't you?"

"I did when I first met him. Now I'm not so certain. I've been here so long I sometimes wonder whether I really see things as they are, or as I want them to be. It might be a good thing to have an outsider come in and take a critical look at us."

"Miriam wouldn't agree with you — and our Nell certainly won't. Beckett won't have women preachers, although he might consider bending just a little and allowing her to teach in Sunday school . . . "

Wrightwick Roberts's grin revealed that he still possessed most of his teeth, "Be thankful for small mercies, Josh. Had it been Lottie who'd taken up preaching instead of Nell both you and Wilberforce Beckett would have had trouble on your hands."

"It's still likely we will. There's a determined side to Nell's character that's not seen too often, but her preaching means a great deal to her. I wouldn't be surprised to see her become a Primitive Methodist. If she goes, Jethro might go too — and half the village with them."

"You could be right, Josh. Yes indeed, you could well be right."

Josh looked at the old preacher in amazement. "You sound neither surprised, nor concerned. After all your years of work . . . ?"

"All my years were spent bringing our people closer to God. I like to think I've had some success. But the years I enjoyed most, and the years when I *know* I was succeeding, were my early years as a preacher. Your pa will remember the miles I'd tramp. In those days I'd hold a service if even two people stopped still long enough to listen to me. Those were rewarding days. What I was doing then is what the Primitives are doing today. Going out and saving souls. Not going to chapel each Sunday to preach to those who are already saved. There was a time when I thought I might become a Primitive Methodist too, Josh. I didn't — but I've never been certain I made the right decision."

"Does anyone else know how you feel?" Wrightwick Roberts's revelation had shaken Josh.

"One or two. Your pa for one. Solomon Bligh as well. He's never felt at ease having me as one of his circuit preachers. Perhaps he and Beckett

346

are right. John Wesley laid the foundation for our Church, and ministers like myself have raised the wall. It might be time to put on the roof and turn our attention to what we have inside. That's where men like Wilberforce Beckett come into their own, Josh. It might be uncomfortable for everyone in the short term, but in the long run God will have his own way."

16

JETHRO SHOVELL was arrested four days after Reverend Wilberforce Beckett denounced trade unionism as 'evil' from the pulpit of the Henwood methodist church.

It had been a cold day with a strong hint of snow in the air and as darkness closed in, Miriam and Josh, with Lottie, Nell and Anne, moved nearer the fire in the warmth of their Sharptor kitchen.

Suddenly the kitchen door opened and Jenny Shovell put her head inside the room. "Hello, is our Jethro here with you?"

"No," Josh replied to her question. "He's worked until very late these last two nights so he could take today off. He's gone to Gunnislake . . . But come in and close the door before we lose all the heat."

Jenny Shovell entered the house. Closing the door behind her she took off the shawl she wore about her head. She had brought the cold into the room with her and, shivering, she moved closer to the fire.

"I knew Jethro was going to Gunnislake but I thought he might have arrived back and come up here to see Lottie."

"*I* haven't seen him for a couple of weeks," declared Lottie sharply. "What's he doing over to Gunnislake anyway? Hawken warned him to keep away from the mines there."

"Strike's captain dropped the wages of the boys and bal-maidens by a penny a day when things were bad. Prices have picked up a bit this last week or two and they've asked to be put back on their old pay scale but the captain's refused. The boys and bal-maidens sent a message asking Jethro to go over there and speak to him on their behalf."

"You don't think he's in any trouble?" Jenny Shovell asked anxiously.

"No, Jethro's far too sensible to find trouble. I could see across to Dartmoor earlier today and it looked as though they've had recent snow that way. It might have come as far west as Gunnislake. He's probably staying with one of the mining families until he's quite sure the roads are clear. But if you're still worried in the morning I'll take a ride over there and bring him back with me."

"Thanks, Josh. You've set my mind at rest. You're right. He'd likely stay if there was any risk of being caught in snow on the way back."

"Of course Josh is right. You'll stay and have a cup of tea now you're here? Or would you like something stronger? You look as though a warming brandy would do you a power of good."

"I mustn't stop. I've left Tom sitting in front of the fire. If he falls asleep he's likely to topple from the chair."

When Jenny Shovell had left the room, Lottie said to Josh, "Do you really think Jethro's staying at Gunnislake for the night?"

"What else do you think he'd be doing?"

"I don't know, but I'm uneasy. *Very* uneasy.

349

Can't we take a ride over there tonight?"

"And risk being caught in snow on a night as black as a hundred fathom level with a gale blowing up? We could pass within ten yards of Jethro and not see him."

Josh could see Lottie was concerned and he put an arm about her shoulders. "Don't worry, Lottie. I'll go and find him in the morning. I don't doubt he'll wonder what all the fuss is about."

"I'll come with you." The offer came from Samuel Coolidge, the one-armed American, who was staying at the Retallick house for a few days. "When we've located Jethro perhaps we could have a look around the mines. I have an idea the Gunnislake mines could increase our supply of arsenic-bearing ore given enough incentive."

"We'll *all* go," declared Lottie. "If Jethro isn't at Gunnislake we'll need to search for him. The more of us there are, the better chance we'll have."

It was a grey, heavy-clouded dawn with an occasional isolated snowflake floating on the wind, hinting of more to come later in the day.

Josh, Lottie, Nell and Samuel Coolidge set off from Sharptor to ride to Gunnislake, leaving Anne Gilmore sulking in the house because Josh would not allow her to join the search party.

Josh had assured the others that Jethro must have decided to remain at Gunnislake for the night, but he was secretly extremely worried. He and Miriam had talked far into the night in the dark privacy of their bedroom. Both agreed Jethro had left early enough to make the return journey quite comfortably. Knowing there was work to be done on the Sharptor miners' pay accounts they felt certain he would not have stayed away. Something unforeseen must have occurred to delay him.

Lottie too was concerned and forced the pace of her pony. Josh frequently urged her to slow down, but by the tine they were nearing Gunnislake he and Lottie were almost half a mile ahead of the others.

Looking back, Josh saw Nell and Samuel Coolidge riding close together, the tall, slim American bending low from his saddle so as not to miss a word his companion was saying. "You know, I think Samuel is fond of our Nell."

Lottie gave an uninterested glance over her shoulder, too wrapped up in her own concern for Jethro to think of anything else, "Don't tell me you're surprised? Samuel's been keen on Nell since he first met her at least year's Liskeard Fair . . . " She had the grace to blush as memories of that day's events returned.

Aware of the reason for her embarrassment, Josh said, "I never have heard the truth of what happened to Nell that day . . . But Samuel Coolidge is probably too old for our Nell to be interested in *him*."

"He's only a few years older than Jethro and Hawken — and she's always shown plenty of interest in *them*."

"I suppose you're right."

Josh looked back at the two riders once more. Because the American had fought and lost his arm in war Josh had always regarded Samuel Coolidge as a much older man. Yet he would have been no more than twenty years of age when he received his wound in the fighting in the Shenandoah valley. The experience of losing an arm in such a manner was enough to age anyone.

Samuel Coolidge was a kindly man with a good family background. He could be a steadying influence on Nell. Her early phenomenal success as a preacher had served to make her wilful and strong-minded. More recently she had shown a tendency towards hot-headedness that had caused Josh and Miriam some concern. Yes, Samuel Coolidge's interest in Nell was something to be encouraged.

"There doesn't seem to be much happening at Gunnislake." Josh's thoughts were interrupted by Lottie's words. "Look, there's only one mine chimney smoking. What can be going on there?"

They had topped a small rise and were within sight of the Gunnislake mines. Not as extensive as the Bodmin moor mining area around Sharptor, Gunnislake nevertheless had a number of very profitable mines. There should have been much more activity.

Lottie urged her horse to a trot and Josh followed suit. Behind them, Nell and Samuel Coolidge shook out their reins and hurried to catch up.

The four riders arrived together at the entrance to the largest of the mines. A thin dusting of undisturbed snow lay on the ground and on the buildings and machinery, a clear indication that no work had been attempted that morning.

A small group of men stood in the deeply rutted road just short of the mine. They seemed uncertain whether or not to challenge the new arrivals.

"What's going on here? Why aren't the mines working?" Josh directed his questions to a squat, black-bearded man who appeared more belligerent than his companions.

"That's between us and Cap'n Vincent," replied the man, his tone of voice in keeping with his appearance. "Unless you've business here you'd best be taking the ladies off somewhere else. We're in no mood for visitors right now."

"We've come from Sharptor looking for Jethro Shovell. He left yesterday morning to come here and didn't return home last night."

"You're friends of his?" There was suspicion in the question.

"I'm Josh Retallick of the Sharptor mine, this is Samuel Coolidge, Lottie Trago and Nell Gilmore."

The squat miner's belligerent expression underwent an immediate change and the others who had been listening to the exchange from a discreet distance crowded about the riders.

"Jethro's in sore need of friends, Mr Retallick. He was arrested yesterday by a police inspector from Liskeard, acting on the orders of Cap'n Vincent."

"*Arrested!* What for?" The cry came from Lottie.

"That's a question you'll need to put to Cap'n Vincent — or perhaps to Mr Strike himself. All

353

I know is it's something to do with persuading the boys and bal-maidens to break their 'terms of employment', whatever that's supposed to mean. Anyway, 'tis a load of nonsense. They'd stopped working before young Jethro got here. All he did to get arrested was try and speak to Cap'n Vincent."

"We're wasting time! Talking together here won't get Jethro out of gaol."

Lottie knew she had to do something to help Jethro. She was not clear what needed to be done, but it was evident that nothing could be achieved at Gunnislake.

"You're right, Lottie. We'll go to Liskeard. Superintendent Coote's there for a week or two, I'll speak to him. If he's unhelpful I'll hire the best solicitor I can find on Jethro's behalf."

"While you're on your way to Liskeard I'll return to Sharptor and tell Mrs Shovell what's happening."

Lottie gave Nell a contemptuous look, "What's the matter, Nell? You scared of getting mixed up in union business because Minister Beckett stood up in the pulpit last Sunday and preached against trade unions? Whether you're for them or not isn't going to make any difference. Beckett will still come out against having women preachers in his church. He's that sort of minister."

Nell flushed angrily. "It's got nothing to do with Minister Beckett. I'll do more good comforting Mrs Shovell than I will riding to Liskeard."

"Nell's right. Will you return with her, Samuel? Tell Miriam what's happening. She'll go down and stay with Jenny until we get back. Come on, Lottie, *we'll* go to Liskeard and find out what's going on there . . . "

"You go by yourself. I'm going to see the man who can do more than either Superintendent Coote, or some old solicitor. I'm riding to speak to Hawken Strike . . . "

17

IT was fourteen miles from the Gunnislake mines to the Strike home, near Launceston. Lottie had covered less than half this distance when the snow that had been threatening Cornwall for days began to fall. It seemed likely it would settle and Lottie urged her horse on.

A strong wind accompanied the snow and by the time Lottie had covered twelve of the fourteen miles its strength had increased so much that Lottie was bowing her head into a blizzard.

Uncertain of the road, the journey rapidly became a nightmare. Twice Lottie's horse strayed from the road and once the horse slipped and both animal and rider crashed to the snow-covered ground. Lottie realised she was hopelessly lost and it came as a great relief when she detected the outline of a cottage at the side of the road.

A woman opened the door to her persistent knocking and Lottie explained she was looking for the Strike home. She was told it was no more than half a mile away. She must have passed the entrance gates along the road.

When Lottie declined an offer to take shelter in the cottage, the woman called for someone named William. After a few minutes a small, grey-whiskered man emerged from the kitchen muttering grumpily. He became even grumpier when the woman ordered him to dress and guide Lottie to the home of Hawken Strike.

His reluctance to leave the warmth of the cottage brought a tirade of abuse down upon him and a coat and hat were taken down from a hook on the door and thrust into his arms. Without further argument the grey-haired man donned the clothes, pulled on a pair of heavy boots and stomped off into the snow without a word to either woman.

For twenty minutes Lottie followed close behind the unspeaking old man. Suddenly the bulk of a large house loomed ahead, effectively shielding them from the icy, snow-laden wind. It was Hawken Strike's home.

She reached the front door and turned to thank her reluctant guide, but he was already heading homeward through the snow to the cottage and his sharp-tongued wife.

Lottie tugged at the bell-pull beside the door and fancied she could hear the bell jingling somewhere deep inside the house. She pulled on the cord once more and the door swung partly open to allow a maid to peep out at the swirling snow and call nervously, "Who's out there?"

When Lottie stepped forward into the faint light slicing through the opening and said she had come to see Hawken Strike, the maid lost her fear of what might be abroad in such a storm. Opening the door wider, she looked at Lottie in awed respect. "What on earth are you doing out in weather like this, ma'am? Why, I wouldn't want to see a rook outside in such snow. Come on inside, there's a nice fire burning in the hall. Give me that wet coat and be warning yourself while I find Master Hawken and tell him you're here."

Lottie stepped inside the house and gave up her coat, at the same time asking the maid to find someone to take care of the horse she had tied outside.

Standing in front of the huge, granite hearth in the hall, Lottie began to realise just how cold she was. As circulation returned to her hands they hurt almost unbearably.

"Who's that down there? Maisie, have you just let someone in?"

The voice of Isabelle Strike came from the top of the stairway leading from the hall.

The maid had already disappeared somewhere inside the house and Lottie called, "It's me, Mrs Strike. Lottie Trago from Sharptor. I've called to speak to Hawken."

"Lottie *who?* I don't know any Lottie. What's your business here, girl?"

At that moment Hawken Strike appeared from one of the downstairs rooms and held out his hands in greeting, "Lottie, my dear! What are you doing so far from home? And in such dreadful weather!"

"Who is it? Hawken, who have you got down there? You know I'm not supposed to keep going up and down stairs. It's not good for my heart . . . "

"It's Lottie Trago, Mother. you remember her. She's the niece of Josh Retallick, my partner in the Sharptor mine."

Considering this explanation sufficient, Hawken Strike said, "Come inside the drawing room, Lottie. I've a drink in there . . . No, don't argue. You've all the time in the world to give me

358

explanations. I don't want you catching a chill."

"That mine girl? The one who *works?* What's she doing here?"

As Hawken Strike led Lottie in the direction of the drawing-room they could hear Isabelle Strike coming down the stairs at a speed that belied the seriousness of her 'condition'.

Hawken Strike was pouring Lottie a large brandy when his mother reached the drawing-room. He would not allow Lottie to reply to his mother's repeated questions until she had drunk enough to put an end to her shivering and bring the beginnings of a glow to her face.

Lottie began her explanations haltingly but as brandy and the injustice of Jethro's arrest combined, she expressed her feelings more forcibly.

While Lottie was speaking, Isabelle Strike's indignation mounted until she could remain silent no longer, "You've ridden for hours through a raging blizzard to plead the cause of one of these . . . seditionists? A known rabble-rouser? Why? What is this man to you?"

"He's been a friend since my early childhood. At times he was my only friend. He also risked his life to save me from certain death in a fire. Jethro's no rabble-rouser. He's an honest, caring, Christian man."

Isabelle Strike began to re-assess the situation. She had no sympathy for Jethro Shovell. Whatever Lottie might say he was a dangerous trade union agitator. A man whose aim was to upset the country's traditional way of life and destroy the natural balance and authority that had been developed over centuries. He deserved to suffer the full wrath of the law.

However there were other, more important, considerations to be taken in to account. Hawken was showing more interest in this working-class girl than he had ever expressed for girls who were 'socially acceptable'. Hawken was a headstrong young man. Isabelle Strike was increasingly concerned that he might be contemplating some quixotic foolishness.

"Hmm! There *is* a possibility I have been misinformed. You are evidently very fond of this young man. Tell me something about him, my dear."

Suspicious of Isabelle Strike's apparent change of heart, Lottie nevertheless told her of Jethro's background. She spoke of his father who had been a trusted mine captain to Isabelle Strike's husband and great uncle. Of Jethro's preaching, and of his help to her when she had no one else to turn to.

For much of the time it seemed Isabelle Strike was not really listening, but when Lottie had finished talking, she said mildly, "Most interesting, my dear. Most interesting. It does sound as though a mistake *might* have been made — "

"Nonsense!" Hawken leapt to his feet angrily. "You were right in your first assessment of Shovell. He's a rabble-rouser who's provoked a great deal of trouble in the mines. A few years ago we'd have been able to haul him before the courts, have him transported, and forgotten all about him. Now, with that weak-kneed Liberal Gladstone in parliament, men like Shovell are *encouraged* to

360

bite the hand that's feeding them."

"There's been precious little 'feeding' at Gunnislake recently, from what I hear," retorted Lottie. "Starving's the word that's been used far more often to describe those who depend on you and your mine for a living. As for 'biting' you . . . " Her gesture encompassed the room and its comfort. "There's little sign of suffering *here*."

"I know you mean well, Lottie, but your sympathy is misplaced. The running of a mine is something you can't be expected to understand."

"Perhaps not, but Jethro is purser of the Sharptor mine. *He* knows."

Hawken Strike seemed momentarily lost for words, but not for long. "It's high time Jethro Shovell made up his mind whose side he's on. He's either with management, or he's against us. He can't be both. Anyway, that will in all probability be decided for him. If he goes to jail, Josh Retallick will have to find someone another purser for the Sharptor mine."

Lottie stood up abruptly. "I can see I've wasted both my time and yours by coming here to see you. I thought I could appeal to your better nature. I was wrong. I'll go now."

"You won't be leaving this house today, Lottie. The snow is drifting badly outside. You wouldn't get as far as the entrance gates. Look, why don't we talk about this again tomorrow? You're tired after your ride. I'm tired too. I've been helping the men bring the stock to shelter. Do you play chess? No? Then I'll be delighted to teach you . . . "

The last thing Lottie wanted was to remain in

the Strike house for the night, but Hawken was quite right. It was impossible for her to return to Sharptor in such weather. Josh and Miriam would realise where she was. She hoped Josh had been able to do something for Jethro in Liskeard . . .

Lottie was trying to make up her mind whether to refuse point-blank to consider playing chess until Jethro's future had been settled, when there came the sound of a commotion from another part of the house. A few minutes later a servant hurried to the drawing-room to find Isabelle Strike.

"It's cook, ma'am," said the servant, apologetically. "She's been drinking again. It's her birthday, you see . . . "

"Don't be ridiculous, girl. She's had at least three birthdays already this year! I shall have to lock all the drinks away. All right, all right, I'm coming!" As the noise increased, Isabelle Strike rose to her feet and the servant followed her from the room.

"Will the cook be dismissed?"

"Are you looking for yet another cause to take up, Lottie?" Hawken Strike shook his head. "No. She's been with us too many years and she's an excellent cook — when she's sober. Mother will order her to bed and give her a thorough dressing-down tomorrow. Cook will behave for another couple of months and then get drunk again. It's been going on for years. Now, shall I set out the chess board and show you how to play?"

"No!" Lottie sat looking into the fire, as though seeking inspiration. She glanced up to

362

see Hawken watching her. "You know, Lottie, when you last visited this house I thought you belonged here. Seeing you seated across from me I know you do."

"I belong at Sharptor, Hawken, and tomorrow I'll be returning there."

"You're being far too optimistic, Lottie. If the barometer is right you'll be here for some days."

"A barometer? What's that?"

"You mean you've never seen one? Well, this is your lucky day, my girl. We possess the finest barometer in the whole of Cornwall. Possibly in the country. Come."

Ignoring her protests, Hawken helped her from the armchair and led her outside to the hall. Here, in an alcove hidden from the main hall, a barometer was attached to the wall and Hawken pointed to it with evident pride, "There! It's a Rondeti. Great Uncle Theopilus brought it back from one of his travels."

The alcove was in shadow and Lottie had to peer close to see the dial. "How does it work?"

Reaching past her, Hawken tapped the glass and the pointer inside moved jerkily to the left, past wording that declared it would rain.

Hawken's hand rested lightly on her shoulder as he said, "There! It's still dropping. We haven't seen the worst of the weather just yet."

"How . . ."

Lottie turned to ask Hawken a question and found his face only inches away. She could have moved away from him. She *should* have moved away. As he kissed her she felt the need in his body. Her body reacted to his even as her mind

LT24

363

warned her against him . . .

She pushed him away and moved her face aside as he tried to kiss her again.

"I've been wanting to do that since I first saw you standing in the hall today I'm very happy to know you'll be staying beneath our roof, Lottie."

"It won't be for long. I'm leaving as soon as the weather breaks. I need to help Jethro — "

"*Damn* Jethro Shovell. Let him stay where he is for a while. It will do him good."

Hawken spoke fiercely about Jethro. Had he been anyone else she would have said he was jealous. But for Hawken Strike to be jealous of Jethro — it was laughable!

"He doesn't deserve to be locked up, Hawken. Had he arrived at Gunnislake in time he would have done his best to *prevent* a strike. He and Nell are both trying hard not to upset our new minister. He doesn't think Methodists should involve themselves in trade disputes."

"Are Jethro and Nell on friendly terms?"

"They spend a lot of time together." The question disturbed Lottie. It was something she tried not to think too much about.

"I see," Hawken suddenly smiled. "All right, I'll see what can be done for him."

"You promise?"

"I promise."

A great feeling of relief swept over Lottie. Her journey in the snow had not been wasted after all, "Thank you, Hawken. I'll be very grateful if you can bring about his release — "

Hawken kissed her again and Lottie did not push him away until she heard Isabelle Strike descending the stairs, complaining to the maid that the cook was likely to prove the death of her.

When Isabelle Strike entered the drawing room Hawken was explaining to Lottie the importance of a chess queen.

"Those stairs have quite fatigued me . . ." Isabelle Strike peered across the room at Lottie. "You'd better move away from the fire a little, girl. Your cheeks are looking quite flushed."

That night, in the largest bedroom she had ever seen, with a warming fire burning in the grate, Lottie thought about Hawken Strike. He was an interesting man. An exciting man, and yet . . . Lottie turned the key in the door and slept in a locked room for the first time in her life. Some time in the night she thought she heard a noise at the door, but she could not be certain. It was an old house, full of many sounds.

18

IT had stopped snowing by morning, but the blanket of snow covering the whole countryside was far too deep for Lottie to attempt the journey home to Sharptor.

It was warm in the house and after Hawken had been out to attend to some chores in the immediate vicinity he returned to the drawing-room and resumed instructing Lottie in the wiles of the game of chess.

During the whole of that day Isabelle Strike was a constant presence. She ensured Lottie and Hawken were never out of her sight together. So watchful was she that Lottie began to wonder whether she *had* imagined the noise at her door the previous night.

That evening, although it became increasingly apparent that Isabelle was deadly tired, she refused to go to bed while her son and his guest remained in the drawing-room together. There was no drunken cook to draw her away tonight and she remained a yawning presence in the room until Lottie went to bed.

The temperature rose during the night. By morning it was raining and the snow had turned to slush on the roads. There was no reason for Lottie to remain at the Strike house any longer.

Isabelle said she would order one of the grooms to ride home with Lottie, but Hawken put his foot down. He would ride to Sharptor with Lottie.

366

When his mother protested there were things for him to do nearer home, Hawken said, "I haven't visited Sharptor for some days. It's time I put in an appearance there. After all, a fifth of the mine *is* mine."

On the road Hawken and Lottie met with a Sharptor wagoner, mounted on Josh's own horse. He had been sent to Launceston to check that Lottie was well. Josh had guessed she was sheltering from the bad weather at the Strike home, but had sent the wagoner at Miriam's insistence.

The wagoner reined in his horse beside Hawken and Lottie, it being his intention to ride back to Sharptor with them, but such an arrangement did not suit Hawken Strike.

Handing the wagoner a shilling and congratulating him on the successful conclusion of his mission to find Lottie, Hawken suggested he should return to Sharptor with equal speed and tell the Retallicks their niece was safe and on her way home.

As the wagoner galloped back the way he had come, Lottie said to Hawken, "You realise of course you've just set tongues wagging at Sharptor? The wagoner will go back and tell everyone on the mine you gave him money to ride off and leave us together."

"So what? It's the truth, and I don't care who knows it. I enjoy your company — and I'm not going to share it with *anyone* until we reach Sharptor."

"That may add to *your* reputation, Hawken Strike. Have you no regard what it might do to mine?"

It was evident such a thought had not entered Hawken's mind. "I'm sorry, Lottie. I really didn't think. I just wanted to have you to myself for an hour or two. I found the presence of my mother yesterday utterly frustrating."

"She did work very hard at chaperoning us. But you needn't worry yourself about damaging my reputation. I ran wild around Henwood for so many years it's assumed I'd learned all there was to know about life before I was twelve."

"Did you?"

"I knew which men I should keep away from on pay nights, and learned to run faster than the men who waited for me when I returned from the moor with Elias Barnicoat's goats. As for the rest . . . it will keep until my wedding night."

"You're a strange girl, Lottie." Reaching out, Hawken took hold of her reins and brought her horse to a halt. "You're a strange, fascinating girl and I find myself thinking of you far more than is good for me."

For perhaps the first time in her life, Lottie found herself at a loss for words. "I . . . I'm glad," was all she could manage.

"Really glad?"

Lottie nodded.

"Then you'll not mind if I come calling on you more often?"

"I'd like that. You've been very kind to me, Hawken, and I appreciate your offer to help Jethro get out of jail."

The mention of Jethro Shovell slightly soured the morning for Hawken Strike, but he hid his feelings and the ride to Sharptor was pleasant, despite the rain that began to fall as they neared the moor.

As it happened, Hawken's assistance to release Jethro from police custody was not required. As he sat before the Retallicks' kitchen fire in borrowed clothes, Josh told him he had secured his purser's release but made no mention of the help given to him by Superintendent Kingsley Coote.

"He's only out on bail, of course," said Josh seriously. "But it's a start. Now his future lies in your hands."

"Why mine?" Hawken spoke indignantly, aware that Lottie, clean and tidy in dry clothes, had entered the room and was listening intently to the conversation. "I had nothing to do with Shovell's arrest."

"Whether it was your doing or your captain's, makes little difference. The only offence with which Jethro can be charged is that of inciting your employees to break their terms of contract. If you say he did nothing wrong the police are left without a case against Jethro. That makes it your decision."

Aware of his promise to Lottie, Hawken sat glaring moodily into the fire for some minutes.

"All right, I'll not sanction any charges against Shovell . . . but on one condition. Shovell must stay away from my Gunnislake mine."

"What about your younger workers and their demand to be returned to their old wages?"

Hawken's temper flared momentarily, "Dammit, Retallick, whose side are you on? Are you forgetting you're a mine owner too?"

"No. Neither am I forgetting I was once a

miner — and a bal-boy. Those boys and the maidens work hard for the few pence they're paid. It will cost you far more than their wages if they stay out for long."

Hawken knew Josh was right. He knew something else. That every morning, shortly before setting out for Sharptor with Lottie, the Gunnislake mine captain had arrived at the Strike house. His miners had taken a firm stand. They declared they would not return to work unless all charges against Jethro Shovell were dropped *and* the penny a day that had caused the original trouble was returned to the children. The mine captain was very concerned. The price of tin was still rising and unless he could begin production once again the mine stood to lose a great deal of money.

"All right, I'll agree to everything. As it happens I've already promised Lottie I would do all I could to secure Shovell's release. I'll return home via Liskeard and Gunnislake and sort everything out."

Lottie's warm smile told Hawken Strike he had said the right things. She, at least, was pleased with him.

The police inspector who had arrested Jethro was less pleased with the mine owner. He had wanted Jethro to be sentenced to imprisonment. However, he knew better than to try to put any pressure on Hawken Strike. The inspector was an ambitious man, hoping for promotion. He had learned long ago that profit came before principles. But he felt free to comment on Hawken Strike's surprising about-face.

370

"I do hope you're not changing your policy on the miners' union, Mr Strike. They pose a greater threat to you than to me, you know. For me they're no more than a blasted nuisance, disturbing the peace and posing a threat to public order. Their actions could make a poor man of you."

"I'm not changing my policy — and I take exception to your impertinence. It wasn't me who let Shovell go. If your men had been around to prevent him going to the mine in the first place I would have sorted out my troubles by now. As it is I must appear to be giving in to the demands made by my own employees. I don't like it. I don't like it one little bit. You let me down once more and there'll be a new inspector of police sitting in your chair."

The police inspector said nothing. The Strike family might be only minor gentry, but it was still gentry, and it was they who effectively controlled the affairs of the county. If he set his mind to it, Hawken Strike was capable of carrying out his threat.

"I don't think you'll have any more problems, Mr Strike. I was talking to a senior Methodist minister named Solomon Bligh the other day. He was telling me he's put a new man into Henwood. A minister who cares no more than we do for the trade union movement. I'll go across to Henwood and have a few words with him. This Shovell has a preacher's licence and takes his religion very seriously. A little pressure from his Church will work wonders."

Refusing to take further action against Jethro had

warmed Hawken's relationship with Lottie — but it failed to solve his problems at the Gunnislake mine.

The miners had said they would return to work if Jethro was released and the bal-maidens and boys had their pay deduction of a penny a day restored to them. They kept their word — but the children who worked on the mine had made no such promise.

The exodus of miners from Cornwall during the recent slump in Cornish mining had led to a shortage of skilled miners. As many of the miners had taken their wives and children abroad with them, it meant there was also a shortage of children to carry out work on the surface.

Taking advantage of the law of supply and demand, children on other mines had demanded, and received, a pay *rise* of a penny per day. The children and bal-maidens who worked the Gunnislake mine wanted the same. They refused to return to work until Hawken Strike paid them not one penny extra, but two.

Hawken found the thought of *children* striking for more money laughable. He refused to meet their demands, but his mine captain took the matter far more seriously. He led Hawken on a tour of inspection of the mine, pointing out all the work that was carried out by the children and bal-maidens. Their duties included recognising and sorting the various ores, and preparing them for processing. Many children worked below ground too, helping their fathers by holding and turning a drill as it was hammered home, or trundling ore from the working face to the shaft. In practice many of the most strenuous tasks, and all the tedious ones, were dealt with by the boys and bal-maidens.

In short, as the mine captain pointed out to Hawken, unless he paid them the additional penny they were demanding, none of the ore being mined by the men working below grass would ever reach the market.

Wiser in the workings of a mine, but poorer in pocket, Hawken Strike set off for home, his mood as foul as the weather that accompanied him along the way.

19

TWO Sundays after Jethro's release from police custody, Minister Wilberforce Beckett informed the congregation of the Henwood Methodist Church that he had an important announcement to make. Waiting until a fractious and somewhat indignant two-year-old girl at the back had been hissed into temporary silence, Wilberforce Beckett reminded his parishioners he had been their minister for a full month. During these weeks, he said, he had worked hard assessing the needs of the community. Now, his assessment completed, it was time to make a number of changes he believed would be to their advantage.

Looking over the hushed congregation and satisfied he had their full attention, Beckett continued, "I find a lack of discipline in your society that is, perhaps, only to be expected. Contrary to normal Methodist practice you have had the same minister for fifty years. He has served you well in the past, I have no doubt. Neither do I doubt his integrity. But Minister Roberts is an old man. A very old man. A man of such advanced years does not possess the energy required of a Methodist minister. Neither has Minister Roberts had the advantage of spending time at the very heart of Methodist thinking and discussion, as I have. Our Church is changing. We must change too. It is no longer a Church to be sneered at by the establishment. We have reached maturity. More than this, we have attracted men of substance. Men whose opinions and standing are respected throughout the land. We now speak with a voice that people listen to. A power in the land. These are exciting times for every one of us."

Beaming at his silent congregation, Wilberforce Beckett continued, "Of course, this new status brings with it a new responsibility. A new dignity."

Peering slowly about the crowded little chapel, Beckett drew a deep breath, "I fear such dignity has been sadly lacking in the Henwood Methodist community in recent years . . . " He expelled his breath. There! It had been said — and it had provoked no great eruption of anger. He drew strength from the congregation's continuing silence.

"Yes, indeed! It is time for us to look at ourselves and join this wonderful advance towards the twentieth century. In order to do this we must rid ourselves of those things the community at large finds unacceptable. The first of these is support of a union of labour, in whatever industry it is to be found. Trade unions do not provide the way forward for our working men. They are not the way forward for the Methodist Church. The very idea is anathema to our way of life. We must purge our ranks of those who claim to believe in our country, our Church, yet at the same time support trade unionism. *They are not of us . . .* "

Sitting not six feet from the pulpit where Beckett was spilling out his hatred of the trade union movement, Jethro was stunned by this sudden, unexpected outburst. But Reverend Wilberforce Beckett had more to say. "I must tell you, here and now, that a man cannot support the Methodist Church and a trade union. He must make a choice — and make it today. Support the Methodist movement, and a Christian way of life — or leave. There is no middle way."

Wilberforce Beckett's glance met Jethro's for a moment, before the minister initiated yet another attack.

"There is one other thing that, while it is not *evil,* is at best . . . misguided. I talk of the unauthorised use of women preachers. It must cease. It *will* cease. As I said a few minutes ago, our Church has finally achieved recognition. It is not necessary to resort to the fairground trickery used by those who once called themselves Methodists. We are not Primitive Methodists. We are not Bible Christians. We are none of those many sad and lost souls who have slipped from the straight and firm path of Methodism. You will hear no more women preaching from *this* pulpit . . . "

He paused as Jethro rose to his feet and after inclining his head no more than a fraction in the direction of the pulpit, turned and walked from Henwood Church.

Beckett had anticipated Jethro's departure. It came as something of a relief. It meant he would not need to go through the process of a formal expulsion.

There was more movement in the congregation. Her face scarlet with anger and embarrassment, Nell rose to her feet and followed Jethro to the

376

door. Wilberforce Beckett's declaration had been humiliating. To announce his decision from the pulpit of the chapel without first informing her was unforgivable.

Others thought the same. There was movement in the chapel behind her. Nell turned at the door and saw she was being followed by Josh, Miriam, Anne and Lottie. Behind them others rose to their feet. Ben and Jesse Retallick, Jenny Shovell . . .

Wilberforce Beckett's complacency over Jethro's departure turned to uncertainty as more worshippers deserted him. Soon there was no more than a third of the original congregation remaining. Most were aged villagers who had either not heard or not understood what was happening. They sat in their seats looking about them in confusion. They did not usually leave at this stage of the service, but perhaps the new minister did things differently . . .

Outside the little chapel, the villagers stood around in small uncertain groups, talking loudly in a bid to cover their confusion.

"You didn't all have to leave." Jethro's thoughts were in as much of a turmoil as everyone else's. "Not for me, or for Nell. I'm sure she wouldn't want that . . . "

"You know the cry that goes up when a miner's in trouble, Jethro. 'One and all.' We're all miners here. Minister Beckett's not. He's trying to foist London ways on us. It won't work, not in Henwood."

"What will we do now?" The hot blood had left Nell's face and she looked pale and dark-eyed.

"We go to see the man whose advice Beckett

377

would have sought had he an ounce of sense. Wrightwick Roberts."

The cheer that went up at the mention of Henwood's late preacher could be heard inside the near-empty chapel. Wilberforce Beckett felt more misunderstood than ever.

Wrightwick was appalled that the villagers had walked out of the chapel — *his* chapel — in the middle of a service. Before he would even listen to their reasons for taking such a step, he insisted on taking a prayer meeting there and then, in the street outside his cottage. It was a memorable service, and the voices raised in a song of praise carried to the ears of Minister Beckett.

When the brief, outdoor service came to an end, Wrightwick Roberts, leaning heavily on a stick, announced that he had no intention of having the whole of the village trampling through his house. Only Josh, Jethro, the trustees of the Henwood chapel and some five or six others were allowed to enter the cottage to discuss the crisis that had arisen within the Henwood Methodist Society.

Miriam, Lottie, Nell and Anne walked home together to Sharptor, their thoughts of the happenings at the service and the meeting now underway at the house of Wrightwick Roberts.

"I wonder what they're talking about back there?" Anne was the first to put her thoughts into words.

"They'll be discussing joining the Primitives," declared Miriam. "It's something Wrightwick should have done years ago. He's always agreed with their way of doing things — and he's been

378

none the worse for that."

"Then why has he never become a Primitive Methodist preacher?"

"Wrightwick Roberts puts great store by loyalty. John Wesley was still alive when Wrightwick was born. He regards himself as a link with the beginnings of Methodism and all it meant to people then. By taking Henwood out of Wesleyan Methodism he'd have been removing another stone from the house that John Wesley built. He's refused to face the fact that the Church itself has changed over the years. No longer one man's dream, it's a way of life for tens of thousands of people, all over the world. Minister Beckett is probably right, the Church has grown up. The problem is, Henwood hasn't."

"What will happen now?"

"Wrightwick may be old, but he's not senile. He'll realise we have no alternative but to take Henwood out of the main Methodist movement. It's not *our* Church any longer. We'll be far more comfortable with Primitive Methodism."

"Is there a lot of difference?"

"Some. The Primitives see their most important duty as going out to save souls. They'd as soon preach in the open as in a chapel and they'll give preachers like Jethro and our Nell as much authority as a minister. They also give their support to trade unions."

"It all sounds too good to be true. I'd rather keep things the way they've always been with Minister Roberts, and remain a Wesleyan Methodist," said Nell unexpectedly.

"You couldn't do that, even if things *did* stay

as they were. It wouldn't be fair to Jethro." It was the first time Lottie had aired her view and she spoke with considerable feeling. "Jethro's bound to be expelled by Beckett after the way he led the walk-out from chapel — and Jethro did that for *you,* not for anything Beckett said about him or the trade union. You owe it to Jethro to do whatever he decides to do."

"I'll do what *I* decide is best," asserted Nell. "Especially when it's something as important as which Church I belong to."

Glaring defiantly at Lottie, Nell quickened her pace and walked ahead on her own.

Anne Gilmore hesitated for a few minutes and then she hurried after her sister.

Miriam sighed. "I suppose I should be pleased to see both sisters getting along with each and not arguing the whole time. But I do wish our Nell would stop thinking she needs to be taking on the world the whole time. It's very tiresome."

When Lottie made no reply, Miriam said more gently, "You're still fond of Jethro, aren't you?"

"We've known each other a long time," Lottie replied defensively.

"That doesn't answer my question . . . but no matter. I had great hopes that our Nell and Samuel Coolidge might take up with each other. I know he's very keen on her. It's a pity he had to go back to Mexico when he did. Another month or two and we might have been getting ready for a wedding."

"He'll be back," said Lottie confidently. "But that doesn't mean Nell will marry him. She may be a great one for religion, but she's as fond of men as any bal-maiden."

"Are we still talking of Jethro . . . or would that remark have something to do with Hawken Strike?"

"It doesn't seem to matter very much to Nell. It's whoever happens to be around."

Miriam knew there was some truth in Lottie's statement. Nell tended to monopolise most of Jethro's non-working hours discussing the affairs of the Methodist Church or helping him with prayer-meetings and discussion groups. Yet she also tried hard to be at Sharptor when Hawken Strike called to take Lottie riding and be the one to accompany them. Miriam had encouraged the arrangement, believing Hawken Strike was not to be trusted with any woman, but she accepted that Nell's presence would be resented by Lottie.

"When Hawken Strike calls the next time I'll see our Nell has something else to do. Anne can come out with you instead. It's not going to be quite so straightforward stopping her seeing so much of Jethro though, if that's where your interests lie."

"I don't want you to do anything about Jethro. It's up to him to make the effort to see me, if he really wants to. If he prefers Nell . . . well, that's his business."

Miriam decided that for the time being she would concentrate on stopping Nell from seeing Hawken Strike too often. It was something she had already given some thought to. Nell *was* far too impressionable. An attractive, worldly man like Hawken Strike was capable of turning the head of a far more sophisticated girl than Nell.

"Here's someone who'd be far better off if she had no man at all," Lottie pointed ahead to where Patience waited at the gate of the Retallick House. "Marcus is one man too many for *her.*"

20

PATIENCE was now thirty-six years old – and she looked fifty. She twitched whenever she spoke and there was always bruising on her face. Everyone in the village was aware of her problem. Only a month before, neighbours had rescued her and the three children from a particularly brutal beating at the hands of Marcus.

On that occasion, incensed by what he considered unacceptable 'interference', Marcus turned on his family's rescuers. Before a blow from a pick-handle laid him low Marcus had knocked down three men and seemed set to rout the remainder. He was a powerful and dangerous man. Yet the next day he complained of feeling ill and had not been back to work at the Sharptor mine since. He declared that arsenic fumes from the calciner were affecting his breathing.

Josh offered to find work for him elsewhere, but Marcus refused the offer, insisting he needed to get right away from the fumes. The men who worked with him were not sorry to see him go. They expressed the view that it was honest toil that was poisoning him, and nothing at all to do with arsenic fumes.

Miriam knew the probable reason Patience had called on her. Her suspicions were confirmed when the younger sister asked to speak to her alone.

Sending Lottie and the others off to different

parts of the house, Miriam ushered Patience inside the kitchen. It was a cold day and Patience looked as though she had been waiting outside for a long time.

Raking out the ashes and putting fuel on the fire, Miriam sat her sister down. As she settled pots on the coals, Miriam said, "How much do you need this time?"

Patience looked distressed, "It's not for me, Miriam, it's the girls. There's been no food in the house for two days. When I send them to bed at night I swear I can hear their bellies complaining from downstairs."

Shaking her head in despair, Miriam drew a purse from her pocket and handed over a guinea. "Why do you let Marcus reduce you to such a state, Patience? Leave him and come up here to Sharptor to live. It would be a squeeze with the four of you, but we'd manage."

"I can't, Miriam. He's my husband. I'll pay you back this money, I swear I will. We're all working at the Marke Valley mine. It's in full production now."

"You're all working — except that good-for-nothing husband of yours?"

"He's a sick man, Miriam. The arsenic — "

"Arsenic is affecting no one except Marcus. Where is he now?"

"He's out somewhere. Getting fresh air in his lungs, he says."

"Marcus says! Marcus says! What do *you* say? You know very well what he's doing, Patience. He's in some beershop, drinking . . . But where does he get the money? And why are you broke when you and the girls are all working?"

Miriam stared at her sister as understanding came to her. "He doesn't take money off you and the girls to go drinking?" Patience's expression provided Miriam with the answer. "He took all your money and left you and the girls with nothing for food? What sort of man is he . . . ?"

At that moment Lottie walked into the kitchen, "If you're talking of who I think you are I'll tell you what sort of man he is. Marcus Hooper is the sort of man you hope you'll never meet more than once in a lifetime. *That's* the sort of man he is."

Suddenly, Patience began to weep. Silently at first, but sobs shook her body when she began to speak, "I know . . . I know he's all everyone says he is — and a great many things they know nothing about. But . . . he's my man. I *love* him."

"Of course you do, and no one's blaming you for that." Miriam dropped to her knees beside Patience and held her close. Over her sister's head she motioned for Lottie to leave the kitchen.

Lottie cast a pitying glance at the sobbing woman before leaving. She wondered what perverse seed of self-destruction was sown in a woman to make her fall in love with a man as worthless as Marcus Hooper.

As everyone anticipated, the trustees and senior members of Henwood chapel elected to take their place of worship out of mainstream Methodism and join the dissenting sect known as the Primitives. Jethro was to be their preacher, helped by Nell Gilmore. The ageing Wrightwick Roberts would act as adviser, conducting any ceremonies

385

requiring the services of an ordained minister.

Not everyone in the village approved of the break with the Methodist Society, but the vast majority did. Indeed, they felt a sense of relief to have seceded from a Church that chose to be represented by men like Wilberforce Beckett.

As it happened, the day of their decision also proved momentous for another, very different, reason.

As dusk was falling a lone and unsuspecting rider, travelling along the road from Liskeard to Launceston, was dragged from his horse, beaten unconscious and robbed, not two miles from Henwood village. Bloodied and shocked, he staggered to a nearby inn half an hour later and gasped out his sorry tale.

It was the first incident of its kind ever to occur in the area. The following morning there were as many policemen around Henwood as there had been when the local miners went on strike eight years before.

The police combed fields, copses and moorland, believing the robbery to have been the work of vagrants. But the homeless army had moved to more hospitable countryside at the onset of winter. The searching policemen found no one and at the end of the day were recalled to Liskeard.

It became the responsibility of Superintendent Kingsley Coote to continue the investigation, and one of his first calls was on Josh, at the Sharptor mine.

Nodding to Jethro who was hunched over the mine accounts at his desk, the police superintendent accepted Josh's offer of a cup of tea and came immediately to the reason for his visit.

"You'll have heard of the vicious robbery carried out on the Launceston road, last Sunday evening?"

"Yes, shocking business. Have you arrested anyone for it?"

"No. My first thought was that it had been carried out by a vagrant, but it seems they've all moved into towns for the winter. There hasn't been a stranger seen in these parts for weeks."

Both Josh and Jethro stared at the policeman in disbelief. "Are you suggesting the robbery must have been committed by someone who lives around here?"

"With no vagrants or strangers in the area, how does it appear to you?"

"Why should a miner turn to highway robbery today? A year ago, yes. Six months even. But with metal prices high and still rising there's work for everyone who wants it right now."

"Well, I do believe there are those who don't *want* to work . . . " Superintendent Kingsley Coote eyed Josh and Jethro in turn over the rim of his cup.

"Do you have someone in particular in mind?" Josh asked the question although he believed he already knew what the policeman's reply would be.

Kingsley Coote shrugged. "I'm checking on anyone or anything that might prove of help to me. I thought I'd begin with Marcus Hooper. I hear he spends a lot of time and money in beerhouses. Do you have any idea where I might find him right now?"

"He'll be at home this early, I expect. But I doubt if he's your man. I don't like Marcus — I know of no one except his poor wife who does — but I don't see him as a robber."

"I understand he stopped working for you some weeks ago. Perhaps you'll be able to tell me where he gets the money to go drinking?"

"You're a well-informed man, Superintendent, but, yes, I *can* tell you where his money comes from. His wife and three children, all young girls, are working in the Marke Valley mine. Marcus takes their earnings to spend on his drink. It's deplorable, but unless they all end up in the poorhouse I doubt if it's against the law."

"I've always said that laws should be written by those who understand *life*, Mr Retallick. Until they are, poor policemen like myself have to do the best we can with what we're given. I'll go and have a word with Marcus Hooper. Thank you for the tea, it went down a treat after a chilly ride."

Rising to his feet, Superintendent Kingsley Coote began fastening his coat. As he did so he glanced across the room to where Jethro was busily making entries in the mine ledger.

"There's nothing can beat hard work when it comes to keeping a young man out of trouble, Jethro. You'll be kept busy preaching too when Henwood is welcomed into the Primitive Methodist Church."

"Josh is right, you *are* well informed. Yes, I expect to be doing far more preaching soon. Doing what John Wesley wanted us to do. Going out to save souls."

"Very commendable. But allow me to give you

388

a word of friendly warning. Be careful *where* you preach. Holding a service on private premises has been held to be an offence. Similarly, anyone found preaching on the Queen's highway can be arrested for causing an obstruction. This is not my interpretation of the law, I hasten to add. I'm merely telling you of cases that have been upheld by the courts. I've no doubt a knowledgeable minister like Wilberforce Beckett will know all about the law when it comes to preaching."

Jethro realised with some surprise that the policeman was hinting at the action Minister Beckett would take against those who, until recently, had helped him in his ministry.

"We're preaching Christianity, not sedition. No one should have any cause to complain about that. Where *can* we preach?"

"If you feel the need to hold services outside Henwood chapel you'd be doing no harm to anyone up on the moor."

"Thank you, Superintendent Coote. I'm grateful too for your help in freeing me from the cells in Liskeard the other week. It's reassuring to know not all policemen think the trade unions are trying to bring down the country."

"I disagree with much the unions are doing, but happened to know the truth about your visit to Gunnislake. No man should be arrested for trying to help others. Helping one's self is something very different, especially when it's to someone else's property. That reminds me, I have an investigation to carry out."

When the police superintendent had left, Josh said, "Coote is an honest man — but I'd never

389

be able to rest if I knew he was after *me*!"

Marcus Hooper used belligerence to mask his own uneasiness when Superintendent Kingsley Coote paid him a visit. Patience and the girls were at work and it was almost noon, but Marcus had risen from his bed only a few minutes before. Unwashed, with an aching head, and a voice as rough as a blacksmith's rasp, the last person Marcus wanted to see at his door was a policeman.

"What do you want? You still looking for that slut Jane Trago?"

"If you have some information about her I'll be pleased to hear it. Right now I'm looking into a serious matter that occurred rather more recently . . . Do you mind if I come inside?"

Without waiting for a reply, Kingsley Coote pushed past Marcus and entered the cottage.

"You have no right to force your way into my home. What am I supposed to have done? What would my wife and kids think if they were home . . . ?"

"They're not here, Hooper. They're out earning money you'll take from them to spend on drink. But if you don't like talking to me here perhaps you'd prefer to come to the police station at Liskeard. You'd have no worries that the neighbours might see you there. I could offer you absolute privacy."

As he was talking, Kingsley Coote was looking about the appallingly untidy room for somewhere to sit. He decided to remain standing.

"What is it you want with me?"

"I want to know something of your movements.

390

Let's begin with where you were last Sunday evening."

The question startled Marcus, "Sunday? Why . . . I don't know . . . Yes I do. I was home, here."

"All evening? You didn't spend any time in Widow Mogg's beerhouse, over at Pensilva?"

Pensilva was another mining village on the fringe of the moor — and less than a mile from the scene of the robbery. Widow Mogg's beerhouse was a notorious drinking-place. At the same time, it was far enough removed from the village to ensure that few complaints were lodged about the clientele from the more law-abiding element of the community.

"Now you come to mention it . . . I *did* spend a little time at Widow Mogg's — but I left early."

"How early?"

"I got home before dark."

The robbery had occurred just after dusk. It had been light enough for the robber to see what he was doing, but too dark for the victim to describe his assailant with any degree of accuracy.

"Your wife will verify your story, of course?" There was just a hint of sarcasm in Superintendent Coote's question.

"She was here, and I was here. Why should she want to lie?"

"Why indeed?"

Superintendent Kingsley Coote was making notes in a pocket-book and he said nothing more for at least three minutes, during which time Marcus became noticeably more agitated.

Neatly pressing home the final full stop, Coote

391

closed the notebook and transferred pencil and book to a pocket before treating Marcus to a humourless smile.

"Finding Cornwall a bit quiet, are you? I suppose you must after the high life you led while you were away."

"I didn't lead no 'high life', as you call it."

"Ah! So your memory's returning. What *were* you doing during all those years you spent out of Cornwall?"

"I don't know . . . I was here and there. In the north of England mainly."

"Even in the north of England places have names. Give me one or two of them."

"I can't remember. Anyway, what business is it of yours? A man can do what he likes, when he likes, without having the police questioning him about it."

"Only if he keeps within the law. But a law-breaker . . . someone who carried out a vicious robbery not so very far from Henwood village. Now he *can't* be allowed to do as he likes, can he? What's more, I intend to see that he's brought to justice for his crime."

"I've already told you . . . it's nothing to do with me."

"So you have. You were here with your wife, you say? Well, I shall be checking on your story. There's something else, while I think of it. There's a toughness in you, Hooper. A toughness that honest, God-fearing men and women find frightening. I've seen it before in soldiers who've fought hard in a war — and also in men who've spent time in prison. You've never been in the army, I suppose? No, I know you haven't. Well, perhaps I'll learn a little more about you in London. I'm going there in a week or two's time. To Scotland Yard. I shall be looking through police files and will no doubt find them of great interest. However, I won't take up any more of your tine. We'll meet again soon and continue our little chat."

When the police superintendent had left the cottage Marcus found it impossible to remain still for more than a moment or two. Wandering nervously from room to room he tried not to panic. It was not easy. Superintendent Coote was a ferret of a man. If he delved deeply enough into London police records he might learn of a certain Marcus 'Cornwall' who had served a seven-year sentence in Newgate prison. It would be a short step from there to the unsolved murder of Oskar Gropius in his Hackney Road pawnbroker's shop.

Maisie must have learned of the murder of the old pawnbroker, and she would know who was responsible. There was no reason why she should have remained silent. On the contrary, she would want to have Marcus arrested and put out of the way once and for all. She had been very fond of the old pawnbroker.

Marcus found some consolation in the knowledge that Superintendent Coote would first have to find the file on Marcus 'Cornwall', and make the connection with Marcus Hooper. It was, after all, only a remote possibility.

Marcus's panic began to subside. It was of more immediate importance to ensure that Patience

393

corroborated his alibi for the evening when the highway robbery had occurred . . .

From the saddle of his horse, standing among the trees of a small copse just outside Henwood village, Kingsley Coote watched Marcus as he hurried towards the Marke Valley mine and he thought he understood the reason for his haste.

Kingsley Coote's belief that Marcus had committed the robbery on the Launceston–Liskeard road was based on nothing more than inspired guesswork. The victim was unable to give even the vaguest description of his assailant and arresting Marcus would be out of the question unless indisputable evidence was forthcoming.

Coote's story of travelling to London's Scotland Yard was sheer bluff. However, the Cornish policeman *did* have a friend who held a senior post in Scotland Yard. Kingsley would ask him to make a search of their records, on his behalf. Superintendent Coote was convinced Marcus Hooper was a criminal. He intended to obtain proof.

21

AS the Cornish winter passed into memory, and spring migrants winged their way northwards across the open moor, Hawken Strike's visits to Sharptor became more frequent. He and Lottie resumed their rides together on the high moor, but, as before, either Nell or Anne Gilmore rode with them.

Mostly it was Anne, as Nell became increasingly involved with Primitive Methodist activities in support of Jethro. Life for the young preachers was much easier now. Wilberforce Beckett had been moved to another circuit, still smarting at having lost his chapel and living to the man he had tried to have dismissed from the Methodist Society.

It seemed Henwood had settled down to a pleasant uneventful routine once more. Then, on a mild March day, news was brought to Sharptor that Isabelle Strike had died in her sleep at her Launceston home.

"I must ride over there right away and pay my respects," said Josh when he heard. "Will you come with me, Lottie?"

"Of course. I'll get ready right away."

"I'll come too," declared Nell.

Her decision came as a surprise to Josh, but he accepted it without comment. After all, she was friendly with Hawken Strike too.

Half an hour later Josh and the two girls were

riding through Henwood, en route for Launceston, when they saw one of the boys employed on the mine. Red-faced and hot, he looked as though he had been running hard.

When Josh called to him and asked why he was not on the mine, the boy gasped breathlessly, "I was sent off with the train to fetch a doctor from St Cleer. It's Tom Shovell . . . He's had a stroke."

"Oh! Poor Jethro!" Lottie was distraught. "You carry on," she said to Josh. "I'll go up to the Shovell house and see if I can be of any help."

Josh looked at Nell, but she shook her head. "It doesn't need two of us there. I'll see Jethro when we come back."

Speaking to Lottie once more, Josh said, "Tell Miriam before you go to the Shovells. I'll come to the house as soon as I return from Launceston tonight — and Jethro's not to hurry back to the mine."

Miriam ran to the Shovell home with Lottie. The doctor from St Cleer had arrived some time before. Unfortunately, although the doctor had wasted no time, he had reached the house too late. Tom Shovell had died ten minutes before his arrival.

When Miriam and Lottie entered the house Jenny Shovell was sitting in an old rocking chair in the kitchen, weeping quietly. When Jethro entered the room a few minutes later he too appeared to be on the verge of tears. Lottie clasped his hands in hers, wishing she could hug him to her, as Miriam was holding Jenny.

"I am sorry, Jethro. Really sorry. Is there something I can do? Anything . . . ?"

Jethro shook his head. "Jessie Retallick's up there, with Ben. They're doing . . . all that needs to be done."

Lottie nodded her understanding. Jesse and Ben Retallick had been friends with the Shovells for very many years.

"You can make tea for us all, Lottie," suggested Miriam. "If there's something a little stronger to go with it I'm sure it won't come amiss. What a day this has turned out to be. First Hawken Strike's mother, and now poor Tom. It's a day we'll none of us forget in a hurry."

There was less grief and more formality at the home of the late Isabelle Strike. Carriages, coaches and riders were arriving and departing from the large house every few minutes. To Nell it seemed as though a sombre and somewhat macabre party was in progress.

This impression was heightened when she entered the house. Food and drink were in plentiful supply, and friends, neighbours and acquaintances chatted and gossiped together around large, heavily laden tables.

Josh offered his condolences to Hawken Strike. Apologising for the absence of Miriam and Lottie, he explained they had been obliged to visit a very sick family friend.

In only one room of the house was there a respectful silence. Here Isabelle Strike lay in her coffin in funereal state. Candles burned at her head and feet and black drapes hid the rough wood of the carpenters' trestles upon which her coffin rested.

A steady file of visitors passed through this room, each pausing at the side of the coffin to gaze down at the thin, severe face, softened in repose. Most breathed a brief silent prayer and some recalled a special moment they had shared with Isabelle Strike. All were relieved when, their duty performed, they could leave behind Isabelle, relict of Leander Strike, and rejoin the living world in the adjacent rooms.

After he had been at the house for about an hour, Josh decided it was time to return home. He had timed his departure badly. He and Nell had encountered intermittent drizzle on their ride to Launceston, but while they were at the Strike house the clouds had lowered. It was now raining very heavily indeed.

Hawken Strike stood in the hallway with Josh and Nell, looking out at the downpour. "It's quite ridiculous even to consider going out in such weather," he declared. "Stay the night. Many of those here now will be staying on. You'll not be short of company."

"I must get back to Sharptor. I promised I'd visit Tom Shovell — "

Josh's explanation was interrupted by a lightning flash and a clap of thunder that caused Nell to draw in her breath in sudden fear.

"At least leave Nell here. I'll send one of my grooms to Sharptor with her tomorrow morning."

Thunder echoed around the sky in the distance and Josh's face registered his uncertainty. It was foolish to force Nell to ride back to Sharptor with him in such weather, but he would not feel happy leaving her under the same roof as Hawken Strike, even on such an occasion as this.

As though aware of Josh's doubts, Hawken said suddenly, "If you're concerned about her honour, I think I can find a satisfactory solution . . . " Hurrying off to intercept a large group of men and women who were about to enter one of the many rooms off the corridor, he returned grasping the elbow of a tall, grey-haired woman who must have been in her early sixties.

Introducing the woman to Josh and Nell as Aunt Faith, he explained the situation to her. "Josh is my partner, the senior partner in one of my mining ventures. He has to return home to Sharptor. He's not keen to take Nell with him in this weather, but is equally reluctant to leave her behind. He might feel differently if you offered to act as Nell's chaperone."

"My dear child!" Faith Strike placed a protective arm about Nell's shoulders. "What manner of brute would force a girl to set foot out of doors on such a dreadful day? Of *course* you'll stay. Come, there's another pretty little girl I'd like you to meet. You'll absolutely adore Victoria, everyone does."

Nell scarcely had time to smile her pleasure before she was whisked away by Hawken's aunt.

Josh acknowledged defeat. It *was* far more sensible for Nell to remain here in such foul weather. He would have been less complacent had he stood close enough to Faith Strike to catch the strength of the gin on her breath.

Victoria Hext found Nell a thoroughly boring companion. The Sharptor girl had visited none of the county's top families; talking of fashion left her blank-faced, and she seemed never to have heard of gossip. As if all this was not enough, she actually *boasted* of being a teetotaller!

It was this last claim that gave Nell's bored companion an evil idea. Asking Nell to excuse her for a few minutes, she left the room.

While she waited Nell stood looking out of a window. It had stopped raining now and the leafless trees were festooned with raindrops. She wondered whether Hawken would send her home now if he saw how much the weather had improved.

Victoria Hext was away from the room for a long time. Nell had almost resigned herself to the belief her companion must have found someone else to talk to, when suddenly Victoria was beside her at the window. In her hands were two tall glasses, both filled with an orange-coloured liquid in which tiny bubbles chased each other in never-ending lines to the surface.

"Here you are, Nell. I've brought a couple of drinks for us."

"What is it?" Nell took a glass and sniffed the contents suspiciously. "There's no alcohol in it?"

"Does it smell like alcohol?" Victoria Hext countered. "It's a French drink I discovered when I was in paris last summer. It's made from orange juice and a sort of . . . sarsaparilla. They drink it all the time over there."

Nell took a tentative sip and her doubt cleared instantly. "It's very nice."

400

"Of course it's nice! You don't think I'd have bothered bringing you something that wasn't?"

Unexpectedly, Nell and Victoria Hext seemed to enjoy each other's company more than before and Nell began to relax. She spoke a great deal and Victoria laughed a lot. When two of Victoria's friends joined them they too seemed to find Nell amusing company.

Lost in her own alcoholic haze, Faith Strike beamed whenever she glanced in Nell's direction. "Such dear girls!" she said to a deaf companion who had no idea what she was saying. "How delightful to see them all enjoying themselves so."

Hawken Strike took a different view later that evening when he entered his small library and found Nell slumped in a leather armchair. Most of his visitors had left the house and he had been anticipating a few quiet moments on his own.

In truth, Hawken had forgotten Nell. It had been a strenuous and busy day. It came as a shock to find her sitting in the near-darkness, her feet tucked beneath her, happily humming what sounded like a hymn.

"Nell! I thought Aunt Faith was taking care of you. I'm so sorry you've been neglected so."

Lighting a lamp that stood on a small table, Hawken turned and looked at Nell. Leaning closer, he asked, "Nell . . . are you feeling all right?"

"I feel . . . *lovely,* Hawken. It's been a wonderful party. I can't remember when I've had a happier time."

"Party?!" Hawken was taken aback. "It's not . . . ."

he peered closer. "Nell! Have you been drinking?"

"Certainly not!" Nell's indignation was comical. "I've signed a pledge never to drink. Have you signed a pledge, Hawken?"

Nell beamed up at her host happily, "You've got beautiful brown eyes, Hawken. Has anyone ever told you . . . you've got beautiful . . . brown eyes?"

It had not been a happy day, but Hawken smiled now, "What *have* you been drinking, Nell?"

"Orange juice. French orange juice, with sarsa . . . sarsaparilla. Victoria kept bringing them for me. She's nice . . . Victoria. You're nice too, Hawken. I like you."

Now Hawken began to understand. Victoria Hext spent much of each year in France. She had a taste for champagne. She would drink it on its own or, more usually, mixed with anything that happened to be on hand.

"How many 'orange juices' did you have?"

"I don't know. I wasn't counting . . . I *do* like you, Hawken. You're not like the other men I know . . . except perhaps Samuel. He's nice too — but not as nice as you."

"Come along, put your shoes on, Nell."

"Why, Hawken? Why must I put my shoes on? Are you sending me home? I don't want to go yet. I want to stay here and talk to you."

"We can talk, but put your shoes on first."

Nell swung her feet to the ground, but as she reached down for her shoes she over-balanced and would have pitched to the floor had Hawken not caught her and lifted her to a sitting position once more.

"I think I'd better put them on for you."

It took Hawken longer than he had anticipated. More than once he had to prevent Nell falling from the chair, and he tried not to notice when she stroked his hair.

Eventually it was done and Hawken stood up. "Come along, it's bed-time for you, young lady."

"But . . . you said we could talk!" Nell wailed.

"We will. We will." Putting an arm about her, Hawken heaved Nell to her feet. There was a softness to her that he thought would disappear with the years . . . yet there was a mature roundness too. As Hawken touched her, Nell caught her breath and then pressed her body hard against his hand.

"I really *do* like you, Hawken. Do you like me?"

"Now what sort of talk is this?" Hawken shifted his hand to take a less intimate grip on her. "What would Josh Retallick say if he knew? What would Lottie say . . . ?"

Nell stiffened and for a moment seemed less dependent upon him for support. "What business is it of hers? She'd have come with us today if she really cared for you. Instead she preferred to go to Jethro's house."

"Lottie went to see Jethro?!"

"That's right . . . " Wrestling with her conscience, Nell added reluctantly, "She heard his father was ill."

"But she knew about my mother?"

"Of course she did. We all did. That's why I'm here."

"I know. I'm grateful to you for coming. You

403

and Josh." Hawken felt hurt. Hurt because Lottie had not come with the others, had not sent a personal message of sympathy.

"I really am sorry, Hawken. This must have been a *horrible* day for you. I know how you must feel. I can still remember my own mother dying . . . in Africa."

"Mother's death wasn't entirely unexpected. She's been living on borrowed time for years."

"I think you're being very brave about everything, Hawken."

Without any warning, Nell turned and kissed him. Then she stood away from him and her hands went down to straighten out an imaginary crease in the front of her dress. "I'm all right now. I can manage on my own."

No sooner had she spoken the words than Nell's ankle turned beneath her and she stumbled.

"I think you'd better allow me to help you for a while longer . . . " Hawken's arm went about her once more and his hand was bolder now. Nell made no attempt to free herself from his grip, even when his fingers began caressing her in a way that could not be considered in the least protective.

"This is your room." Hawken stopped at a door in the shadows at the end of a first floor corridor.

"Thank you, Hawken," Nell spoke as though she suddenly found breathing difficult. "I . . . I'll be all right now."

"Nonsense! Unless I see you safely tucked up I'll lie awake worrying about you."

The room was large and there was a fire burning

404

low in the grate. There was a lamp alight beside the bed too, but it was smoking badly.

Gently lowering Nell to the edge of the large bed, Hawken turned to the lamp. Cupping his hand about the top of the tall glass chimney Hawken blew out the ragged flame. Then, grumbling about the laziness of the maids, he turned his attention to the fire, transferring two large logs from a basket to the grate, pushing them well into the red ashes.

When he moved away from the hearth Hawken could see Nell sitting stiff and ill at ease on the edge of the bed where he had left her.

"Not in bed yet? Come, let me take those shoes off for you. We can't have you losing your balance again."

He lifted her legs higher than was comfortable, but Nell managed to keep her balance until the second shoe dropped to the floor. Then, unable to remain upright any longer, she fell backwards on the bed.

As Nell lay there unmoving Hawken Strike became aware that his body was responding to the opportunity she offered and he leaned over and kissed her. He kissed her a second time then lay down beside her. His hands moved over her body, stroking her.

"Don't, Hawken . . . please don't."

Nell was not really certain what he was doing, but she was aware that her body was doing strange things, as though it no longer belonged to her.

"No, Hawken! What are you doing . . . ?" In spite of the question she knew exactly what he

405

was doing now. He was removing her clothes. She knew she should be stopping him, but her body had taken on a life of its own. It was responding not to her brain, but to Hawken's hands . . . and then his body.

His full weight bore down upon Nell, crushing the breath from her. Then she felt pain, a remote, searing pain . . . and yet she did not want it to stop. Then she was holding him, pulling him to her, and crying at the same time.

When Nell woke, grey light was framing the curtains and she knew it was morning. It took her some minutes to remember where she was. She moved her head — but not too much. It felt as though there was a full-size set of mine-stamps hammering in her brain. Suddenly she remembered all that had occurred the previous evening.

As her memory filled in the details, Nell thought it must have been a dream — a nightmare. Then, as she struggled to sit up, other aches and pains made themselves known and she knew it had been no dream. She had encouraged Hawken Strike, and he had made love to her.

She sank back on the bed once more. He had made love to her, and then he had left her. He had gone from her as a man would walk away from a woman he had used. For whom he had neither love nor respect.

She, Nell Gilmore, had committed the very sin she had so often scathingly condemned in other girls. She had behaved no better than a common bal-maiden. Yet even *this* would not have mattered quite so much had Hawken Strike only stayed with her until morning.

Hiding her face in the pillow, Nell clenched the bed-clothes in her hands and wept bitter tears.

22

DURING the weeks after the question of Henwood's form of Methodism had been settled, Jethro worked hard as their senior preacher and there was no shortage of helpers. His biggest disappointment was that as time passed he found he could no longer count on Nell's assistance. She still took classes and Sunday school, but she refused to preach.

Jethro thought he must have offended her in some way, but when he spoke to the Retallicks he learned they were equally puzzled by her sudden lack of enthusiasm for evangelism. They decided it must have something to do with the return from Mexico of Samuel Coolidge.

The one-armed American was paying a great deal of attention to Nell. She never went out of her way to encourage him, but neither did she discourage his attentions.

Samuel Coolidge had brought disturbing news from the New World for Josh. There had been a massive re-organisation of government officials in Mexico. For many years the country had been bedevilled with revolution and counter-revolution but the present government was popular and far more stable than most in recent years. Because of this it felt strong enough to take a stand against the widespread corruption that had long riddled the Mexican administration.

As part of their re-organisation the government

was preventing its funds leaving the country until it could be proved they were to be used for essential expenditure.

Samuel Coolidge told Josh the government would eventually agree that protection of the country's cotton crop was of vital importance to the Mexican economy, but it might mean payment for the arsenic produced by Josh would be delayed.

This was serious news for Josh. Any prolonged delay would pose problems for the Sharptor mine. Tin and copper prices were falling sharply once more and the mine depended heavily on its arsenic sales.

Yet, although the future of the mine might be in some doubt, the future of those in the Retallick household seemed more secure. While things were going well Josh had invested heavily in the booming china clay industry, which was rapidly replacing metal mining in central Cornwall. Profits from these investments were soaring, but they would support only the family, not the Sharptor mine.

Samuel Coolidge expressed an interest in this new venture and, early in May, Josh took Miriam, Anne and the American off for the day. They were to join fellow china clay investors celebrating the opening of a new clay pit.

Lottie remained in the house hoping Hawken might come visiting and go riding with her.

For some weeks after the death of his mother Hawken had not been seen at Sharptor. Lottie believed he was offended because she had not gone to Launceston to pay her last respects to

409

Isabelle Strike and she sat down and laboriously wrote a long letter to him. In it she expressed the hope he was recovering from his loss and explaining why she had chosen to remain with the Shovell family when Tom died. She told him how much she owed to them for their help in the past and ended the letter by telling Hawken that while her duty had been with the Shovells, her thoughts had been with Hawken.

The day after he received Lottie's letter, Hawken had come to Sharptor. He seemed quieter than before, at least he was when the Retallicks or Nell were around, but Lottie put it down to grief at the death of his mother. She liked him no less because of it and was happy his visits had resumed.

Today Nell had remained behind at Sharptor too, pleading that she had agreed to check an important sermon for Jethro.

He was preaching at a 'camp' meeting on the moor the following Sunday. It was hoped the meeting would attract at least five thousand people.

Lottie was in the stables behind the house, grooming her horse, when she heard the door open. She turned quickly, thinking it might be Hawken. Instead it was Nell. Disappointed, Lottie resumed her task without speaking. She and Nell had not quarrelled for many months now and Nell no longer made a nuisance of herself during Hawken's visits, but the two girls had very little in common.

"I thought you had work to do for Jethro, or was that just an excuse because you didn't want to go and see the china clay pit?" Lottie finally broke the long silence.

"It's not my idea of an exciting day out."

Lottie stopped brushing her horse's coat and pushed back a lock of hair that hung in front of her face. "Is there something you want, Nell? You don't usually come and watch me when I'm working."

Nell looked suddenly desperately unhappy. "I . . . I wanted to talk to you, Lottie. I need your help."

"You need *my* help? I don't believe it! You've never needed anybody's help. Had you been born a hundred years earlier you'd have probably ended up writing John Wesley's sermons for him."

Nell turned and would have walked from the stables had Lottie not reached out a hand and brought her to a halt.

"I'm sorry, Nell. That was unkind."

Lottie had seen the raw agony on Nell's face as she turned away. There had been many tines when she, too, desperately needed someone's help. "Wait while I swill my hands off in a bucket of water and we'll take a walk on the moor. There's no place quite like it for unloading your troubles. When I was younger I'd go up there and tell my troubles to myself, out loud. I still do it sometimes. It's far better than keeping things knotted up inside."

The two girls walked until the houses on Sharptor were far behind them. Picking their way through budding ferns that appeared to be tacked to the grass like outsize green staples, Nell said abruptly, "You were right what you said back there . . . About me telling everyone what they should or shouldn't be doing."

Lottie shrugged, "You're a preacher. Preachers *always* tell people how they should live their lives. It's expected of them."

"I know, but that only makes what I have to say even worse. Lottie . . ." Nell hesitated, as though still not certain whether or not to unburden her soul.

"Lottie . . . I'm pregnant."

It came out in such a rush that for a stunned moment Lottie believed she must have misheard her.

"You're *what*?!"

"I'm expecting a baby, Lottie. Oh! what can I do?"

"It sounds as though you already know far more than me what to do!"

"I'm frightened, Lottie. Really frightened. I . . . I was hoping you might be able to help me."

"Get rid of the baby, you mean? How many months are you gone?"

"Three months now."

Lottie winced. It must have happened about the time Tom Shovell had died and Lottie had been helping Jethro overcome his grief. Lottie and Jethro had moved closer to each other as a result and she found it humiliating that Jethro should have been making love to Nell during all that time. She tried to put such thoughts behind her.

"Is this why you haven't done any preaching lately?"

Nell nodded mutely.

"Well, at least there's some shame left in you, but what do you expect me to be able to do about it?"

"I don't really know. I thought . . . Well, it's well known that most bal-maidens . . . do it. What do they do if they fall pregnant?"

"You're asking the wrong bal-maiden. Contrary to what you believe, not *all* bal-maidens 'do it', as you so delicately put it. You're talking to one who doesn't — and who never has."

Nell's eyes filled with tears. "I'm sorry, Lottie. I'm not suggesting you're like that. It's just . . . I'm absolutely desperate. I've just got to get help from someone."

Lottie might have felt more sympathy for Nell if her mind had not been haunted by a mental picture of Nell and Jethro lying together, perhaps on this very part of the moor . . .

"What does . . . the *father* think about it?" She could not bring herself to use Jethro's name.

"He doesn't know. I don't want to tell him."

"Well, that's your business, I suppose."

Lottie had no intention of pursuing that particular aspect of Nell's sordid story, but she would never feel the same about either of them again. In spite of all their religious clap-trap and sermonising they were no better than anyone else. It was obvious Nell was desperately unhappy and Lottie could not help feeling sorry for her. She was far too young to have to face such a situation on her own.

"What have you tried so far?"

"Nothing. I wouldn't know where to begin, although I do remember hearing of a woman living at Liskeard who carries out abortions."

"You've probably heard of her because two of her 'patients' have died in the last twelve months. Superintendent Coote caught up with her and she's serving a life sentence in prison now. You keep well clear of abortionists. There's a herbalist who makes something up for unmarried girls in your condition. I'll try to find out who she is."

Nell's relief was almost overwhelming. With tears filling her eyes, she said, "I am grateful, Lottie. *Really* grateful. I've worried myself sick for weeks. I thought everyone who looked at me must be able to tell."

"I still think the baby's father should know . . ."

"No! He must *never* know. No one must ever know. Promise you won't tell anyone, Lottie?"

"It's the last thing I'd want to pass on — but if I do find this herbalist she'll want paying. I don't suppose such remedies come cheap."

"I've got money. As much as you need . . ." The Retallicks had been generous to both Nell and her sister, and Nell spent little. "I don't care what it costs. You'll do it soon, Lottie?"

"If Hawken doesn't arrive to take me riding I'll make enquiries today."

Nell seemed alarmed. "Hawken's coming here?"

"He might. What's the matter, Nell? I've promised not to say a word to anyone. That includes Hawken."

"I . . . I can't face anyone right now. I'll go on back to the house. You won't forget to find out about this woman?"

"You being pregnant's not easily forgotten, Nell. Anyway, if I do find out where this woman lives I think it will be better if *I* go and see her. As far as

414

she's concerned I'm just another bal-maiden and most folk think as you do. *You're* different. You go around preaching and people respect you and the Church because of it. Whether you ought to be preaching after what you've done doesn't matter to me — but it would to Miriam and Josh. They're proud of you and after all they've done for me I don't want them hurt. No doubt you feel the same way."

"I do, Lottie. I'm so ashamed. Truly I am."

"Do you love him?"

Lottie could still not bring herself to speak the name of the man she thought to be the father of the baby Nell was carrying.

"No. I thought I did, once, but I don't. He doesn't love me, either."

Lottie gained little comfort from Nell's confession. "Well, it takes two to make a baby, or so I'm told. You'd better go on home now. I want to stay up here on the moor for a while and do some thinking."

"All right . . . and thanks, Lottie."

Hawken Strike did not visit Sharptor that morning and Lottie went to the Sharptor mine to speak to Emma Hobbs during the midday break.

Seated amidst piles of rock and unsorted ore, Lottie asked Emma the name of the herbalist used by women and girls with unwanted pregnancies.

Emma Hobbs looked at Lottie in astonishment. "You haven't got yourself in the family way, Lottie? Who's the father? Is it Jethro, or your rich friend Strike?"

"I haven't got myself pregnant, and I don't

415

intend doing anything with anyone to get myself that way."

"It's me you're talking to, Lottie. More than half of Mother Kettle's customers are there 'for someone else'. Even those who've left it far too late and have the baby on her doorstep on the way out."

"Well I'm not one of them. Are you going to tell me where I can find this Mother Kettle, or do I need to ask someone else?"

"If you value what reputation you have left you won't even breathe her name to anyone else. She lives just outside North Hill, in a small cottage on its own along the road to Trebartha. If you wait until I finish work tonight I'll come with you."

"Thanks for the offer, but I'll go now and get it over with."

"Please yourself — but I do think you ought to tell me who it is wants Mother Kettle's potion. Is it your Aunt Patience? It's high time she saw some sense . . ."

On her way from the mine Lottie encountered Jethro. They had not met for more than a week and he seemed so pleased to see her that it cut into her like a knife to think of what he had done with Nell. Lottie walked past him without answering his greeting, or even looking at him. He was left gazing after her, thoroughly bewildered.

Jethro would have run after her had Malachi Sprittle not come from his office and called to him. A tin-buyer had arrived to settle an account. He wanted to check his records against the mine's books.

Mother Kettle was a short, heavily built woman of considerable age who suffered from arthritis. Opening the door to Lottie she hobbled ahead of her into the cottage without asking a single question.

Once inside a tiny sitting-room, Mother Kettle lowered herself painfully to a wooden chair at the table. Safely seated, she sighed with relief and looked closely at Lottie for the first time.

"Um! You're not pregnant, so you must be here to have your fortune told. Sit yourself down and we'll get started. Will it be your palm or the cards? And I'll see the colour of your silver before I begin."

"I've not come to have my fortune told. I'm here for a friend. She's landed herself in trouble."

"Why didn't you tell me before I sat down? Now I need to get up again . . ."

Mother Kettle struggled to her feet painfully after a number of attempts. It must have been a full five minutes before she stood with her hands on the table, breathing heavily.

"I don't know what the girls of today are coming to, I'm sure. When I was young a girl was expected to keep herself for her husband. If she didn't she'd be condemned by the vicar from his pulpit and have to face the disapproval of the whole community. Things are different today, and no mistake. Girls have no respect for themselves or their bodies. It's the age we live in that I blame. With all the mines closing young girls have too much time to wander around looking for ways to get into mischief, or worse. As for the vicars we've got . . . There's no sense calling

417

one of *them* in to speak to a girl who's in trouble. Likely as not he's the one who got her that way in the first place."

"Well, it gives *you* a good living, so you've no reason to complain." Sensitive of her own fatherless childhood, Lottie was stung to a swift reply.

"I perform a Christian service," retorted the arthritic old woman. "If it wasn't for me a girl's misery would spread to a whole lot more people. Now, how many weeks pregnant is this friend of yours?"

"I'm not absolutely certain . . . about twelve weeks, I should think."

Mother Kettle was rummaging in a cupboard and she snorted her approval, "At least she's more sense than some. I won't do anything for a girl who's more than six months gone. You'll likely lose both baby and mother if you do. There's some who aren't fussy about doing it, though. A dead girl can't come back and complain, they say, but I'm not one of them. How heavy is this girl? Heavier or lighter than you?"

"Heavier, not by much though." It was difficult to judge. Nell was not as tall as Lottie, but she was plumper.

"Just you stay here. I'll be back in a while."

Her arms filled with small bottles and jars, Mother Kettle waddled her way stiffly from the room."

As she waited, Lottie could hear the rattling of pots and pans from the kitchen. Once she looked through the window and saw the old woman, bending with difficulty to collect herbs from a

418

patch of cultivated but overgrown garden.

Mother Kettle was absent from the room for half an hour. When she returned she was shaking a large bottle filled almost to the top with a cloudy liquid in which floated a pot-pourri of cut-up leaves and fragments of roots.

"Here it is. Tell your friend to take it all in four doses during one day. The first in the morning, as soon as she wakes up, the last when she goes to bed. She'll feel like death during the night and had better not be too far from a privy. If she's got family who don't know what's going on she should try to keep them away from her during the night. More important, be sure a doctor doesn't come near her until at least twelve hours after she's taken the last dose. After that he might make a lot of guesses, but he'll be able to prove nothing."

Holding the bottle out towards Lottie, she said, "That will cost three guineas — and your friend will never spend money more wisely. Not only will it get rid of the baby, it'll put her off men for a few months." The old woman cackled merrily. "I ought to charge twice as much."

Lottie placed the money on the table and stood up to leave.

"What's your hurry, lovey? She can't take the first dose until morning and I don't suppose you've come from so far away you won't be home before then. Stay and have your fortune told."

"I've no money to waste on such nonsense."

"I've asked for no money . . . and nonsense you say? Give me your hand. Come on now."

Lottie decided she had nothing to lose by

humouring the old herbalist for a few minutes. She held out both her hands.

Mother Kettle took Lottie's hands in hers, looked at the backs of them, then turned them over, appearing to compare the palms of each. Releasing Lottie's left hand, she peered more closely at the right.

"You've known what hard work is, lovey, I'll give you that, but you're knowing better times now."

Lottie was unimpressed. Years of working as a bal-maiden had left scars, but the state of her hands now would have told any fool she had not broken or sorted ore for a long time. Mother Kettle peered more intently at the hand. Suddenly she said, "Come over here." Without releasing Lottie's hand, the old woman led her closer to the window and turned her palm towards the light. As her gnarled, rough-skinned finger traced the lines she found there, Mother Kettle's glance occasionally shifted to Lottie's face.

When she spoke again there was a new respect in her voice, "It's been many years since I last looked at a hand like this, lovey. More than twenty. That one belonged to a girl from over Henwood way. Good-looking, she was — just like yourself. Now what was her name? I can't remember, but she was wild — just the way you were as a girl. Left to find her own way. But I knew her wildness would never change . . . I wish I could remember her name! Your hand now . . . I can see your fortunes took a turn for the better when you were about thirteen, or maybe fourteen. Mind you, the wildness is still there. You'll need to keep it under control if you're not to go the same way as the last one . . . "

Mother Kettle looked up to see what effect her words had on her visitor. Lottie revealed none of her very mixed emotions and the old woman bent to her study of Lottie's palm once more.

"You've known unhappiness in your life. The loss of someone close to you. The only person ever to have been close to you. That's strange, I'd have expected it to be your mother . . . or even your father. Yet your mother is no more than a shadow — and I can't see a father at all . . . "

Lottie suddenly pulled her hand away. "This is all silly nonsense."

"Oh no, me dear. 'Tis no nonsense, as well you know. I've told you what I can see of the past, don't you want to know what your future holds? It's a foolish girl who doesn't care about such things — and you're not foolish, lovey. No, not by any means, even though it *is* your heart and not your head that guides you."

In spite of her reluctance, Lottie allowed the woman to take her hand once more.

"I see a long life, lovey, and a familiar path, but you're not walking it yet. You'll stumble more than once, too, before you find it. There's confusion here as well . . . " Mother Kettle's fingernail scratched the palm of Lottie's hand, as though she was trying to remove something from the skin. "*Such* confusion I've never seen before. There's money and position . . . but it's all going away from you!"

Mother Kettle released Lottie's hand. "You'd better go now. I've been standing for far too long. My legs are paining me."

Lottie took out a shilling and offered it to the woman. "It's usual to take silver for telling fortunes, so you said."

"I've not *told* your fortune, lovey — and I won't, neither. Not for silver, nor for gold. You've got what you came here for. Go."

Thoroughly confused, Lottie made her way across the room. She had almost reached the door when Mother Kettle paused in the laborious task of lowering herself to the chair.

"I remember . . . I remember now! The name of the girl who came to me all those years ago. The wild one. Seeing you walk towards the door reminded me. She had a walk just like yours. Trago, that was the name. Jane Trago . . ."

23

LOTTIE was seen at Mother Kettle's cottage by a Henwood woman on a visit to her sick father in North Hill. When the woman returned home a week later she lost no time informing Miriam.

By then Nell had recovered from the illness that had laid her low for a few days. A doctor called from St Cleer had diagnosed it as 'a woman's malady'. It was, he said, part of Nell's 'growing-up'.

When Miriam said that Nell's condition had been far more severe than any so-called 'woman's malady' she had ever encountered, the doctor informed her that Nell was a growing girl, and growing girls developed in different ways. All she needed was to marry and fulfil the role for which she had been placed upon God's earth. That would cure all her problems.

Miriam was still angry at the doctor's pompous and condescending attitude when she tackled Lottie about her visit to Mother Kettle.

"I went there to have her tell my fortune," declared Lottie. "There's nothing wrong with that, is there?"

"There's *everything* wrong with it. That woman's notorious for . . . other things. Going to her will blacken your name quicker than you can say Mother Kettle."

"How do you know of her?" Lottie asked the

question in apparent innocence.

Momentarily taken aback, Miriam recovered quickly. "Mother Kettle's been selling her herbal potions to girls for as long as I can remember — and her mother was doing it before her. You forget, I was a bal-maiden once and I knew what went on. Keep away from her, Lottie."

Miriam was still not convinced Lottie was telling her the truth, even though she knew Lottie was a far more moral girl than others believed her to be.

"Mother Kettle remembered my ma. She told her fortune too."

"A fat lot of good knowing the future did your ma! You just keep away from Mother Kettle, Lottie. If you don't you'll earn yourself a reputation you don't deserve."

Lottie nodded, satisfied she had successfully diverted attention from the real purpose of her visit to North Hill. Not that anyone would ever have suspected she had gone there on behalf of Nell Gilmore. 'Holy Nell' . . . !

Nell was slow recovering from the induced miscarriage. She was up and about soon enough, but seemed not to want to leave the house. She also tired easily and would burst into tears if anyone was thoughtless enough to speak sharply to her.

Then Miriam received a mysterious letter from a woman in Portsmouth, who signed herself Phoebe Gilmore. In the long and somewhat rambling letter the writer explained she was the sister of a Roger Gilmore and his wife Lizzie, missionaries who had gone to Southern Africa with their two young children almost eleven years before. Their families had never heard from them again and, in spite of numerous enquiries, nothing certain had been learned of their fate.

Phoebe Gilmore had even spoken to Robert Moffat, the famous missionary from Kuruman, on his return to England two years before. He had told them that Lizzie and Roger had died while taking the gospel to tribesmen on the Zambezi River, but he could tell them nothing about the two children.

More recently, whilst visiting the poor in a Portsmouth workhouse, Phoebe Gilmore met a dying Cornish woman named Mrs Batley. During a conversation they had, Phoebe Gilmore mentioned her missionary brother. Much to her surprise, Mrs Batley told her of Josh's and Miriam's return to England about eight years before with two young girls. The Cornish woman believed the girls to be the orphans of African missionaries.

Mrs Batley had been unable to give any more details, and Phoebe Gilmore had become used to disappointment in her search for her missing brother and his family. However, she wondered whether someone would be kind enough to reply to her letter, if only to put an end to the faint flame of hope the dying Cornish woman had kindled.

The news caused great excitement in the Retallick household and Nell began to take an interest in something for the first time in weeks.

Josh had tried to discover details of the Gilmore family upon his return from Africa. He had been handicapped by the fact that the Gilmore missionary party had gone to Africa without the backing of any known society. No doubt this lack of organisation contributed to their tragic end miles from civilisation, with no one aware of their whereabouts.

Miriam and the girls sat down and composed a letter by return. The result was a flurry of letters between Sharptor and Portsmouth which confirmed beyond all doubt that Phoebe Gilmore was the aunt of Nell and Anne. It also transpired that the two girls had other aunts and uncles as well as a great many cousins, all in the Portsmouth area.

When Samuel Coolidge informed the family he had to return to Mexico for a while Miriam decided to take the girls on a visit to Portsmouth. Samuel would be sailing from Southampton, only fifteen miles from the home of Phoebe Gilmore. He would act as an escort for Miriam and the girls. Her announcement did much to lessen Nell's unhappiness at Samuel Coolidge's news.

Before leaving Samuel Coolidge had spoken to Josh and Miriam about his feelings for Nell. He wanted to marry her and had been awaiting the right opportunity to ask her.

The matter had been on his mind for a long time, but he had been reluctant to ask a young girl who had such a zest for life and evangelism to tie herself to a one-armed man. However, since her illness she seemed to have matured a great deal, accepting perhaps that she could not change the world on her own. In the last few days, especially, she had been far more responsive to his attentions.

Josh and Miriam were fond of the American and they both hoped an opportunity might arise for him to propose to Nell during the journey to Portsmouth but, as they pointed out to him, the discovery that the two girls had a family might mean he would need to seek permission from someone else.

Josh and Lottie went as far as Liskeard to see the others begin their journey on the train. They were travelling first class and their carriage was fitted out in dark red leather, in the manner of a luxuriously appointed carriage.

As the train, pulled by a hard-working locomotive, rolled out of the station Lottie and Josh stood waving until the last carriage trundled by. Lottie could not help noticing the sharp contrast between the comfort of the first-class passengers and the over-crowded conditions inside the wooden-seated third-class carriages.

A fleeting, sad smile crossed Lottie's face as she wondered what Jethro would have had to say about such a discrepancy. No doubt he would have commented indignantly that working-class bottoms were just as sensitive to discomfort as those of the men and women who could afford to travel seated on cushions. At least, that was what the Jethro she *thought* she knew would have said. Now she was no longer certain she really knew him.

Lottie had not spoken to Jethro since Nell's revelation. She tried to convince herself she hated him but without success. It hurt more each time she passed him by, head held high, ignoring his pleas for her to tell him what was wrong, what she believed he had done.

One day Jethro had waited for her to return from a lone ride on the moor. He stood in the middle of the path, refusing to move, believing she would have to stop in order not to knock him down. Lottie urged her horse to a canter, not believing he would hold his ground and risk injury. But this was exactly what he did. He did not budge an inch until her horse cannoned into him, knocking him to the ground.

Had Jethro possessed the presence of mind to lie still, Lottie would have jumped from her horse and run back to him, full of remorse for what she had done. Instead, all sense and breath knocked from him, Jethro picked himself up painfully and stood looking after her in bewilderment as Lottie rode away. Lottie justified her action by telling herself Jethro must know why she was behaving in such a manner. He must realise his secret was out.

Jethro's actions seemed to confirm this belief. After this incident he had not come to the Retallick house again and he made no further attempt to speak to her.

" . . . There's no need to look so sad, Lottie. They'll all be home again soon."

Lottie nodded. If it pleased Josh to think she would miss everyone she would not disillusion him. In fact, she was looking forward to the house being quiet for much of the day. She would be spared too from having to look at Nell's wan, miserable face, remembering what she and Jethro had done.

In the carriage on the way back to Sharptor, Josh said, "It's going to feel strange not having

Miriam and the girls about the house."

"Perhaps I should ask Emma Hobbs to bring some of her friends over one evening? I understand they're a pretty lively crowd."

Josh smiled, "That isn't quite what I meant — but if it's what you want to do I don't mind. It's your house too, Lottie. You can bring who you like there, but I think you know that already."

"Yes."

Somehow the simple statement was not enough. "You and Miriam have been very good to me, Josh. I may not always show it as much as I should, but I *am* grateful to you both."

"We don't expect you to ooze gratitude every minute of the day, Lottie — but we both hope we've been able to offer you a little more happiness than you might otherwise have known."

"I'm happy enough."

"Are you? Are you really, Lottie? Miriam and I have been wrapped up in Nell's illness and this business of her aunt, but we've been watching you too. There's been precious little happiness in you these past few weeks."

When Lottie made no immediate reply, Josh knew his surmise had been right. Lottie *was* unhappy.

"What is it, girl? Is young Hawken Strike giving you any bother?"

"Hawken? No! He's been kindness itself these past few weeks. I've grown quite fond of him."

Josh sighed. "Then it must be something to do with Jethro. I thought as much. He came to me a week or two back. Said you wouldn't so much as speak to him and he couldn't think of anything he'd done. He asked me if I knew what he was supposed to have done wrong."

"He flatters himself if he thinks I care what he's done. As far as I'm concerned Jethro can go his way, and I'll go mine."

"It hasn't always been that way, Lottie. There was a time when I believed you and Jethro were made for each other. You've always been good for one another. Jethro's an over-serious young man. You're the only one I know who can remind him he shouldn't go through life trying to imitate Wrightwick Roberts. Wrightwick Roberts is in his eighties. Jethro's sixty years younger. He should be getting some enjoyment from life. Having *fun*."

"Oh, you don't have to worry about Jethro. He has his fun, you can be sure of that. No, none of us need worry about Jethro Shovell any more. He doesn't go short of anything."

Josh hoped Lottie would say more, but she had said too much already. Turning away, she gazed moodily out of the carriage window.

"Well, it's a great pity, but perhaps it's all for the best. I doubt if Jethro will be at the Sharptor mine very much longer."

The speed with which Lottie returned her attention to Josh gave the lie to her declared lack of interest in Jethro. "What do you mean? Where's he going? What's he going to do?"

"There's nothing certain yet, but he's been asked to advise some of the clayworkers over at St Austell in a dispute they're having with their management. When I was last in the clay country I heard rumours that every man there was ready to join a trade union. They've asked that Jethro be appointed to represent them full-time. There are a few thousand men over there now. If Jethro takes the position he'll wield a great deal of power, but there'll be precious little humour attached to the job."

"What about his preaching . . . and his mother? She won't be happy here alone if he leaves Henwood."

"There's a new Primitive Methodist minister coming here soon, from Plymouth. As for Jethro's mother, she's told Miriam she's thinking of going to live with Gwen, her daughter by her first husband. It's another reason for Jethro to move to the clay country. He wouldn't want to live in the cottage by himself either, would he?"

Lottie said nothing, but she could not help thinking bitterly of the course fate had taken. She believed Jethro would have asked her to marry him years before had it not meant Lottie sharing the cottage with his strong-minded mother. Now, when marriage between them was out of the question, this barrier was being removed.

A sudden disconcerting thought came to her. Perhaps Jethro would ask Nell to marry him! She wondered who Nell would choose, Jethro or Samuel Coolidge?

Lottie quite enjoyed the not-too-onerous responsibility of looking after the house and cooking meals for Josh. It still left her plenty of time to go off riding with Hawken.

With Miriam and the girls away, Hawken became a daily visitor. He seemed far more relaxed without the others around. When Lottie

431

commented on this he said it was because he and Lottie were beginning to understand each other more. As for the increase in the frequency of his visits, he did not want her to be lonely.

One day, although Hawken made the ride from Launceston, the weather on the moor was too blustery for them to go riding. Instead they sat in the warm kitchen of the house on Sharptor, talking about themselves and the very different lives each had led.

Hawken, it seemed, had seen little of his parents during his childhood. Sent away to a boarding-school when he was seven he had gone straight from school into the army.

"I don't think I'd like that for any children of mine," declared Lottie. "I want to keep them around me and make sure they enjoy a better life than I had. Do you feel the same?"

"Oh, I didn't have a bad life, Lottie, not when compared with yours. I always had a roof over my head, good — if unimaginative — food in my belly, and I enjoyed a first-class education. Isn't that what life for a young child is all about?"

"No. I'd put love and a sense of belonging at the top of my list of what children need. A feeling of being wanted and cherished for themselves. Not to feel they were an unfortunate product of something their parents did without thinking too much of the end result."

"My, you *do* have firm views about things! I must say, I admire a girl who knows her own mind. Do you have equally rigid ideas about the man who'll father these paragons of yours?"

"Yes. He'll need to be a man I both love and

respect. One who'll take my views seriously. Not a man who'll pat me on the head, tell me what a bright girl I am — and would I please hurry to get his supper so he can go out to the beerhouse with his friends."

"You can do better than a man who frequents beerhouses, Lottie. Look, come over to my place for a few days. See what it's like to have servants look after you and prepare your meals. I'd enjoy having you as a guest in the house."

"I don't doubt it! And what would folk say about it? What would Josh say? He'd have no one here waiting on him and cooking *his* meals."

"He can come too — although I'd prefer to have you all to myself for a few days. We'd have fun, I promise you."

"*You*'d have fun, you mean. Oh no, Hawken Strike. If it's fun you want you only have a couple of weeks to wait. Liskeard Fair will be here again then and you can have *fun* with your widowed actress — but not with me!"

"You're a puzzling mixture, Lottie. I've never known a girl to be quite so frank and open in her conversations with a man. Yet you're reluctant to translate such free-thinking into deeds. It's both confusing and frustrating. You're not a girl who *could* hold back if you really loved someone. I must assume you don't feel the same about me as I do about you."

"No one has made any mention of *love*. You're annoyed because I won't become your mistress. Well, you'll need to remain annoyed with me. I'll not be mistress to you, nor to any other man. I intend keeping my body for the man

433

I marry — and it's *not* because marriage is the price I set on my virginity. That's just another form of prostitution. I'll keep my body for my husband because it's the only thing I have that's truly mine to give. I'll have only that — and my love — to take into marriage."

The shrug that followed this statement was Lottie's way of showing her embarrassment over opening her heart to Hawken in such a manner. "I don't expect you to understand me. There are some days when I'm not certain I really understand the way I think myself, but that's the way it is with me."

Hawken Strike looked at Lottie for a very long time without saying anything. Then he said abruptly, "All right, if that's the way it must be."

His reply baffled Lottie, "What's that supposed to mean?"

"It means that if I can't have you any other way, then we'd better be married."

"Now you're being foolish."

"Foolish? I propose to a girl for the first time in my life — and what does she say? She tells me I'm being 'foolish'."

"You can't be serious, Hawken."

"Of course I'm serious. *Damned* serious. Perhaps you think I should be on one knee if I'm proposing. All right, how will this do you?"

Dropping to one knee, Hawken took her hand and looked up at her. "Lottie Trago, I want you to share my life. To live in the ancestral home of countless Strikes as my wife."

Rising to his feet without releasing her hand, Hawken said, "Was that better? Perhaps now you'll give me an answer."

"I'll accept that you're *half* serious — but the whole idea is too ridiculous for words! I've met some of the people you're used to mixing with. Girls like the Weston sisters. They'd never accept me."

"To hell with the Westons. They're two of the most boring people in the world. We'll make new friends. People we both like. People who'll like you for what you are."

Lottie was still protesting that Hawken was being ridiculous when they both heard the sound of footsteps crunching on the path that led to the kitchen door. A few moments later the door opened and Josh entered the house.

Only the slightest of frowns betrayed Josh's disapproval at finding Hawken and Lottie standing so close together. He had complete trust in Lottie, but very little in Hawken Strike.

"I hoped I might catch you before you went out for a ride. I'd like to speak to you in the mine office before you return home, Hawken. With no cash received for arsenic we're running into trouble . . . "

"Later, Josh. Business can wait for a while. Lottie and I have something important to tell you. I've asked her to marry me."

Surprise rendered Josh speechless as his glance moved from his business partner to Lottie.

"Hawken's asked me, but I haven't accepted yet."

"She will, Josh. Of course she will. I'm probably the best catch in the whole of the county. Tell her, Josh."

"No, tell *him* he's being foolish, Josh. I have."

"You come from very different backgrounds, certainly, but if Hawken can overcome the problems that poses I guarantee he'll never find a finer girl for a wife."

As Lottie listened to Josh, her eyes brimmed with tears and she flung her arms about him. "That's the nicest thing anyone's ever said to me. I love you for that, Josh."

Hawken Strike looked on and rubbed his chin ruefully. "That's more than she's said to me, but no doubt my time will come."

"No doubt, but this calls for a celebration. I must have something in the house worth drinking . . . I wish Miriam was here to share this moment. We must have a real celebration when she returns . . . "

Later that evening when Hawken had returned to Launceston and Josh was out of the house visiting Wrightwick Roberts, Lottie received a surprise visit from Jethro.

He knocked at the door and waited for it to be opened. This in itself was something out of the ordinary. In mining areas visitors neither knocked nor waited. They walked into neighbours' homes as though they were their own.

Lottie opened the door and saw Jethro in the light from the lamp inside the room. There was a heavy moorland drizzle outside and Jethro was soaked. However, she maintained the unusual formality by not inviting Jethro into the house.

"What are *you* doing night-visiting? If you want to come calling I suggest you call in the

436

daytime, when all the family's here — including our Nell."

"I haven't called before because I no longer feel welcome in the house, especially by you."

"Don't tell me you're *surprised*, Jethro Shovell?"

"I'm more than surprised, Lottie. I'm hurt, and totally bewildered. Won't you tell me what I'm supposed to have done?"

For the briefest of moments Lottie could almost have believed him. "That's a question you should be asking Nell, not me."

"Why? Stopping preaching was her idea, not mine. I'd be pleased to have her going out to prayer meetings with me again."

"I'm *sure* you would."

"I've done nothing to upset Nell . . . but I haven't come here to talk about her. I'm here because I heard this evening that you're likely to marry Hawken Strike . . . but this isn't something to be discussed on the back doorstep. Can I come in?"

"Anything you have to say can be said as well outside as in. Yes, Hawken has asked me to marry him."

When Lottie saw the hurt and bewilderment on Jethro's face she almost weakened. She wanted to ask him point blank about the relationship there had been between himself and Nell. But she had promised Nell she would say nothing and Lottie did not break a promise lightly.

"Have you thought about what you're planning to do, Lottie? Really thought about it? I realise Strike set out to charm you from the very first moment he set eyes on you, but he's not your sort of man. You won't find a lifetime of happiness with him."

"You name me any woman around here who's had a lifetime of happiness with her man. Wrightwick Roberts has told us often enough from his pulpit that we've no right to expect happiness. At least I'll never have to worry about being poor again if I marry Hawken."

"There's more to life than money, Lottie. Especially for you. I don't want to see you get hurt — "

"Oh, that's great coming from *you!* You should have thought about not hurting me a long time ago."

Jethro appeared more bewildered than ever at this latest outburst. "I honestly don't know what I've done to you Lottie. Whatever it is, I'm sorry. If you'll only *tell* me what it is I'll try to put it right — "

"It's too late for that. Hawken's asked me to marry him — and I intend to accept."

Jethro was silent for a very long time, unhappiness oozing from every pore in his body.

"I had hoped . . . " Jethro's voice faltered, then gained strength as he said, "I wish you all the happiness in the world, Lottie. Far, far more than Hawken Strike can ever give you."

With this, Jethro turned away and disappeared in the darkness.

Miriam returned from Portsmouth far sooner than was expected — and she was in no mood for celebration.

Her carriage did not arrive at Sharptor

until dusk was falling. The driver dumped her unceremoniously at the gate of the house together with all her baggage, then promptly set off on the return journey to Liskeard. He intended being clear of the moor's indifferent roads before darkness fell.

Josh was delighted at her return, but his first question was of Nell and Anne.

"They're staying at Portsmouth. Samuel's boat has been delayed at Southampton for a week so Nell would prefer to be there. Anne's meeting enough cousins to fill a chapel . . . but that has nothing to do with the reason I'm home so soon."

"The reason doesn't matter. Lottie has some very exciting news for you — "

"The reason *does* matter — and I have news for Lottie. In fact, it's news that concerns you deeply. You'd best sit down to hear what I have to say."

Miriam sounded so serious that Lottie sat down without a word.

"While I was in Portsmouth I thought I should go to the workhouse to see this dying Cornish woman who told Phoebe Gilmore about the girls . . . this Mrs Batley. I saw her — and she's Cornish all right. Neither is there any doubt that she's a dying woman . . . but I wouldn't care to swear to the Mrs Batley part of her story . . . "

Miriam looked at Lottie almost pityingly, "Lottie, the woman in the Portsmouth workhouse hospital is your ma. She wants to see you . . . "

24

WHEN Jane Trago left Henwood by night with a sizeable sum of ill-gotten money in her possession, her intention was to buy a grog-shop, somewhere many miles from Cornwall. She had never seriously contemplated sharing this new life with Marcus and any doubts she might have entertained disappeared on their first night together in London. Marcus was an adequate lover, but he was a fool. When he was drinking heavily he became a *dangerous* fool. While wasting their money on some drunken spree he was likely to boast of what they had done.

Jane had put much scheming and a lot of hard work into obtaining Waldo Davey's money. She was not going to watch it all slip through her fingers. Lovers were easy to find. Money was not.

She used similar logic when she decided to take Marcus's union money in addition to the cash she had stolen from Waldo Davey. If she left it behind Marcus would undoubtedly squander it. In a matter of weeks it would be no more than a fading memory to him.

Jane believed the money should be put to better use. She was doing Marcus a favour by forcing him to use his wits now, before strong drink permanently dulled his senses.

Leaving Marcus in a drunken sleep she took a hackney-carriage from the inn to Paddington railway station. Here she had a railway porter transfer her luggage to another carriage. This time she went to *Euston* railway station.

There was good reason for such guile. The first hackney-carriage driver had been on familiar terms with the landlord of the inn she had just left. She had no intention of leaving a trail that *anyone* could follow.

From Euston, Jane took a train to Liverpool. She had visited the sprawling, bustling great sea port once before, on her return from India with part of the regiment she was with. As a customer in one of the many crowded beerhouses she had watched money flow from newly returned soldiers and sailors to the beerhouse owner. Jane had decided there and then that if ever she had enough money she would open a grog-shop close to the docks in Liverpool. Now she had the money and was on her way to realise the dream.

Jane moved into an inn on the fringe of the dock area that was just expensive enough to raise it above the seedy level. There were few home comforts and the landlord was surly to the point of rudeness, but it would suffice until she found what she was seeking.

One of the first things Jane did was to deposit all the money she was carrying in a local bank, using the name Jane Davey. Using Waldo's name was a quixotic gesture that appealed to her, although the landlord of the Cheesewring Inn might not have shared her amusement.

Four days after Jane's arrival in Liverpool she found a property ideally suited to her purposes. The downstairs might once have been a shop, although there were enough upstairs rooms for it to have been a lodging-house. When Jane learned it had in fact been a beerhouse a few years before she knew her search was over.

Jane's informant was a toothless crone she found sitting on the floor of an outhouse at the rear of the building. The woman's only possessions appeared to be a verminous blanket and a cracked jug partly filled with flat ale.

After passing on her information, the woman added, "But if you're looking for a place to buy this isn't it. You wouldn't like it here, dearie."

"What you really mean is *you* don't want me to buy it because I'll probably throw you out on the streets."

The crone lifted the jug to her lips and studied Jane over the rim as she downed the flat ale. Registering distaste as she lowered the now empty jug to the floor, she belched, sniffed noisily, and cuffed a dribble of ale from her chin.

"What you do is your business, and me and the street is old friends. But this house is haunted by the ghost of old Charlie Dack who had the beerhouse here. He hanged himself from that hook up there on the beam just above your head. That's why the place has been empty this three years. It's unlucky."

Jane resisted the urge to look up at the makeshift gallows. "Then no doubt the owner will be anxious to make a quick sale."

Before she left Jane Trago threw a shilling in the lap of the old woman, "Here. Don't spend it all on drink. Use some of it to get yourself cleaned up — and throw that lousy blanket away.

I'll buy you a new one, but if you're going to live out here and eat my food I'll expect you to earn your keep."

"You want me to *work*?"

"No one mentioned work. This will be a grog-shop again when I buy it. If I'm to make money I'll need to attract sailors in here, men back from a long voyage with money in their pockets. Put a sailor, a woman and a drink together and there's good money to be made. I'll provide the drink, what I want you to do is tell the drabs they're welcome here. If they bring a customer in with 'em we'll come to some arrangement about their drinks."

"Oh! A *clever* one, are we? Well, you'll need to get a licence first — and they don't give them to anyone. You need to prove you've a good character. I doubt that'll be easy for anyone as familiar as you are with the ways of a drab."

"You let me worry about that. What's your name, old woman?"

"Lil's me name, dearie. Lil Tooley — and if you get a grog licence I'll come and dance on a table for your sailors."

The old crone's amused cackle followed Jane as she walked out through the yard.

The owner of the premises was a solicitor with a gloomy little office above a saddler's shop on the fringe of the dockyard area. A tarnished brass name plate on the wall at the foot of the stairs named the occupant of the office as one 'Ignatius Snade, solicitor'.

Ignatius Snade was slight and bespectacled,

with a spinal deformity that hunched his body and raised one shoulder higher than the other.

He greeted Jane cautiously, sat her in a chair and when she stated her business he said, "Ah yes, the premises in Waterloo Road. It's a highly desirable building. A sound business investment for the right person. It has attracted a great deal of interest, of course . . . " Ignatius Snade shuffled ineffectually through a large and untidy pile of papers. "As a matter of fact I believe I have an offer right here from someone who is very keen to purchase, very keen indeed."

Jane had made a number of enquiries before coming to the solicitor's office. She knew the property had lain idle for three years and had twice been offered at auction without attracting a buyer. It was also rumoured that Ignatius Snade was in dire need of money to meet a series of mounting debts.

Rising to her feet, she said, "I didn't realise you already had a buyer for the property, Mr Snade. I'm sorry for wasting your valuable time — "

Ignatius Snade's reaction bordered on panic. Scuttling across the room he succeeded in intercepting Jane before she reached the door.

"Wasting my time . . . ! My dear lady, if anyone is wasting my time it is the other party. One day he wants it, the next he's unsure. You'd think he would be eager to snap up such a bargain — "

"The property is grossly over-priced," interrupted Jane abruptly. "Reduce it by a hundred pounds and I'll buy it."

"A hundred . . . ? I don't know . . . " Ignatius Snade tried to hide his glee. He had obtained the property by somewhat dubious means when the previous owner, his client, committed suicide leaving no next-of-kin. Now Snade played for time as he mentally balanced Jane's offer against his outstanding debts.

"Perhaps twenty pounds . . . or even thirty pounds less might be acceptable. But a *hundred* . . . !" He shook his head dubiously.

"A hundred — and I'll pay cash. Think about it, Mr Snade. If I haven't found anywhere else that suits me better in a week or two's time I'll call again and see if you've made up your mind."

"My word, it's a pleasure to do business with someone who knows exactly what they want, Mrs . . . Davey, did you say? Yes indeed, a real pleasure. The property shall be yours. If you care to be seated I'll draw up the agreement immediately."

Seating herself once more, Jane said, "There's one more thing. I intend applying for a grog-shop licence for the premises and I shall need a character reference. I trust you'll oblige me, Mr Snade. After all, anyone who can afford to pay you in cash for a property must be of good character, I'm sure you agree . . . "

Jane's grog-shop opened its doors to customers exactly a month later. She had employed two carpenters to work every day as well as half through the night to furbish it exactly as she intended it to be.

Jane did not keep Lil Tooley to her promise to dance upon a table at the opening, but she ensured the old woman spread the news of the opening among the women of the Liverpool streets.

Lil Tooley performed her task well and Jane's grog-shop was packed with customers from the moment it opened. The prostitutes who worked the streets in the dockside area made their way there. So, too, did young girls: chambermaids, nannies and seamstresses among them. Following the example of their professional sisters it was an accepted means of supplementing their meagre incomes. It was this group of customers who gave Jane the idea of increasing her profits even more.

She decided to put the empty rooms above the grog-shop to good use. A bed, a blanket or two, wash-stand, bowl and jug were the only requirements for each room. Now the young, part-time prostitutes — the 'dolly-mops' — would not need to leave the premises and run the risk of being seen with a man and reported to employers, or families.

A young girl and her beau for the evening would be guided up the uncarpeted stairs by a grumbling Lil Tooley, complaining she was far too old to be expected to climb so many stairs each night. Usually a generous tip from a sailor and plentiful drink from Jane ensured she never complained *too* loudly.

Then, only three months after Jane opened her grog-shop, the premises were raided by the Liverpool police. They crowded in through the doorway at the busiest time of the evening. Brushing aside the protesting customers a number of them pounded noisily up the wooden stairs.

The constables had timed their raid well.

Seven of the upstairs rooms were occupied by copulating couples. Three of the occupants were hardened prostitutes who had already served terms of imprisonment for pursuing their trade. They complained of police 'insensitivity', declaring they were merely bidding farewell to 'loved ones', who would be off braving the perils of the deep on the morrow. The dolly-mops, less ready with their excuses, could only weep, swearing they 'had never done such a thing before', and promising never to come near Jane Trago's place again.

Everyone found occupying a bed, sailor, prostitute or dolly-mop, was led away to the police station. So too was Jane Trago — or Jane Davey, as she was known to the police.

The next morning all the women were led into court to face the censure of the magistrates and to suffer the penalties decreed by the laws of the land.

The weeping dolly-mops were fined, as was one of the youngest prostitutes. The remainder were sentenced to a month's imprisonment.

Jane went to prison for three months for keeping 'a disorderly house'. Far more serious for her, the licence enabling her to sell intoxicating liquor was withdrawn. This was the bitterest blow of all. It meant that her career as a grog-shop proprietor was at an end.

Jane survived the rigours of prison far better than Marcus Hooper. She had met up with hard men and women in many parts of the world and she had learned to fight and swear better than most men. When she was picked on by the woman regarded as 'queen of the convicts',

Jane left the other woman lying face down on the flagstone floor, with injuries to her face that would mark her for life.

No one else troubled Jane during the remainder of her sentence and she was accorded due deference by fellow prisoners and warders alike.

The raid on the grog-shop was a serious set-back to Jane, but she refused to treat it as a disaster. One of the first things she did upon her release was to arrange the sale of her property. Luck was on her side. She found a customer who wanted to open a lodging-house in the Waterloo Road district. A visit to the property by solicitor and client was all that was needed, and the agreed price was considerably higher than Jane had paid.

But Jane's luck did not rest on its laurels. She remained in Waterloo Road until the new owner took possession and two days before she was due to move one of the prostitutes who had shared her prison cell paid her a visit. Some of the grog-shop's stock remained and Jane opened a bottle of London gin by way of a farewell celebration.

The prostitute stayed no longer than an hour before standing up somewhat unsteadily and announcing her departure.

"But there's almost half a bottle left! Are you ill?"

The prostitute shook her head, "You know me, Jane. I'd down what's left in that bottle and be calling for another by evening-time, but I'm not a woman of leisure like you. I've a living to earn."

"Forget it for today. Here, let me top up your glass — "

The prostitute's hand capped the empty glass. "Another time, perhaps. There's a troopship out in the river with soldiers just back from India. It'll be docking on this afternoon's tide. A whole regiment of men who won't have seen a white woman for years — all with money jingling in their pockets."

Jane accepted the other woman's excuse for not drinking the day away. It would not be fair to ask her to miss such an opportunity. Every prostitute in Liverpool would be at the dockside today. Such opportunities were rare these days.

"Does anyone know which regiment it is?"

"Why . . . ? Oh, of course, you were in India for years, love, weren't you? I've heard you say so. Yes, it's a regiment with some Indian name, although all the soldiers are English. I remember because an officer came ashore by boat this morning and someone spoke to him. Let me think. It's the first, something or other — First Bengal Light Infantry. Yes, that's it."

"Are you sure?"

"Pretty sure, why?"

"That's *my* regiment. I was with them for years out in India!"

"Then give yourself a treat, Jane. Come down to the docks and see 'em in. It's better than sitting here with only a half-bottle of mother's ruin for company."

25

REGIMENTAL Sergeant Major William Batley formed his men up on the dockside, barking orders as though he were on a parade-ground. He was smart, ramrod-stiff and looked every bit as fierce as any self-respecting regimental sergeant major should. Yet beneath the military exterior William Batley felt as though his heart was breaking. Today was his last day of service with the regiment that had been home, mother, father and mistress to him for twenty-five years, man and boy.

Officially, the regiment no longer existed. Formed by volunteers, from Suffolk and Norfolk regiments serving in India many years before, the regiment had been disbanded on the ship bringing them home from the country where they had served with considerable distinction.

The majority of the men would make their own way home from Liverpool. The remainder, a mere handful of younger men, were travelling on to garrison towns to join new regiments.

Regimental Sergeant Major Batley had trained every man standing on parade today. He had taught each soldier to be proud of the regiment in which he served. Under his guidance new recruits, immature young men unfamiliar with so much as the sharp edge of a razor, had become soldiers. Each man ready to fight anywhere, at any time, for the glory of queen, country — and the regiment.

Many had been called upon to put their readiness to the ultimate test. The graves of soldiers of the 1st Bengal Light Infantry were scattered among the bare hills and defiles of the Himalaya mountains, where they had won honours from their country, and respect from their enemies.

"First Bengal Light Infantry . . . atten*tion*!"

Regimental Sergeant Major William Batley's voice carried to every soldier on parade. The sound of heels striking the stone-flagged ground echoed from the warehouses at the edge of the quay. Sergeant Major Batley marched stiffly to where the colonel of the regiment stood flanked by his officers.

There was just the hint of a break in Batley's voice as he saluted his commanding officer and reported the regiment 'present and correct' for the last time.

The colonel shared his regimental sergeant major's emotion for the occasion. After returning the salute, his hand reached out and rested for a moment on William Batley's shoulder before he and his entourage moved closer to the parading soldiers.

His message to them was brief but highly emotional. He had served as their colonel for twelve years and been with the regiment for even longer than their regimental sergeant major. He reminded them of battles fought and won: of unforgotten comrades they had left behind in a foreign land. He vowed he could not have wished for braver or more loyal soldiers. Finally, his voice barely audible, he wished them 'God speed!' Then,

451

with a bow of his head, he ordered William Batley to 'Dismiss the regiment.'

The order was given, the regiment performed a half-turn away from their colonel, then hesitated, as though in a vain bid to delay the inevitable. Then the 1st Bengal Light Infantry broke ranks and was no more.

For a long time ex-Regimental Sergeant Major William Batley remained at the dockside, waiting until the last farewell had been said and only a handful of uniformed men remained, waiting for transport to take them to their new depots. Then, throwing a heavy bag containing all his worldly possessions into a carriage with a few others, he walked alone from the dockside. His baggage would be carried to an inn where he and a few other NCOs had booked accommodation. But for now he preferred to be alone with his thoughts.

Jane Trago located William Batley in one of the few 'respectable' grog-shops in the dock area. She saw him sitting alone at a table, staring moodily into the tankard of ale standing on the table before him.

Seating herself on the far side of the table, she looked across at the strong, sun-tanned face of a soldier in his early forties and saw his unhappiness.

"Hello, Bill. It's been a long time."

Looking up, William Batley's face registered amazement, swiftly followed by honest delight. "Jane Trago, as I live! What are you doing in Liverpool? I thought your home was somewhere in the West Country?"

"It's a long story, Bill, and one for another time. Today belongs to you and the regiment. It's been good to greet so many old friends on the streets of Liverpool. But I didn't expect to find you drinking on your own. Not today."

"I'll need to get used to being on my own. There's no Bengal Light Infantry now and I'm no longer Regimental Sergeant Major Batley. I'm just Bill Batley, an ex-soldier who'll never quite belong anywhere any more . . . But let me get you a drink. What'll it be? Gin? Ale?"

"I'll have a glass of Old Tom, with a splash of bitter and water. Thanks, Bill."

Jane watched the uniformed man as he pushed his way through the crowded room to the counter from which the owner served drinks. He was a fine, upstanding man who drew more than one admiring glance from the few women allowed in by the proprietress. Bill Batley had been respected in the regiment as a man who was honest and scrupulously fair to everyone. He had steered clear of the many money-making fiddles that most NCOs regarded as their due. He was a brave man too, as the colourful array of medal ribbons affixed to his chest attested. She had heard soldiers of the Bengal Light Infantry declare that having RSM Batley beside you in battle was a sight more reassuring than a whole regiment of native infantry.

"There you are." William Batley returned to the table and placed the drink in front of her. "I said to make it an extra large one. It saves me keep getting up. Now tell me about yourself. What have you been doing since you came

453

back to England? What was it now, eighteen months . . . two years ago?"

"Something like that. I haven't done a great deal. I visited my family for a while, but I'd been away too long." Jane had no intention of going into any detail about her return, but her words struck a spark from William Batley's own thoughts.

"That's pretty much the way I feel. My parents are both dead. The sister I can barely remember lives in America with her husband and I'll have long been forgotten by those in the village where I was born."

"So what are your plans? A man of your age can't be considering retirement."

"I'm not. I've been a careful man with my money and I have a tidy sum put by. I had hoped to buy a small country inn at Shotley Gate, in Suffolk. There's an innkeeper there — and ex-regiment man — who's wanting to sell. But he's asking too much. Colonel Holbrook's offered to lend me money, but I don't want to be beholden to any man for my livelihood."

"How much more do you need?"

"Close on six hundred pounds. It's a forlorn hope. I couldn't hope to repay that amount, even with a good pension added to anything I'll be earning."

Suddenly, Jane said, "Are you hoping to meet up with some of your friends, or are you content to sit drinking and chatting with me?"

"I've spent twenty-five years of my life with soldiers. Now I need to get along without them. I'm happy enough talking to you."

"Then I'll take you to where we can talk without all this noise about us — and I'll cook you a home meal to show you what you've been missing all these years. Come on, Bill. Down your drink and we'll go."

The size of Jane's property in Waterloo Road made a great impression upon William Batley. He was even more impressed when she took him inside.

"I came home from India with the same dream as you, Bill. I wanted to own a tavern. The closest I came to it was buying this place and running it as a grog-shop. Now it's sold I'll be moving on again."

"Where did you get the money to buy a place this size?" William Batley looked about him incredulously. Jane Trago had run beershops in India. She had also laundered, nursed and, if regimental rumour was to be believed, done a great many other things in order to live. Yet nothing she was reputed to have done would have made enough money to buy an establishment of such size.

"I was left some money by my uncle — Uncle Waldo. I've put it to good use. You help yourself to something to drink, there's a few bottles left over there. I'll pop out and buy us a couple of nice beefsteaks. By the time this evening's over you'll wish you'd come back to England years ago . . . "

When William Batley woke in the morning he remembered Jane's words and thought there was a great deal of truth in them. Jane had made up a bed for him in one of the spare rooms, using sheets he suspected had come from her own bed. He had gone to sleep with a full belly, and as much drink inside him as he could comfortably hold.

He stretched himself luxuriously and looked across the room to where his uniform was folded tidily over the back of a chair. He would need to buy new clothes today. He was surprised to find the thought did not fill him with as much gloom as it had yesterday.

The door opened and Jane Trago entered the room. She was carrying a tray on which were eggs, bacon and toast, together with a small piece of steak saved from the previous night.

"Here you are, a gentleman's breakfast. You shouldn't expect it every morning, but today's special. You're back in England — and for the first tine in twenty-five years you're not a soldier. How do you feel about it this morning?"

"Better than I did yesterday — and it's all thanks to you."

William Batley raised himself to a sitting position and took the tray from her. "I'll never be able to thank you enough, Jane."

Putting the tray in front of him, Jane said, "That's where you're wrong. I think there's a way you *can* thank me — and do yourself a good turn at the same time."

"How?"

"Don't let your breakfast get cold. I can talk while you eat, even if you can't — and that's a good thing too. I'd like you to listen to what I have to say, and then think carefully about it before you make up your mind." Jane glared pointedly at the plate in front of William Batley. He began to eat, although curiosity affected his enjoyment of the meal.

Seating herself on the edge of the bed, Jane said, "You told me yesterday about the village inn you'd wanted to buy but couldn't afford, and I told you how owning an inn had always been what I wanted."

William Batley nodded wordlessly, his mouth filled with steak.

"Well, think about it. You haven't got enough money to buy a tavern, and neither have I — but put our money *together* and we'll have more than enough to buy a tavern and make us *both* happy. Not only that, we'll be left with enough to set it up just the way we wanted."

William Batley had difficulty swallowing the steak on which he was chewing. He succeeded at his third attempt and said in a strangled voice, "Are you suggesting we get wed, Jane?"

"Don't be so daft! Why should we marry? I'm talking of a workable business arrangement. You and me equal partners. You'd be the landlord and I'd help you run it, supervising the kitchen, the chambermaids, and the like. It would work, Bill, I *know* it would. You just think about it."

Jane had not reached the door when Batley called out, "The answer's yes, Jane."

"I asked you to take your time and *think* about it. Really think."

"Why? Up in the hills, ambushed by Afghan tribesman I couldn't say, 'Wait. Stop shooting while I think what to do.' I made a decision right there and then. I'm still the same man I was there, Jane. I've made my decision — but there's a condition."

"Oh, and what's that?" In Jane's experience a condition always meant the side agreeing to it needed to concede something.

"I'll go along with you only on the condition you agree to marry me."

"Returning to England's affected your brain. No, I won't marry you."

"Then it seems we'll both need to find another dream to fulfil."

"That's stupid, Bill. It would be a very good *working* arrangement. We'd both be doing what we want to do, without any ties. Besides . . . " Jane hesitated before adding, "You don't really know anything about me. I'm not the sort of woman men *marry*."

"I'm not a man who cares very much what others do or think. I know far more about you than you realise — especially the things you did in India. You're no angel, Jane, I know that — but neither am I. Come to think of it, I can't see a couple of angels making a go of running a Suffolk inn, can you? I'll take you up on your offer, but only if we go into the inn as man and wife."

"You're making no sense, Bill. You must see that. Look, you've not been back in England twenty-four hours. I'm the first Englishwoman you've set eyes on — "

"I've given you my decision, Jane. Yes, I'd like to run an inn with you — but, I repeat, it will be as man and wife or not at all. Now it's *your* turn to go away and think about it — but I warn

458

you. Say no to me and I'll ask you again, and again . . . and again."

"All right."

There was something in the way Jane spoke the words that made William Batley forget all about his breakfast.

"All right, you'll give the matter careful consideration?"

"No, you're not the only one able to make up his mind quickly. It means . . . all right, Bill Batley, seeing as how you're daft enough to ask me . . . I'll marry you!"

26

WILLIAM BATLEY and Jane Trago were married a week before they moved to the country tavern at Shotley Gate. The small village was on the tip of a spit of land. On one side flowed the river Orwell. On the other the river Stour. Across the Orwell was Felixstowe, with Harwich sprawled along the far bank of the Stour. Both towns guarded the entrance to a natural harbour favouring Harwich, to which town a ferry operated from Shotley Gate.

When winter storms raged along the East coast, ships sought shelter in the harbour, and many sailors chose to spend a night ashore in Shotley in preference to the more commercial delights on offer in Harwich.

William and Jane renamed their inn the Star of India. It soon became a focal point for soldiers who had served in the Bengal Light Infantry, and any other Suffolk man who had ever served in the large and colourful country of India.

The first three years of marriage to William were the happiest of Jane's life. He was a kind, considerate and loving husband, and Jane responded with a warmth and faithfulness that surprised herself. The only cloud on her horizon was the rector, the Reverend Desmond Tilley.

Mr Tilley's brother was the husband of William Batley's only sister — and Desmond Tilley took an immediate and unreasonable dislike to Jane. He

460

wrote to William's sister in America, suggesting her brother had made a lamentable mistake in his choice of a bride.

The result was an emotional letter from Alexandra Tilley, William's sister, suggesting he emigrate to the United States and begin a new life there, far from all 'unhealthy' influences — and making no mention of his wife, or even his marriage.

William Batley laughed the letter away, telling Jane he was hardly likely to pay attention to a sister he had not seen since she was a young girl — and who had not written to him once during all the years of his service in India.

It was not difficult to forget all outside influences. The Star of India was popular with local people and travellers alike, due in no small measure to the geniality of William Batley, and his fund of stories of service life in India.

In the early days a somewhat unruly element frequented the inn during the evenings. Jane encouraged them at first, arguing that they spent good money in the bar. William Batley disagreed, offering the opinion that they were keeping away customers who would pay far more in board and lodging.

In spite of Jane's misgivings he barred anyone from the tavern who was inclined to be noisy or quarrelsome. Jane soon had to agree her husband was right. They began to attract a higher class of clientele and the inn became a meeting place for the local gentry.

The only rowdy nights at the inn occurred when reunions were organised for officers and men of the Bengal Light Infantry. These were the only nights Jane ever had to help her husband to bed because he was the worse for drink.

Yet, drunk or sober, William Batley was a surprisingly gentle man. Most of the men in Jane's life had been men of violence and she learned to love her husband for his patient and quiet ways. Jane's love for William Batley showed clearly to everyone except the Reverend Desmond Tilley. William and Jane Batley were looked upon as an ideally suited couple by their friends.

Early in their fourth year at the star of India, William became ill. At first it was no more than a vague listlessness. A tiredness that came upon him unexpectedly. A few minutes' rest would be sufficient for him to return to work looking somewhat sheepish and apologising for his lack of stamina.

Then gradually his bouts of tiredness occurred with increasing frequency and a few minutes' rest was no longer sufficient to bring about a full recovery. Soon he was spending half the day lying on his bed and customers began commenting on the amount of weight he was losing.

One day, when for the first time William felt too ill to rise from his bed in the morning, Jane ignored her husband's protests and sent for a doctor. By the time he arrived William had left his bed and, protesting that he felt fine was tackling the day's chores.

The doctor told Jane, somewhat condescendingly, that it was perfectly natural for a wife to be concerned for her husband's health. Nevertheless, he believed William Batley was a perfectly healthy man. He dismissed the tiredness as being nothing more than the body's reaction to a lifetime spent in the army.

"Your husband has been a courageous and disciplined soldier," the doctor told Jane. "He has pushed his body to its limits. When he left, instead of relaxing, he took on the challenge of this inn. He has worked exceptionally hard to build up a good trade — and has succeeded. In his mind he is aware of his success and the mind is telling his body the tine has come to relax and enjoy life."

The doctor beamed at Jane, "I've seen such cases before. The trouble with working hard for many years is that you don't know when it's time to stop. Fortunately for you and your husband you have sought my professional advice — and it's this. Now you are successful let others do the work. You and your husband sit back and learn to enjoy life and I promise you'll have many years of good living ahead of you."

When Jane told her husband of the doctor's advice he agreed to heed his words and take life more steadily.

Only a few weeks after the doctor's cheering words William Batley suffered a stroke which left him paralysed down one side of his body and able to speak only slowly and indistinctly.

Jane had doctors brought in from nearby Ipswich and, in final desperation, she turned to London for the finest medical practitioners in the land. It was all to no avail. Early in 1869 William Batley suffered another stroke. He died in his wife's arms one morning as the dawn sun laid a golden path for him across the confluence of the two tidal rivers.

William's death came as a devastating blow for Jane. She wandered about in a state of shock, quite incapable of coping with the daily routine of running an inn.

On the day before the funeral, his sister Alexandra arrived at the inn with her husband, Quentin Tilley. Many months before, the Reverend Desmond Tilley had written to tell Alexandra her brother was ailing. He suggested that if she wished to see him alive she should consider a visit at the earliest opportunity. She and her husband had come as quickly as business and distance would allow.

Alexandra Tilley's bitterness at not seeing her brother alive was directed at Jane, but her anger was wasted. Jane was so overcome with grief she hardly registered anything going on about her.

After the funeral her condition deteriorated even more. Caring nothing for the running of the inn, she remained in her room day and night, emerging only to call for more gin to be sent up to her.

There were important decisions to be taken. The Star of India had been in William's name. If Jane wished to take on the running of the inn she would need to apply to have the licence transferred to her.

The task of running the inn had fallen to the cellarman, but making decisions was beyond his limited capabilities. He tried to discuss the situation with Jane, but was driven from the room by a torrent of incoherent abuse.

Finally, from sheer desperation, the cellarman took his problem to the Reverend Desmond

464

Tilley. The rector listened to the tale of woe, as did his rather vacuous brother and tight-lipped sister-in-law. Thanking the cellarman, Desmond Tilley assured him the matter was in hand. Indeed, he was merely awaiting a reply to an inquiry he had made. He felt confident he would then be in a position to set the affairs of the Star of India to rights.

Three weeks after William Batley's funeral, Desmond, Quentin and Alexandra Tilley arrived at the Star of India in the rector's trap. Handing the reins of the pony to an under-groom, the trio marched in through the door, 'Looking for all the world . . . ' quoted a chambermaid who saw them, ' . . . like three avenging angels, only they didn't have no wings nor haloes, and their looks favoured Old Nick more.'

The trio went straight to Jane's room and entered without bothering to knock at the door. In the doorway they stopped, noses wrinkling in disgust and exchanging I-told-you-so glances.

Jane sat in a chair close to a log fire. Shoeless, she was dressed in a grubby housecoat. Her hair looked as though it had not come into contact with a brush for days, and there was a strong and sickly smell of stale gin hanging in the air.

"Disgusting!" Alexandra Tilley was the first to speak. "How William ever became involved with such a slut, I'll never know. She must have bewitched him."

Turning red-rimmed, lack-lustre eyes upon the trio, Jane gave no sign she had heard Alexandra Tilley's words.

465

"Jane whatever-your-real-name-is, we've come here to have a serious talk with you."

Still there was no acknowledgement of their presence from Jane and she returned her gaze to the fire burning low in the grate.

"The woman's *drunk*." Quentin Tilley pulled out a silk handkerchief from his pocket and held it to his nose. "She's no doubt been in this condition since the funeral."

" . . . And for a long time before if the rumours I've heard are true," declared Desmond Tilley. "I've no doubt your poor brother *worked* himself to death, my dear."

"Fortunately *she's* not going to benefit from all William's work, thanks to you, Desmond."

Alexandra advanced to where Jane sat hunched in the chair, "We're here to talk to you and it's no good you pretending to be so overcome with drink, or whatever, that you can't hear us."

"Go away. I don't want to talk."

"That doesn't surprise me in the least — but you're going to *have* to talk to us."

"I don't want to talk to anyone. Go away — and on your way out tell Rose to bring me up another bottle of gin."

"You disgusting slut," Alexandra Tilley towered above Jane, her body quivering with the strength of her indignation. "The sooner you're out of William's inn the better."

"It's my inn now."

This was the first indication Jane had given that she understood anything of what had been said and the Tilleys exchanged triumphant glances.

"Oh no it's not." The Reverend Desmond

Tilley drew a letter from his pocket and brandished it in front of Jane's face. "I've believed all along you weren't all you've pretended to be. Here I have my final piece of proof."

Opening up the sheet of paper, Desmond Tilley said, "Shall we begin with your name: Jane 'Trago', 'Deeble', 'Hooper', 'Davey' . . . Which is it now?"

"It's Batley, as you know full well — " Jane spoke defiantly, although each name mentioned by the Reverend Desmond Tilley punched a hole through the drunken cocoon encasing her brain and she tried desperately hard to marshal her scrambled thoughts.

"Oh no! It wouldn't surprise me if you laid claim to many more names than I've already mentioned, but I doubt if Batley is among them. You gave your name as Davey when you were sent to prison in Liverpool for running a disorderly house. It was Deeble when you went to India with your *husband* — and Trago was the name you used when you went through a wedding ceremony with poor William. You certainly gave false information to the man who conducted the ceremony — and I wouldn't be surprised to learn you have actually committed bigamy."

"I've never been married to anyone before. Deeble was the name of the soldier who took me to India, using his wife's marriage certificate. *He* was married, I wasn't."

"Oh? No doubt you drew the other woman's marriage allowances too? And what about the other names?"

Jane made no reply and once again Alexandra

Tilley spat out a single word.

"*Disgusting!*"

"I think the best thing you can do is leave this inn right away. Tonight."

Jane came as close to being sober as was possible in that moment. "I married Bill properly. In a church. And I gave him half the money to buy this inn. It *is* mine."

"Perhaps you'd care to explain where you got the money to buy a half-share in an inn?"

Desmond Tilley gave his companions a quick, triumphant smile, " . . . or would that have something to do with the reason an Inspector Coote of the Cornwall police requested the help of Scotland Yard to trace your whereabouts a few years ago. I've written to this Inspector Coote and am awaiting his reply with great interest . . . "

"Get out! GET OUT!"

Jane picked up an empty gin bottle and hurled it at the Reverend Desmond Tilley. It missed his head by no more than an inch and shattered against the stone wall.

Another bottle pursued the trio across the room to the door as Jane screeched obscenities at them.

In the doorway, an arm held up to shield his face, Desmond Tilley turned to face the furious and dangerous woman.

"We're going now, but if you have any sense you'll be gone from the Star of India by the time I return this evening with a constable. I doubt if you'll find him as gullible as poor William Batley."

27

IT was fate . . . an accident . . . or perhaps no more than an excess of gin that led Jane to Chatham, two nights later.

As soon as the three members of the Tilley family had left the Star of India, Jane packed a trunk, took all the money from the safe and the cash drawers, and had the groom drive her in the hotel carriage to the railway station ten miles away in Ipswich.

Jane was giving up her legitimate claim to the ownership of the inn she and Bill had bought, but she still had money in a bank. Receiving recognition as the rightful owner of the Star of India would mean little to her if she was locked in a prison cell — and Jane had no doubt that would be her fate if Police Inspector Kingsley Coote caught up with her. Besides, the loss of the inn mattered little when compared with the loss she had so recently suffered.

Jane caught a train to London, although she had no intention of staying there. In truth, she had no idea where she was heading. Her only tangible thought was to put as much distance as possible between herself and Shotley Gate.

The bottle of gin she consumed between Ipswich and London helped neither her thinking nor her speech. When her trunk was loaded on a hackney carriage and she stumbled inside and called her instructions to the driver, 'Station' was the only intelligible word he heard. Three times he tried without success to clarify her instructions. In the end he gave up. He had a regular passenger to pick up soon in the Victoria area. He would drop her off at Victoria railway station. It was unlikely to matter very much. One railway station would be much the same as another to a woman as intoxicated as was his passenger.

At Victoria station the hackney-carriage driver helped himself to his fare from the purse Jane waved beneath his nose, taking more than four times the normal amount for the journey. Then he espied a number of young sailors being shepherded into the station by a naval recruiting petty officer, en route to the naval barracks at Chatham.

Calling to the sailors, the resourceful carriage driver said, "Give this lady a hand, will you, lads? She's on her way to Chatham, but I fear she's been celebrating too well along the way. Get her ticket and put her on the train and you'll no doubt earn her undying gratitude."

The hackney-carriage driver winked at the sailors. "You'll find money for her fare in a bag about her neck — and there's a bottle or two of gin in the top of the trunk. If she were sober she'd want to show appreciation for your assistance, so just help yourself to anything you want."

The petty officer gave the driver a contemptuous look. "Get on your way and find someone else to rob, cabbie. If this lady's going to Chatham we'll see she gets there safely — with her money *and* her gin."

Turning his back upon the hackney-carriage driver, the recruiting petty officer detailed two of the sailors to carry the trunk before speaking to Jane for the first time.

"I'll be happy to be of assistance to you, ma'am. The cabbie said you were going to Chatham. So are we. If you have money for your fare I'll be happy to get a ticket for you, and see you on the train."

Jane peered at the speaker, but found it difficult to focus her eyes. He was bearded and she had the impression of a wide-eyed, honest face, but this was all.

"Thank you . . . be much obliged . . . " She fumbled for the soft, pigskin bag hanging on a leather cord about her neck. She succeeded in finding and opening the neck of the bag and a number of sovereigns fell to the floor.

"This should suffice, ma'am. I'd tighten the drawstrings again if I was you. You don't want to lose any more than you already have."

The petty officer was about to go off and buy her a ticket, when Jane reached out and grasped his arm, "You think . . . I'm drunk?"

"I think you've probably had a fair amount to drink, begging your pardon, ma'am. But that's none of my business. I'll get your ticket."

"I'm a *widow*, sailor. I was widowed only two weeks ago . . . or was it three? He was a soldier . . . in India. A *brave* soldier . . . a regimental sergeant major. He was given a medal . . . a *gold* medal. The Indian Order of Merit. For *valour* it says on the medal. I've got it here . . . somewhere."

The petty officer's hand reached out when she began fumbling in her bag. "You don't have to

471

prove anything to me, ma'am. I was in India, with the navy." He pointed to a red and white medal ribbon, worn on his chest. "I got that when we relieved Lucknow. If your husband was out there I respect him for a brave man. The least I can do is make certain his widow comes to no harm. You just go along with my men, they'll take care of you while I buy you a ticket."

Petty Officer Jack Sparling was a man of his word. He bought Jane's ticket, put her trunk on board the train, then he and the sailors travelling with him shared her carriage to ensure no one took advantage of her drunken condition.

On the journey, Jane insisted upon taking two bottles of gin from her trunk and passing them among the sailors. After only a momentary hesitation, Petty Officer Sparling agreed his men could share her drink. He thought they were probably doing her a favour. If she drank any more Jane Batley was likely to fall victim to alcohol poisoning.

Long before the train came to a halt at the main station for the Medway towns, Petty Officer Sparling had ascertained that Jane knew no one in Chatham. He could learn nothing of her reasons for travelling to the naval town, but he determined she would not suffer as a result of her inebriated condition.

Chatham station was a hive of activity. As well as the large naval dockyard and barracks, the headquarters of the Royal Engineers was nearby and soldiers and sailors milled about the platforms in large numbers.

Despite the crowds, Petty Officer Sparling was

able to secure a hansom-cab for Jane. He gave the driver instructions to take her to an address close to the Royal Engineers barracks, where a Mrs Brown would be found. The driver was to tell her that Jane had been sent by Petty Officer Sparling and was to be looked after. He would explain as soon as he was able to leave the naval barracks.

Jane Batley awoke in a strange room, not knowing where she was, or why she was there, or even what time it was.

From somewhere nearby she could hear street noises. There were sounds from nearer at hand too. House noises. People talking and laughing . . .

She lay for a long time trying to remember, but her last *clear* memory was of holding her beloved Bill in her arms. He was dead. Undeniably dead. At the recollection of his last moments Jane's insides screwed up and two tears escaped from her eyes.

She sat up in bed and saw the outline of her trunk on the floor close to the window. Her mouth felt dry and leathery. Her head ached, so too did most of the muscles in her body. She needed a drink.

Tottering unsteadily to the trunk, Jane opened the lid and rummaged through the contents. There were no more bottles here. She searched the room, but with the same result.

Muttering curses, Jane wondered about calling for a maid, but it would appear from the room that she was not inside an inn. She suspected she was in someone's house. Opening the blinds a few inches, she was able to confirm it quickly. Outside was a steep street, lined with terraced houses, their doors opening directly on to the pavement.

There was an air of grey drabness about the street, the sky, the houses . . . even the people. It was morning, but not early. People were going about their daily lives. Here and there women stood talking. Higher up the hill two women knelt side by side, scrubbing their respective doorsteps.

Jane returned to the bed and sat down heavily, the weight of the events of past weeks returning to her.

There came a knock on the door and a plump, motherly woman entered the room. In her hand she carried a mug of strong tea.

"I thought I heard you moving about up here, lovey. You'll be ready for a nice cup of tea, I daresay, after all your travelling."

"Where am I? Who are you?"

"I'm Ethel Brown, lovey. I'm a widow-woman, like yourself. This is my house, in Dale Street. It's not as posh as some parts of Chatham, but there's nice people as lives here, and nice neighbours are worth a whole parkful of pretty trees, that's what *I* always say — "

"Chatham . . . ?" Vague, fragmented memories rose like mountain peaks through the fog of Jane's mind. Trains and stations . . . sailors.

"How did I get here?"

Ethel Brown's expression was one of amused indulgence. "You must have been in a worse state than I thought, lovey. Jack Sparling brought you here. He's a sailor. A petty officer like my late husband. They was mates for years."

The woman's words conjured up a face. A bearded, blue-eyed, round face. An *honest* face, like Ethel Brown's own.

"Did he spend the night here with me?"

"That he did not!" Ethel Brown's expression was one of stern disapproval. "I'd not have such goings-on in *this* house. Besides, Petty Officer Sparling isn't that sort of man. Not that sort of man at all!"

Jane raised the cup of tea to her mouth and her hand trembled alarmingly, threatening to spill the contents. She succeeded in bringing it under control and took a mouthful of tea. It was hot and strong and sweet. She drank it all without removing the cup from her lips.

"I feel much better for that. Thank you, Missus Brown. I don't really know what I'm doing here in Chatham. I seem to have become totally confused these past few weeks."

Ethel Brown could have commented that Jane's confusion undoubtedly owed much to the amount of gin she had consumed. Jack Sparling had removed two and a half bottles from Jane's bag when he called at the house, the previous evening.

"You've been widowed recently, lovey?"

Jane suddenly felt thoroughly dejected and alone, "Just a few weeks. He was a soldier once . . . "

Ethel Brown became sympathetic once more, "I know just how you're feeling, lovey. I lost my Bert four years ago, yet sometimes it seems only yesterday he was sitting in the old chair across the fire from me. Do you have any family?"

Jane shook her head.

"I don't know what I'd have done without mine. They was a God-sent comfort, and no mistake." Ethel Brown was a compulsive tidier and busily straightened objects in the room as she spoke. "But never you mind, lovey. You're welcome to stay here for as long as you feel you need to."

Picking up the empty mug, Mrs Brown said, "I'll leave you to clean up. Come downstairs when you've a mind. There's no hurry."

"I'll pay you for my keep . . . "

"That will be a help, lovey, but only if you can afford it. My Bert left me a little bit of money — not that it goes very far these days."

That night Petty Officer Jack Sparling came to the house. He politely enquired after Jane's health and seemed genuinely pleased to see her 'looking so much better', as he tactfully put it.

Ethel Brown had prepared a large roast meal for the petty officer. Jane shared it with them, but quickly realised she was intruding upon their cosy little evening together. As soon as she could she pleaded tiredness and retired to her bedroom. She felt a desperate need for a drink, but another search of her baggage produced nothing. Petty Officer Jack Sparling had been thorough in removing all temptation from her reach.

Jane lay on the bed thinking over the events of recent weeks, and within minutes she was asleep.

The next day began as before for Jane, with a mug of tea brought up to her room by Ethel Brown. The remainder of the day followed the same pattern. By the time Petty Officer Jack Sparling came to the house that evening, Jane felt she would scream if anyone called her lovey once again. Ethel was a kind and generous person, but she had the personality of a sponge. Her conversation revolved about her home and ensuring Jack Sparling was made comfortable and amply fed when he paid his daily visit.

As the petty officer settled into the armchair vacated by the late Bert Brown, Jane announced her intention of taking a walk.

"On your own? Where will you go?" Ethel sounded horrified.

"I don't know, but I haven't been out of the house for two days. A walk will do me good."

"She'll come to no harm in Chatham. Unlike some parts of the world I could mention," Jack Sparling's smile travelled from Ethel to Jane. "All the same, if you walk as far as the main town you'd do well to keep clear of the streets down by the river. The fleet's home from the Far East and they've brought their supply ships with them. The supply ship crews are a tough crowd so they've been moored upriver, well clear of the dockyard. They'll be causing all manner of trouble in the riverside beerhouses tonight."

Jane could hear the rowdy singing from the riverside inns and grog-shops when she was still a street away. There were top-hatted policemen here, standing about in nervous groups, but she saw none when she turned the corner. The mud of the river glistened to one side of the road.

477

On the other one, in three of the houses, was a licensed grog-shop.

Out in the river a line of pot-bellied merchantmen were anchored in a ragged line, their yard-arms denuded of canvas. She could see few seamen on their decks; most appeared to be ashore. For some it was the first time they had set foot on English soil for three years. They had returned with money in their pockets and seemed intent upon spending it.

Jane's progress along the street was attended by catcalls and whistles, together with loud invitations to 'come here and have a drink . . . ' But Jane chose her drinking establishment carefully. The noise coming from some of the grog-shops was too much, even for her. She made for a tavern halfway along the riverside street where she had seen a number of ships' officers entering. She felt the need for company more mature than the bawdy, ribald wit of the predominantly younger seamen in the beerhouses.

Getting acquainted with the man of her choice was a routine with which Jane was familiar. She paused in the doorway and gazed around the room as if looking for someone she expected to be here. Then, with a disappointed and slightly apprehensive expression, she approached the table of her choice and gave the name of a fictitious cousin she was expecting to meet here. Perhaps they knew him . . . ?

Five minutes later, a drink on the table in front of her, the introductions were over and she and the men about the table were chatting as though they had known each other for years.

Jane did not return to the terraced house in Dale Street until the next morning. Then it was only to settle up with a tight-lipped Ethel Brown and collect her trunk from the house.

"I thought you might have had more respect for poor Petty Officer Sparling than to go off like you did. Worried out of his mind, he was. He was all for going out and searching the town when you hadn't shown up by eleven o'clock."

"I met a cousin. I knew he'd be here somewhere. I remembered that was why I came to Chatham in the first place."

Jane's lies slipped off her tongue easily, but Ethel Brown's loud sniff conveyed disbelief.

"Now I suppose you'll be moving out to stay with this 'cousin' of yours?"

"That's right. I have a carriage waiting outside, I'll be leaving as soon as I've collected my things."

"Without bothering to stay long enough to say a thank you to Petty Officer Sparling after all he's done for you?"

"*You* say thank you for me, Mrs Brown. I'm sure he'd prefer it came from you. The pair of you really ought to get married, you know. You're ideally suited to each other."

"I don't need advice from *you.* Me and Petty Officer Sparling are quite happy with things the way they are, thank you very much. You need to sort your own life out before you go around telling other people how to run theirs . . ."

Ethel Brown was still grumbling about 'ungrateful women who try to tell others their business' when Jane left the house.

Jane instructed the driver of the hired carriage to take her to the victualling quay in the Royal Naval Dockyard. Not until she saw the ship's boat alongside the jetty with Hugo Moran waiting patiently in the stern was she really certain he would be here waiting for her.

Hugo Moran was first mate of the supply ship *Mermaid.* Jane had spent the previous night on board with him. This morning the ship was sailing to Portsmouth to take on stores. In due course it would join up with the ships of the Home Fleet. Moran had suggested Jane might like to sail to Portsmouth with the vessel.

It made no difference to Jane whether she was in Chatham or Portsmouth. Moran was good-looking and pleasant company. When he was no longer around there would be someone else. There was no permanence in Jane's life any more. Now William Batley was dead life had become no more than a series of temporary experiences.

28

PORTSMOUTH was a disaster for Jane from her very first day there. Many times during the ensuing years she deeply regretted not recognising the warning signs. If she had had any sense she would have caught the first train out of the south coast naval town.

Mermaid was berthed alongside the wall in the dockyard and Hugo Moran suggested that Jane leave her belongings on board and remain on the ship. It would save her paying out money for lodgings.

Jane agreed readily enough. Hugo was as much of a man as she wanted for now and she would need all her money for the new scheme taking form in her mind.

Circumstances had forced her to give up the Star of India to William Batley's family, but she still had some of the money put by from the sale of her Liverpool grog-shop. To this she had added a great deal of the profits from the Star of India, given to her by her late and generous husband.

Jane intended to open another grog-shop in Portsmouth if she could find a suitably cheap property. It would, of necessity, be smaller than her Liverpool venture, but that would be a good thing. She would not be tempted to make a similar mistake to the one she had made there. Jane believed she could make a modest but comfortable living from such a venture.

The first evening in Portsmouth was spent in a beerhouse close to the docks. Suddenly there was a cry of "Jane!" from across the room and a large seaman pushed his way between the customers to the table where she sat with Hugo Moran.

"Jane . . . It *is* Jane Davey?" The drunken seaman leaned closer. "Of *course* it is. I'd never forget your face. Don't you remember me . . . Arthur Scrimshaw? I was one of your best customers when you had the grog-shop in Waterloo Road, in Liverpool."

Jane's spirits sank. In view of her plans the last person she wished to meet here was anyone who had known her in the Liverpool days. But there was worse to come.

"It was the best little grog-shop this side of Hong Kong — and *I* should know. We had some great times together there, remember? Of course you do."

The fact that Jane had no recollection of the man at all made no difference to him.

"I got the shock of my life when I came back from a voyage and found the grog-shop closed and you in prison. Running a disorderly house, they said — now there's a laugh! There wasn't one *orderly* grog-shop in the whole of Liverpool!"

"I'm sorry, I think you've mistaken me for someone else." Jane stood up abruptly and spoke to Hugo Moran, "Can we go now? This man's embarrassing me."

Hugo Moran was looking at Jane peculiarly, but he stood up.

The big, drunken seaman was indignant. "Of

482

course I'm not mistaken. You must remember me."

"You heard the lady. She said she didn't want to hear any more."

Hugo Moran spoke sharply and the drunken seaman looked at him, as though seeing him for the first time. Pushing his face close to Moran's, the seaman said insultingly, "If I'd wanted to hear you speak I'd have called Pretty Polly! Sit down until I do."

As the seaman put out a hand to push Hugo back into his seat, the *Mermaid*'s first mate hit him. The seaman staggered back into the customers across the room. Cheering, they promptly threw him back for Moran to hit again. Seconds later the bar erupted in a free-for-all.

Hugo Moran guided Jane clear of the mêlée. Rubbing the knuckles of his right hand, he said, "I think we'd better go back to the ship and have a look at this hand. I hope I haven't broken anything."

"I'm sorry, Hugo. It was all my fault . . . "

"You weren't to know he'd be there — but I don't think he'd mistaken you for anyone else."

"No."

"Perhaps you'd better tell me all about it."

Before marrying William Batley, Jane would never have dreamed of telling anyone *anything* about herself, but now she told Hugo Moran all that had happened to her, beginning with her arrival in Liverpool. Her only lie was the same one she had told her husband. She said the money for the grog-shop had been left to her by an uncle.

Hugo Moran listened in silence until her story was ended. Then he said, "This grog-shop licence, will you get it if the Portsmouth authorities learn you've been convicted of running a disorderly house?"

"No. But with any luck they'll never find out. My name was Davey then. It's Batley now."

"Would it help if *I* were to write a character reference for you?"

"It might. It would certainly do me no harm."

"Right, that's what I'll do — but do you have enough money to buy a property and do whatever's needed to set up a grog-shop?"

"I have a banker's draft for more than enough."

"Then you have nothing to worry about. Let's go back on board and I'll open a bottle of the captain's best brandy and drink to your future success."

The next week sped by. In the dockyard *Mermaid* continued to take on stores during the day, keeping Hugo busy but Jane did not mind. She was busy searching for a property that would be suitable for a grog-shop.

She and Hugo spent their evenings drinking in the Portsmouth taverns and beerhouses. Jane feared meeting up with the seaman who had known her in Liverpool, but he seemed to have left the town.

By the end of the week Jane thought she had found a suitable property and she took Hugo to see it. He seemed favourably impressed and suggested they should go to an inn he knew and celebrate the end of her search.

The evening ended in disaster. It was evident that *Mermaid's* first mate was familiar not only with the tavern but also with one of the serving-girls. His attentions to the girl became so blatant and embarrassing that he and Jane had a furious argument which resulted in Jane throwing a tankard of ale over the first mate. Followed by the cheers of the other customers, she stormed from the tavern.

Hugo caught her at the door. He was very, very angry. "You're behaving like a stupid young virgin — something you've probably *never* been. Come on back to the ship, it's time I taught you a lesson."

"You go back to the ship — and you can take your serving-girl with you for all I care. I'll find somewhere else to sleep."

Hugo did not pursue Jane beyond the door and she found accommodation for the night in a lodging-house where she suspected she was the only female without a sleeping-partner.

The following day, still smarting over Hugo's unreasonable behaviour, Jane kept away from the dockyard until the late afternoon. Then, requiring a change of clothes, she made her way to the victualling quay.

By now she had thought very carefully about the previous evening's incident. Although she still felt Hugo's behaviour had been unreasonable, she could hardly expect him to have led a celibate life before meeting her. He was too good-looking a man for that. No, if he was prepared to apologise to her, she would forgive him. If not . . . well, there was always her grog-shop.

When Jane reached the victualling quay she received a shock that stopped her dead in her tracks. The *Mermaid* was no longer berthed there!

At first she thought she must have been so wrapped up in her thoughts that she had made a foolish mistake and come to the wrong jetty. She had even begun to retrace her steps before she stopped herself. There was no mistake. She had walked to the jetty at least twice a day for the past week.

A stores clerk in the office at the end of the jetty confirmed that *Mermaid* had indeed sailed.

"Went out on this morning's tide," said the clerk nasally, sniffing his way through a heavy cold. "Gone off with the Home Fleet."

"Gone *where*?" Jane was in a panic. Not only were all her clothes in the trunk on board — but the banker's draft was there too.

"Gone to sea." The clerk's sniff served both a cold and his disdain at having to answer such a stupid question.

"When will they be back? I have a lot of property on board."

The clerk shrugged, "Search me. I'm not the bleedin' admiral. Might be next week . . . next month. Next year even."

Jane went cold. Her whole future was on board *Mermaid*.

"Is there any way I can find out about the *Mermaid's* plans?"

"You can make enquiries at the Admiral's office. They might tell you there."

Jane turned to leave the clerk's office. She

would learn nothing more here. Then she had a sudden thought. "When did the orders arrive for the *Mermaid* to sail?"

"Must have been some time yesterday. I can't tell you exactly. I was off sick with this cold . . . " he sniffed yet again to emphasise his condition, "but there was nothing about it the day before."

Once outside the office Jane tried to think things out without panicking. Her trunk was locked and Hugo Moran probably thought it contained only clothes. In any case, even if he found the banker's draft he would be unable to do anything with it while the ship was at sea.

It took Jane two visits to the admiral's office before she was given the information she wanted. A weekend had intervened between her calls, by which time *Mermaid* had been gone four days.

Jane was eventually shown into the office of a commander, who treated her as though he suspected her of being a dangerous spy. He questioned her in great detail about her reasons for wishing to know the movements of Her Majesty's Home Fleet.

He finally accepted Jane's story, but what he had to say dismayed her. The fleet would be absent from Portsmouth for at least six months. They were at this moment on their way to Gibraltar. One of the supply ships was expected to return in about three months' time, the other might be away for a year. He could not tell her which ship would be doing what.

"But . . . everything I have in the world is in a cabin on board *Mermaid*."

"The Royal Navy cannot be held responsible for

that, Mrs Batley. I do not approve of women being carried on board *any* ship that sails with the fleet. However, *Mermaid* is outside my jurisdiction. But as a matter of interest, what is the name of the officer who, er . . . *entertained* you on board the ship?"

"Hugo Moran."

"The first mate? Then I am afraid your problem is two-fold. While your possessions may be on board *Mermaid,* First Mate Moran is *not.* He left the vessel shortly before it was due to sail and failed to return. One of my lieutenants was loaned to them as first mate. This friend of yours would seem to be a thoroughly unreliable type."

Jane knew in her heart even before she went to the bank that Hugo Moran was not only unreliable, but thoroughly dishonest. Her enquiry was a hollow formality.

The bank draft had been cashed on the day *Mermaid* set sail. If there was something irregular in the transaction, the bank manager suggested to Jane she should go to the police immediately.

Jane knew she could do nothing about the theft. If she went to the police their enquiries would lead back to William Batley's family in Shotley Gate. They in turn would identify her as Jane Trago, one time serving-girl at Henwood's Cheesewring Inn, who had absconded with three months' takings. It was a risk she could not take.

For the second time in little more than a month, Jane had been robbed of a small fortune.

She was back where she had started. Penniless and with only one thing she could sell to earn a living. Her body.

29

MIRIAM and Lottie set off for Portsmouth three days after Miriam's return to Sharptor with news of her sister. It had taken Miriam this long to persuade Lottie to accede to her mother's wish and agree to see her.

Lottie pleaded she had no love left in her heart for the mother who had twice deserted her. She still felt very bitter too about her mother's callous indifference to Jacob when he was dying.

Miriam's entreaties eventually won the day, but it was a very uncertain and unwilling daughter who set off early in the morning to visit her mother in the naval town. Lottie could not help feeling her mother had brought most of her problems upon herself.

Even her mother's potentially fatal illness would seem to be a direct result of the life she had been leading in Portsmouth. Miriam would not tell Lottie exactly what it was, but her very reticence left no doubt in Lottie's mind.

The journey took all day, and involved four changes of train. They were on the final one and actually within sight of Portsmouth when Lottie said for the umpteenth time, "I wish I hadn't let you persuade me to come, Miriam. No good will come of this. I just know it won't."

"You had to come, Lottie. When I told your mother you'd been seeing a lot of Hawken Strike she got so excited about it I thought she was going to have a fit on the spot."

"She hasn't brought me all this way just to wish me luck. She'll spoil things for me. I know she will."

"You shouldn't speak like that, Lottie. I know she's done some terrible things, but she *is* your mother. Besides, there's little she can do about anything now. My only hope is that she's still alive when we get there."

Miriam and Lottie went first to the home of Phoebe Gilmore. She was a tall, gaunt and somewhat forbidding woman, but she showed her true nature by hugging Lottie warmly when she greeted her, "You must be very excited at the prospect of seeing your mother again after all these years. However, I must warn you, she's in a very serious condition. Acting upon Miriam's instructions we've moved her from the workhouse to a hospital and she's receiving the best possible care, but ... " Phoebe Gilmore paused, and carefully chose her next words. "Your mother has not taken care of herself in recent years and is now paying a very heavy penalty. I won't try to fool you, Lottie. The doctor has said it's only her will — and the will of God, of course — that's keeping her alive. I'm not being unduly pessimistic, but I do want you to be prepared for what you'll see when you go to the hospital."

"Lottie will have some news to tell her too," declared Miriam. "Hawken Strike has asked her to marry him."

Anne Gilmore squealed with delight. It was

not until she and Phoebe Gilmore had expressed their congratulations that it was noticed Nell had left the room without saying anything to Lottie at all.

"She'll be feeling sorry for herself," explained Phoebe Gilmore. "Samuel Coolidge sailed for Mexico only yesterday. She's missing him dreadfully. Before he left he asked her to marry him. It would seem marriage is in the air."

"Did Nell accept him?" Miriam asked.

"She said what any sensible young girl would say to such a nice young man. She said yes."

"I'm delighted for her. He *is* a nice young man — but she'll need permission to marry. That might prove difficult now we've discovered she and Anne have a family . . . "

"Nothing has changed as far as the two girls are concerned. We had a family conference while you were away in Cornwall, and the two girls were included in our discussions. Both said they wished to remain with you and your husband. The family are happy for you to become their legal guardians, if you so wish. Indeed, we are all grateful beyond words to you and Mr Retallick for rescuing Nell and Anne and bringing them up to be such splendid girls."

"Josh and I love them both as though they were our own daughters," said Miriam, hugging Anne. "We'd be very unhappy to lose them now — unless it was in marriage."

"They are very lucky girls," said Phoebe Gilmore. "And now they've gained a great many aunts, uncles and cousins too. One of their uncles is a solicitor. He's drawing up papers to make you their legal guardians. He's also looking into a rather strange story told to me by your sister Jane. It would seem she is probably the legal owner of an inn somewhere in Suffolk, but she has been cheated out of it by a number of her late husband's relatives. One of them a man of the cloth, I believe."

Marcus Hooper returned to Henwood in the evening of the day Miriam and Lottie left for Portsmouth. He had been drinking, but he was not drunk. He gave no reason for his absence, and his first words to Patience were, "I'm hungry. I'll have a meal — and be quick about it."

Patience wrung her hands apologetically. "There's no food in the house, Marcus. The girls have had nothing to eat since yesterday and I haven't been able to get any money from our Miriam."

Reaching inside a pocket, Marcus threw a number of coins casually on the table. Among them were four golden guineas.

"Go out and buy something — and be quick about it. I don't intend spending the whole evening in the house listening to you moaning about all that's been going on while I've been away."

"Nothing's been going on . . . except that our Jane's turned up again. Miriam's seen her."

Patience announced the news with a sidelong glance at her husband. It was eight years since he had supposedly gone in pursuit of Jane Trago. She wanted to see his reaction now.

She was totally unprepared for the effect it had upon him. The blood drained from his face and he turned on her fiercely. "What do you mean, she's 'turned up'? Is she here, in Henwood?"

"No."

Marcus's reaction to news of Jane was even worse than Patience had feared. Now she was certain that he had gone off with her, that he still cared for her.

"Then where is she, woman? Where is she now? Tell me!"

"No! You're not going off with her again. I knew you was lying. I knew you'd gone off somewhere together — "

Marcus's fist shot out and Patience crashed back against the wall of the room. She fell to the floor, blood spurting from a badly cut lip.

Kate, youngest of the Hooper girls, was in the room and she began screaming, but Marcus seemed oblivious of anyone but his unfortunate wife. Gripping Patience by her hair he pulled her up from the floor. "Where is she? Tell me where she is!"

"She's ill. Dying. It'll do you no good . . . "

Patience spoke with difficulty, her split lip had swollen alarmingly.

Marcus hit her again, this time on the nose, and blood spread across her face. As Patience fell to her knees a vicious kick took her in the ribs and sent her sprawling on the floor again. Marcus kicked her yet again, this time on the stomach and Patience's screams joined those of her daughter.

The screams became a pathetic sobbing as Patience begged Marcus not to kick her any more. Suddenly Kate fled from the room and, stumbling out on to the street, appealed for help to the rapidly growing crowd outside the house.

"Help . . . please help my ma! Pa's killing her."

Marcus Hooper was not a man any miner there would have tackled willingly. But each miner would have to face the scorn of his wife later, in the quiet of his own home — and there were enough men in the crowd to take him.

The first two miners hesitated for a moment at the open door of the Hooper cottage, until they were propelled inside by the weight of those behind. Once started there was a rush of men into the house and in a moment Patience's screams were lost in their shouts.

At the height of the fight inside the house there was the sound of breaking glass and a man's arm came through the window. It was withdrawn immediately but the violence inside continued for many more minutes.

When the noise finally died down, a cheer went up from inside. Moments later miners appeared at the door, dragging a bloody Marcus on his knees between them.

When their men threw Marcus into the street some of the women spat on him until he rose shakily to his feet and glared at them through the one eye that was still open.

"Some of you had better get inside and tend to Patience. She's taken a bad beating."

The miner who spoke to the women dabbed at a bloody nose. Marcus had been beaten to the ground, but he had gone down fighting.

"What was it all about?" One of the women

put the question to Kate.

"Ma told him Aunt Jane had been found and was in a workhouse but she wouldn't tell him where."

"Did she tell him in the end?"

"Yes, but he still wouldn't stop beating her."

"He's a bad 'un and no mistake, for all he's your pa. I shouldn't say it to you, but what he gave your ma will be nothing to what Jane Trago will get if he catches up with her."

That night, as soon as it was dark, Marcus collected the clothes he would need for his journey to Portsmouth from the cottage. Patience and the children were staying with a neighbour, but Marcus was not looking for them. He was going to find Jane Trago — but he had a score to settle with the men who worked at the Sharptor mine before he left Henwood.

There was no one at the mine at this time of night and no lights burning, but Marcus knew his way around. It was not the first occasion he had relied upon darkness to cloak his activities here.

It took him no longer than twenty minutes to complete his task and he went on his way towards Liskeard railway station well satisfied with his work. Marcus ached in every limb and his face pained him but his ills would be nothing compared with what the Sharptor miners would suffer the next day.

The Portsmouth hospital was an unprepossessing place. With its dark stone walls and small windows it might have been a prison, or a workhouse. The

495

inside confirmed this impression, being stark and gloomy.

Seeing Lottie shudder, Miriam said, "Your ma's much better off here than she was in the workhouse. Compared to that place, this is a palace."

Lottie shuddered again, "I wouldn't wish a workhouse on anyone. Let's get on and see Ma. I want to get this over with."

They found Jane was in a ward with seven or eight other women. Each was in the final stages of her life.

In spite of all the warnings she had been given and her own determination to show no sympathy for the woman who had deserted her and Jacob, Lottie was shocked by her mother's appearance.

Jane Batley lay in bed, the sheet pushed down almost to her waist. Her arms and what could be seen of her body were of skeletal proportions. The flesh of her face, too, was wasted away leaving her with the sunken eyes and cheeks of a mummified skull.

Suddenly the eyes flickered open and Jane's glance settled upon her daughter.

"Well, well! So you've come to see your old ma after all, eh? I was beginning to think you wouldn't come." The voice was as aged and wasted as the body from which it had come.

Jane's eyes closed again momentarily, but she continued to speak, "I wouldn't have blamed you had you *not* come. I did you no favours by bringing you into this world, and I've done little for you since."

The eyes opened again. "Mind you, I could

496

surprise you yet. I told that solicitor who came to see me about the Star of India, at Shotley Gate, in Suffolk. It belonged to me and Bill. We were married properly, in a church spent three happy years there. It'll be yours when I die."

"I don't want any inn — or anything else of yours."

There was the trace of a smile on Jane Batley's face when she said, "You sound just the way you did when I came back to you the last time. When you were up on the moor with someone's goats, and Jacob ran to fetch you . . . "

Jane closed her eyes and remained silent for so long Lottie thought she had dozed off. Then the thin, cracked voice said, "I was sorry to hear about Jacob, our Lottie. He was a good boy. I honestly didn't know he was so ill, or I'd never have left him that night."

"If what everyone has been telling me is true then you're too close to your Maker to be telling lies like that now. If it's sympathy you want you've got it. I wouldn't want to see a sheep looking as ill as you. But as for caring what happened to Jacob . . . You never gave a damn for him, nor for me neither. You've never cared for *anyone* except yourself — and by the look of you now you didn't do a very good job of *that*!"

Lottie spoke so fiercely that all other conversation in the ward came to an abrupt end.

"Lottie! That's no way to talk to your ma — "

"It's all right, Miriam. What she's saying is no more than the truth. We all know it."

Looking up at her daughter, Jane grimaced,

as though in pain. "You're a good-looking girl, Lottie. *Too* good-looking — and too much like me in your ways . . . "

Suddenly Jane began fighting for breath. When the struggle had gone on for some minutes Miriam looked around for a nurse, but none could be seen. The attack gradually subsided and when it ended Jane lay on the bed breathing shallowly. When she opened her eyes again her next words were to Miriam.

"Where's our Patience? I thought she might have come to see me — or hasn't she forgiven me yet for ridding her of that no-good husband of hers?"

"Patience wanted to come, but Marcus was away. He'd been gone for a few days and she wouldn't dare to come without telling him what she was doing."

"He went back to her?"

"Marcus returned to Henwood last year, after more than seven years away. It took us all by surprise."

"Has he changed his ways?"

"Can a fox learn to sing like a skylark?" Lottie spoke scornfully. "Marcus Hooper will never change."

"No more will a lot of other folk I could name — and that includes the Strike family. Leander Strike was never any good to any woman — and his son's no better. Miriam tells me you've been seeing a lot of him lately."

"It's a bit late for you to tell me you're worried about the company I'm keeping."

"Not when it's one of the Strike family we're

talking about. They're no good. Keep away from them."

"I'll be a Strike myself before long. Hawken's asked me to marry him — and I've decided to say yes."

Suddenly Jane tried desperately hard to speak, but she was suffering another attack of breathlessness. This one went on for much longer than before and during the attack Jane writhed helplessly on the bed. Fortunately there was a nurse at hand now and she came and swiftly hauled Jane to a sitting position.

Talking over the head of the gasping woman to Miriam and Lottie, she said, "You'd better go now. We'll give her something to make her relax and help her breathing. She'll sleep for a long while afterwards. Come back and see her in the morning . . . "

30

THE next morning seven men and two bal-maidens were taken violently ill at the Sharptor mine before Josh realised there was something seriously wrong with the drinking-water.

All the victims had collapsed with severe stomach pains only minutes after drinking water from the tank outside the men's changing-room. Two, an aged miner and one of the bal-maidens, were also violently sick.

While Josh was on the tank, looking inside, Malachi Sprittle hurried across to him. He had been below grass when he received news of what was happening.

"What is it — contaminated water? Sometimes it stands for too long and becomes brackish."

"This has nothing to do with nature. Someone's put arsenic in the tank. I've found traces of it around the cover and one of the arsenic stores has been broken open."

Malachi Sprittle stared at Josh in disbelief, "Who'd do a thing like that? Why, it's tantamount to murder!"

"I don't know . . . "

Suddenly the two men realised they *did* know — and they both spoke his name together.

"*Marcus Hooper!*"

"Does anyone know where he is now?"

"No . . . but I can hazard a guess. He has

500

an obsession about Jane Trago. He beat poor Patience nigh to death until she told him where Jane was. He'll be well on his way to Portsmouth by now."

"What can be done about him?"

"Send someone to fetch a doctor — then have that water tank emptied and cleaned out. Save some of the water though, we'll need to have it analysed. While you're doing that I'll ride to find Superintendent Coote. Marcus Hooper has got away with a great many things in his lifetime, but he's gone too far this time. This is attempted murder."

Marcus reached Portsmouth late on the day when Miriam and Lottie had paid their first visit to Jane. He went first to the workhouse where she had been, only to be told Jane had been removed to a hospital half a mile away.

At the hospital Marcus found the matron less helpful. His appearance did not help him. One eye was closed and discoloured and his face cut and bruised. The matron refused permission for him to see Jane, saying she was far too poorly to receive any more visitors that day. She added that if Marcus cared to contact Jane's relatives they would no doubt allow him to accompany them when they visited her again the next morning.

Marcus left the hospital, but ten minutes later he was back inside, having entered the building by the door used by kitchen and cleaning staff.

Once inside the hospital the injuries he had received at the hands of the Sharptor miners proved an advantage. Any member of the medical staff who saw him assumed he was a patient. Not until he reached the women's wards was he challenged by a nurse.

"I've been sent with some money for Jane Trago. She's expecting it — but I've forgotten which ward she's in."

"Trago? I can't recall anyone of that name in here. What's wrong with her?"

"No one told me, although I heard them say she's very ill."

"Then you'd better try the ward upstairs. They have the incurable cases."

Marcus made his way up the stairs and came to a ward where the door was wedged open with no nurse in sight. There were a number of women in here, all but two of them lying in their beds. The two exceptions were sitting on a bed at the far end of the ward, talking. One was old, the other younger but hunched over as though in permanent pain.

Marcus tried to look confident as he walked between the two lines of beds looking at their occupants. The face of Jane Trago was burned into his memory, but he could see no one who looked like her here.

"Who you looking for?" The question was hurled at him by the younger of the two women.

"Jane Trago — 'though she's probably using her married name again now."

"There's no one named Trago in here. The only Jane is Jane Batley. You passed her on the right as you came in through the door. She was brought in a couple of days ago."

"Oh, then I must have the wrong ward."

Marcus walked back down the ward but as he was about to go out through the door he looked again at the patient named by the woman as Jane Batley. Her eyes had been closed when he came in. Now they were open and there was something about them that made Marcus pause and look again.

He took in the sunken cheeks and eyes. The wasted arm outstretched on the sheet. It couldn't be . . . and yet those eyes . . .

"Hello, Marcus. You've come a long way to see me."

The voice was hardly more than a whisper, but it was a voice he had never forgotten. He had heard it in his mind every day of his life.

Crossing to the bed he looked down at the dried-up husk of the woman he had been seeking for so long.

"Don't you want to kiss me, Marcus? For old times' sake? You never used to be so shy. A fool, yes, but never shy."

Jane's attempt at a laugh caused her to cough. When she stopped and was no longer fighting for breath, Marcus hissed, "Kiss you? I came here to *kill* you, Jane Trago. I spent seven years in prison because of you. Seven years out of my life, while you spent the money you pinched from me."

"And where did *you* get it from, Marcus? Where did we *both* get it . . . and for what? It's all gone now, Marcus. Stolen by others who'll be damned in their turn, I don't doubt."

"I searched everywhere for you. Every new place I went I hoped I'd find you there. On good nights I'd dream I'd found you and had my hands around your throat, like this — "

Marcus put his hands about her neck. It felt so frail he knew he could have broken it with little more than a flick of his thumbs.

Looking down at her, he could see no fear in her eyes. Only a fierce elation.

"Do it, Marcus. Kill me and put an end to my pain."

Marcus took his hands away, "You'd like that, would you? You'd like me to strangle you so you could die happy, knowing I'd dangle at the end of a rope because of it. Well I've got a better way. You see this?" Marcus pulled a small, paper-wrapped package from his pocket. "Do you know what this is? It's arsenic, fresh from the container at Sharptor mine. There's enough here to kill everyone in this ward."

"Give it to me, Marcus. Do what you've come all this way to do. Kill me and put me out of my pain. I'll thank you with my dying breath."

Marcus stood looking down at Jane for a long time. Then he said slowly, "I believe you're serious. I think you really *do* want to die. I *would* be doing you a favour."

Putting the packet back in his pocket he said, "I don't want to do that. Perhaps I'll stay and talk to you for a while. Tell you of the world outside. What I'll be doing while you lie here waiting to die. Of the beerhouses I'll visit and the girls I'll enjoy myself with. Girls who look as you once did. Plump, happy, good-looking girls with enough flesh on their bones to make a man feel comfortable. While I'm out there enjoying life you'll be lying here like some dried-up autumn leaf, waiting to be blown away."

"Is that what you think, Marcus? Is that what you really believe? Then let me tell you something. While you're sitting getting more stupid with every drink, hating the world about you, I'll be lying here *thinking.* I'll be thinking of the things *I've* had. The laughs and the fun I've known. The love of a good man who made me feel like a queen whenever he looked at me. Yes, I'm dying, and in pain, but deep inside I've got memories. Happy memories. What will you think about when *you're* dying, Marcus? What memories will you have?"

Before Marcus could reply he heard the sound of heavy footsteps coming along the corridor towards the ward. A woman's voice was saying, " . . . this is the ward I sent him to, but there's no one named Trago here . . . "

The nurse who had spoken to Marcus appeared in the doorway. She was accompanied by a uniformed police inspector and two tall constables.

"There he is! That's him!"

Marcus straightened up and backed away from the bed, looking about him. There was nowhere to go. The ward had only one door, and it was blocked by the policemen.

"Marcus Hooper?" The inspector spoke from the doorway. He would not give Marcus the opportunity to make a dash for freedom. "I've had a telegraphed message from Superintendent Coote of the Cornwall county constabulary. He wants to question you about the attempted murder of a number of men and women at a Cornish mine. My advice to you is to come quietly. Cause trouble

505

and you'll only make things worse for yourself."

Marcus weighed his chances carefully. He knew they were very slim indeed. If the police took him he would go to prison for a very long time. There was more than attempted murder involved. In his pocket he carried a watch he had stolen from one of the many victims he had robbed on the highways of Cornwall. It was a distinctive watch, but he had taken a fancy to it . . .

From the bed beside him there was weak but audible laughter from Jane Batley, "You're going to have to wait for that drink, Marcus — and the plump, good-looking girls. You'll go back to prison, Marcus Hooper — or is it still Marcus Cornwall you're calling yourself?"

Jane's voice was not strong, but it carried to the policemen, and Marcus knew she had put a rope about his neck as surely as if she were a hangman standing beside him on a scaffold. Marcus Cornwall had murdered a pawnbroker in Hackney Road in London. It would not take the police long to discover his secret.

"You bitch! I *should* have killed you."

"Give yourself up, Hooper. Don't make things any worse for yourself."

Worse! Marcus knew he was a dead man already. He backed away from the bed, moving farther down the ward, away from the policemen. Only the inspector moved after him, the constables remaining in the doorway.

"Come along, Hooper. There's no escape for you. Give yourself up peaceably."

Marcus reached inside his pocket and his hand came out clutching the small paper package.

Breaking it open he crammed the contents into his mouth. The arsenic powder was dry and difficult to swallow. Snatching up a glass of water from a nearby bedside table he washed the powder down his throat. The inspector watched him uncertainly, unaware he was watching Marcus Hooper cheat the due processes of temporal law.

No more than sixteen hours after Marcus Hooper's contorted death throes came to an end, Jane Batley took the same path. But she died peacefully, with a priest's blessing in her ears.

Lottie and Miriam arrived at the hospital only minutes too late to be present at the end and met the priest on his way from the ward. They might have been at the hospital earlier had the police inspector not called to tell them of the happenings there. Miriam was still pale-faced after formally identifying the body of her brother-in-law.

As Miriam shed a tear for her errant sister, the priest said, "It's a blessed release for her, the matron tells me. She'll be in no more pain — yet I am pleased to know someone cared enough for her to shed a tear."

Patting Miriam's hand reassuringly, the priest next turned his attention to Lottie. "You'll be Jane Batley's daughter?" The priest was an elderly man who had been a servant of God for far too long to question why a daughter should not shed a tear at news of the death of her mother.

"That's right, Lottie *Trago*."

"I have a letter here for you. Your mother knew she was dying and she asked me to write the letter. I found some of the things she had to say puzzling, but she repeated them so I know I have them right. Matron witnessed the letter too. Your mother's mark is at the bottom of the page. That too was witnessed by the matron."

"Why should she want to write to me? It's the first letter she's ever sent and she's been away for most of my life."

"I never questioned her motives, child. I merely wrote what she told me. No doubt you'll find an answer in the letter. Here . . . "

The priest handed over a sheet of paper which was covered with writing in a neat, small hand.

Lottie began to read. She was sceptical when she read her mother's expressed sorrow at not being all she should to her only daughter. It was almost as though it had been written to gain the approval of the priest, but Lottie felt she knew her mother well enough to put such a thought aside.

There was mention in the letter too of the Star of India inn. Jane reiterated it was legally owned by her. Should the Gilmore family establish her ownership she wished the inn, or the money realised by its sale, to go to Lottie.

It was still the sort of letter that might have impressed a priest more than it did Lottie — but then those about her saw the blood drain from her cheeks and she looked up at Miriam with disbelief. "No! I don't believe it. She only did this to hurt me. She always hated me. She blamed me for everything that happened to her. This is her way of paying me back — "

"What is it, Lottie? What does it say?" Miriam grasped Lottie by the shoulders, fearful for a moment that she was about to fall to the ground in a faint.

"I can assure you there was nothing vengeful in Jane Batley when she died," said the priest. "She was at peace with herself, and with the Lord. I know the part to which you are referring, it is one of the details I asked her to repeat. She did — and she also said I was to tell you she was sorry, *deeply* sorry for what she had to say."

"What is it, Lottie? What has your ma said?"

Miriam still held Lottie tightly and she suddenly felt her slump in her grasp, as though all the strength had gone from her. Miriam tried to lead her to a chair, but she broke away. Turning to Miriam, she thrust the letter at her.

As the priest tried to calm Lottie, Miriam read the letter hurriedly, passing over the platitudes she came to the final paragraph.

" . . . What I have to tell you now is of more importance than anything else I have said. When you have read my words you will hate me more than before, and yet it is the greatest service I have ever done you. You must not marry Hawken Strike. You CANNOT. You and he were fathered by the same man, Leander Strike. In the certain knowledge that I am a dying woman I swear that what I tell you is the truth. Hawken Strike is your half-brother . . . "

31

HAWKEN STRIKE'S reaction to Lottie's decision not to marry him was one of petulance, rather than heartbreak.

"But dammit, Lottie, at least tell me *why,*" he demanded for the third time. "I have a right to know the reason, surely? If you think it's too soon after the death of your mother, we can put off a decision on the wedding for a few months."

"It has nothing to do with her death," Lottie lied. "It's simply that . . . I don't want to marry now, that's all."

"That's *all?* You devastate my life, ruin my future happiness and all you can say is, 'I don't want to marry now, that's all?' What manner of girl *are* you to behave so heartlessly? Have you met someone else, is that it? You've met someone else while you've been away at Portsmouth, but don't want to tell me? Or has your uncle Josh and that adopted daughter of his been feeding you with false rumours about me?"

"Josh . . . and Nell? What could they tell me?" Lottie looked at him sharply.

"That's right, pretend you don't already know." Hawken Strike's anger caused him to say far more than he intended. "The Strikes have money and influence, remember? There are always rumours circulating about us among the workers — you were once a bal-maiden, you should know all about *that.*"

"I don't think you're being very pleasant, Hawken."

Lottie and Hawken Strike were on a path on the slope of Sharptor, looking down upon the mine. Lottie had brought him up here to break the news that she would not marry him. She did not want to tell him the reason. He had done nothing to deserve the added unhappiness it would cause him.

"You spring the devastating news on me that you'll not marry me, refuse to give me a reason — then complain because I'm not being *pleasant?* My God, Lottie! What sort of a make-believe world are you living in?"

"I'm sorry, Hawken. I'd hoped we might at least be able to part as friends — "

"Lottie, I've been expecting us to become man and wife. You can't suddenly say,'Can't we just be good friends instead?' Good God! You must be as cold as a winter's day inside. Perhaps it's as well I've found out now, rather than in the marriage bed."

The hurt on Lottie's face should have told Hawken how wrong he was about her, but he was far too angry to notice such details.

Suddenly Lottie turned and ran blindly back towards the house. It had taken both courage and a strong will not to tell Hawken the truth about his father — *their* father — and his anger hurt her. She was feeling far from calm — and certainly not cold.

She crashed in through the kitchen door of the house at Sharptor and ran upstairs to her room, ignoring those sitting in the kitchen. The door to her room crashed shut behind her too, but when Miriam would have gone up the stairs after her, Josh put a restraining hand on her arm.

"Leave her alone, Miriam. It's hard for the girl, but she has to work it out for herself."

Hawken had left his horse at the mine and he was on his way to fetch it when he found Emma Hobbs blocking the pathway.

"Well, well! Have you and Lottie quarrelled already? That bodes ill for your future marital bliss."

"There will be no marital bliss — or marital anything else. The marriage is off."

Emma Hobbs's eyebrows disappeared beneath her fringe, "Don't tell me Lottie's finally found out what you're really like, Hawken? I wonder who could have told her?"

"If you've had anything to do with this — "

"Me? Why should I say anything to upset my best friend? No, you'll need to look elsewhere to find out who's been telling the truth about you. But does this mean I'll be seeing more of you now — or less?"

"There's nothing to bring me to Sharptor any more."

"Oh, but there *is*. Let's take our usual walk farther up the tor, Hawken. I'll put you in a good mood again — and then I'll tell you my news . . . "

Lottie had been hurt by Hawken Strike's accusations, yet she accepted he had every right to be angry. Strangely enough, now Hawken had been told she would not marry him Lottie discovered she was not as upset as she might have been. Indeed, there was a vague feeling of relief inside her.

Lottie had not really liked any of the people she had met on her visits to the Strike home and knew she would never be fully accepted by any of them. This would not have mattered too much had Hawken loved her enough to dull the cynicism of his friends, but she had never been *entirely,* satisfied his offer of marriage was anything more than an attempt to weaken her resistance and make her his mistress. Had she succumbed, she suspected he would have found some reason why the marriage should not take place.

Lottie was lying on the bed late in the evening, after remaining in her room all day, when there was a knock at the door.

"You can come in, it's not locked."

Lottie called the invitation, expecting Miriam to enter the room. To her surprise it was Nell. She carried a mug of hot milk and some meat and bread on a plate.

"I thought you might be hungry, Lottie. I've brought you these."

"I don't feel like eating."

"I didn't think you would . . . but I wanted to talk to you."

Lottie looked up apprehensively at the other girl, "You're not pregnant again?"

Nell quickly closed the door behind her, "No . . . but what I have to say is to do with that. Lottie . . . who do you believe made me pregnant?"

Lottie sat up on the bed, "Why, Jethro. You told me so yourself."

Nell shook her head, "No, Lottie. You *assumed* it was Jethro. I let you go on thinking that."

"You mean it *wasn't* him?" Lottie's confusion turned to dismay as she remembered some of the things she had said to Jethro and the way she had treated him. "But if it wasn't him, then who . . . ?"

Suddenly it all came together. Nell had spent a night at the house of Hawken following the death of his mother — and Lottie remembered the angry accusation he had made earlier that day.

Lottie fell backwards on to the bed once more and stared up at the ceiling, "What a *fool* I've been. It was Hawken all the time."

"Yes."

"Why, Nell? Why *you,* of all people?"

"I'm sorry, Lottie. I didn't mean it to happen. One of his friends gave me lots to drink. I thought it was just orange juice. I learned afterwards she'd put champagne in it."

Lottie sat up again. "You mean he made love to you when you were drunk?"

Nell nodded miserably.

"Why didn't you *tell* me? Why didn't you say anything when you learned I was going to marry him?"

"I didn't want to spoil things for you if you really loved him. I thought perhaps he'd been drinking too and it was something he'd never do again . . . "

Lottie thought that drunk or sober, single or married, Hawken Strike would not hesitate to take advantage of a girl if the opportunity arose. If she were perfectly honest with herself, this was something she had always known.

Yet Hawken, the man she had been going to marry occupied only a small corner of her thoughts. Her next words startled Nell.

"Poor Jethro."

"Jethro? What does he have to do with this?"

"I thought he was the father of the child you were expecting. I've been very unkind to him as a result."

"Jethro?" Nell looked at Lottie disbelievingly. "He'd have been deeply shocked had he suspected I was pregnant. Besides, when it comes to girls, he's never had eyes for anyone but you."

Lottie remembered how Jethro had come to the house to see her, after he had heard the news of her engagement to Hawken Strike. "He didn't try too hard to stop me marrying Hawken," she said, perversely.

"Would you have taken any notice of him if he had? Anyway, Jethro would have thought it all out before saying anything. If he thought it was what you really wanted he'd have backed off. Jethro's a very special man, Lottie."

"Yes, I really believe he is."

"I'm glad we've had our chat, Lottie. I feel a lot better about things now. I hope you do too."

Lottie lay back on the bed again. "I'll feel better when I've put things straight with Jethro. I'll go and see him tomorrow."

"Oh! Hasn't Josh said anything to you? Jethro's not here. There's a new minister and his wife come to Henwood from Plymouth. They're staying at

Wrightwick Roberts's house. It means Jethro's freed from his responsibilities to the chapel here and he's working over at Josh's new clay works, near St Austell. He'll be there for a week or two, then he's going up north to a meeting of trade unionists. Jethro's becoming an important man in the county now."

Lottie was bitterly disappointed. She wanted to put things right with Jethro as quickly as possible. However, her apology would be all the better for the waiting. It would give her time to put her thoughts into some vestige of order.

The following morning Lottie walked to Henwood village to bring Patience Hooper's three daughters to Sharptor for a while.

Patience had taken the death of her husband very badly, even though Superintendent Kingsley Coote had revealed details of Marcus's past. Evidence had also come to light linking Marcus Hooper with at least sixty robberies throughout the county, most accompanied by some degree of violence.

Patience did not care what other people said, or thought. Marcus had been her husband. Her man.

As Lottie went down the hill towards the village she saw a number of bal-maidens walking disconsolately away from the Sharptor mine, Emma Hobbs among them.

"What's going on? Is there no work today?" Lottie put the question to her friend.

"No. Malachi Sprittle's sent a few men below grass to carry out maintenance work, but they're

516

bringing up no ore. All production's come to an end. The Sharptor mine's finished, I reckon, just like the others around here."

Lottie thought Emma was probably right. Josh had been saying the price of tin had dropped so low there wasn't a mine in Cornwall could hope to cover its costs. The prospects for arsenic were uncertain too. Josh had not been paid for the last shipload and all his storage space was full, awaiting news from Samuel Coolidge and the Mexican government.

"They say Josh Retallick has no more interest in the mine. That he's taken all his money out and put it into china clay."

"I wouldn't let Josh hear you say that. No one could have done more to keep the Sharptor mine working — and he hasn't given up yet. He's hoping to start up again when he's heard from Samuel Coolidge."

"By the time that happens I don't suppose I shall care very much. I doubt if I'll be taken back on as a bal-maiden."

"Why not? Josh has never forgotten how you and your family helped me find Jacob when he was lying ill. As long as there's any work to be had there'll be a place for you at the Sharptor mine."

"What I meant was . . . by the time the mine's working again I'll be too far gone to do a bal-maiden's job. I'm in the family way, Lottie."

Lottie was horrified. "You're pregnant? How long have you known — and who's the father? Have you been to see Mother Kettle yet?"

"I'll be going nowhere near Mother Kettle."

517

Emma patted her stomach smugly. "This is going to give me a life of ease for the rest of my life."

"How? Are you marrying a man who's going to keep you at home?"

"Who said anything about *marrying?* All I've got to do is be a good girl and smile every time anyone asks me the name of the father and I'll be well looked after."

"Are you trying to tell me the baby has a rich father? Who do you know who'd pay you to keep quiet . . . ?"

Lottie knew the answer before she finished asking the question, "*Hawken Strike!* You've let Hawken make love to you."

"*I've* not said it was him. It was you who mentioned his name, you remember that, Lottie Trago. Anyway, you're not marrying him, so it doesn't matter to you what he does."

"You were letting Hawken Strike make love to you while he was courting me? You . . . my *friend.* To think, I almost married him . . . He must have made love to every bal-maiden working at the Sharptor mine."

"I don't think he's taken Sally Coombe up on the moor yet . . . " Sally Coombe was a spinster of at least sixty years of age, who had spent her whole life working as a bal-maiden. She hated all men.

Totally unrepentant, Emma Hobbs said, "I was meeting Hawken Strike up on the moor long before you began to take a serious interest in him. A girl's got to look after her own these days."

Emma inclined her head in the direction of the Sharptor mine, "It won't be long before the

518

last mine has closed down. For every house with money coming in there'll be a hundred without. Rather than see their kids starve women will be ready to lie down in the bracken with any man for sixpence. I was just thinking ahead, that's all."

32

A FORTNIGHT after Lottie's revealing meeting with Emma Hobbs, a long letter reached Josh from Samuel Coolidge. It contained only bad news. There had been a number of ministerial changes in the Mexican government. The minister responsible for importing arsenic for the cotton crop had been replaced. The new man did not like the idea of a 'gringo' representing his office and Samuel Coolidge had been dismissed.

Before giving up his appointment, Coolidge had 'persuaded' the Mexican authorities to pay for the last shipload of arsenic about to be unloaded in the Mexican port of Tampico. He had used the simple expedient of threatening to send the ship elsewhere unless the money was paid in advance.

Rather than risk having their cotton crops devastated by the boll weevil the government had paid up, but they informed Samuel Coolidge they had made 'other arrangements' for future imports of arsenic and he would no longer be welcome in their country.

While he was winding up his own affairs in Mexico, Samuel Coolidge had tried to learn the name of the new supplier, in the hope he could persuade him to include arsenic produced at Sharptor in his shipments. Unfortunately, it seemed the deal was still being negotiated via the new transatlantic cable and Samuel could learn nothing.

Coolidge intended returning to Cornwall after visiting his home in the United States where his own family owned cotton plantations. He promised to make enquiries there. If there was a market for arsenic in America he would inform Josh immediately.

There was also a letter for Nell. Samuel hoped she would marry him as soon as possible after his arrival in England and return with him to America. He was confident Nell would be both comfortable and happy living on the large estate he owned there. His family was not as wealthy as it had been before the recent disastrous civil war, but they had always invested their wealth wisely. Enough remained to maintain a standard of living undreamed of in a Cornish mining village.

Jethro was away from Henwood village for more than a month. He returned brimming with enthusiasm and confidence for the future of the trade union in Cornwall. All too often those who were working hard to improve pay and conditions for the Cornish working man felt they were fighting a lone battle. Hated by the employers and castigated by the Churches, they were frequently scorned by the very men they were trying to help.

However, a tour of coal mines in the north of England convinced Jethro that the unions had an important part to play in the future of his county.

In the mines of the north he had seen the improved conditions brought about by the unions. Miners were at last being treated as human beings. They had recently won a living wage for the first time and succeeded in bringing their working day down to ten hours — with many mines agreeing to an eight-hour shift system. There was anew mood of optimism and hope in the air.

This mood was reflected at the trade union conference Josh had attended with delegates from every county of England, representing a wide variety of trades.

Conference officials were especially interested in the development of the china clay industry as outlined by Jethro. Before the conference came to an end Jethro was asked to look into the possibility of bringing the clay workers together under the banner of a single trade union, of which he would be the official representative.

So excited was Jethro when he came to Sharptor to tell Josh of developments in the movement, Lottie felt her apology to him had passed almost unnoticed. She was left wondering whether Jethro even remembered the way she had treated him.

She had her answer later that same evening. When it was time for Jethro to leave, he said his goodbyes to the others before asking Lottie to walk to the end of the path with him, adding, "It's a beautiful moonlit night, you'll have no trouble finding your way home again."

Miriam and Josh exchanged delighted glances. A reconciliation between Lottie and Jethro was something for which they had both been hoping. Lottie said nothing but followed Jethro to the kitchen door, putting on her coat before going out into the night with him.

As they walked from the house, Jethro asked, "Can you tell me now what caused our misunderstanding?"

"No. It's not because I don't want to, but someone else is involved and I've promised I'll say nothing."

After a few minutes' silence, Jethro accepted her refusal to explain, saying, "You're throwing away a lot by not marring Hawken Strike."

"Yes — trouble mostly."

"You could find trouble with whoever you decide to marry. You only have to look at Patience to realise that. If you married Hawken Strike you'd have luxury and status and would never have to worry about going hungry. There are few families in a mining community can hope for as much. You said so yourself."

"Are you trying to persuade me I *should* marry Hawken Strike now?"

"Of course not. Strike wouldn't make you happy. I doubt if he'd even try very hard. I simply want to be certain you know what you're doing, that's all."

"Why?"

"Because I care for you, Lottie. I care very much. I've been miserable these last few months, believing you were going to marry Hawken Strike and being unable to talk to you."

"I've been miserable lately too, just thinking of the way I behaved to you."

They had reached the end of the path now and they stopped walking, standing together in an awkward silence for a few minutes.

"Lottie — "

"Do you — "

They both spoke together and laughed foolishly.

Jethro tried again. "I'm glad we're friends again, Lottie. I know it's too soon . . . after Hawken Strike, but I'd like to feel I could talk to you about the future soon. *Our* future."

"I'd like to feel you could too."

"That's all right, then," Jethro sounded suddenly very relieved. His nervous uncertainty would have astounded his trade union colleagues. It might also have astounded those who had heard him preach a sermon to a camp meeting of thousands. "You'd best get home now, before you catch cold."

"Yes. I am glad we're friends again, Jethro. *Really* glad, and thank you for being so understanding about everything."

Lottie leaned forward and kissed Jethro before turning away quickly and hurrying home. She felt happier than she had for very many weeks. Later, as she lay in bed and thought of the events of the week, she realised she had known Jethro all her life yet they had never kissed before tonight. She hoped it marked a new beginning for both of them.

The Sharptor mine had been idle for three months when Samuel Coolidge returned to Cornwall to claim his bride. Nell was so overjoyed to see him that the few doubts Miriam and Josh had entertained about the marriage were quickly banished. Watching Nell and Samuel Coolidge together no one could doubt the couple were very much in love with each other and had a real chance of sharing a happy married life together.

Even Lottie, who had always felt Nell was too

immature and fickle for marriage, admitted they were a well-suited couple.

Samuel Coolidge had brought presents for the whole family, and letters from his mother for Nell and for Josh and Miriam. Celebration was in the air and it was not until late that afternoon that Coolidge was able to suggest that he and Josh should take a walk to the Sharptor mine.

Nell had hardly left his side for a moment during the day. She was reluctant to do so now, but she knew the two men wanted to talk business, something that would affect the future of Henwood. With the closure of the mine an air of depression had descended upon the village. There was no work and very little hope in any of the villages of Bodmin Moor.

As the two men walked down the hill, Josh pointed to the slopes of another hill no more than half a mile away, where a copper mine had shut down its engine in a slump that had occurred eight years before. "You see that mine, Samuel. Only a few years ago it was bringing ore to grass and giving a living to a hundred families. Yet today you'd need to look hard to find it. In twenty years' time all the mined ground will have been reclaimed by the moor. There's a patient timelessness about it. You're always aware it's here, waiting to reclaim its own, whether it takes a year, ten — or a thousand."

"I'm afraid it's likely to reclaim a great many mines during the course of the next few years, Josh. I visited some of the mines being worked in Mexico. They've increased production tenfold since I was last there. They're producing even more in Chile and labour costs are negligible. This is the reason the price of copper has fallen — and will fall even more. Cornwall can't hope to compete."

"Some of us realised years ago what was happening. I've managed to build up a large investment in the china clay industry but others haven't been so lucky. As for the miners . . . they face a bleak future unless we can produce something else the world wants. Something like arsenic."

"That's what I wanted to speak to you about, Josh. I've discovered who's been given the Mexican government's contract for arsenic."

Pausing to adjust the collar of the coat he wore, using his one hand, Samuel Coolidge said, "The arsenic's being supplied to them by Hawken Strike."

Josh was startled. "He's said nothing to me. If we're to fulfil a contract we ought to be in full production now — "

"The Sharptor mine hasn't been mentioned, Josh." Samuel Coolidge was deeply sympathetic. "The contract was negotiated on Strike's behalf by his cousin who's on the staff of the British ambassador in Mexico. According to him, Strike is building a calciner at Gunnislake that will be the largest in the country."

Josh was thunderstruck as the full impact of Coolidge's words came home to him, but so many things made sense now.

"He has the mines, and no transport problems," Josh was speaking his thoughts aloud. "All his arsenic can be barged straight downriver to Plymouth."

Unless Josh's own production increased, the narrow gauge railway linking Sharptor with the port of Looe would soon have to close. It seemed circumstances and Hawken Strike were combining to sound the death knell for the Sharptor mine. Strike was taking a grim revenge for his rejection by Lottie.

"You've had no luck finding an American market for our arsenic?"

Samuel Coolidge shook his head unhappily, "The market will come, Josh. Texas and Mexico are so close the boll weevil must reach America one day soon. When it happens all the calciners in the world won't be able to produce enough arsenic for the needs of the cotton growers. It may be next year, or it may be ten years away. You can't cling to hope that long."

They had arrived at the Sharptor mine where Jethro had been working all day to list the mine's assets and total up its debts. When the two men entered the office Jethro was putting papers and ledgers away in the drawers of his desk.

"Jethro, have you heard anything of Hawken Strike building a calciner at Gunnislake?"

"Not until a few minutes ago." Jethro inclined his head towards a chair in the corner of the office where a stranger sat slumped in the shadows, both hands to his face. Neither Josh nor Samuel Coolidge had noticed him when they came in.

"He's from the Gunnislake mine. There's been a serious accident. It seems Hawken Strike acted against all advice and ordered his captain to produce arsenic before the calciner and equipment was properly checked. There's been an explosion

527

and a serious leak of arsenic fumes. Seven men are dead and children are choking in half the houses in the area. The Gunnislake men are so angry they're marching on Strike's house — and they've taken the dead men with them. Some of the older men are frightened of what might happen. They've asked me to go and speak to the men — and to Strike."

Josh pointed to the still figure in the corner, "How did he get here? I saw no horse outside."

The Gunnislake man spoke for the first time, "I walked — when I wasn't running. What Jethro didn't tell you is that the Gunnislake men have been joined by every unemployed miner around those parts. By the time they get to Strike's house they'll have half of Cornwall with them — and every one an angry man."

"They must be almost at Strike's house by now. Take one of the horses, Jethro. I'll come with you."

"Count me in as well, although I'm not sure which side I'm on. I have a dislike of mobs, but I believe Strike deserves everything that's coming his way."

"My concern is for the Gunnislake men. They've been treated shabbily by Strike for so long they're at breaking point. It only needs a couple of hotheads to spark them off and it'll take the army to deal with them. That will mean bloodshed, and give yet another victory to Strike."

Locking his desk drawer, Jethro added grimly, "Our only hope is to get to them before they reach Strike's house."

33

IT seemed Jethro's worst fears had been realised when the three horsemen arrived at the home of Hawken Strike. They had heard the chanting of the mob from almost a mile away but the size of the crowd still took them by surprise. There must have been close to two thousand men crowding on the lawns in front of the Strike house, some carrying lighted torches to ward off the onset of darkness.

In front of the house a space had been cleared and here were laid out the bodies of the seven workers killed in the explosion and subsequent gas leakage. One of the bodies was that of a boy aged no more than ten.

As the three horsemen approached the house a lighted torch flung from the crowd arced through the air and hit the house wall only inches from a partly opened window. It fell in a flower bed where it lay sizzling and spluttering amidst the green undergrowth.

A cheer went up from the men from Gunnislake but as another torch crashed against the wall and erupted in a shower of sparks Jethro urged his horse to the front of the crowd. Jumping to the ground, he mounted the steps leading to the main door of the house.

Raising his arms he shouted, "Stop! Stop, I say!"

Jethro's sudden arrival took the mob by surprise.

Taking advantage of the lull in their shouting, Jethro lowered his arms and looked straight out over the heads of the crowd, most of whom recognised him.

"What do you think you're doing? Have you all gone mad? I've ridden here to see how I can help miners who were reported to be in trouble — only to find they've become a mob, a mindless, unruly mob bent on mischief."

"We've seven dead here, killed by the greed of Hawken Strike. Talk won't bring any one of them back to life."

"Neither will violence," Jethro shouted as loud as he could. Even so, his voice was heard by only a few of the men standing closest to him.

It was some minutes before he succeeded in silencing them sufficiently to make himself heard again. This time he singled out the miner who had shouted to him from the crowd.

"You . . . The man who spoke just now. Come up here and let's hear what you have to say. Come along, let him through."

The subject of Jethro's attentions was reluctant to come forward, but he was propelled through the crowd by the hands of his colleagues.

"That young man knows how to control a crowd."

Josh and Samuel were standing with the horses at the rear of the crowd and Samuel spoke admiringly as the Gunnislake miner climbed the steps to Jethro.

"It's what he does now that will decide the outcome," murmured Josh. "A mob is like a thin branch in a wind. It can blow in any direction. . . . "

"Why are you here?" Josh put the question to the man he had chosen to be spokesman for the Gunnislake men. "What do you hope to achieve?"

"We want Strike to see what his greed and penny-pinching have done."

"No doubt Hawken Strike's been watching your every move from one of the windows above us. He'll have seen the dead men. Now what do you intend doing?"

The question took the 'spokesman' by surprise. "I . . . we . . . Well, what's he going to do about it?"

"What *can* he do? An accident's happened — and there won't be a miner here who's not familiar with such things."

"This is Strike's fault. What's he going to do about it?"

"What do you *want* him to do?" Jethro countered.

Once again the question took the reluctant spokesman by surprise, "I don't know . . . you're the trade union man who goes around sorting out other people's problems. You tell us what we should be doing."

Jethro had succeeded in what he had set out to do. When he had arrived he had been faced with a leaderless and volatile mob, ready to follow the most reckless element among them. Now Jethro had them looking to him for leadership.

"How many of you are trade unionists?"

There was a show of hands among the crowd.

"Less than half. All right, how many of you would like me to negotiate with Strike on behalf of the dead men's families?"

This time twice as many hands rose in the air.

"Good. I'll see if Strike is prepared to see me. In the meantime there's a man here I would like you to listen to. No one knows better than Josh Retallick the dangers of trying to achieve your aims — whatever they might be — by a show of unorganised force such as you have here tonight. He suffered wrongful conviction and transportation because of it. Josh, will you come up here and say a few words?"

After a surprised silence the miners erupted in a roar of approval as Josh pushed his way through the assembled men. Many of them reached out to pat him on the back as he passed them. Meanwhile, Jethro tugged hard on the bell-pull behind him, hoping fervently that someone in the house had been listening to what had been said.

They had. The door opened just as Josh reached the top step to stand beside Jethro.

"I'm sorry to let you in for this, Josh. But if they haven't got something to occupy their minds while I'm inside they'll get restless and we'll have serious trouble. Unless Strike's an absolute fool he'll have sent a servant out of the back door to call out the police and militia from Launceston. I don't want there to be any excuse for bloodshed."

"I understand. You've done well, Jethro. Get inside and do what's necessary. If you're gone for too long I'll call on Samuel Coolidge to come up here and say something. Off you go now."

Inside the house Jethro was guided upstairs by a servant-girl who was so nervous she was in grave danger of dropping the candle she carried before them.

Hawken Strike was standing in front of a partly

532

open window in a darkened room overlooking the main entrance and Josh's voice carried clearly up to the two men.

"Put that candle out!" Hawken Strike hissed the order angrily at the servant-girl. Before it was extinguished Jethro had seen the double-barrel sporting gun placed against a chair by the window.

"I don't think you'll be needing your gun tonight, Mr Strike."

"Perhaps not. All the same, I'll keep it to hand."

After a brief pause, Hawken Strike said grudgingly, "You headed off a situation that was potentially very dangerous. Thank you. But it doesn't excuse their disgraceful conduct. I've sent someone to inform the police in Launceston. They should be here soon."

"Not *too* soon, I trust, Mr Strike. An unsympathetic police presence is all that's needed here to provoke a riot. There are seven dead men lying on your lawn. You're being blamed for their deaths. If any violence erupts this house will be the target for those men out there. It's a magnificent house. I'm sure neither of us would like to see it burned to the ground."

"Are you threatening me, Shovell?"

"I'm trying to bring some common sense into the situation. I don't want your property suffering damage — but I'm even more concerned for the men outside. Their community's suffered a grievous loss and they're angry. I want to persuade them to go home peacefully, but I'll need your help. As I see it the men have two

533

main grievances, the first being the dead men, the second the hasty and shoddy work that caused the accident. Promise compensation to the relatives and say you'll have the calciner inspected and put to rights and I'm confident I can persuade the men to return to their homes."

"Considerably enhancing your own reputation and that of your dammed trade union too, I've no doubt. No, Shovell. I'll not let a rabble dictate to me."

"No one's *dictating* to anyone. I'm trying to resolve a situation that was created by you and has been made worse by angry and frustrated men. Unless you make some gesture to them now you're never going to produce arsenic at Gunnislake. There are more than two thousand men outside. They'll picket your works — with the backing of the unions — and I guarantee not one ounce of arsenic will be produced."

"This is blackmail!"

Even as he blurted out the accusation Hawken Strike was assessing the consequences of such a dispute. His cousin in the Mexican embassy had made a number of rash promises in order to secure a contract with the new Mexican government for Hawken. The accident in the Gunnislake works would mean a delay in meeting the terms of the contract. He could not afford to have delivery held up still further by an industrial dispute.

Jethro said, "You've tried to cut corners and it's resulted in the deaths of seven men. I think you owe something to their relatives. The men out there owe you nothing at all."

"How much would I be expected to pay by way of compensation?"

Successfully hiding the elation he suddenly felt, Jethro shrugged, "That's a matter for negotiation — although the men would expect you to be generous."

"Where could I find someone to inspect the calciner and have it put to rights? I doubt if there's anyone in the county in possession of the expert knowledge it would require."

"Wrong. The man you want is out there talking to the men right now. One of the best engineers in the south west of England."

"Josh Retallick? I couldn't expect him to help me! My calciner has put him out of business. He would laugh in my face."

"Not if you offered him something in return. Your share of the Sharptor mine, for instance."

Hawken Strike was about to protest that Jethro was asking too much of him, but he stopped in time. The Sharptor mine had ceased production. It would probably never produce tin or copper again, though he doubted whether Josh Retallick would agree to put the machinery up for sale. Jethro Shovell was asking him to part with a fifth share of nothing in exchange for away out of the embarrassing and expensive dilemma he was in.

Jethro waited patiently for Hawken Strike to reach a decision. Because he kept the accounts, Jethro knew more about the Sharptor mine's financial position than anyone else. He believed that if it was not necessary to pay a share of all profits to Hawken Strike the Sharptor mine could be kept running, using a reduced work force and stock-piling ore to take advantage of the fluctuations in the ore market. This would please Josh and still leave him free to invest in china clay — where he was hoping to employ some of the out-of-work miners from Henwood.

"Do you *really* believe you could persuade Josh Retallick to advise on the rebuilding of the calciner at Gunnislake?"

"Yes."

Jethro spoke with confidence. There was no market for arsenic from the Sharptor mine calciner and with the closure of so many other mines in the Bodmin Moor area there would not be sufficient ore to keep it running.

"Then I accept your terms for a return to work by the men. When do you think Josh Retallick will be able to go to Gunnislake?"

"As soon as you've agreed the amount of compensation with the dead men's relatives."

"Tell the men I'll meet their next of kin in the Gunnislake mine office the day after the last man's buried but tell them to be off my land within the hour, or I shall consider our agreement null and void."

Jethro ignored Hawken Strike's attempt to exert some control over the situation outside. The mine owner had suffered a defeat — and they were both aware of it.

Jethro, Josh and Samuel Coolidge remained on the steps of Hawken Strike's mansion until the last of the Gunnislake miners made their way along the long driveway and out through the gate. Carrying their dead colleagues, they were singing a Charles Wesley hymn.

The men were so evidently peaceful that the magistrate from Launceston, hurrying to the scene with a motley force of police, yeomanry and county gentlemen drew to the side of the road and allowed them to pass on their way unmolested.

As the last of the Gunnislake men passed from view, Josh rested a hand on Jethro's shoulder. "I said it before, and I'll say it again. If I hadn't been here to see what happened with my own eyes I would never have believed the way you handled that mob. You had two thousand men eating out of your hand — Hawken Strike too, by the sound of it."

Jethro moved away, heading towards the horses. Embarrassed by Josh's praise, he was also aware that Hawken Strike was in the upstairs room, able to hear every word being spoken.

As they reached the trees where the horses were tethered, Josh spoke to Jethro once more, "Your pa would have been proud of what you did tonight, Jethro."

Before Jethro could reply, a voice from the darkness said, "I'm proud of him too," and Lottie rode into view from the shadow of the trees.

"What are you doing here?" Josh asked the question before Jethro had recovered from his surprise.

"Malachi Sprittle found the man from Gunnislake sitting in the mine office and brought him up to the house. When he told us what was happening Miriam said it sounded just like the miners' march on Looe, when you were arrested for trying to prevent them rioting. I've heard the story so many times I went cold at the thought that the same thing might happen to Jethro."

"You rode here in darkness, on your own?"

"There's a moon up, it wasn't so bad."

"You care enough for me to do that?" There was something in Jethro's voice that galvanised Josh to sudden action.

Untying the reins of his horse, he said, "Come on, Samuel. The night's activities have given me an appetite. We'll get back to Sharptor and leave these two to follow us in their own time."

Josh was answered with a knowing smile from Samuel Coolidge, but neither Jethro nor Lottie seemed to notice.

As the two men rode along the road, heading for home, Samuel Coolidge looked back. Jethro and Lottie were only just visible, riding very close to each other and engaged in very deep conversation.

"You know, Josh. Nell might not be the only bride you'll be sending out from Sharptor in the near future."

"I've never doubted it for a minute. Every man, woman and child in Henwood has known for years that Lottie and Jethro were made for each other. The difficulty's been convincing *them*."

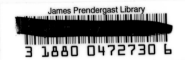
LARGE PRINT
Thompson, E. V., 1931-
    Lottie Trago

		DATE DUE	

JAMES PRENDERGAST
LIBRARY ASSOCIATION
JAMESTOWN, NEW YORK
Member Of
Chautauqua-Cattaraugus Library System